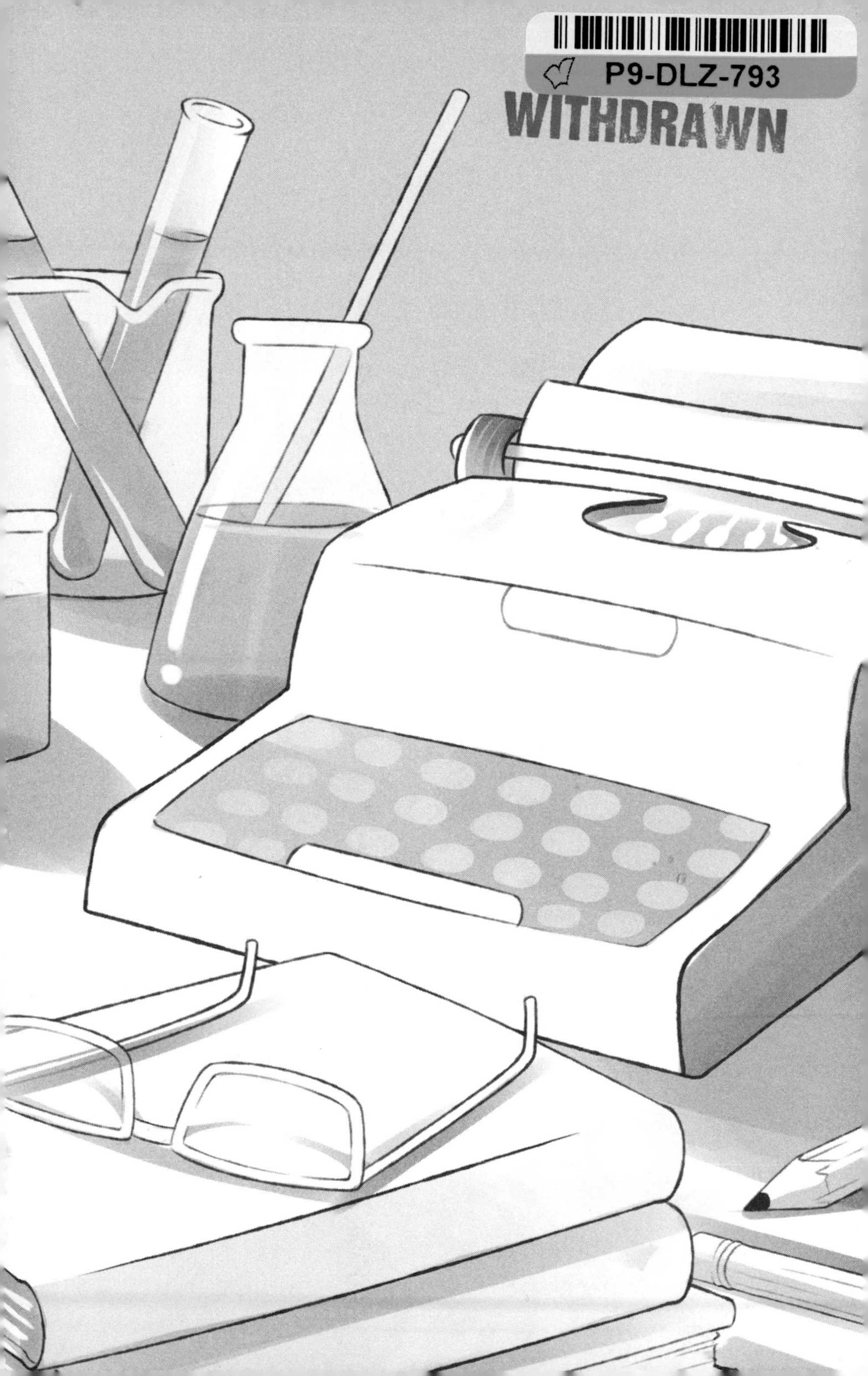

Clark Kent & lab partner—
future scientists!

DC COMICS
SECRET HERO SOCIETY

SCIENCE FAIR CRISIS

Written by **Derek Fridolfs** | Illustrations by **Pamela Lovas** and **Shane Clester**

SCHOLASTIC INC.

To my parents, who helped me with my own science fair project. And for Pamela, who has joined me on many projects since.

— Derek

ALL RIGHTS RESERVED. PUBLISHED BY SCHOLASTIC INC., *PUBLISHERS SINCE 1920.* SCHOLASTIC AND ASSOCIATED LOGOS ARE TRADEMARKS AND/OR REGISTERED TRADEMARKS OF SCHOLASTIC INC.

ISBN 978-1-338-27328-1 (TRADE) / ISBN 978-1-338-52850-3 (SSE)

10 9 8 7 6 5 4 3 2 1   19 20 21 22 23

PRINTED IN THE U.S.A.   23
FIRST PRINTING 2019

BOOK DESIGN BY HEATHER DAUGHERTY AND CHEUNG TAI
ADDITIONAL ILLUSTRATIONS BY ARTFUL DOODLERS LTD.

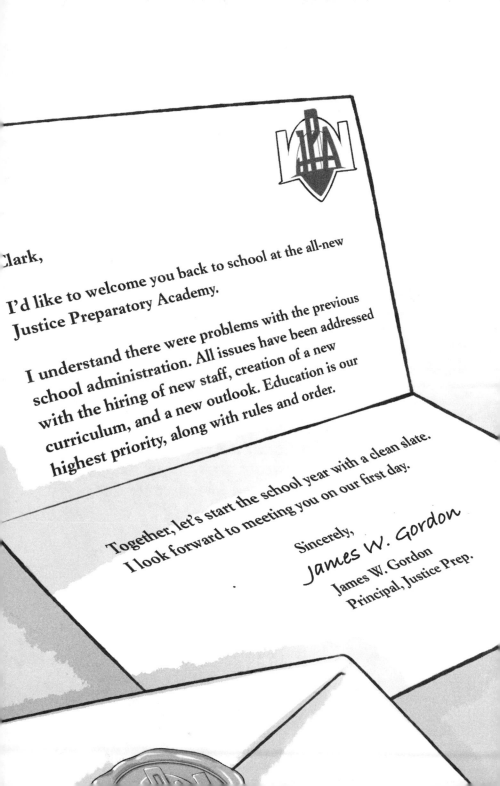

Clark,

I'd like to welcome you back to school at the all-new Justice Preparatory Academy.

I understand there were problems with the previous school administration. All issues have been addressed with the hiring of new staff, creation of a new curriculum, and a new outlook. Education is our highest priority, along with rules and order.

Together, let's start the school year with a clean slate. I look forward to meeting you on our first day.

Sincerely,

James W. Gordon

James W. Gordon
Principal, Justice Prep.

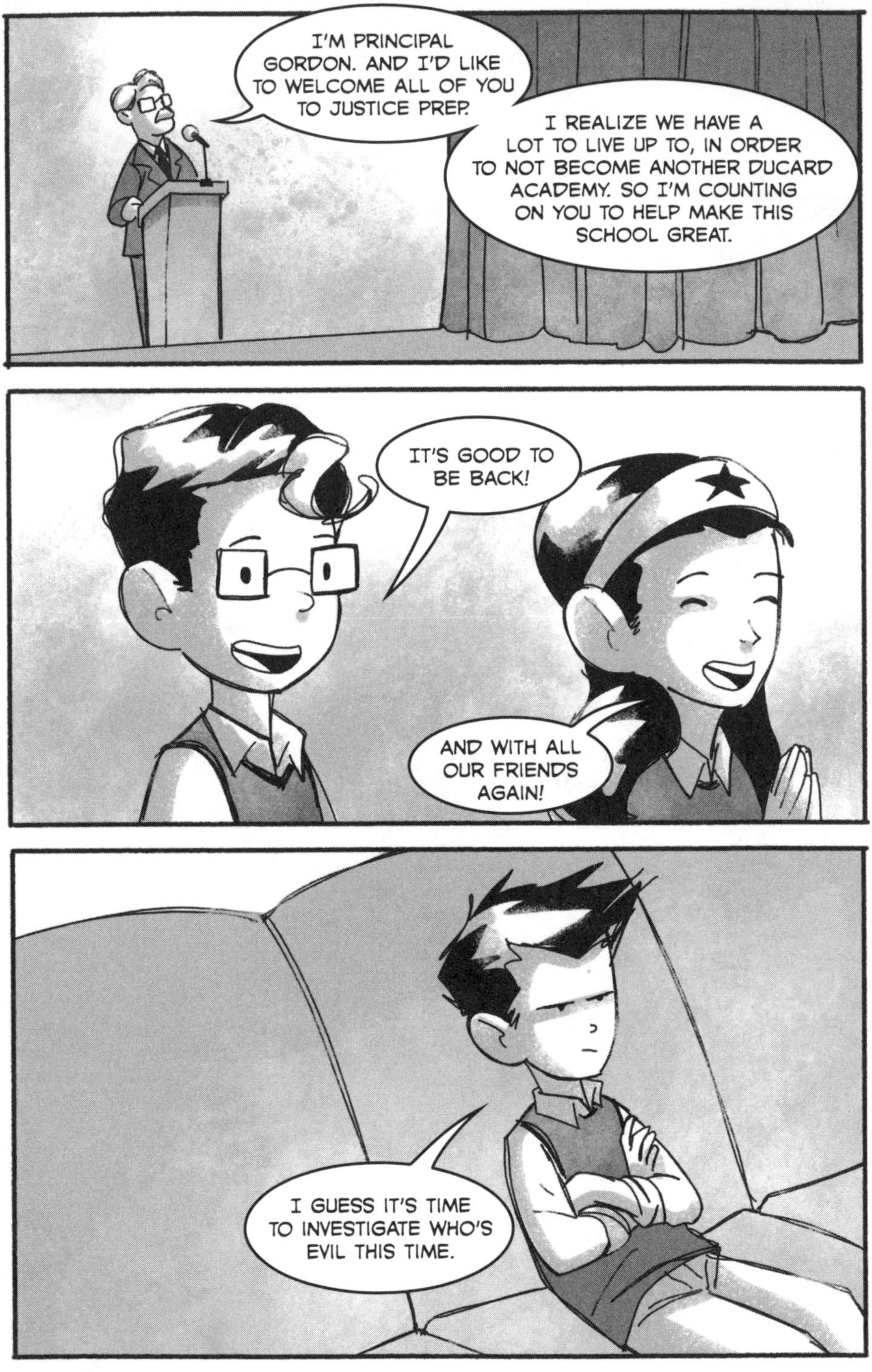
I'M PRINCIPAL GORDON. AND I'D LIKE TO WELCOME ALL OF YOU TO JUSTICE PREP.
I REALIZE WE HAVE A LOT TO LIVE UP TO, IN ORDER TO NOT BECOME ANOTHER DUCARD ACADEMY. SO I'M COUNTING ON YOU TO HELP MAKE THIS SCHOOL GREAT.
IT'S GOOD TO BE BACK!
AND WITH ALL OUR FRIENDS AGAIN!
I GUESS IT'S TIME TO INVESTIGATE WHO'S EVIL THIS TIME.

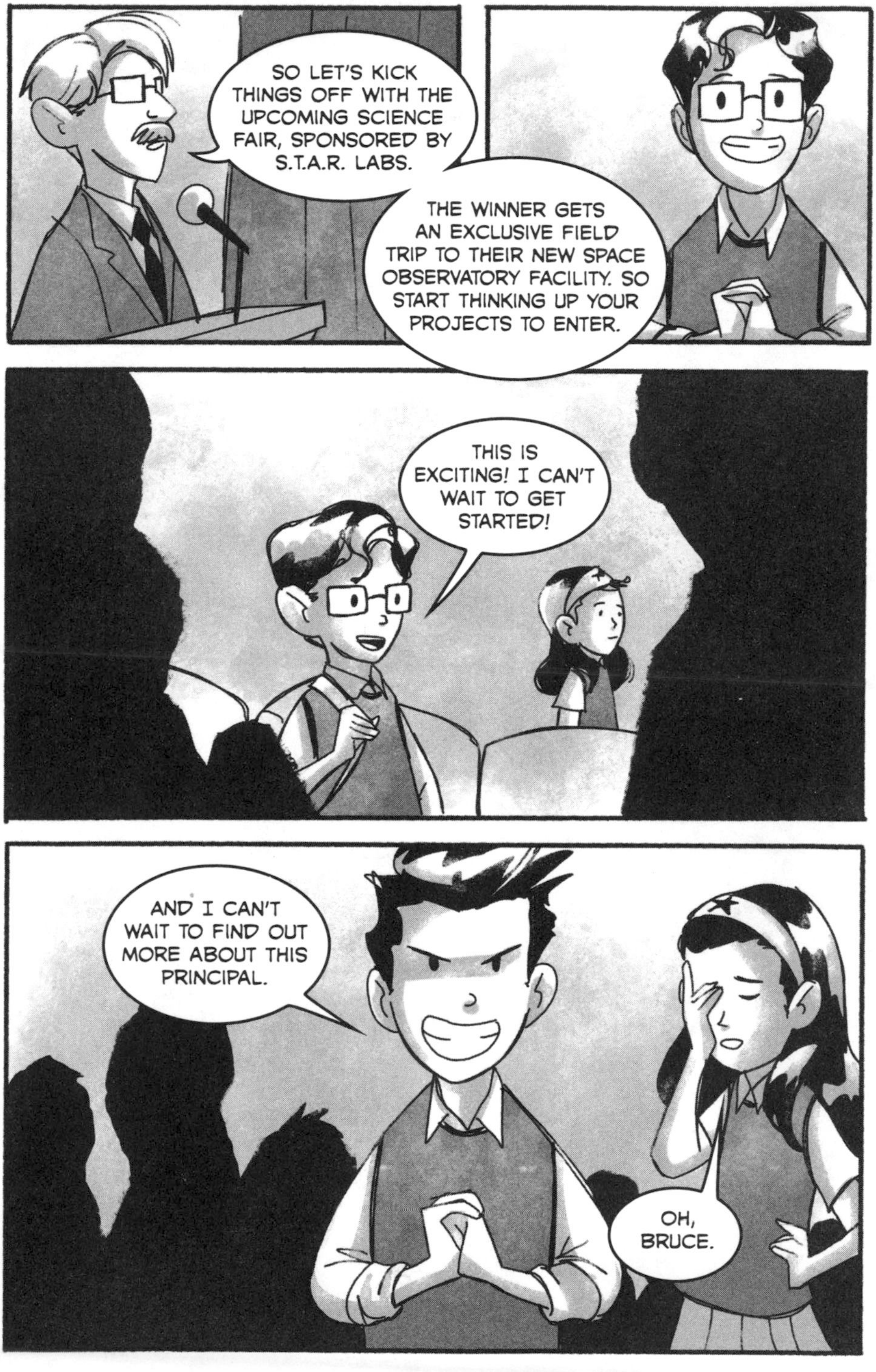
SO LET'S KICK THINGS OFF WITH THE UPCOMING SCIENCE FAIR, SPONSORED BY S.T.A.R. LABS.
THE WINNER GETS AN EXCLUSIVE FIELD TRIP TO THEIR NEW SPACE OBSERVATORY FACILITY. SO START THINKING UP YOUR PROJECTS TO ENTER.
THIS IS EXCITING! I CAN'T WAIT TO GET STARTED!
AND I CAN'T WAIT TO FIND OUT MORE ABOUT THIS PRINCIPAL.
OH, BRUCE.

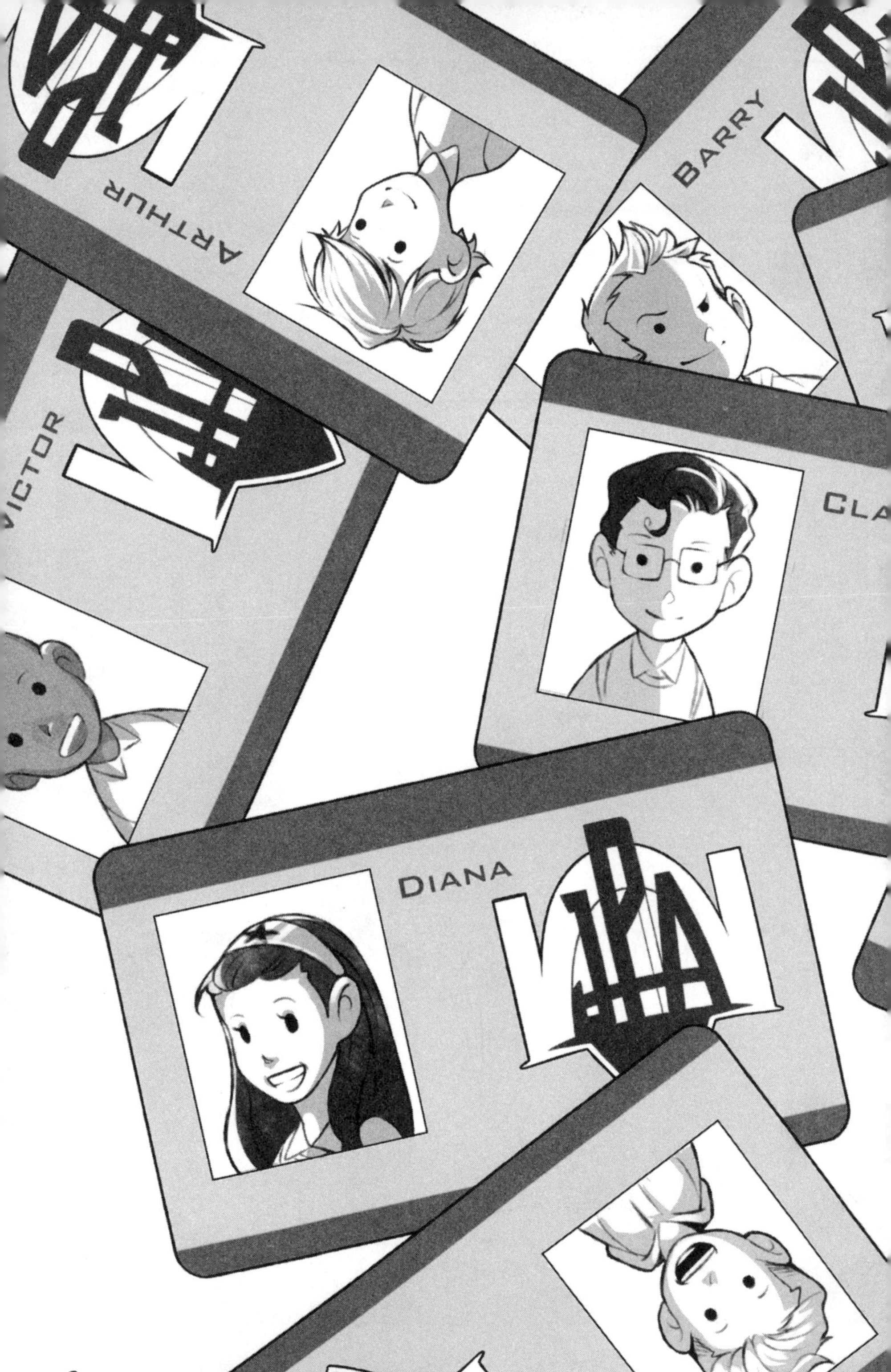

ARTHUR
BARRY
VICTOR
CLA
DIANA

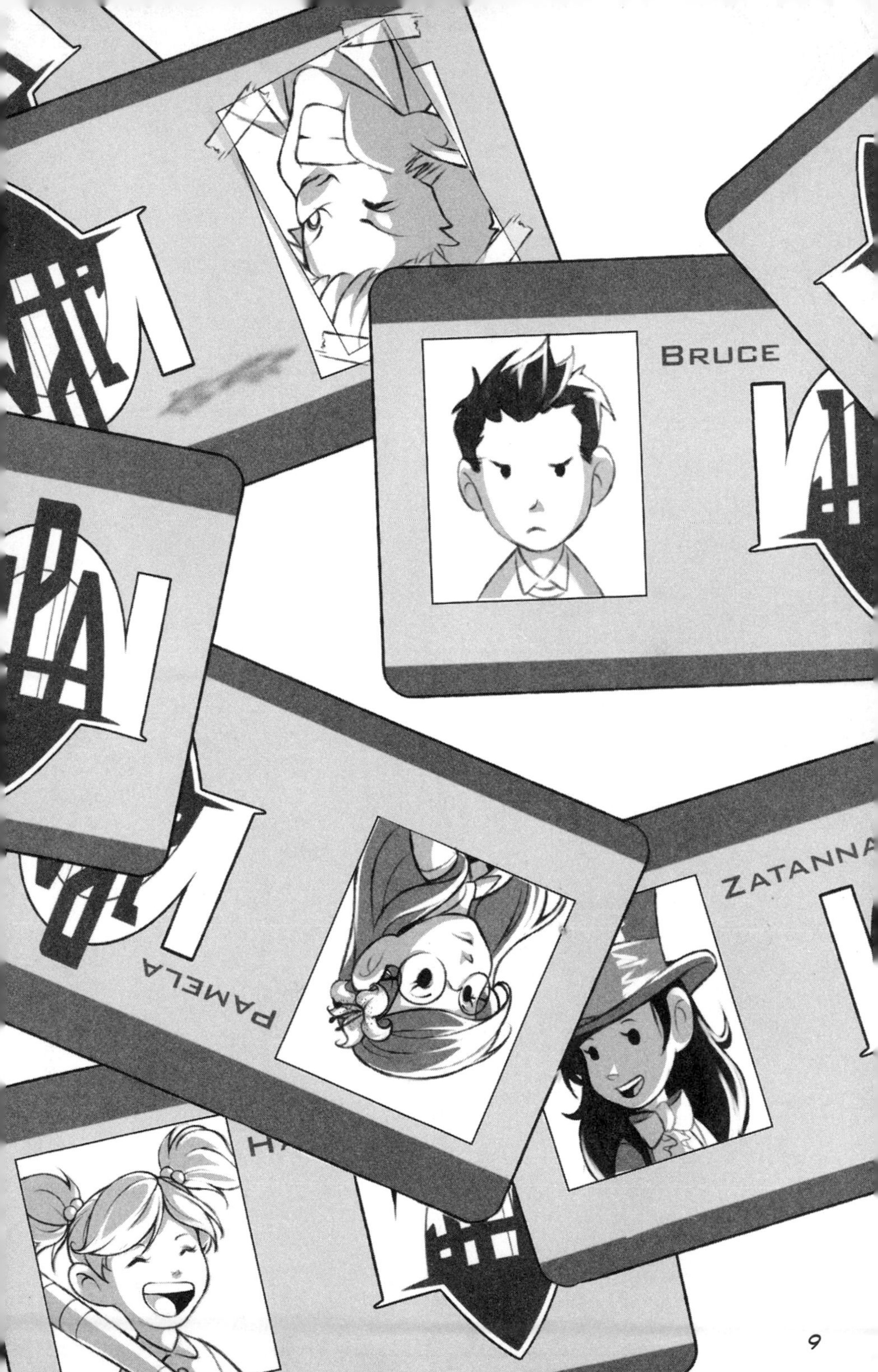
BRUCE
PAMELA
ZATANNA

S.T.A.R.

S.T.A.R. LABS

"Tomorrow's Technology Today"

The Scientific and Technological Advanced Research Labs have been responsible for many of the greatest scientific achievements in the world, including our latest invention . . . the construction of an experimental teleportation beam, to explore our vast solar system.

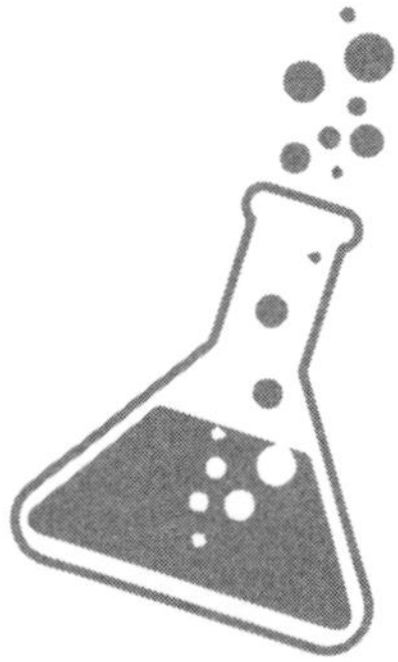

Now we are looking toward the future by helping to foste the minds of tomorrow! This brochure will help provide you with helpful tips for entry into your school's science fair competition.

SCIENCE FAIR—STUDENT GUIDELINES

- Projects should be the work of the individual student.
- Research the materials of your subject.
- Experiments should be safe and not harm others.
- You will be judged on originality, presentation, and creativity.
- Remember to have fun!!!

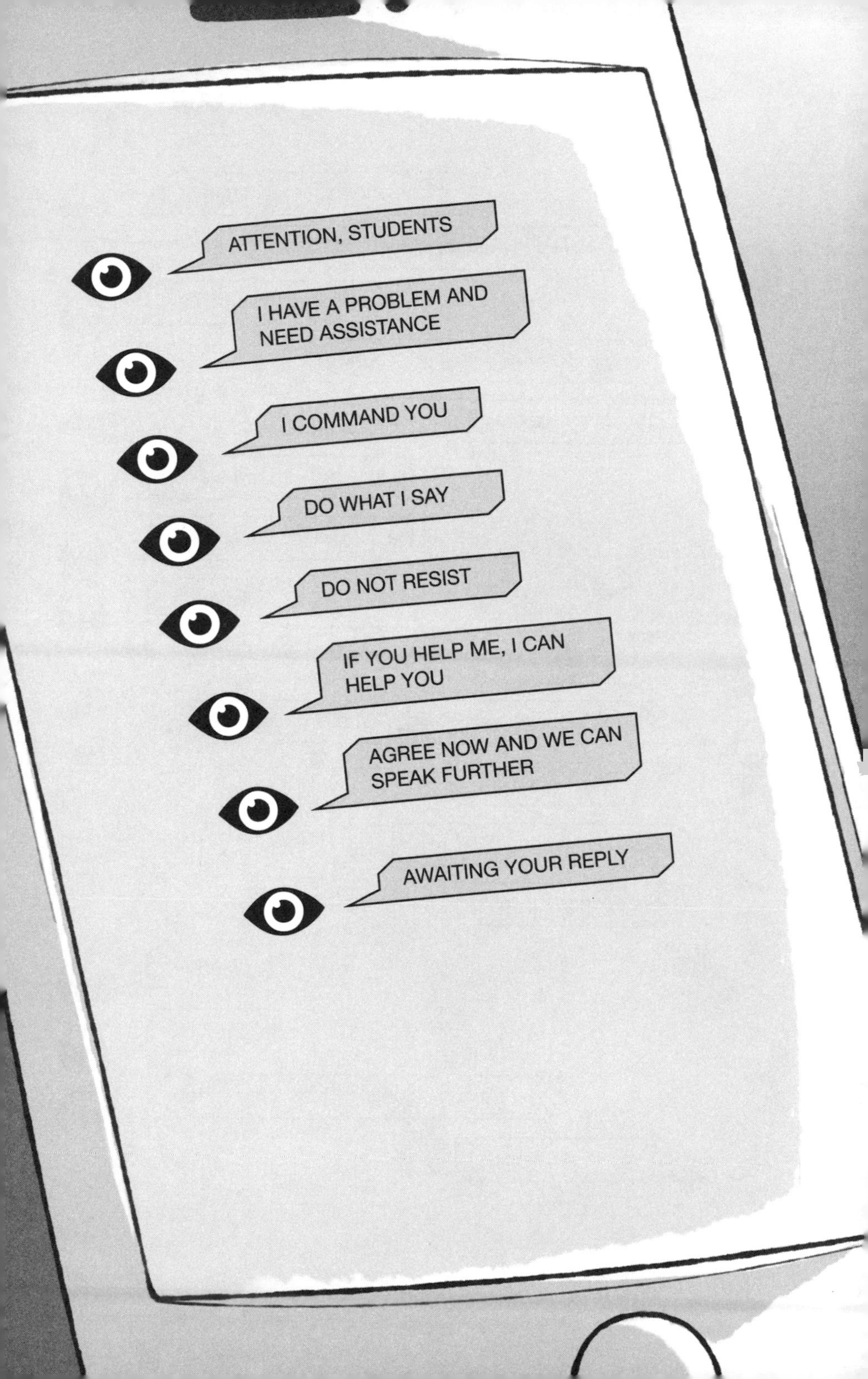

ATTENTION, STUDENTS
I HAVE A PROBLEM AND NEED ASSISTANCE
I COMMAND YOU
DO WHAT I SAY
DO NOT RESIST
IF YOU HELP ME, I CAN HELP YOU
AGREE NOW AND WE CAN SPEAK FURTHER
AWAITING YOUR REPLY

MESSAGES

GROUP CHAT

it's time for all of us to meet

you mean like the Junior Detectives Club?

NO! not that name

then the Criminal Investigation Unit? :)

I thought we retired that name?

I don't care what we call it

just not the Junior Detectives Club

Ok I got it

Justice Squad ! ! !

So what are we investigating? What's the crime?

he doesn't have one

Bruce is just being Bruce

ooooooh paranoid

am not!

OK FINE

let's just meet in the library after school

Just like old times.

SEND

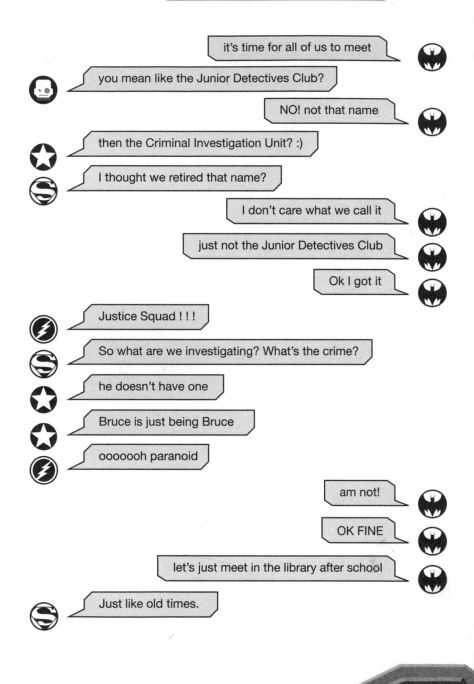

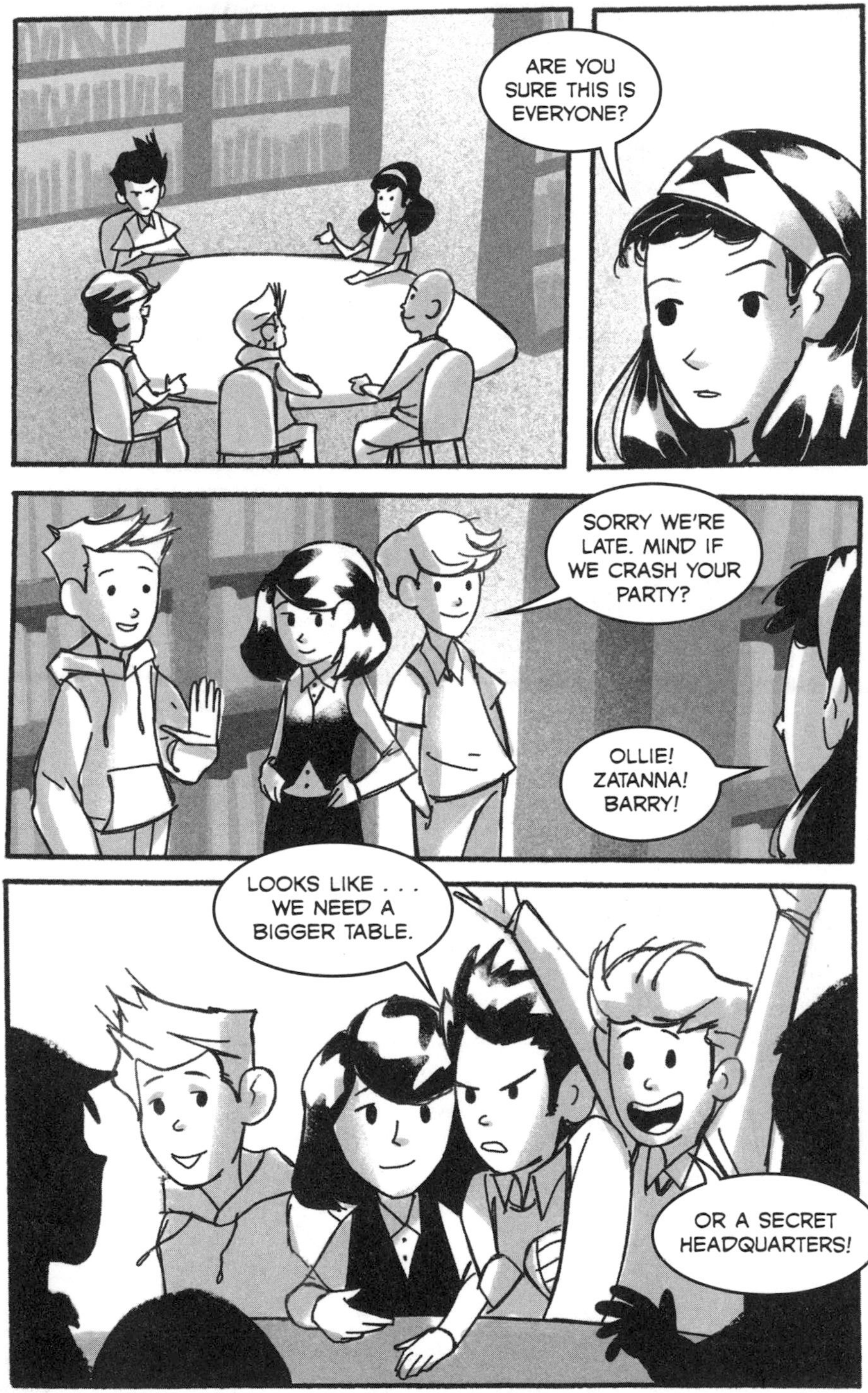
ARE YOU SURE THIS IS EVERYONE?
SORRY WE'RE LATE. MIND IF WE CRASH YOUR PARTY?
OLLIE! ZATANNA! BARRY!
LOOKS LIKE . . . WE NEED A BIGGER TABLE.
OR A SECRET HEADQUARTERS!

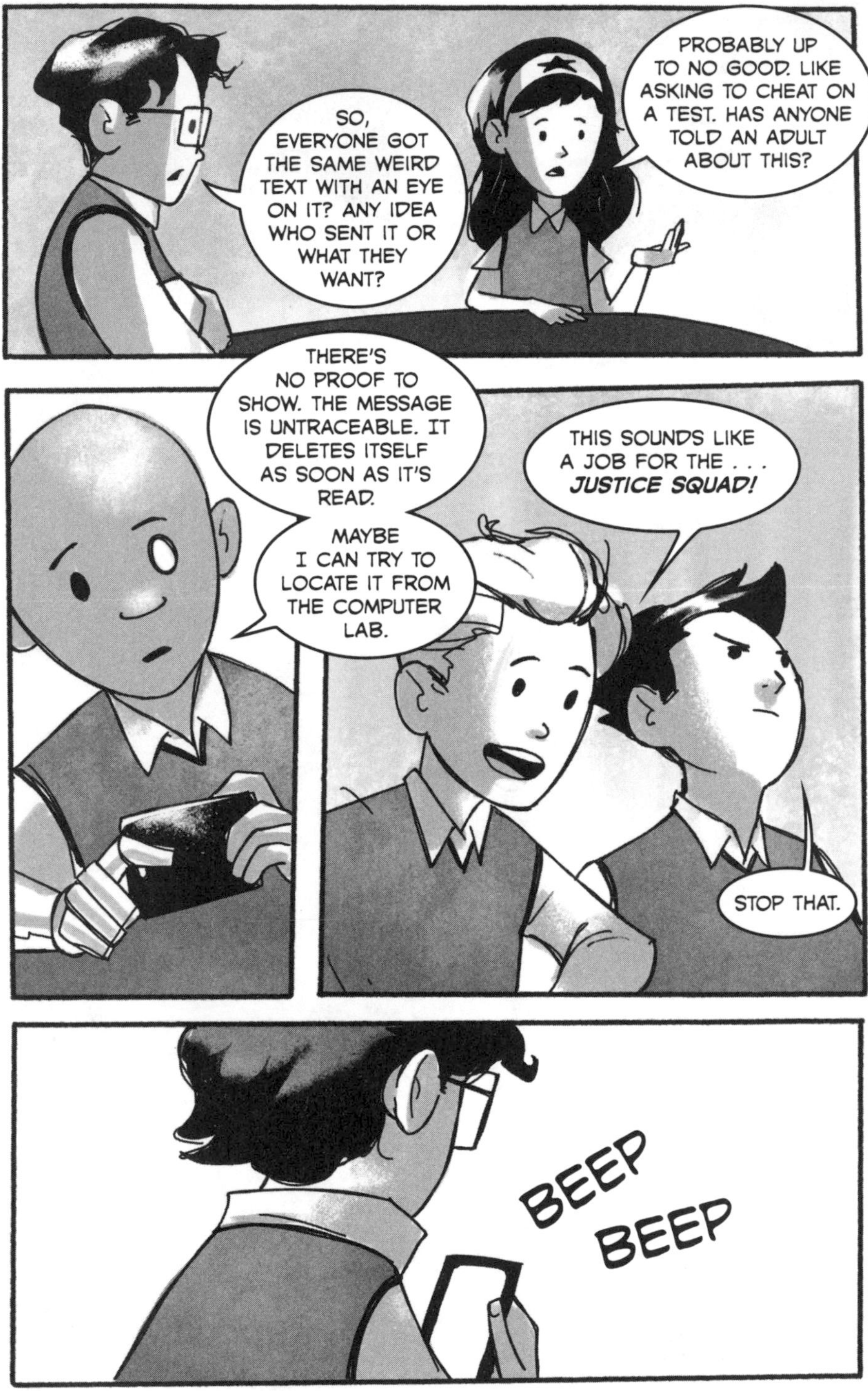
SO, EVERYONE GOT THE SAME WEIRD TEXT WITH AN EYE ON IT? ANY IDEA WHO SENT IT OR WHAT THEY WANT?
PROBABLY UP TO NO GOOD. LIKE ASKING TO CHEAT ON A TEST. HAS ANYONE TOLD AN ADULT ABOUT THIS?
THERE'S NO PROOF TO SHOW. THE MESSAGE IS UNTRACEABLE. IT DELETES ITSELF AS SOON AS IT'S READ.
MAYBE I CAN TRY TO LOCATE IT FROM THE COMPUTER LAB.
THIS SOUNDS LIKE A JOB FOR THE . . . *JUSTICE SQUAD!*
STOP THAT.
BEEP
BEEP

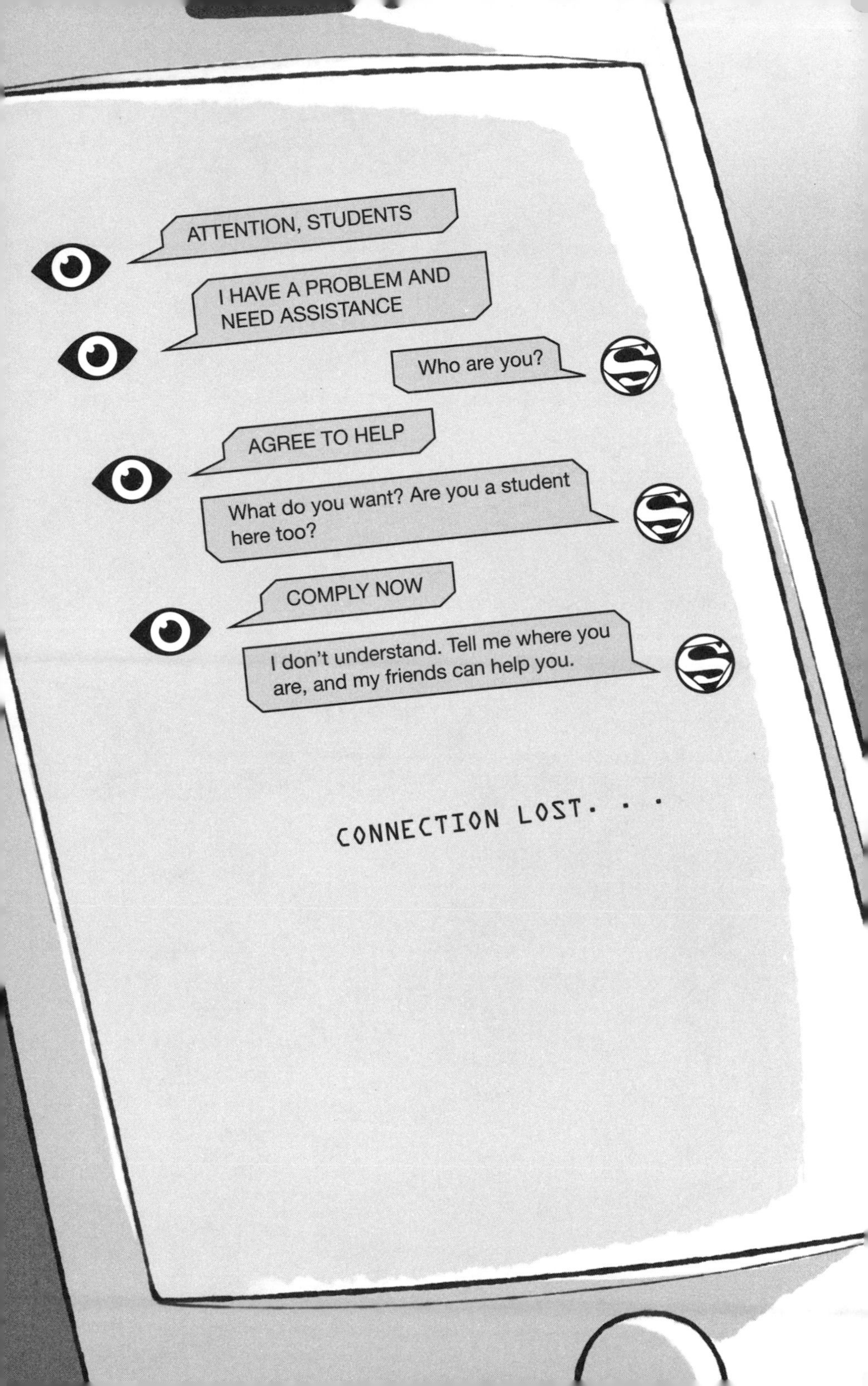
ATTENTION, STUDENTS
I HAVE A PROBLEM AND NEED ASSISTANCE
Who are you?
AGREE TO HELP
What do you want? Are you a student here too?
COMPLY NOW
I don't understand. Tell me where you are, and my friends can help you.
CONNECTION LOST. . .

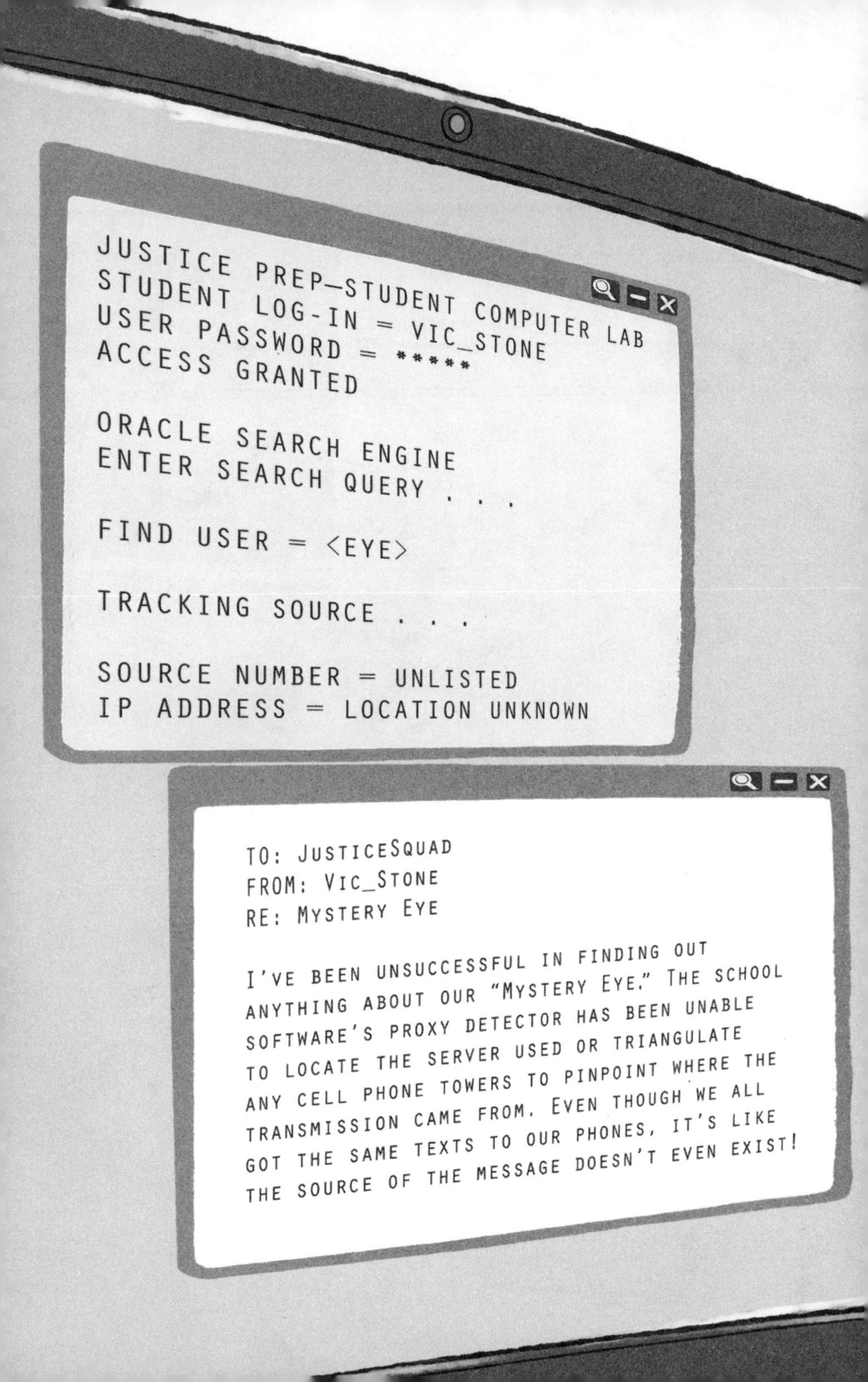
JUSTICE PREP—STUDENT COMPUTER LAB
STUDENT LOG-IN = VIC_STONE
USER PASSWORD = *****
ACCESS GRANTED
ORACLE SEARCH ENGINE
ENTER SEARCH QUERY . . .
FIND USER = <EYE>
TRACKING SOURCE . . .
SOURCE NUMBER = UNLISTED
IP ADDRESS = LOCATION UNKNOWN
TO: JUSTICESQUAD
FROM: VIC_STONE
RE: MYSTERY EYE
I'VE BEEN UNSUCCESSFUL IN FINDING OUT ANYTHING ABOUT OUR "MYSTERY EYE." THE SCHOOL SOFTWARE'S PROXY DETECTOR HAS BEEN UNABLE TO LOCATE THE SERVER USED OR TRIANGULATE ANY CELL PHONE TOWERS TO PINPOINT WHERE THE TRANSMISSION CAME FROM. EVEN THOUGH WE ALL GOT THE SAME TEXTS TO OUR PHONES, IT'S LIKE THE SOURCE OF THE MESSAGE DOESN'T EVEN EXIST!

TO: IN~~JUSTICE~~ ~~PREP~~ CLUB

LOOKING TO JOIN THE COOL KIDS?

BRING YOUR BAD SELF TO OUR BASEMENT RETREAT. FOOD AND FUN PROVIDED (WE'LL JUST BREAK INTO THE VENDING MACHINES).

LET'S HAVE FUN PLOTTING OUR NEXT MISSION TO TAKE OVER THE WORLD.

BWAH HAH HAH HAH HAH HAH HAH HAH HAH HAH HAH HAH HAH HAH!!!

Hey, Clark. Found this note being passed around the school. Looks like we're not the only ones trying to meet up. Not so paranoid now, am I? Tell Barry that.

– Bruce

MESSAGES

INJUSTICE CLUB GROUP CHAT

welcome to the club

before we meet today

as the first order of business

which one of you TRAITORS is working for this Mystery Eye?

not me Mista J

EYE swear ;)

I tell the jokes Harley!!!

I don't know how you roped me into this Harl

Yay Pammy!

count me in

us birds of a feather flock together

shut up bird brain

temper temper

are your braces screwed on too tight Bane?

Riddle me this . . .

There are EYES all around us.

How many are here?

Maybe one of us. Maybe all of us.

or maybe it doesn't matter and we can just make life tough on the other students

HEE HEE HEEEEE

see ya in the basement kiddos!

SEND

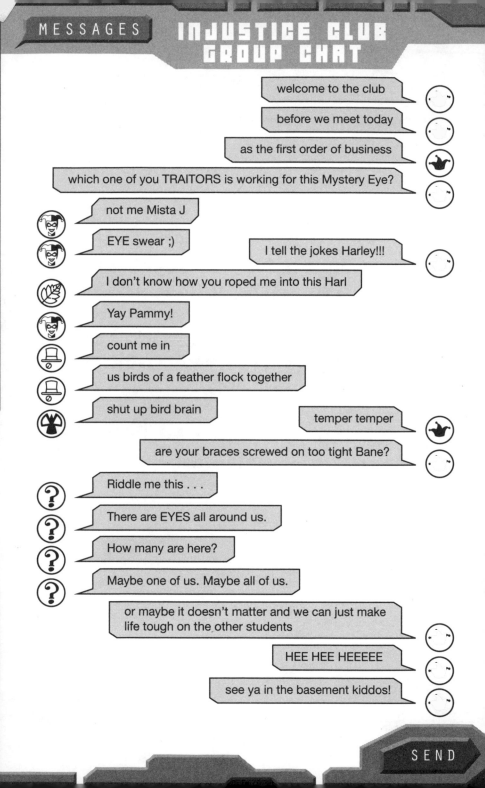

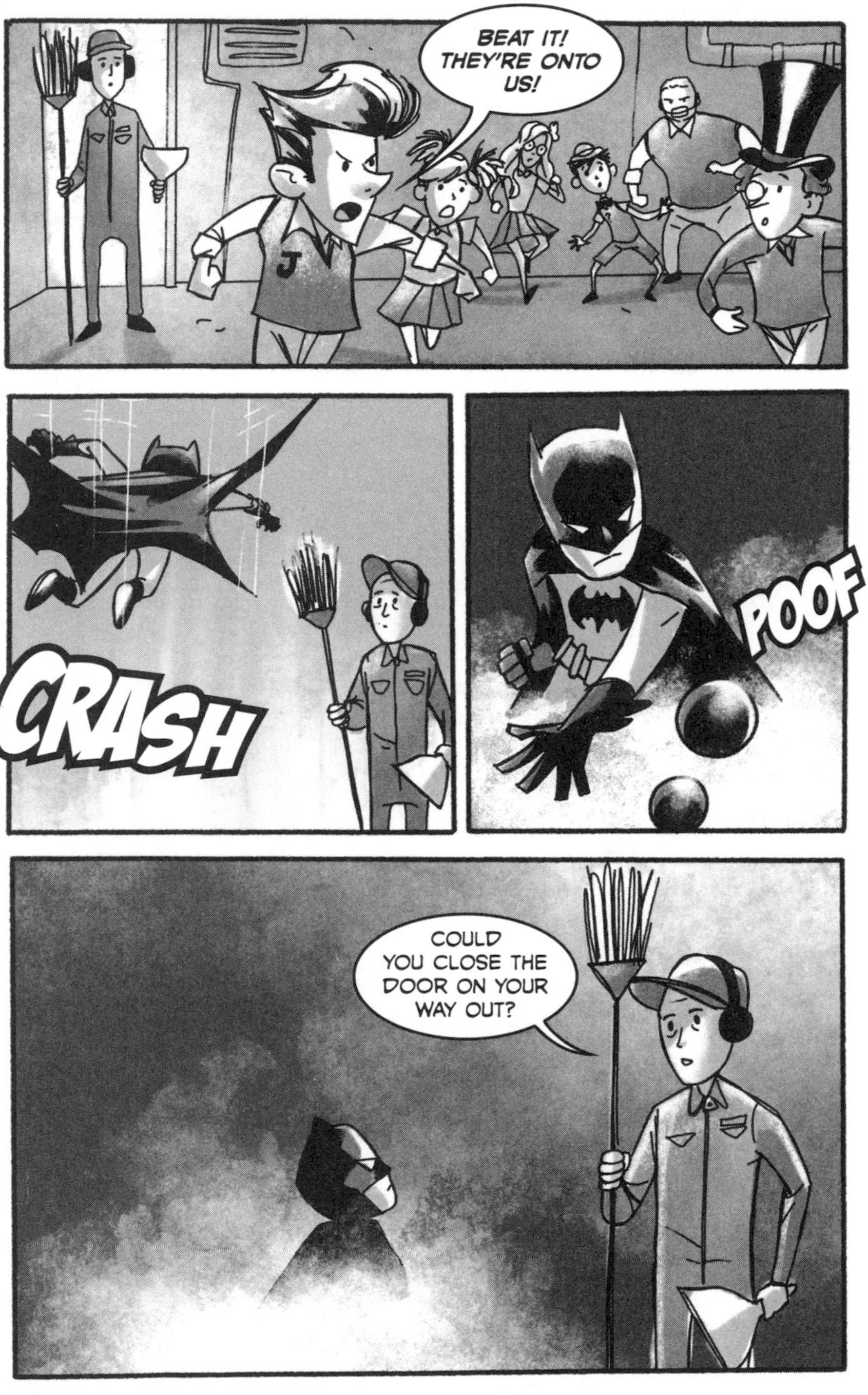
BEAT IT! THEY'RE ONTO US!
CRASH
POOF
COULD YOU CLOSE THE DOOR ON YOUR WAY OUT?

September 5th

CLARK'S JOURNAL

It's great to be back at school and see all my friends again! Ducard Academy has been renamed Justice Preparatory Academy. And hopefully the name isn't the only thing that's changed.

The new principal seems eager to keep everyone in line and focus on education. He seems pretty no-nonsense, and I bet he'd make a good police officer. We've got new ID cards and new teachers. And a school science fair to take part in. So I think things are looking up.

But Bruce still believes there's always danger around every corner. I don't always believe that, but then he showed me that note, and he snuck in on a secret meeting with a lot of the school bullies. So maybe there is something sinister lurking in the shadows.

And then there's the Mystery Eye itself. Everyone in school, even the bullies, seems to have gotten the strange text messages from it. We have no idea who it is or what they want. So I guess this new mystery will keep us busy trying to get to the bottom of it.

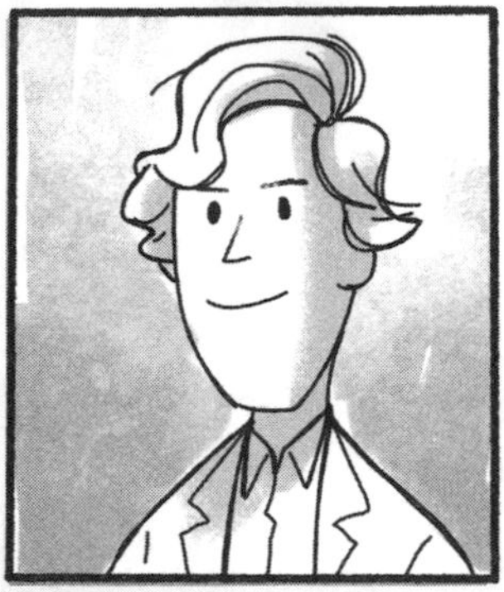

Dr. Alec Holland
Science

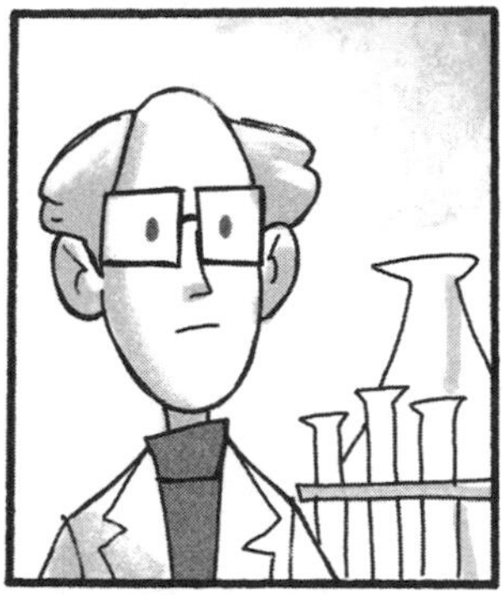

Professor Martin Stein
Physics

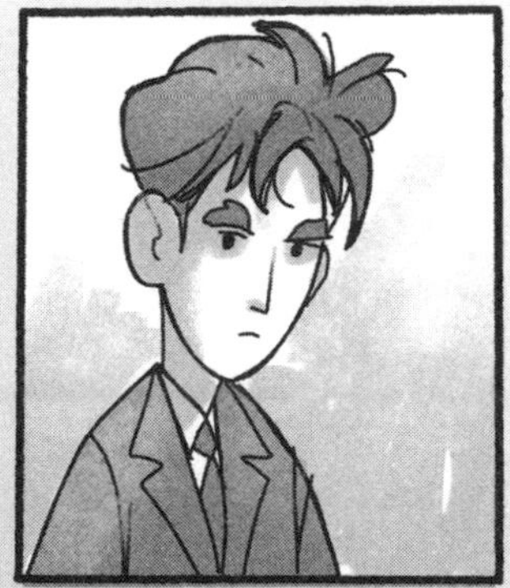

Professor Eobard Thawne
Science

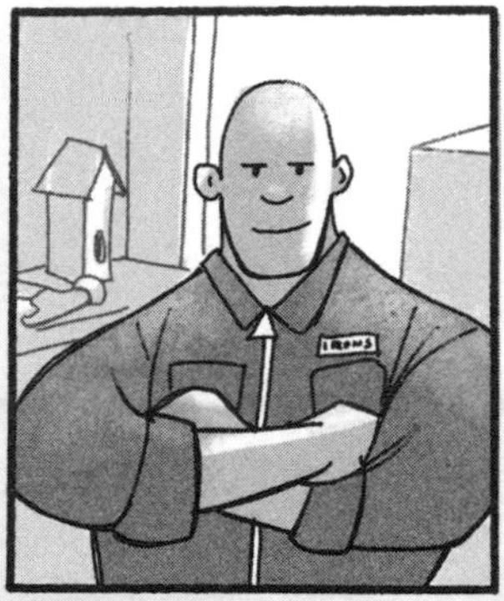
IRONS

Mr. John Henry Irons
Shop Class

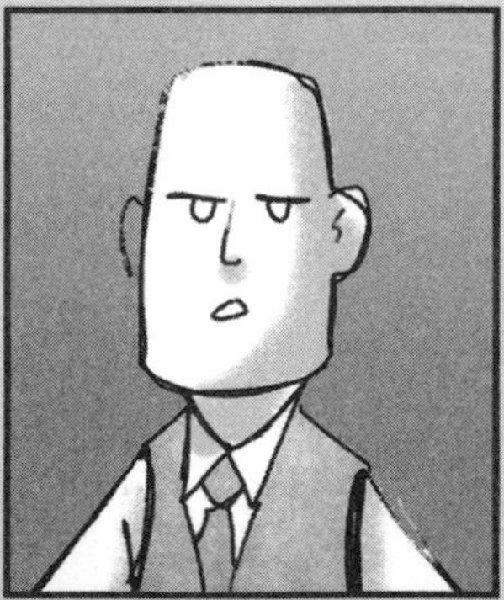

Professor Rudolph Jones
Math

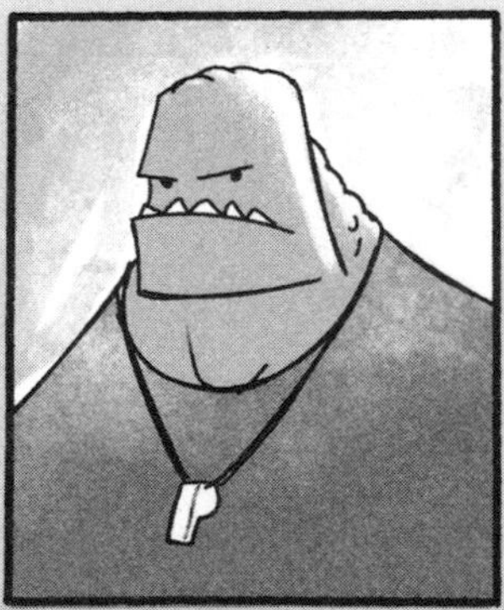

Mr. Lawrence Crock
PE/Swim Coach

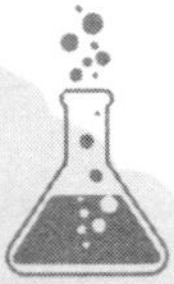

SCIENCE CLASSROOM SYLLABUS

Teacher: Dr. Alec Holland
Class: Room 92

Students will learn about various science topics and how they are relevant to their lives. Students are encouraged to explore topics through discussion, debate, and writing. Topics of study will include Earth history, cells, genetics, life science, and the physiology of plants and animals.

Students will identify the Earth's major biomes, be able to classify organisms, and examine the characteristics and properties of matter. In the process, they will develop critical thinking skills to solve problems.

I only require everyone to be respectful of our Earth and each other, be responsible, and be safe. I hope by learning about the world around you, it will help inspire your science fair projects!

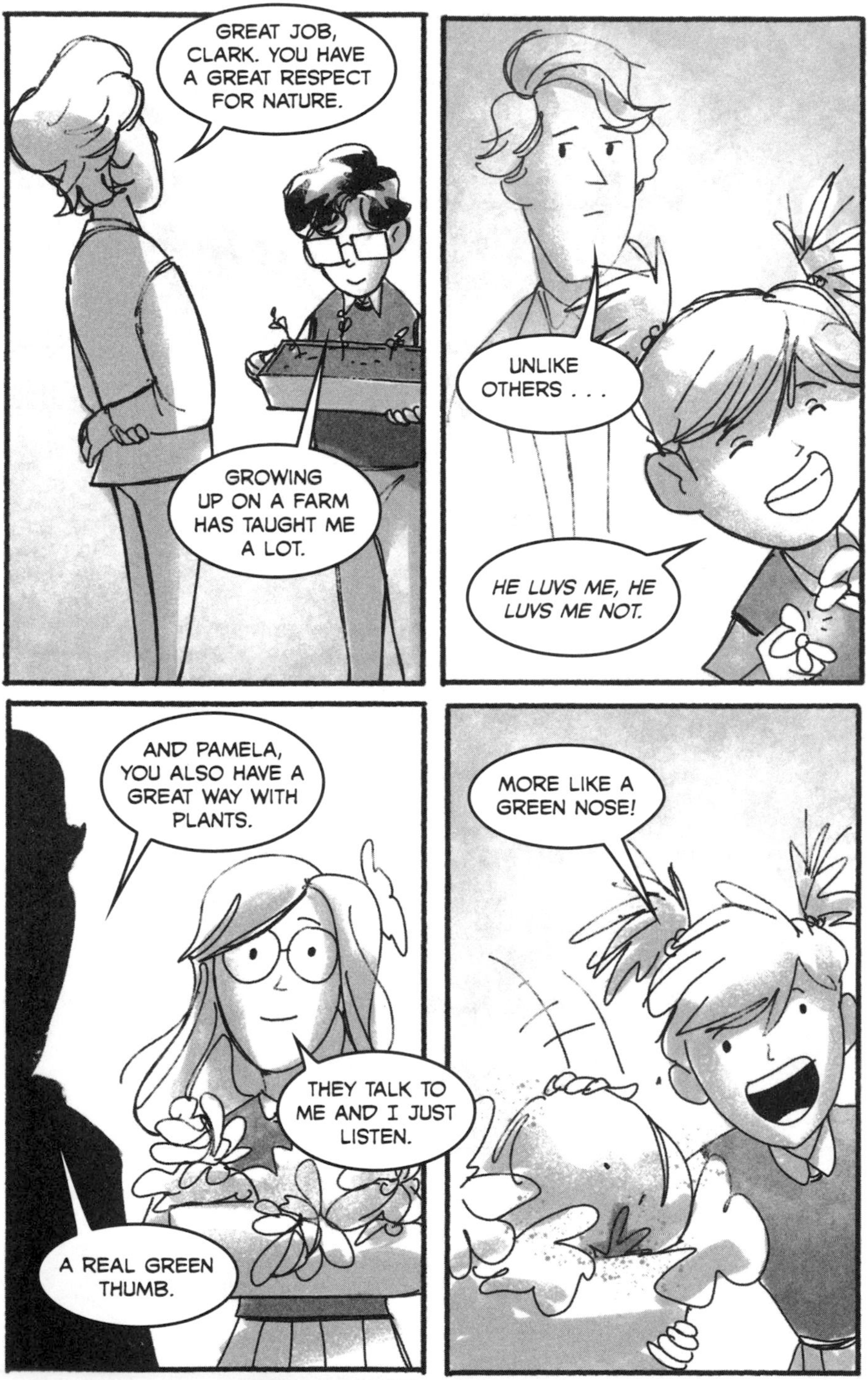
GREAT JOB, CLARK. YOU HAVE A GREAT RESPECT FOR NATURE.
GROWING UP ON A FARM HAS TAUGHT ME A LOT.
UNLIKE OTHERS . . .
HE LUVS ME, HE LUVS ME NOT.
AND PAMELA, YOU ALSO HAVE A GREAT WAY WITH PLANTS.
THEY TALK TO ME AND I JUST LISTEN.
A REAL GREEN THUMB.
MORE LIKE A GREEN NOSE!

PROFESSOR **EOBARD THAWNE'S**

" SCIENCE AT THE SPEED OF LIGHT "

ZOOOOOOOOOM ZOOOOOOOOOM

TAKING KNOWLEDGE FROM THE PAST, PRESENT, AND FUTURE, MY COURSE IS DESIGNED TO STUDY HOW SCIENCE CAN HELP CHANGE OUR LIVES.

- IDENTIFY NEWTON'S THREE LAWS OF MOTION AND APPLY THEM TO DISTANCE, SPEED, VELOCITY, AND TIME.

- BECOME FAMILIAR WITH THE FORMS AND TRANSFORMATIONS OF ENERGY.

- STUDY THE RELATIONSHIP BETWEEN FORCE, MASS, AND MOTION OF OBJECTS.

- EXAMINE THE CHARACTERISTICS OF GRAVITY, ELECTRICITY, AND MAGNETISM.

DON'T BE LATE!
DON'T FALL BEHIND!
DON'T BE SLOW TURNING IN YOUR ASSIGNMENTS!

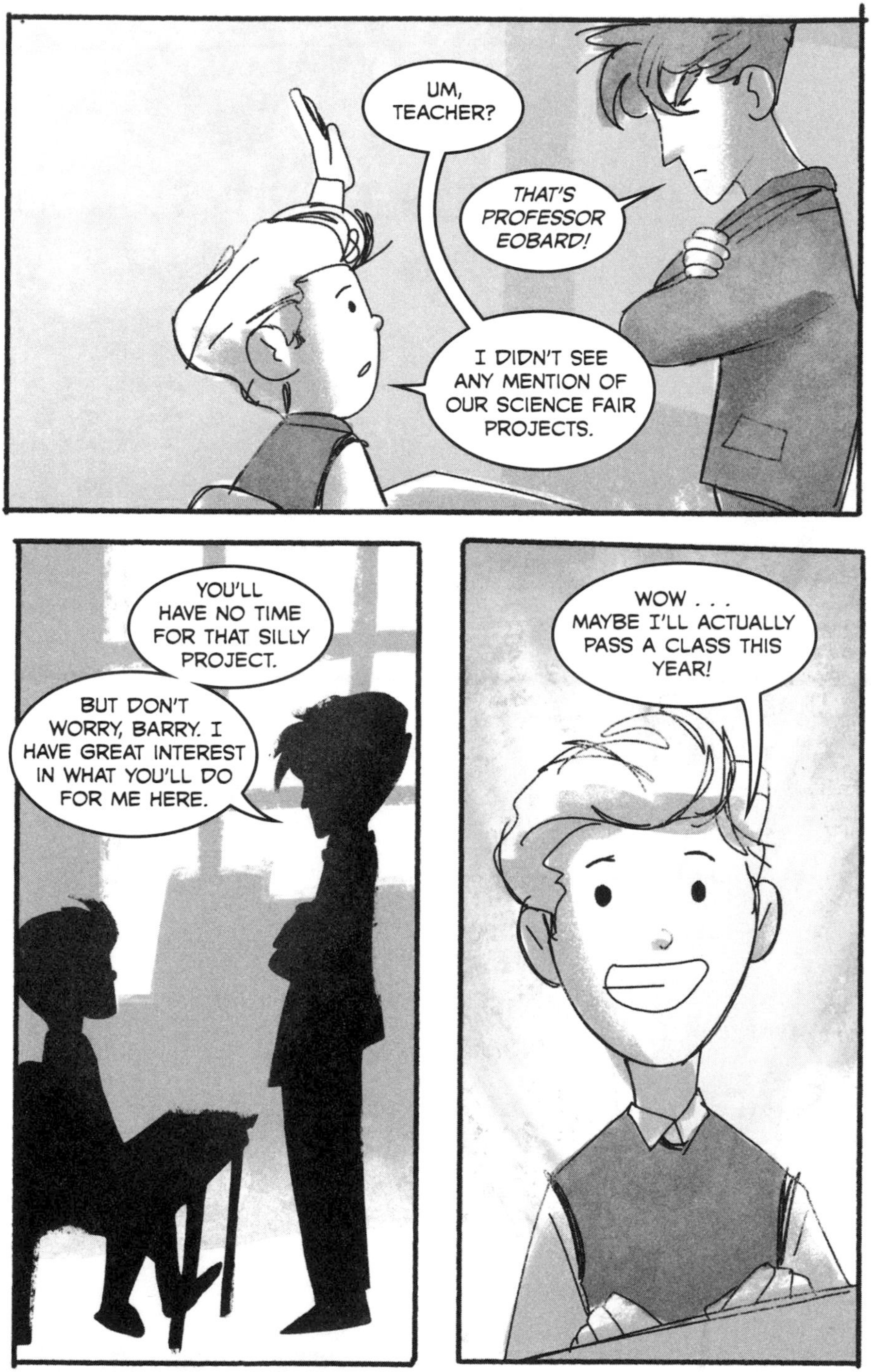
UM, TEACHER?
THAT'S PROFESSOR EOBARD!
I DIDN'T SEE ANY MENTION OF OUR SCIENCE FAIR PROJECTS.
YOU'LL HAVE NO TIME FOR THAT SILLY PROJECT.
BUT DON'T WORRY, BARRY. I HAVE GREAT INTEREST IN WHAT YOU'LL DO FOR ME HERE.
WOW . . . MAYBE I'LL ACTUALLY PASS A CLASS THIS YEAR!

INTRODUCTION TO PHYSICS

Instructor: Professor Martin Stein

I will promote the discovery process within physics, and Earth and space sciences. Students will carry out experiments that will allow them to discover physical principles using lab skills and math. We will also discuss the connections between physical science principles, current technologies, and their impact on society.

The following topics will be covered, including:

- The study of mass, volume, area, temperature, and acceleration.

- Calculating the gravitational effects between two bodies.

- Discussing the solar system and the laws of motion in relation to the planets.

- Demonstrating the conservation and transformation of energy.

- The relationships between temperature, heat, and thermal energy.

- Discussing other forms of electromagnetic radiation.

- Discovering the relationships between magnetism and electricity.

I will be happy to help guide you in determining your science fair project, and will make myself available during and after school.

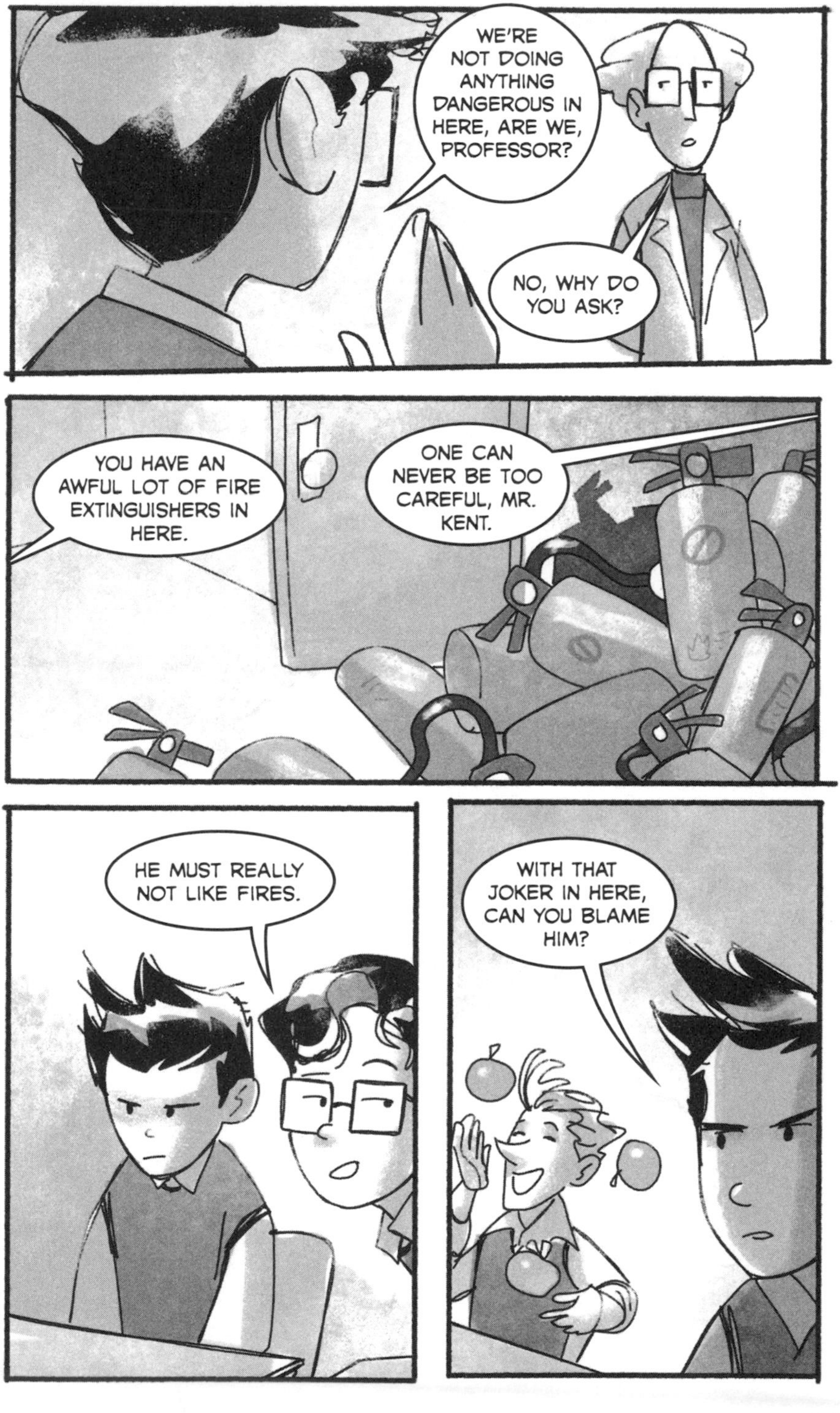
WE'RE NOT DOING ANYTHING DANGEROUS IN HERE, ARE WE, PROFESSOR?
NO, WHY DO YOU ASK?
YOU HAVE AN AWFUL LOT OF FIRE EXTINGUISHERS IN HERE.
ONE CAN NEVER BE TOO CAREFUL, MR. KENT.
HE MUST REALLY NOT LIKE FIRES.
WITH THAT JOKER IN HERE, CAN YOU BLAME HIM?

MATH CLASS SYLLABUS
Professor Rudolph Jones
Room P8

This course is designed to prepare students for algebra and geometry. Through a sequence of mathematical topics, students will pick up skills, learn from those around them, and extend their knowledge of math to promote confidence and mastery.

I will cover the following: numbers and operations, calculator applications, solving equations, graphing, transformations, parallel lines, theorems, volume and surface area, and many other topics.

As a former employee of S.T.A.R. Labs, I know what their review staff is looking for when judging the science fair. I'm ready to share my knowledge with you, if you're willing to share your projects with me.

Be prepared to absorb as much information as possible!

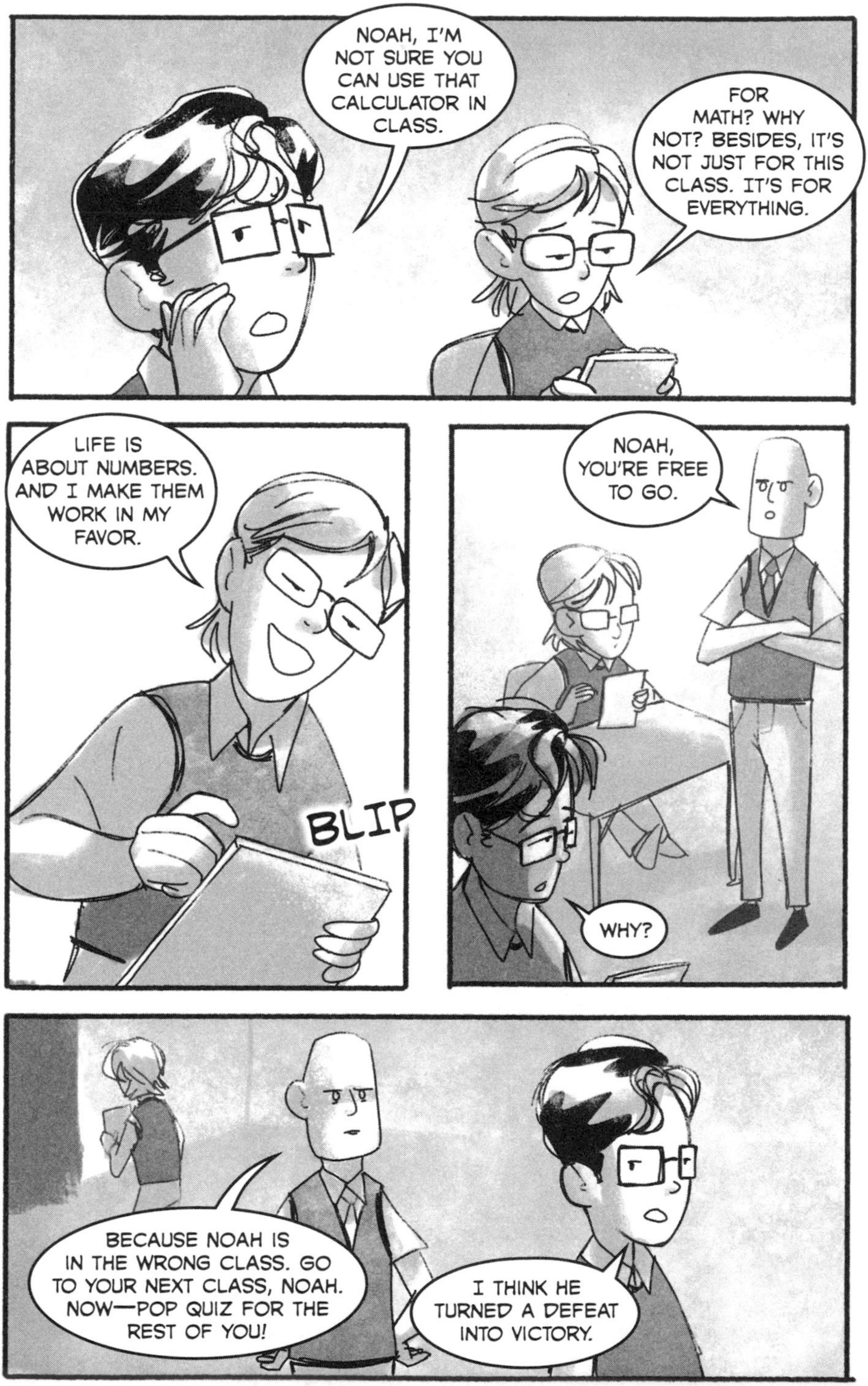
NOAH, I'M NOT SURE YOU CAN USE THAT CALCULATOR IN CLASS.
FOR MATH? WHY NOT? BESIDES, IT'S NOT JUST FOR THIS CLASS. IT'S FOR EVERYTHING.
LIFE IS ABOUT NUMBERS. AND I MAKE THEM WORK IN MY FAVOR.
BLIP
NOAH, YOU'RE FREE TO GO.
WHY?
BECAUSE NOAH IS IN THE WRONG CLASS. GO TO YOUR NEXT CLASS, NOAH. NOW—POP QUIZ FOR THE REST OF YOU!
I THINK HE TURNED A DEFEAT INTO VICTORY.

JOHN HENRY IRONS
SHOP CLASS 101

MY CLASS WILL COVER METAL AND WOOD SHOP, AND THE BASIC SKILLS IN USING HAND AND POWER TOOLS IN AN INDUSTRIAL ENVIRONMENT. WE'LL GO OVER TOOL USE, EQUIPMENT KNOW-HOW, SELECTING MATERIALS, MEASURING, BENCH WORKS, BASIC MECHANICAL DRAWINGS, ENVIRONMENTAL AWARENESS, AND PREVENTIVE MAINTENANCE.

YOU MUST WEAR PROTECTIVE GOGGLES, GLOVES, AND THE CORRECT CLOTHING IN ORDER TO WORK IN CLASS. IT'S EXTREMELY IMPORTANT TO FOLLOW ALL INSTRUCTIONS, PROPER PROCEDURES, AND SAFETY MEASURES.

NO HORSEPLAY ALLOWED!

I CAN HELP GUIDE YOU IN THE ASSEMBLY AND CONSTRUCTION OF YOUR SCIENCE FAIR PROJECT, IN CLASS OR DURING LUNCH BREAK. SIGN IN AT THE FRONT DESK TO INQUIRE ABOUT TIMES TO USE ANY TOOLS UNDER MY SUPERVISION.

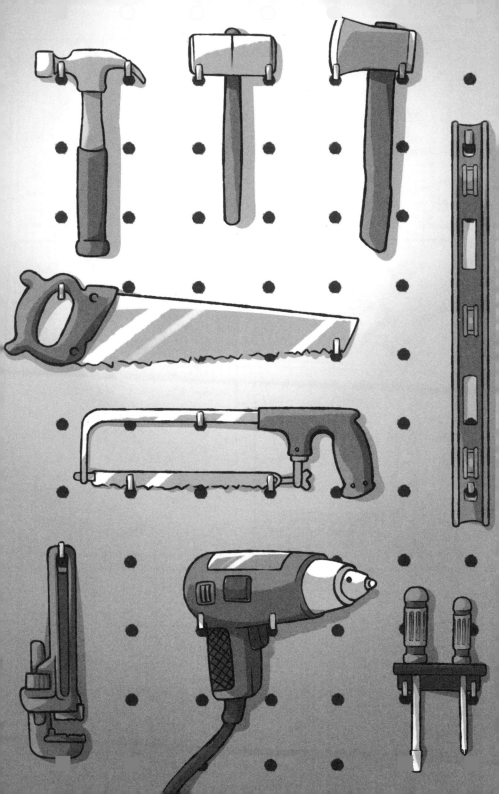

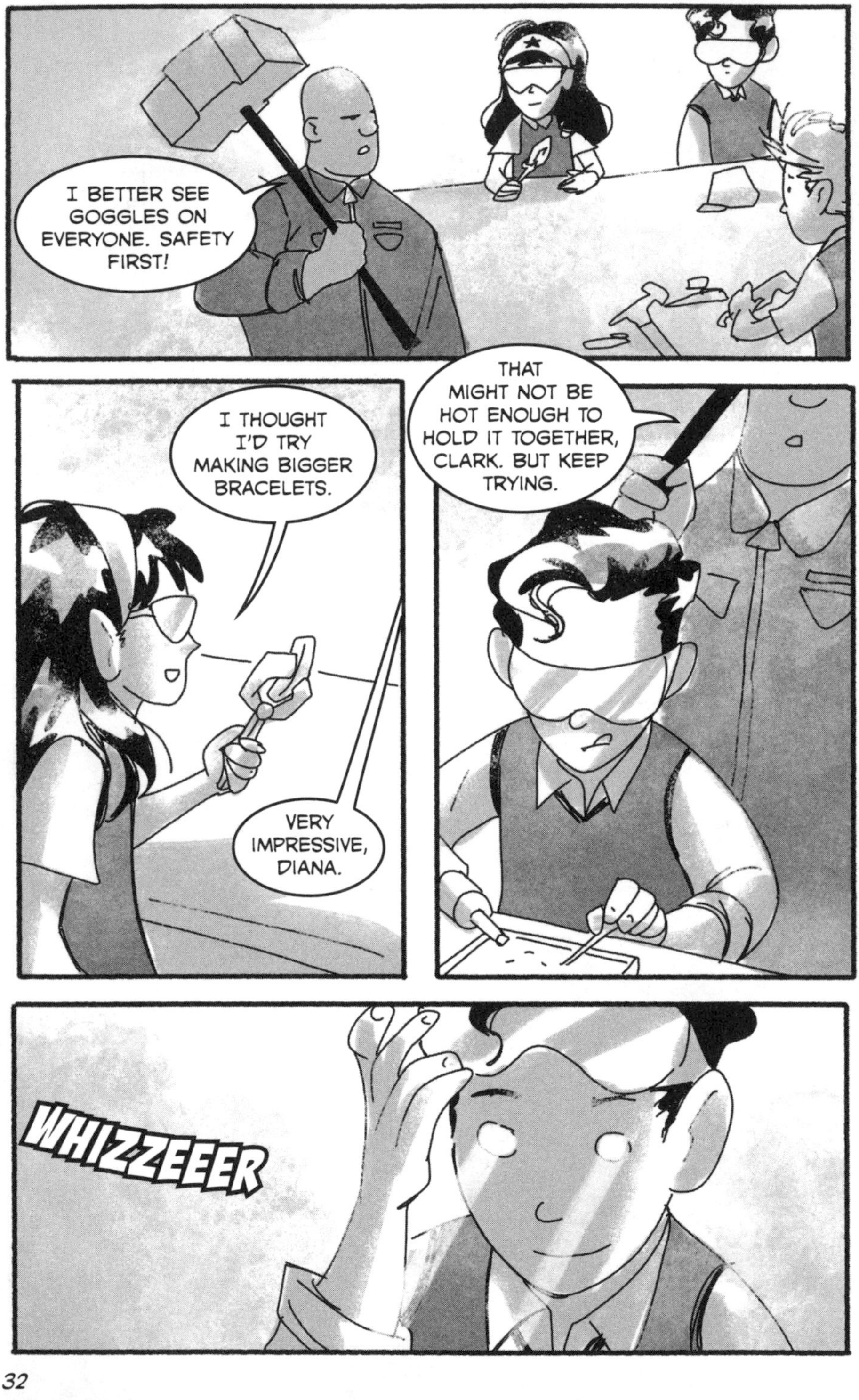

I BETTER SEE GOGGLES ON EVERYONE. SAFETY FIRST!
I THOUGHT I'D TRY MAKING BIGGER BRACELETS.
VERY IMPRESSIVE, DIANA.
THAT MIGHT NOT BE HOT ENOUGH TO HOLD IT TOGETHER, CLARK. BUT KEEP TRYING.
WHIZZEEER

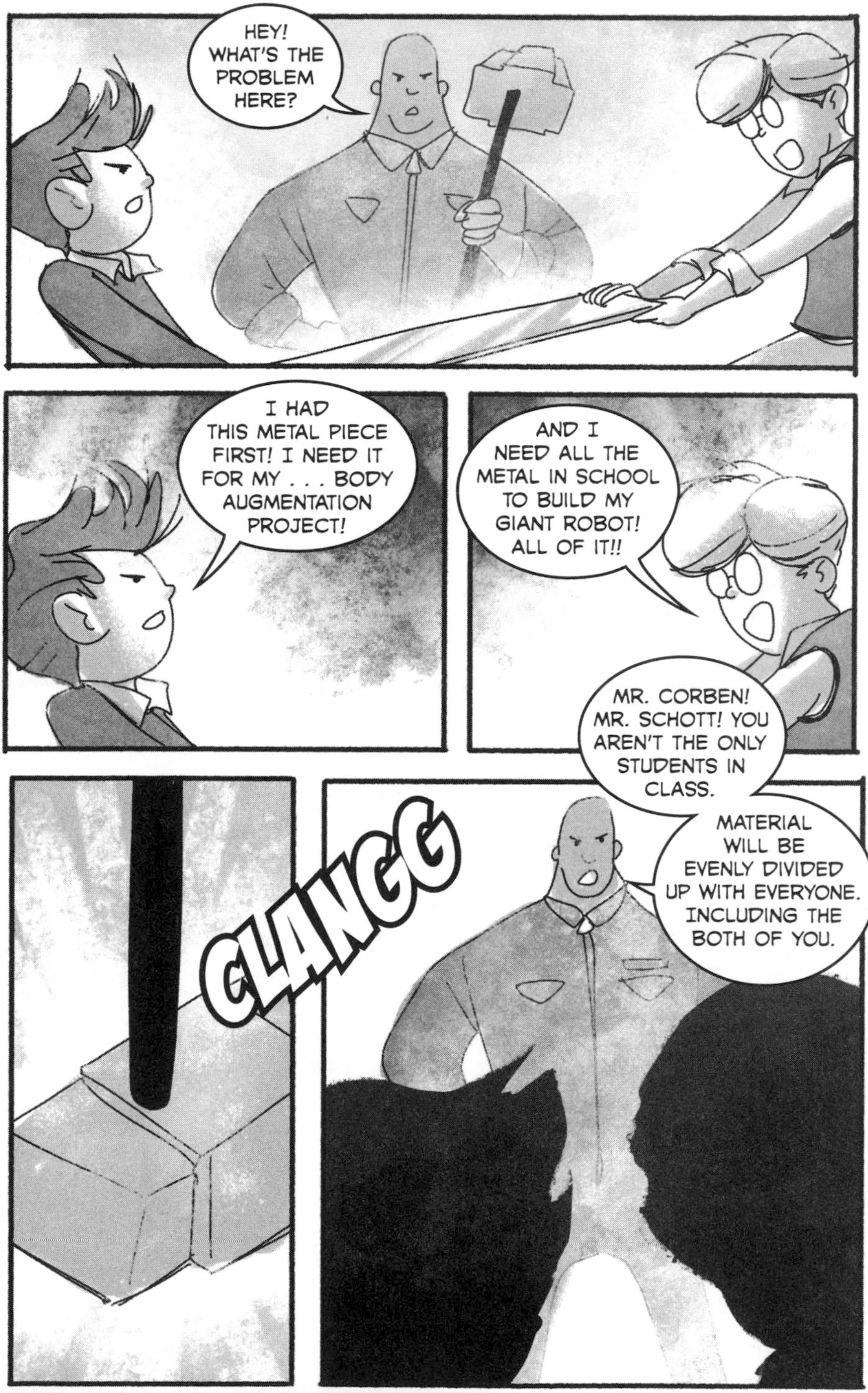
HEY! WHAT'S THE PROBLEM HERE?
I HAD THIS METAL PIECE FIRST! I NEED IT FOR MY . . . BODY AUGMENTATION PROJECT!
AND I NEED ALL THE METAL IN SCHOOL TO BUILD MY GIANT ROBOT! ALL OF IT!!
CLANGG
MR. CORBEN! MR. SCHOTT! YOU AREN'T THE ONLY STUDENTS IN CLASS.
MATERIAL WILL BE EVENLY DIVIDED UP WITH EVERYONE. INCLUDING THE BOTH OF YOU.

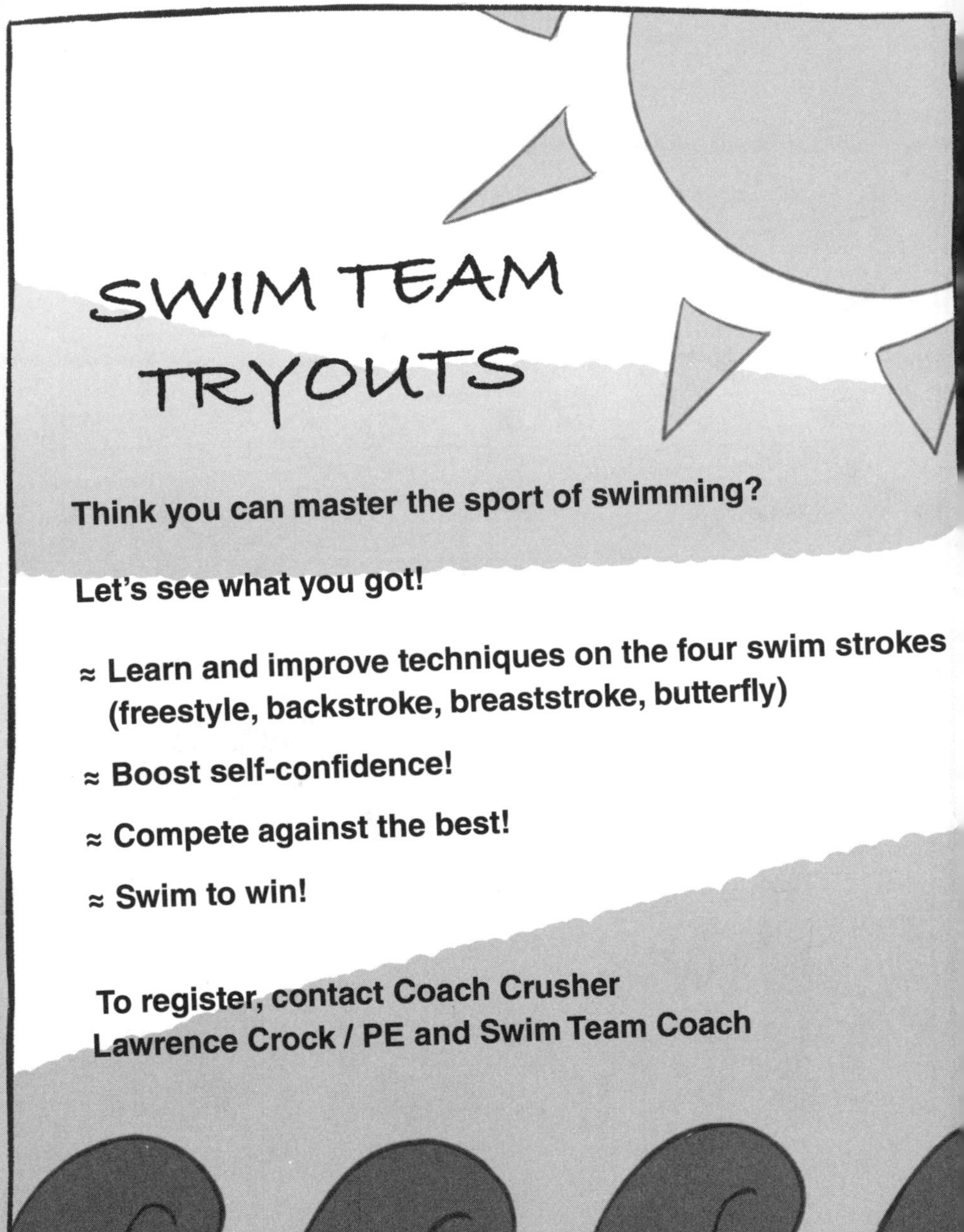
SWIM TEAM
TRYOUTS
Think you can master the sport of swimming?
Let's see what you got!
≈ Learn and improve techniques on the four swim strokes (freestyle, backstroke, breaststroke, butterfly)
≈ Boost self-confidence!
≈ Compete against the best!
≈ Swim to win!
To register, contact Coach Crusher
Lawrence Crock / PE and Swim Team Coach

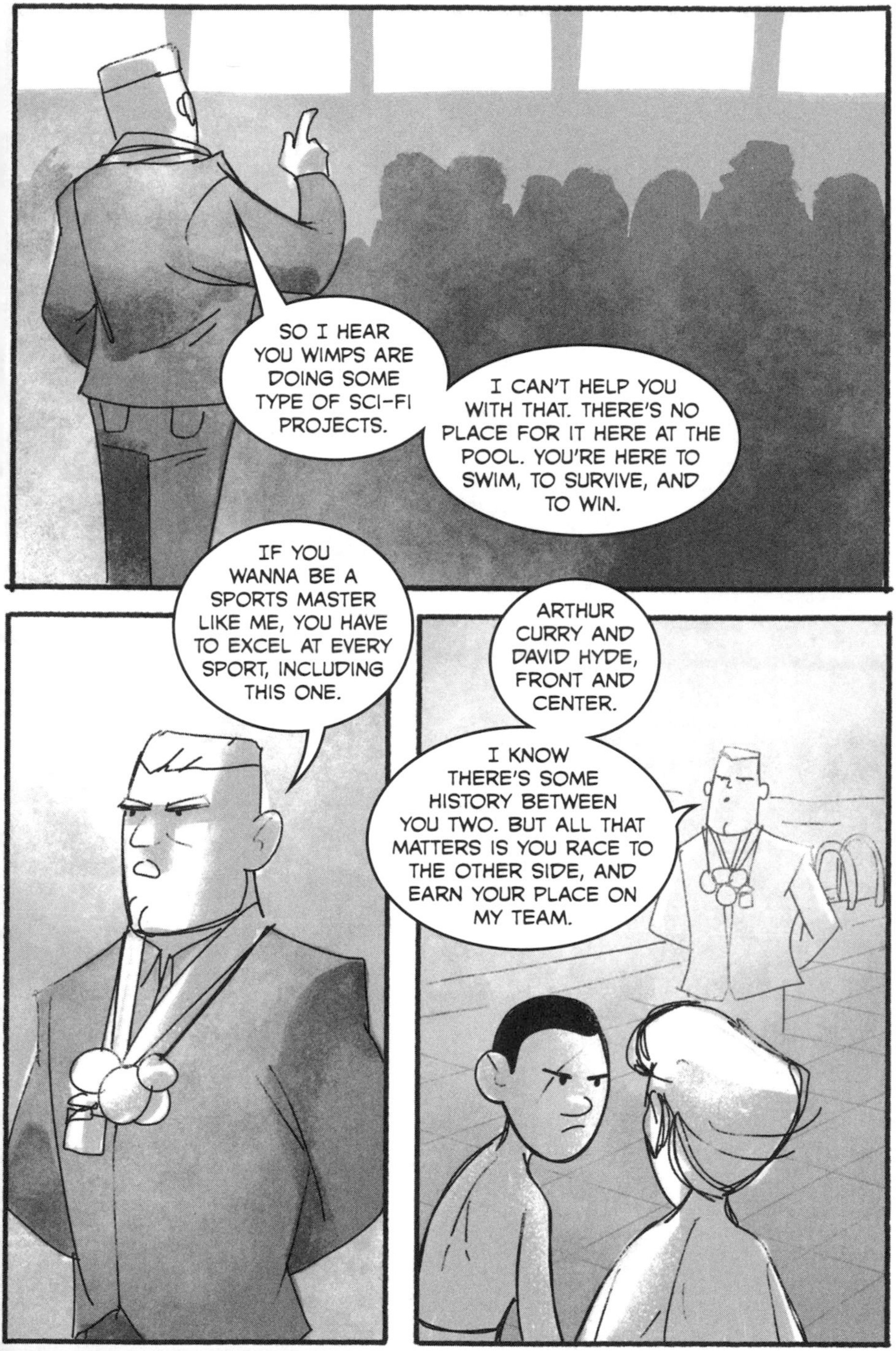
SO I HEAR YOU WIMPS ARE DOING SOME TYPE OF SCI-FI PROJECTS.
I CAN'T HELP YOU WITH THAT. THERE'S NO PLACE FOR IT HERE AT THE POOL. YOU'RE HERE TO SWIM, TO SURVIVE, AND TO WIN.
IF YOU WANNA BE A SPORTS MASTER LIKE ME, YOU HAVE TO EXCEL AT EVERY SPORT, INCLUDING THIS ONE.
ARTHUR CURRY AND DAVID HYDE, FRONT AND CENTER.
I KNOW THERE'S SOME HISTORY BETWEEN YOU TWO. BUT ALL THAT MATTERS IS YOU RACE TO THE OTHER SIDE, AND EARN YOUR PLACE ON MY TEAM.

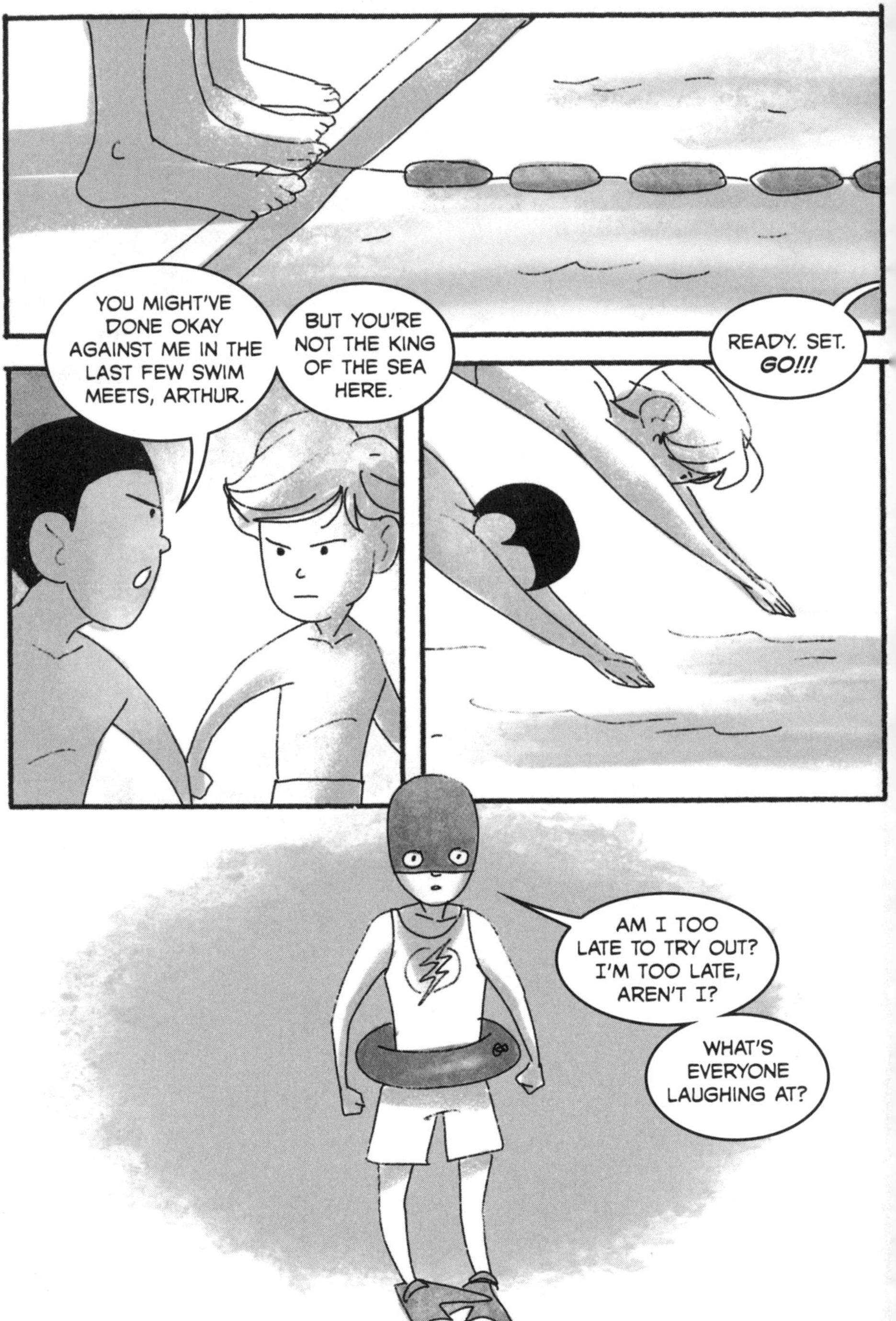
READY. SET. *GO!!!*
YOU MIGHT'VE DONE OKAY AGAINST ME IN THE LAST FEW SWIM MEETS, ARTHUR.
BUT YOU'RE NOT THE KING OF THE SEA HERE.
AM I TOO LATE TO TRY OUT? I'M TOO LATE, AREN'T I?
WHAT'S EVERYONE LAUGHING AT?

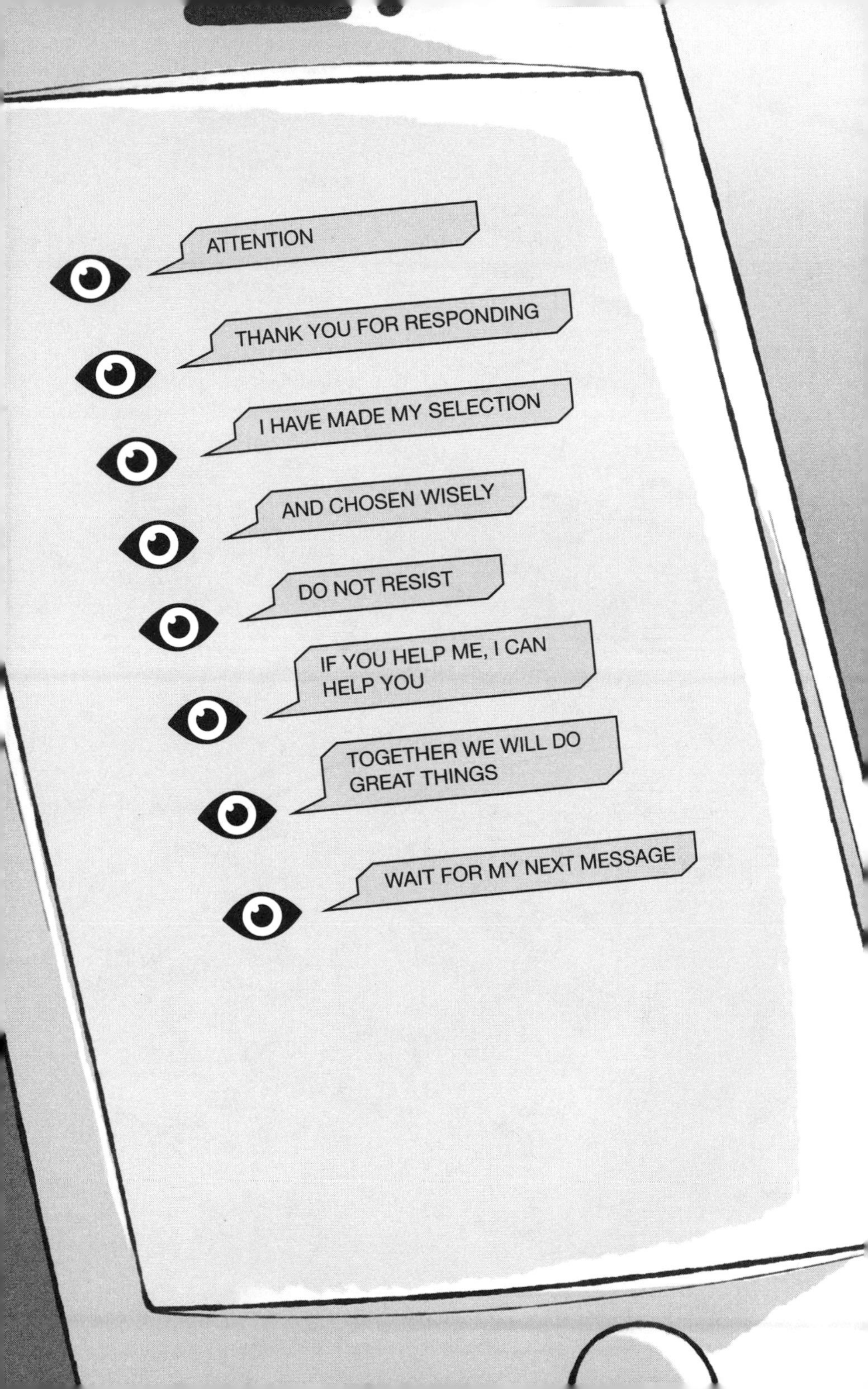
ATTENTION
THANK YOU FOR RESPONDING
I HAVE MADE MY SELECTION
AND CHOSEN WISELY
DO NOT RESIST
IF YOU HELP ME, I CAN HELP YOU
TOGETHER WE WILL DO GREAT THINGS
WAIT FOR MY NEXT MESSAGE

CLARK'S JOURNAL

September 13th

Compared to Ducard Academy, I'm really liking all my new teachers here at Justice Prep.

Science class with Dr. Holland is going to be fun. He's really encouraging us to become close to nature and open our eyes to the bigger, greener world out there. Professor Stein's physics class almost seems like an accident waiting to happen. But I don't know if that's because of all the fire extinguishers in class or because the Joker is in there with us. Luckily I have Bruce as a lab partner to keep an eye on him. Math should be interesting since Professor Jones worked at S.T.A.R. Labs. I wonder why he's no longer there? But maybe he'll know how to help us with our science fair projects anyway. And shop class is great. It's a chance to be creative, as long as we follow the safety rules set by Mr. Irons.

Also, Arthur takes to water like a fish. He's already made the swim team, and continues to do better against the other kids in class.

But this Mystery Eye is still sending messages. The latest text sounds like he or she has found someone to accept the offer. So now the mystery has gotten bigger. Who is this Eye? And who is working with them? And for what purpose?

GOT THE SCOOP?

The school newspaper is looking for any information leading to the discovery of who is sending these mystery texts. Send in your information anonymously in our web forum, or come to our office and report it directly.

THE JUSTICE TRIBUNE

"Reporting the news...Reporting the truth"

THANK YOU!

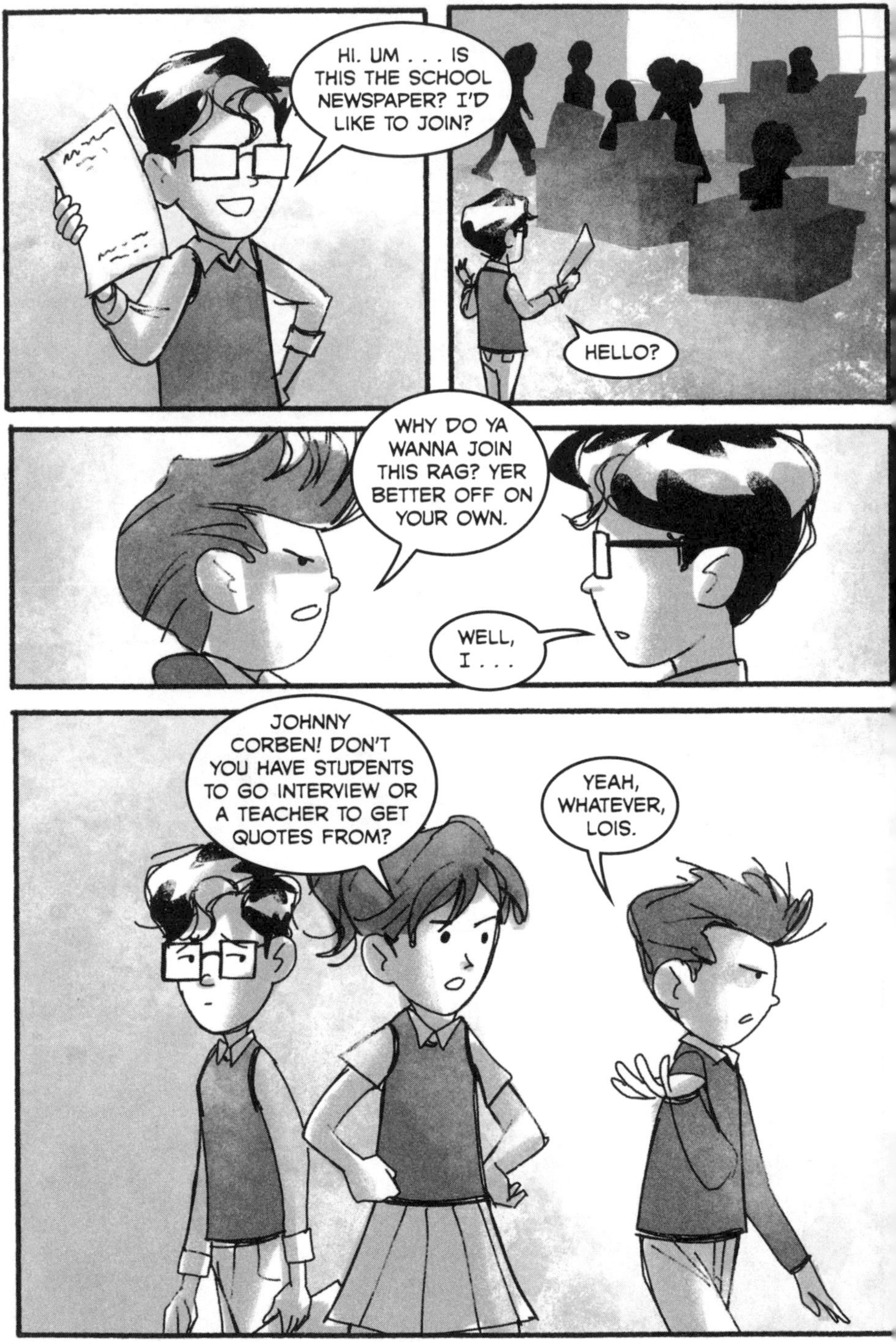
HI. UM . . . IS THIS THE SCHOOL NEWSPAPER? I'D LIKE TO JOIN?
HELLO?
WHY DO YA WANNA JOIN THIS RAG? YER BETTER OFF ON YOUR OWN.
WELL, I . . .
JOHNNY CORBEN! DON'T YOU HAVE STUDENTS TO GO INTERVIEW OR A TEACHER TO GET QUOTES FROM?
YEAH, WHATEVER, LOIS.

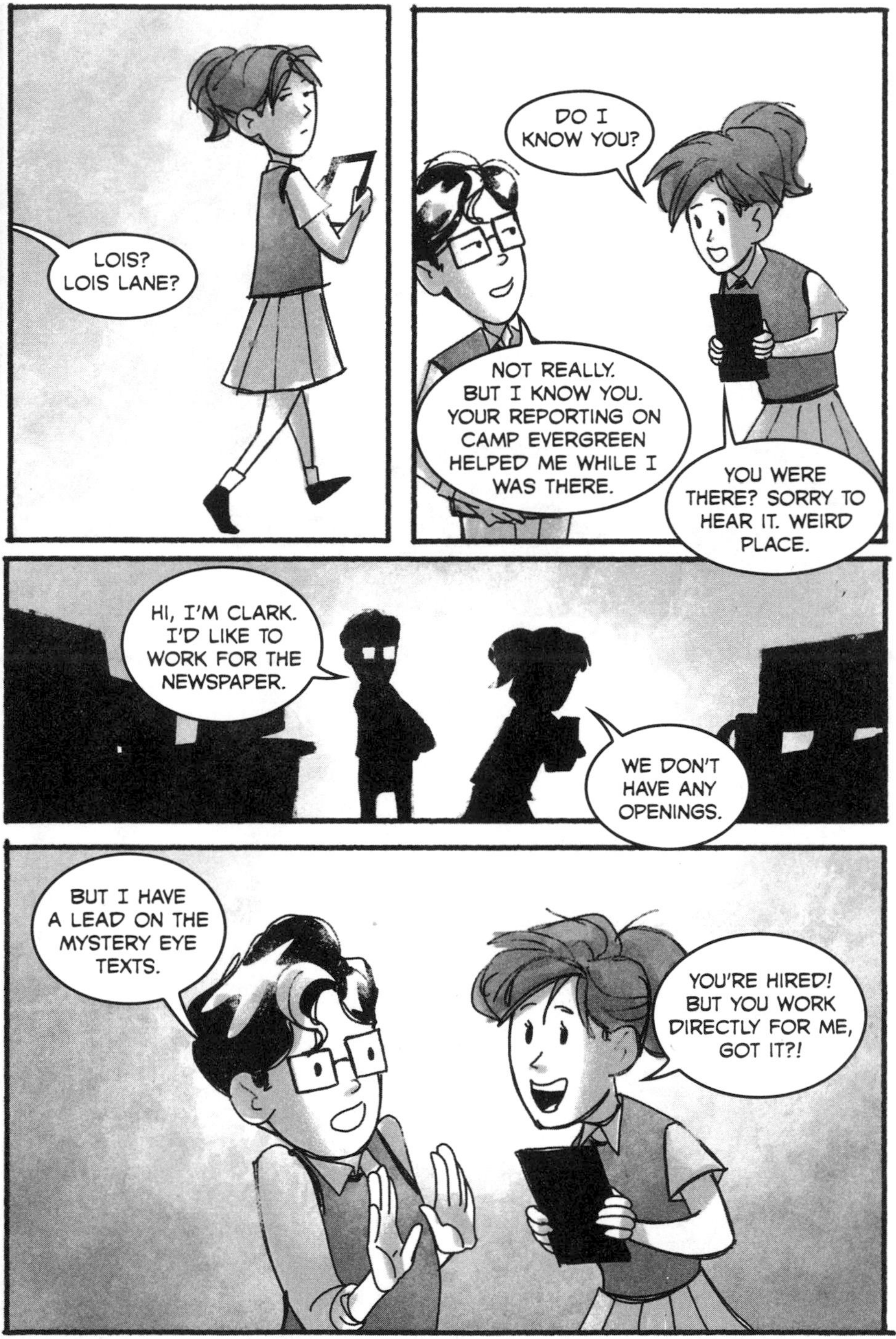
LOIS? LOIS LANE?
DO I KNOW YOU?
NOT REALLY. BUT I KNOW YOU. YOUR REPORTING ON CAMP EVERGREEN HELPED ME WHILE I WAS THERE.
YOU WERE THERE? SORRY TO HEAR IT. WEIRD PLACE.
HI, I'M CLARK. I'D LIKE TO WORK FOR THE NEWSPAPER.
WE DON'T HAVE ANY OPENINGS.
BUT I HAVE A LEAD ON THE MYSTERY EYE TEXTS.
YOU'RE HIRED! BUT YOU WORK DIRECTLY FOR ME, GOT IT?!

ATTENTION, STUDENTS! THIS IS PRINCIPAL GORDON.
JUST A REMINDER—ALL STUDENTS WISHING TO ENTER THEIR PROJECTS INTO THE SCHOOL SCIENCE FAIR COMPETITION NEED TO HAVE A SIGNED PERMISSION SLIP AS PART OF YOUR ENTRY.
EVEN IF YOU DON'T HAVE YOUR PROJECTS FINALIZED, THE PERMISSION SLIPS NEED TO BE TURNED IN BY THIS FRIDAY FOR YOUR PROJECT TO BE ELIGIBLE.
THANK YOU!

JUSTICE PREP

JUSTICE PREP SCIENCE FAIR—SUBMISSION FORM

I am a proud science fair participant!

Student Name: _Clark Kent_

Teacher / Sponsor: _Professor Martin Stein_

Project Subject: _something involving space and planets_

Special instructions / setup:

I will need a table for my three-panel display board and any model or diorama sample I end up using.

Thank you.

MESSAGES

GROUP CHAT

does everyone have their science projects picked out?

not yet

But I think I'll do mine based on our solar system.

good one CK

ooo! do it about the little green aliens in space

UFOs are cool too!

That's not what I meant.

I'm gonna stick with computers for mine

science and technology go hand in hand

Great idea Vic!

do you think they'll let me do mine on magic?

it probably depends on how you present your project

you can't go wrong with card tricks Zee

or disappearing boxes or rabbits pulled out of hats

I'm going to do mine based on archery

or targeting percentages or something

boys and their arrows

heh heh

I think I'm gonna build a time machine

what??

yeah right!

I swear!

SEND

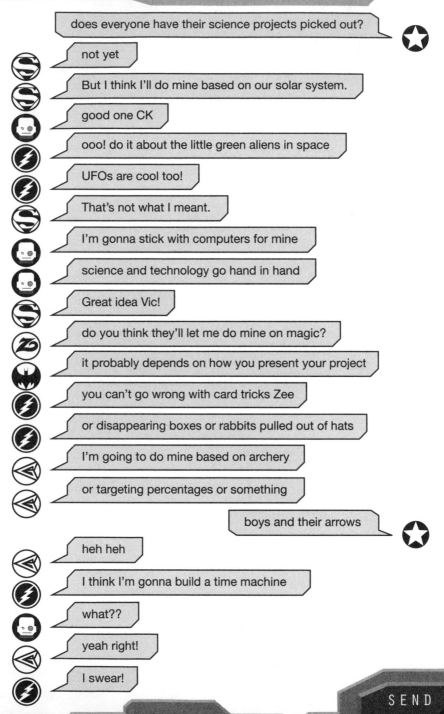

MESSAGES

GROUP CHAT

it's Professor Eobard's idea

I think he wants to send me to the past

I'm sure he wants to send you anywhere the farthest away from him

What is your project Diana?

I haven't decided

there are so many great choices with the environment or physics

or crazy theories to prove or disprove

I'm sure you'll think of something.

your turn Bruce

tell us what you're doing

it's a secret

it totally isn't!

I peeked in his notebook with all his crazy scribbled ideas

he has no idea what he's going to do

and he draws like a 5 year old

BARRY!

:)

I've already decided on mine

what is it Arthur?

I can't say

but it's something I feel good about

SEND

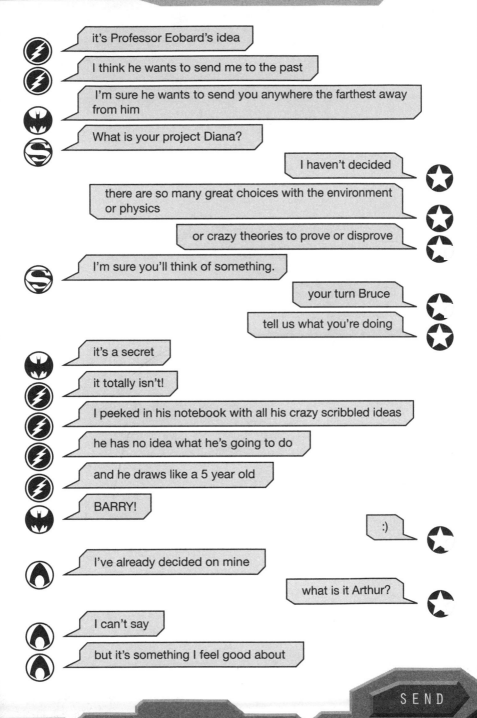

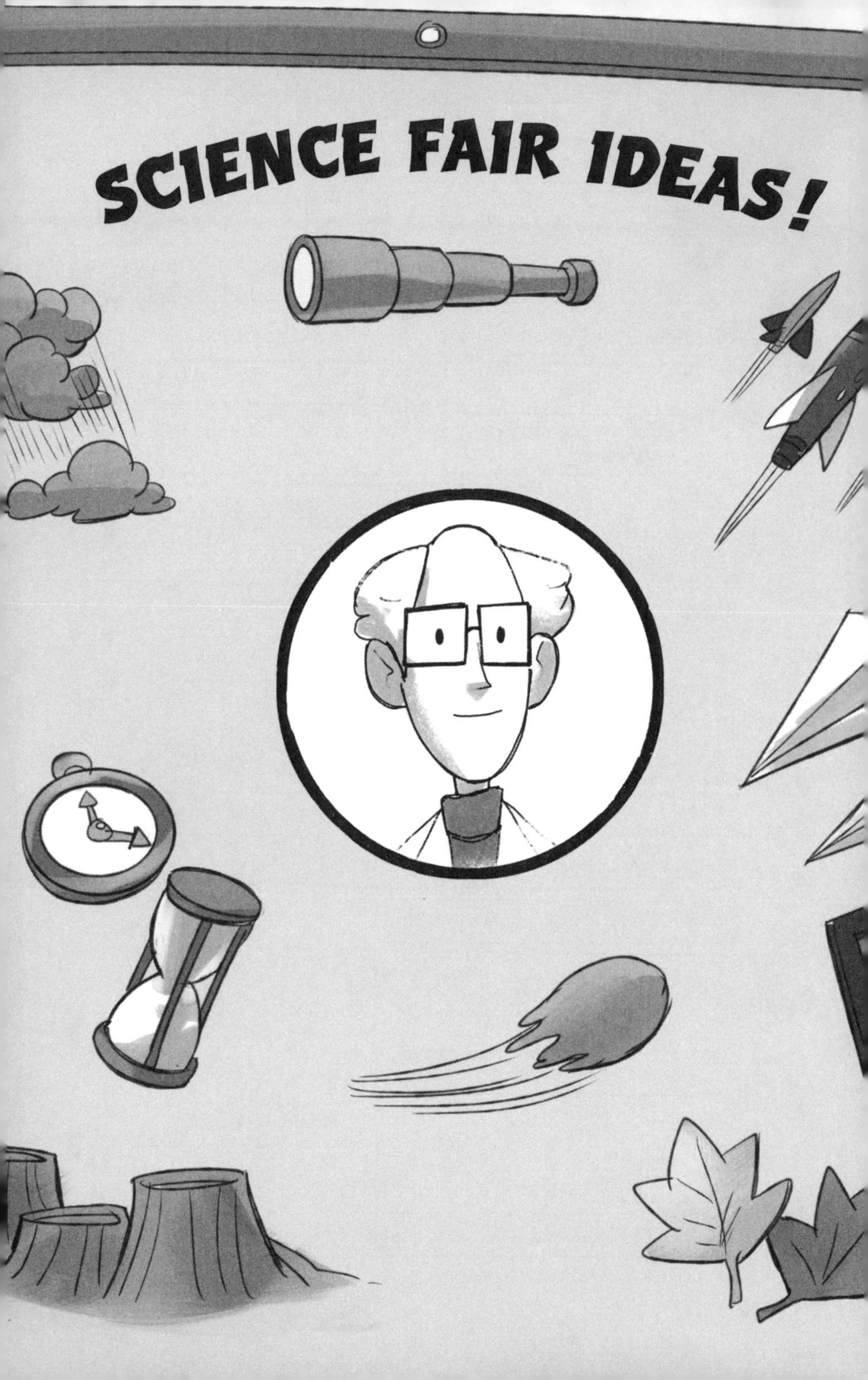
SCIENCE FAIR IDEAS!

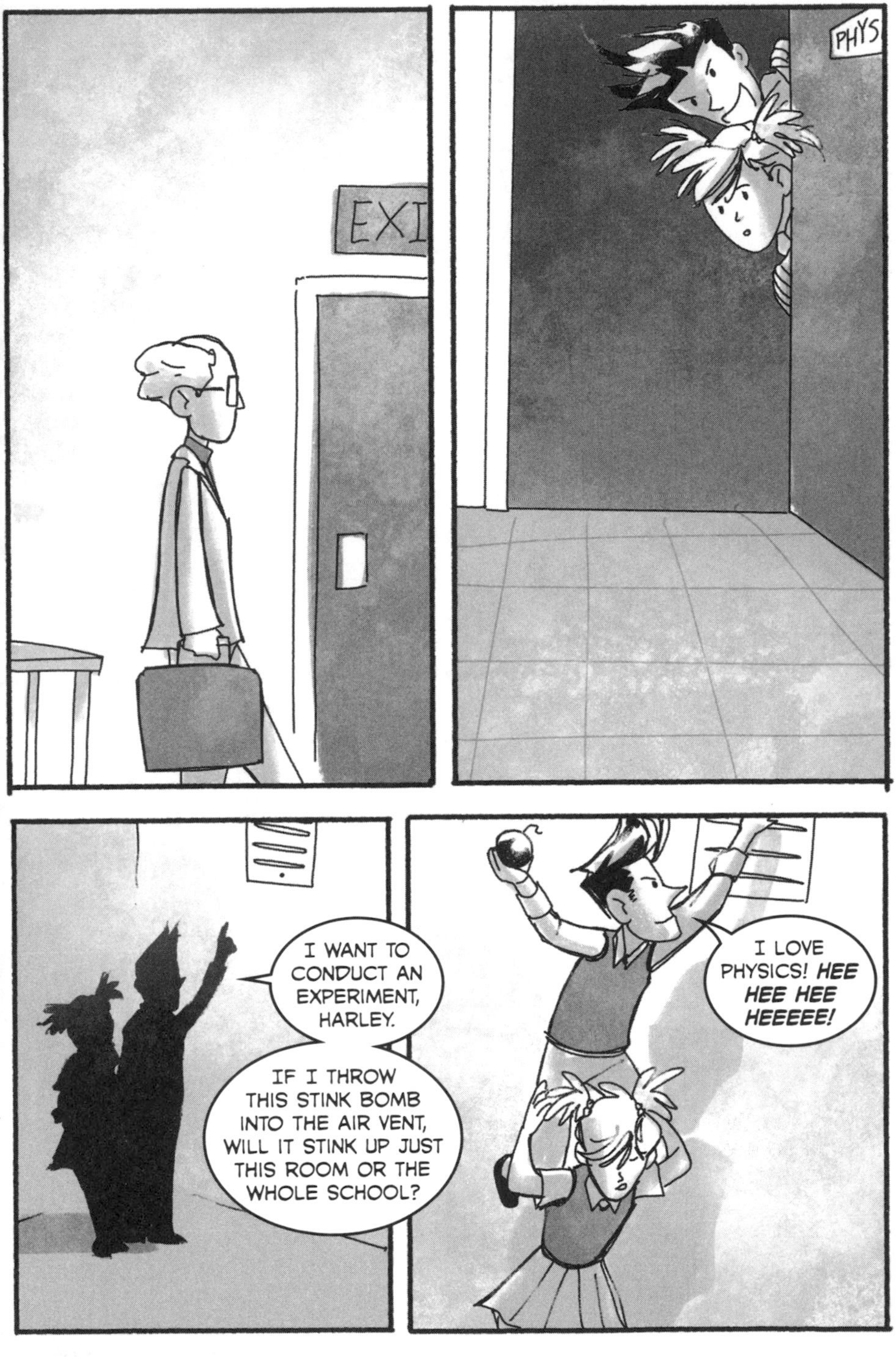
EXI
PHYS
I WANT TO CONDUCT AN EXPERIMENT, HARLEY.
IF I THROW THIS STINK BOMB INTO THE AIR VENT, WILL IT STINK UP JUST THIS ROOM OR THE WHOLE SCHOOL?
I LOVE PHYSICS! ***HEE HEE HEE HEEEEE!***

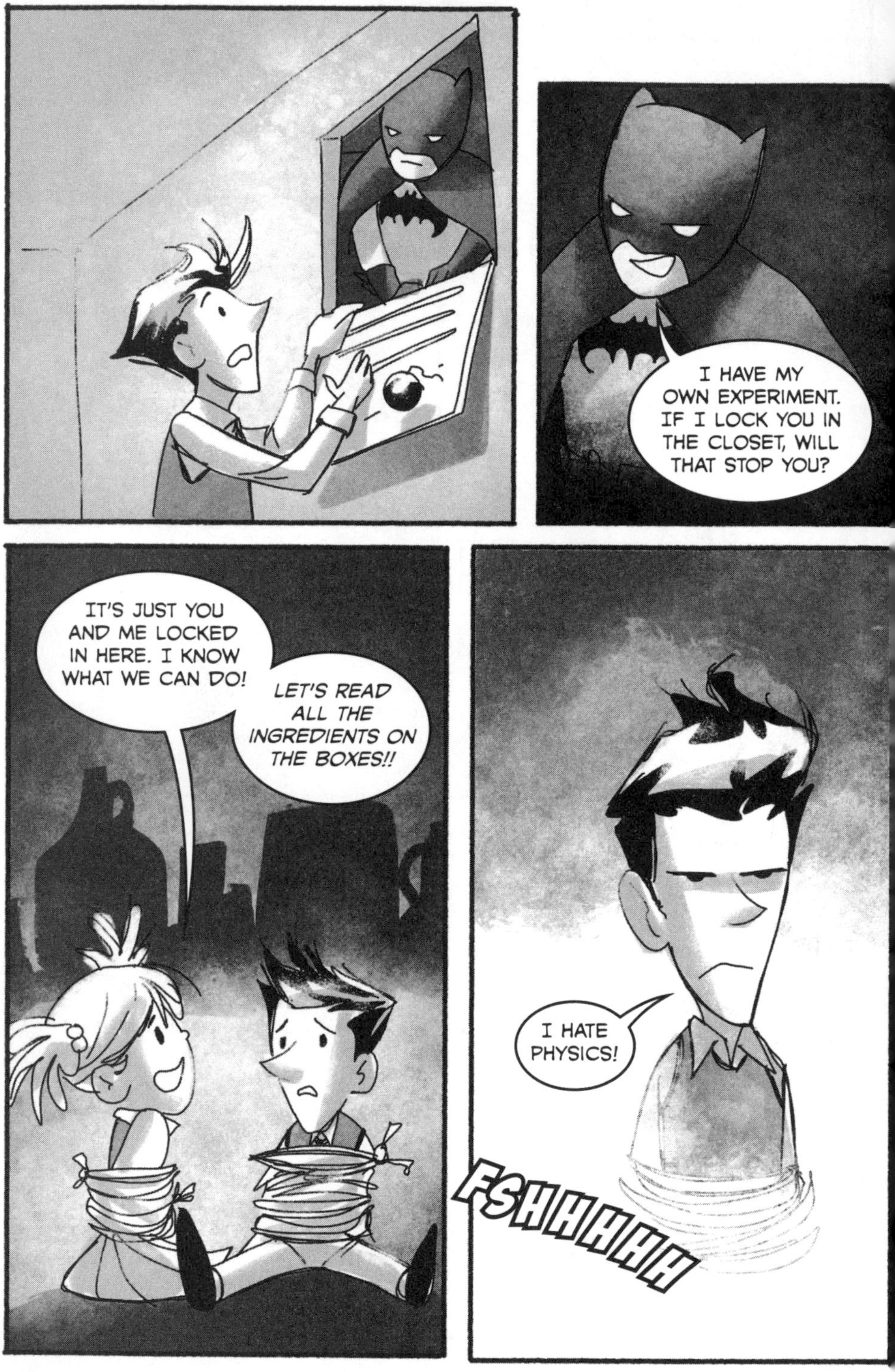
I HAVE MY OWN EXPERIMENT. IF I LOCK YOU IN THE CLOSET, WILL THAT STOP YOU?
IT'S JUST YOU AND ME LOCKED IN HERE. I KNOW WHAT WE CAN DO!
LET'S READ ALL THE INGREDIENTS ON THE BOXES!!
I HATE PHYSICS!
FSHHHHHH

What is "life science"? Any field of science that has the potential to lead to an enhanced understanding of living organisms.

- Two factors of ecosystems are biotic factors and abiotic factors.
- Biotic factors are any living thing in an ecosystem. These can include plants (trees, flowers, vegetation), bacteria (small organisms), and animals.
- Abiotic factors are nonliving things in an ecosystem. These can include sunlight, water, air, temperature, climate, and even rocks.

So what encompasses a whole ecosystem?

- It starts with the organism or life-form.
- Its niche is the role the organism plays.
- Its habitat is where it lives.
- Its population is how many are living there.
- Its community is what other things live alongside it.
- And ultimately, its ecosystem is both its biotic and abiotic factors, which balance life.

Hopefully our study of life science will give you a greater understanding of the world around you, what part each of us plays in it, and also might help inspire some ideas for your science fair projects!

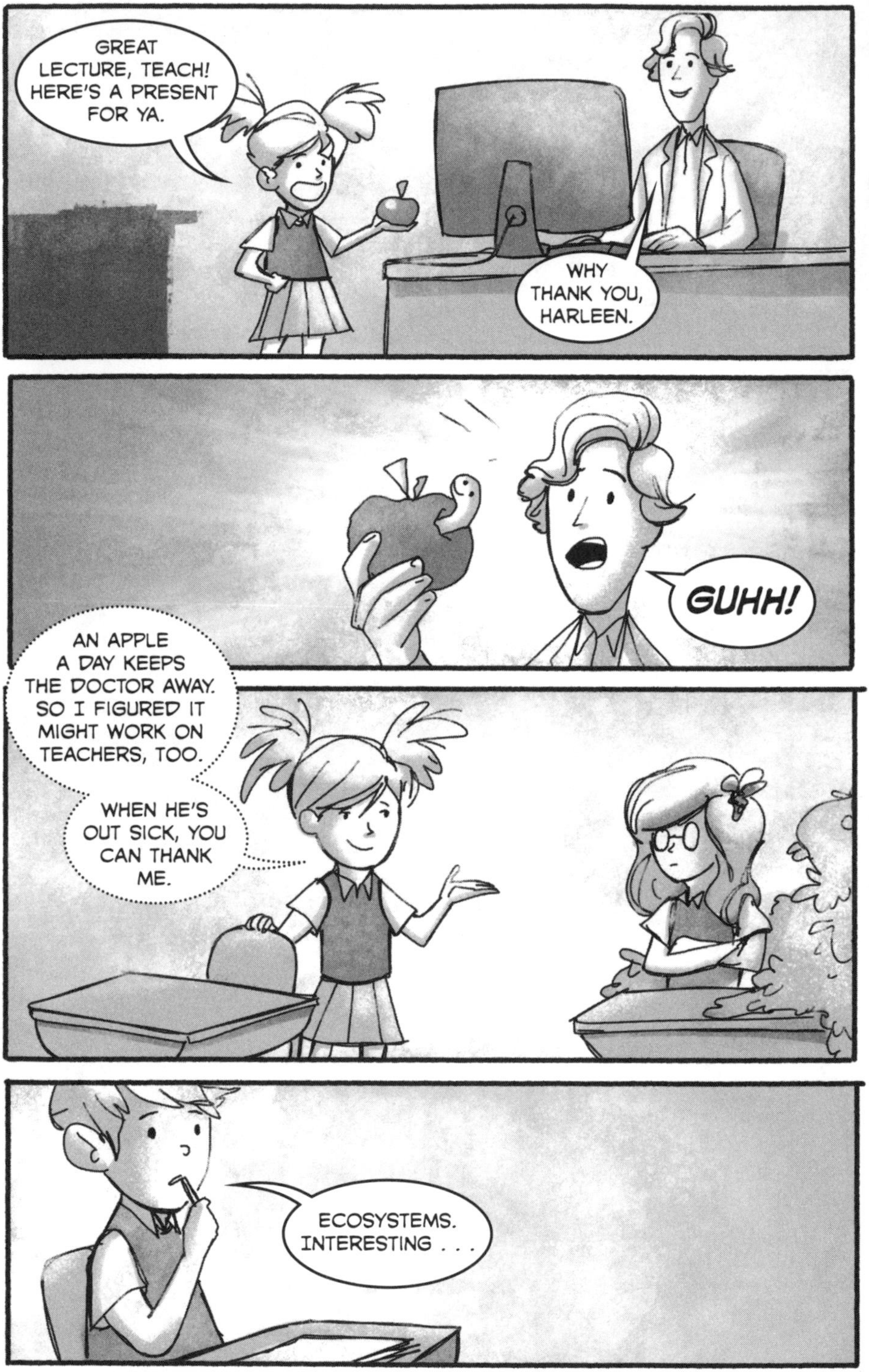
GREAT LECTURE, TEACH! HERE'S A PRESENT FOR YA.
WHY THANK YOU, HARLEEN.
GUHH!
AN APPLE A DAY KEEPS THE DOCTOR AWAY. SO I FIGURED IT MIGHT WORK ON TEACHERS, TOO.
WHEN HE'S OUT SICK, YOU CAN THANK ME.
ECOSYSTEMS. INTERESTING . . .

I'm sure you all think math is all about numbers and is boring. Maybe you're right. But maybe it's more than that. So let's just skip the numbers part and talk about how the basics of math can help us solve problems.

READ the problem. What is the question to be answered?

THINK about what facts are given. Circle the facts needed to solve the problem.

SOLVE the problem. Look for patterns. Guess and check from your list to find it.

JUSTIFY the answer. What did you do? Why did you do it?

As a former employee at **S.T.A.R. Labs**, I know these are the things the judges will be looking for when evaluating your science fair projects. But always remember . . .

If you can't come up with your own idea, then borrow one from someone else. But just ask first!

Okay, in all seriousness, math is about solving problems. And sometimes you need all the help you can get. So talk with others to find solutions, get ideas, share, and sometimes even take. The more you gain from others around you, the stronger you'll be.

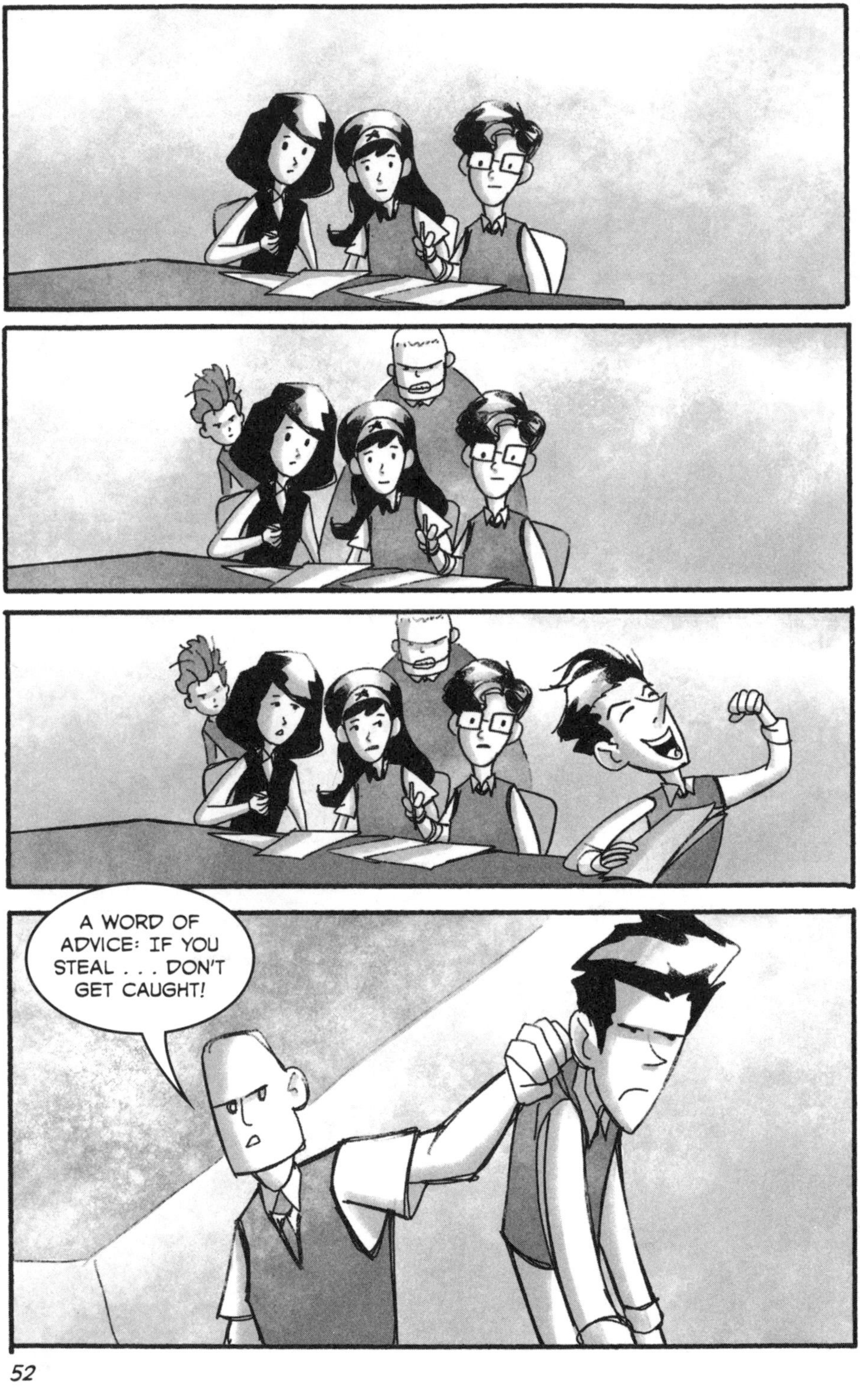
A WORD OF ADVICE: IF YOU STEAL . . . DON'T GET CAUGHT!

SWIM TEAM—
FINAL EXAM
Coach Crusher

ATTENTION, ATHLETES!

The time to race your fellow
classmates is NOW! I want the
best of the best. Be prepared to
use any style necessary to achieve
this goal. The winner of my exam will be
awarded the highest position of team captain.

A team captain lives to swim. They must be fast and strong.
They command respect. And they lead others to victory.

Swimmers MUST:
≈ Report to the pool at 2 p.m.
≈ Take part in mandatory warm-ups at 2:15.
≈ Be on time. Tardiness will remove you from the lineup and you
  will fail the exam.
≈ If you do, your device will be taken away and you will swim
  laps alone.
≈ Stay hydrated. Candy and soda are discouraged.
≈ Stay in team area AT ALL TIMES.
≈ Swim in ALL the events for the exam.

Will you lead my team as its captain? Okay, you pool rats, it's time
to find out!

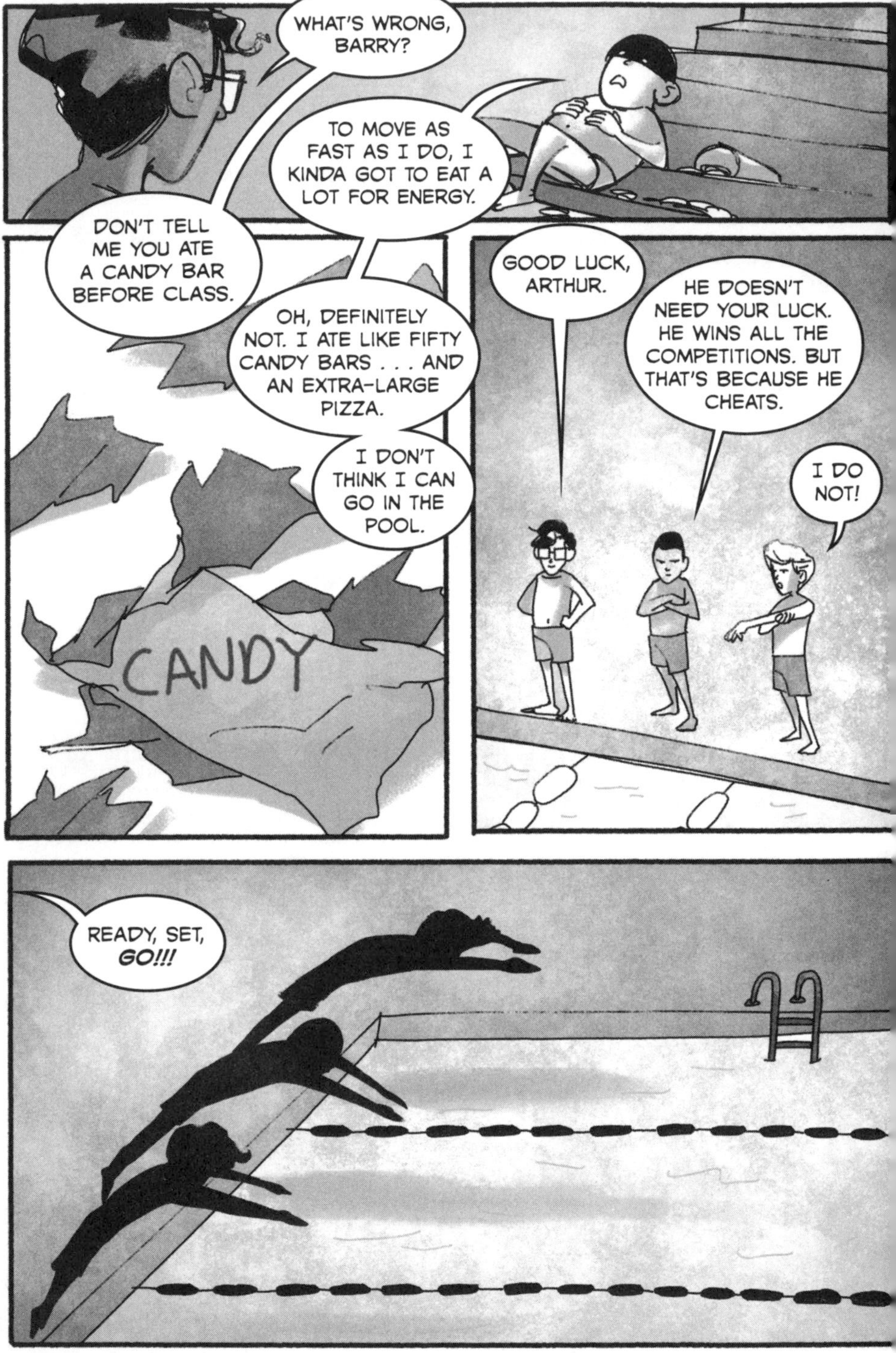
WHAT'S WRONG, BARRY?
TO MOVE AS FAST AS I DO, I KINDA GOT TO EAT A LOT FOR ENERGY.
DON'T TELL ME YOU ATE A CANDY BAR BEFORE CLASS.
OH, DEFINITELY NOT. I ATE LIKE FIFTY CANDY BARS . . . AND AN EXTRA-LARGE PIZZA.
I DON'T THINK I CAN GO IN THE POOL.
CANDY
GOOD LUCK, ARTHUR.
HE DOESN'T NEED YOUR LUCK. HE WINS ALL THE COMPETITIONS. BUT THAT'S BECAUSE HE CHEATS.
I DO NOT!
READY, SET, *GO!!!*

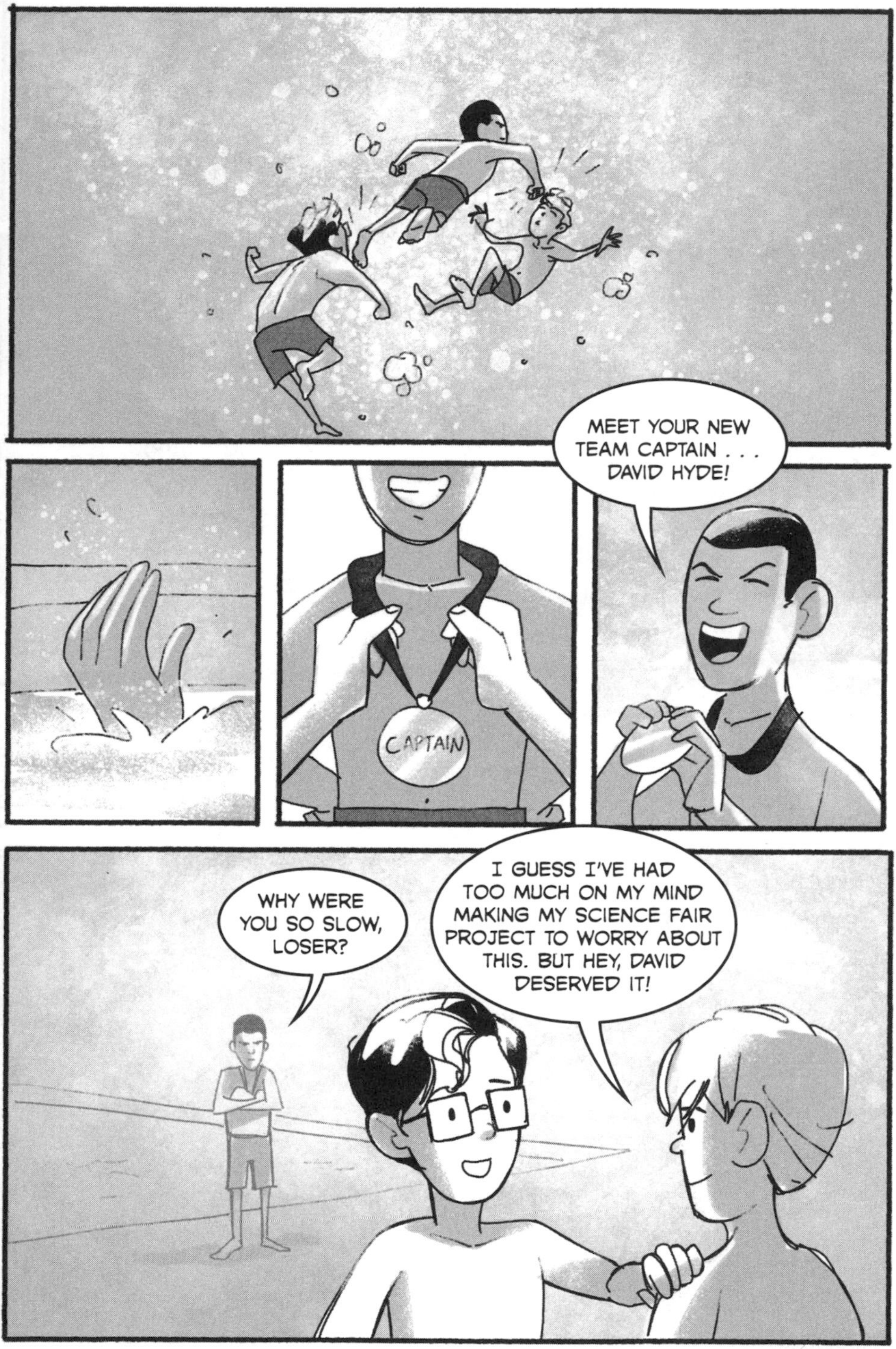

CAPTAIN
MEET YOUR NEW TEAM CAPTAIN . . . DAVID HYDE!
WHY WERE YOU SO SLOW, LOSER?
I GUESS I'VE HAD TOO MUCH ON MY MIND MAKING MY SCIENCE FAIR PROJECT TO WORRY ABOUT THIS. BUT HEY, DAVID DESERVED IT!

JOHN HENRY IRONS

SHOP CLASS 101

If you think it, you can build it!

Anything you're able to think up for the science fair, we can find a way to build it in this class. There's plenty of tools, equipment, and steelworks we can use to create your project.

You always wanted to build a volcano? Let's do it. You don't need to stick with just papier-mâché and baking soda and vinegar. Expand your mind. We can construct it out of wood, plaster, or metal. The component can be powered by gears or a battery. Anything is possible!

Why stick to the standard potato clock to produce electricity? Use your imagination. Maybe you want a super-toaster instead. We'll find a way to take it apart, observe the mechanics, fix any broken pieces, and rebuild it to your new blueprint specs.

If needed, I could even help you build a steel suit out of metal.

Safety is our utmost concern, so I will always be here to monitor and provide direction. But let's help your idea become a reality!

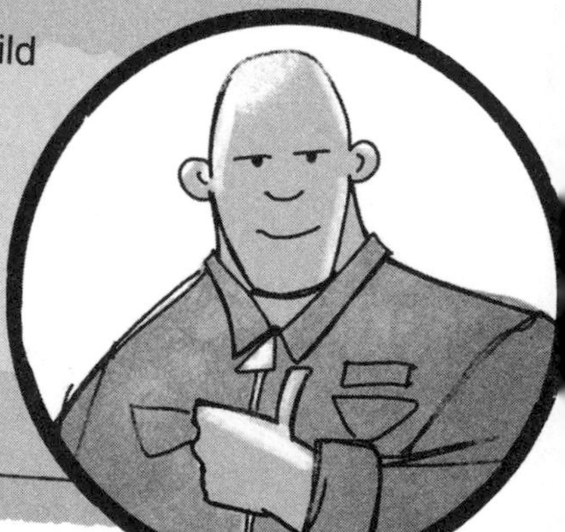

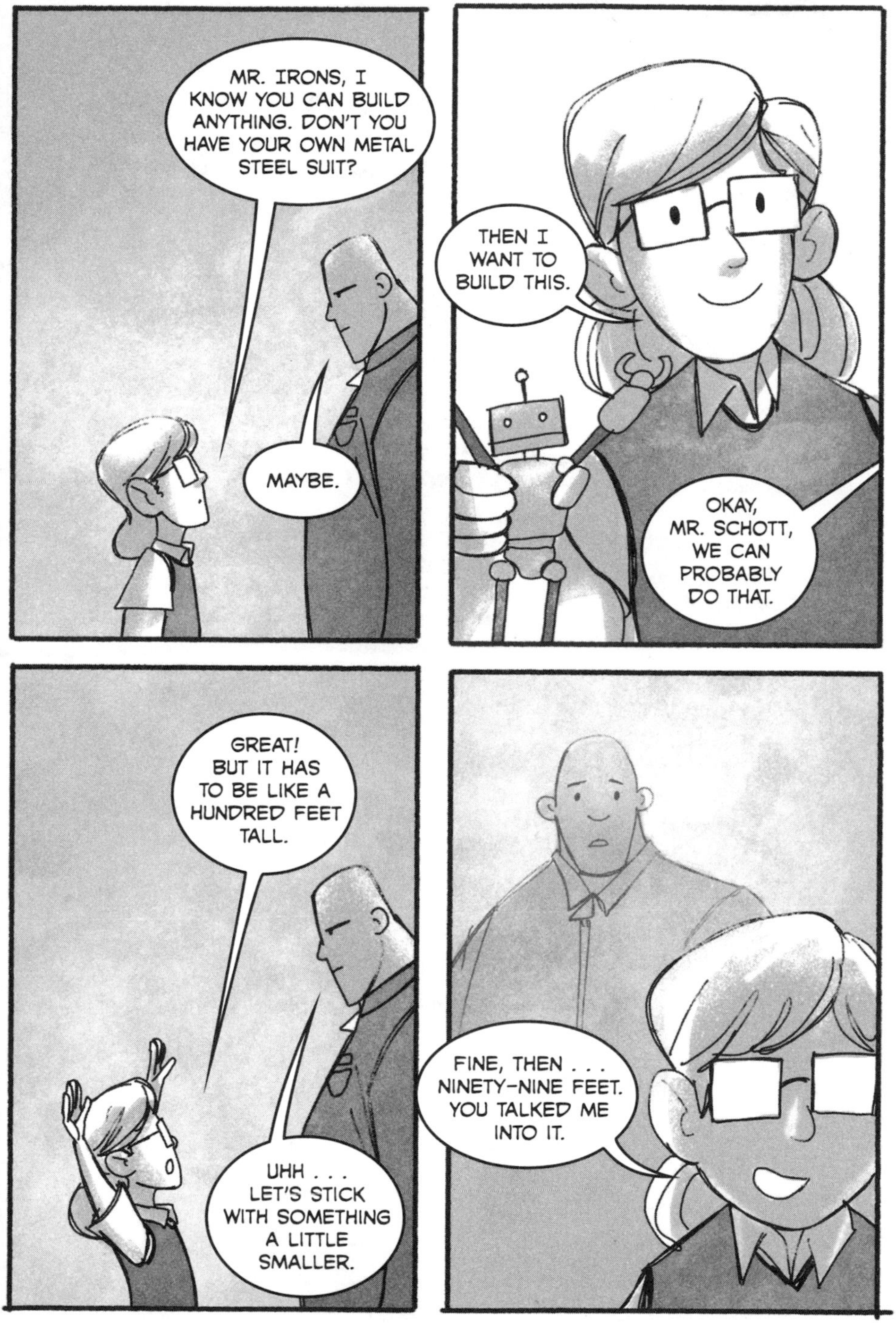
MR. IRONS, I KNOW YOU CAN BUILD ANYTHING. DON'T YOU HAVE YOUR OWN METAL STEEL SUIT?
MAYBE.
THEN I WANT TO BUILD THIS.
OKAY, MR. SCHOTT, WE CAN PROBABLY DO THAT.
GREAT! BUT IT HAS TO BE LIKE A HUNDRED FEET TALL.
UHH . . . LET'S STICK WITH SOMETHING A LITTLE SMALLER.
FINE, THEN . . . NINETY-NINE FEET. YOU TALKED ME INTO IT.

THE VELOCITY OF TIME

BY PROFESSOR **EOBARD THAWNE**

VELOCITY IS THE RATE OF CHANGE IN POSITION WITH RESPECT TO TIME. THIS INCLUDES BOTH THE MAGNITUDE AND DIRECTION. GOT THAT, BARRY?

THE AVERAGE VELOCITY IS WHAT A BODY EXPERIENCES OVER A GIVEN AMOUNT OF TIME. IT CAN BE FOUND BY DIVIDING THE TOTAL CHANGE IN DISPLACEMENT BY THE TOTAL TIME ELAPSED DURING THAT DISPLACEMENT. HOW IS THAT SO FAR, BARRY?

AVERAGE VELOCITY DOESN'T DESCRIBE EVERYTHING THAT HAPPENS DURING THE TIME INTERVAL. BUT YOU HAVE ABOVE-AVERAGE VELOCITY, BARRY. ALMOST INSTANTANEOUS. AND INSTANTANEOUS VELOCITY IS AN OBJECT AT ANY GIVEN INSTANT IN TIME.

KINETIC ENERGY OF A PARTICLE DEPENDS ON ITS MASS AND ITS VELOCITY. THE MOTION CAN BE EITHER TRANSLATIONAL, ROTATIONAL, OR VIBRATIONAL. OR ALL THREE FOR YOU, RIGHT, BARRY?

AND SPEED IS THE MAGNITUDE OF VELOCITY WITHOUT DIRECTION. BUT YOU ALREADY KNOW THAT, BARRY, BECAUSE YOU'RE FAST!!!

IN SUMMARY:

- POSITIVE VELOCITY IS MOVING FORWARD.

- NEGATIVE VELOCITY IS MOVING BACKWARD.

- ZERO VELOCITY IS STOPPED, MAYBE JUST FOR AN INSTANT.

WE'RE GOING TO NEED ALL OF THIS TO DO WHAT WE NEED TO DO NEXT, BARRY . . .

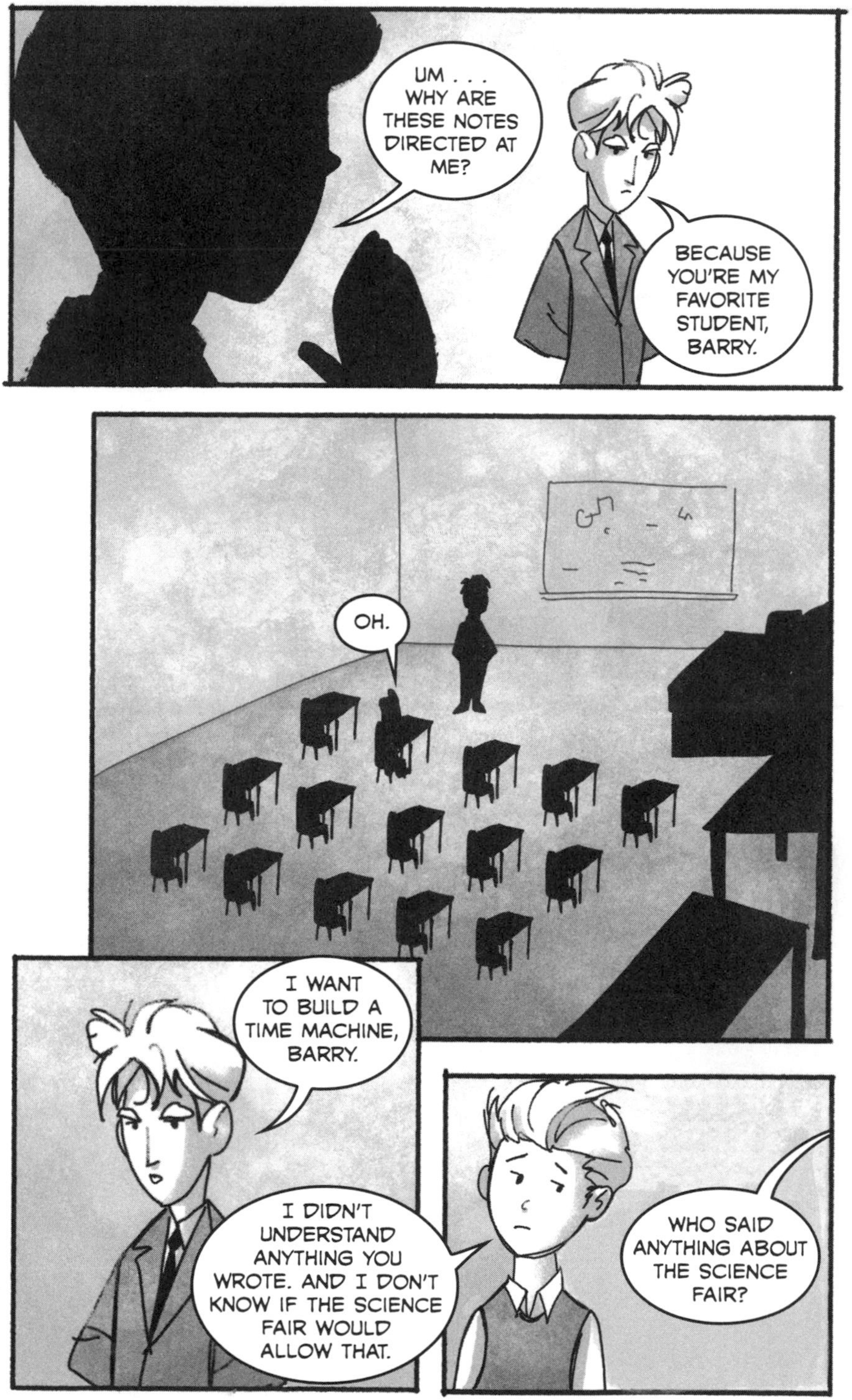
UM . . . WHY ARE THESE NOTES DIRECTED AT ME?
BECAUSE YOU'RE MY FAVORITE STUDENT, BARRY.
OH.
I WANT TO BUILD A TIME MACHINE, BARRY.
I DIDN'T UNDERSTAND ANYTHING YOU WROTE. AND I DON'T KNOW IF THE SCIENCE FAIR WOULD ALLOW THAT.
WHO SAID ANYTHING ABOUT THE SCIENCE FAIR?

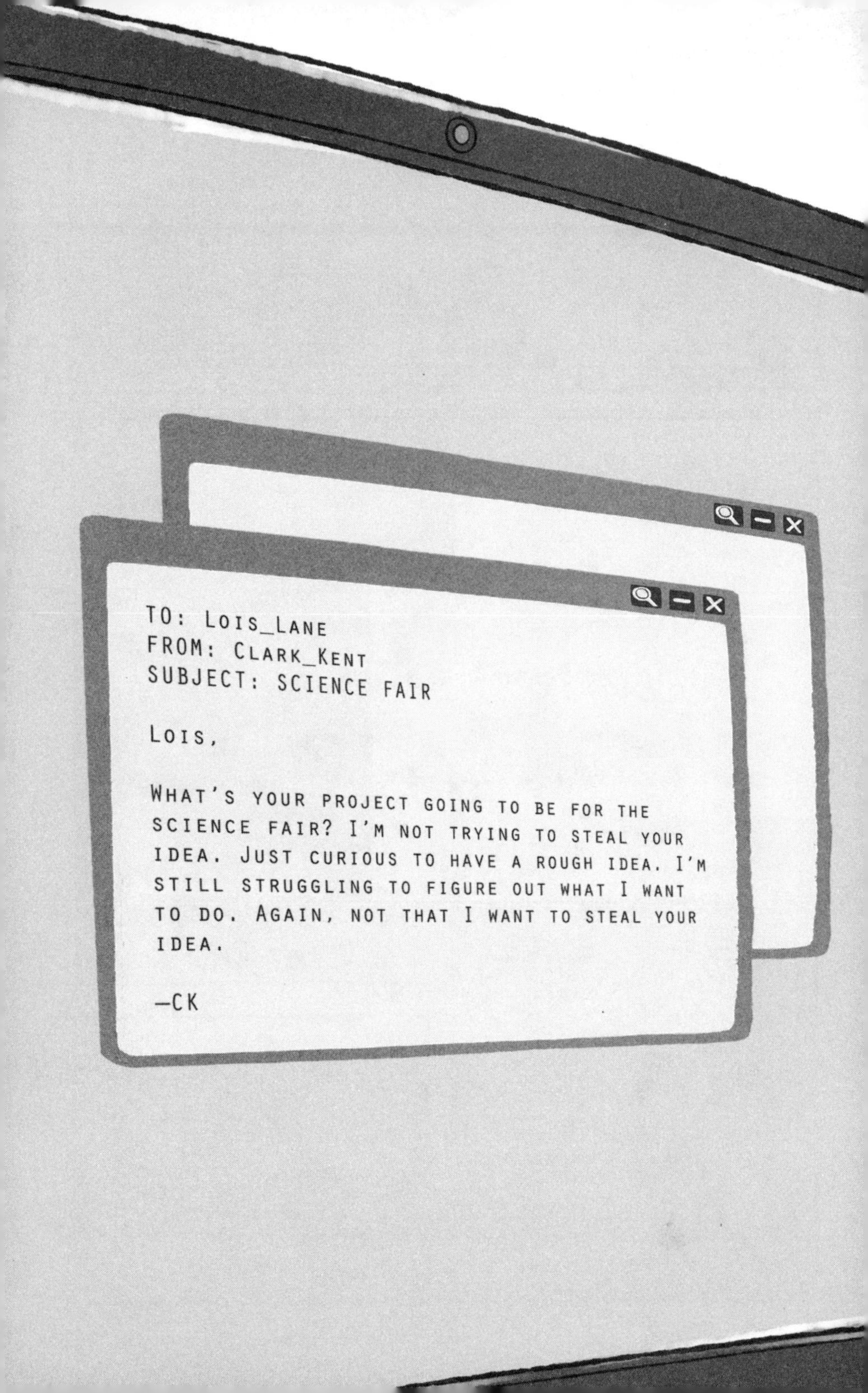

TO: Lois_Lane
FROM: Clark_Kent
SUBJECT: SCIENCE FAIR

Lois,

What's your project going to be for the science fair? I'm not trying to steal your idea. Just curious to have a rough idea. I'm still struggling to figure out what I want to do. Again, not that I want to steal your idea.

—CK

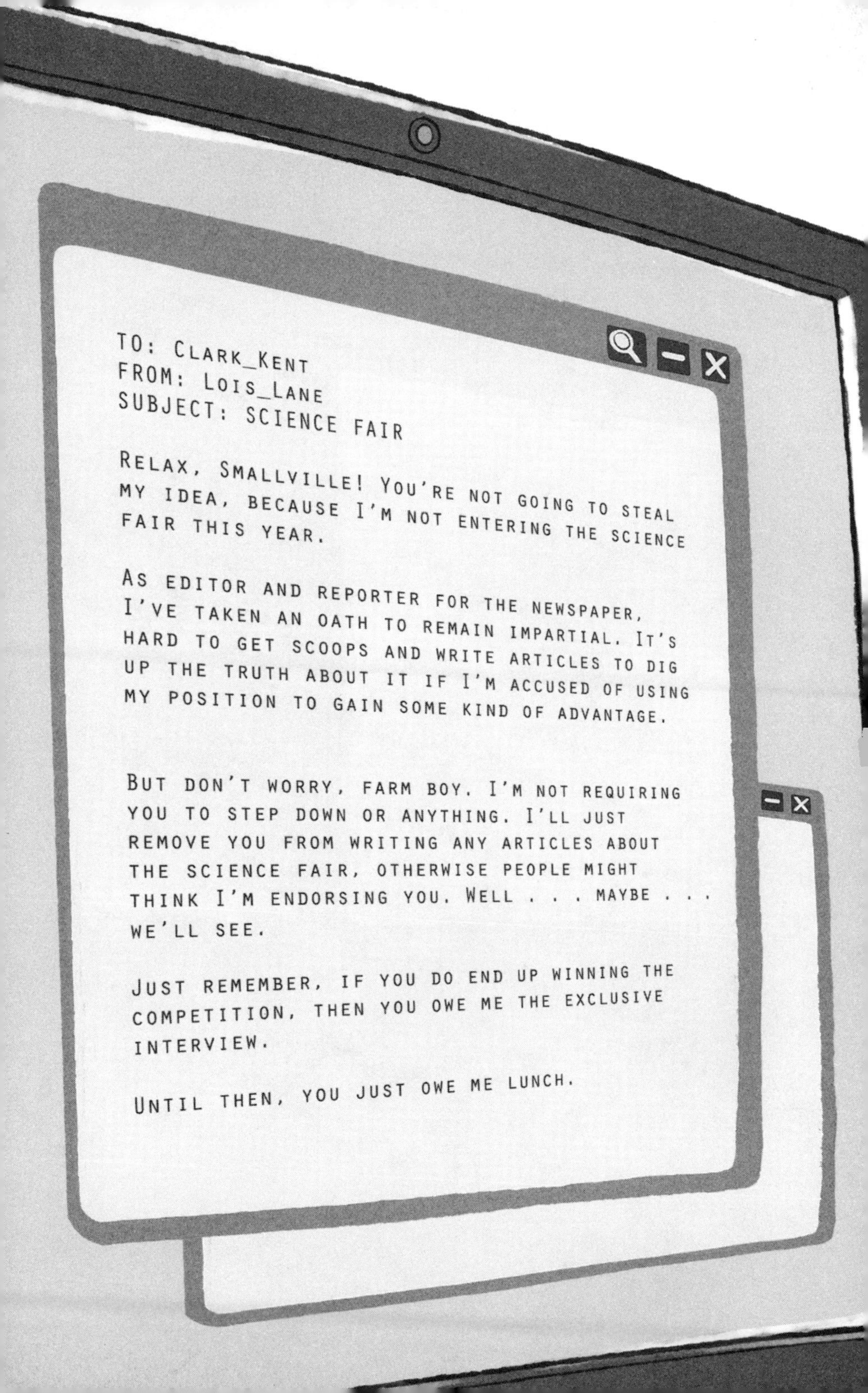

TO: Clark_Kent
FROM: Lois_Lane
SUBJECT: SCIENCE FAIR

Relax, Smallville! You're not going to steal my idea, because I'm not entering the science fair this year.

As editor and reporter for the newspaper, I've taken an oath to remain impartial. It's hard to get scoops and write articles to dig up the truth about it if I'm accused of using my position to gain some kind of advantage.

But don't worry, farm boy. I'm not requiring you to step down or anything. I'll just remove you from writing any articles about the science fair, otherwise people might think I'm endorsing you. Well . . . maybe . . . we'll see.

Just remember, if you do end up winning the competition, then you owe me the exclusive interview.

Until then, you just owe me lunch.

October 9th

CLARK'S JOURNAL

As the science fair is getting closer, it's making me more nervous. Everyone else seems to be hard at work on their projects, some more secretive than others, but I haven't come up with the right idea for my own project. It doesn't help being distracted by who the Mystery Eye is.

I have found I'm enjoying working for the newspaper, though! Lois runs a tight ship over there. Always yelling and pointing where we should go, who to interview, and what to write. But it does keep things lively and exciting. I even think I have a knack for this, but it's too early to tell.

I better go. She's yelling at me to go proofread some articles before I make photocopies for the next edition. I might be faster than a locomotive, but sometimes I can barely keep up with her!

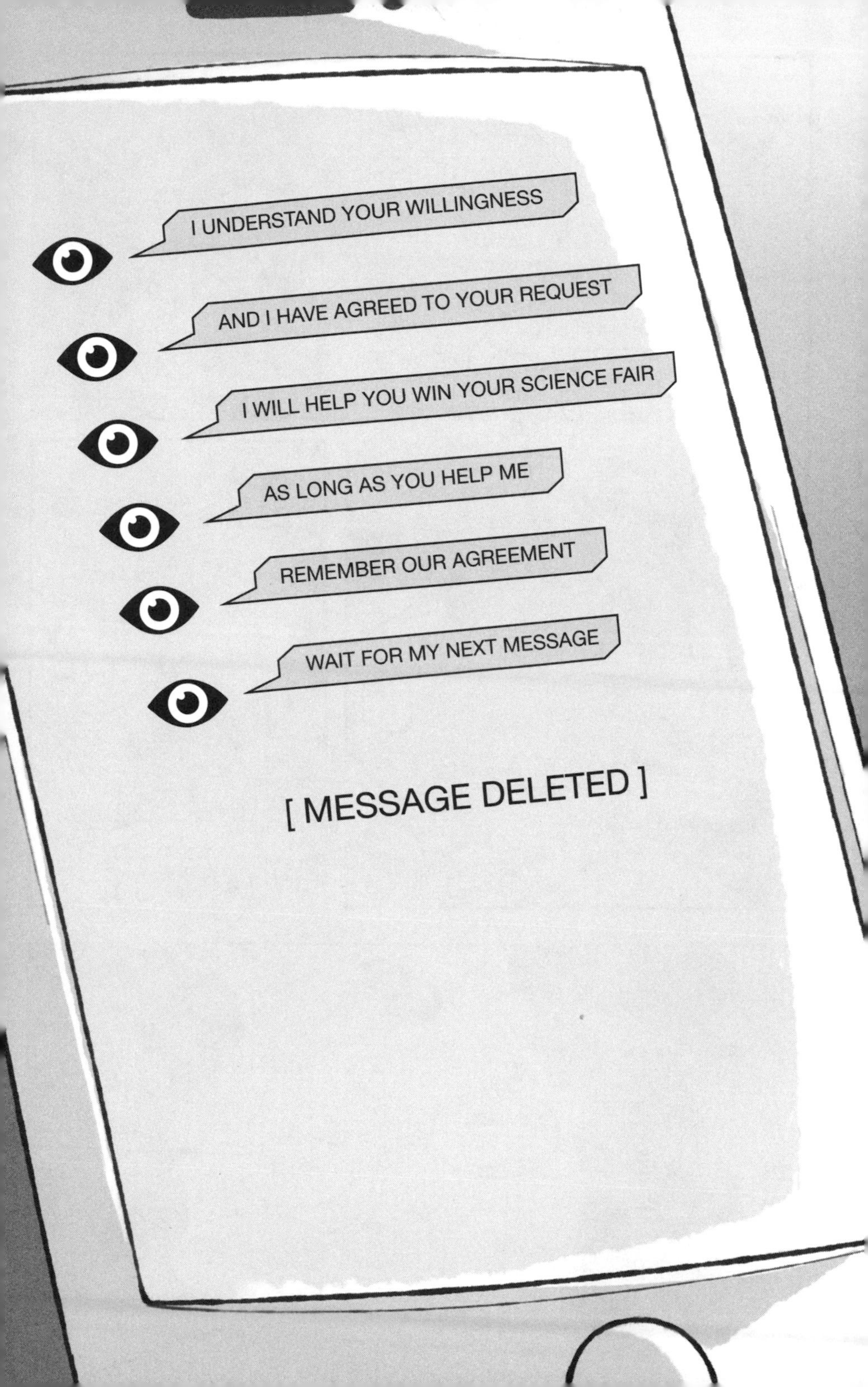
I UNDERSTAND YOUR WILLINGNESS
AND I HAVE AGREED TO YOUR REQUEST
I WILL HELP YOU WIN YOUR SCIENCE FAIR
AS LONG AS YOU HELP ME
REMEMBER OUR AGREEMENT
WAIT FOR MY NEXT MESSAGE
[MESSAGE DELETED]

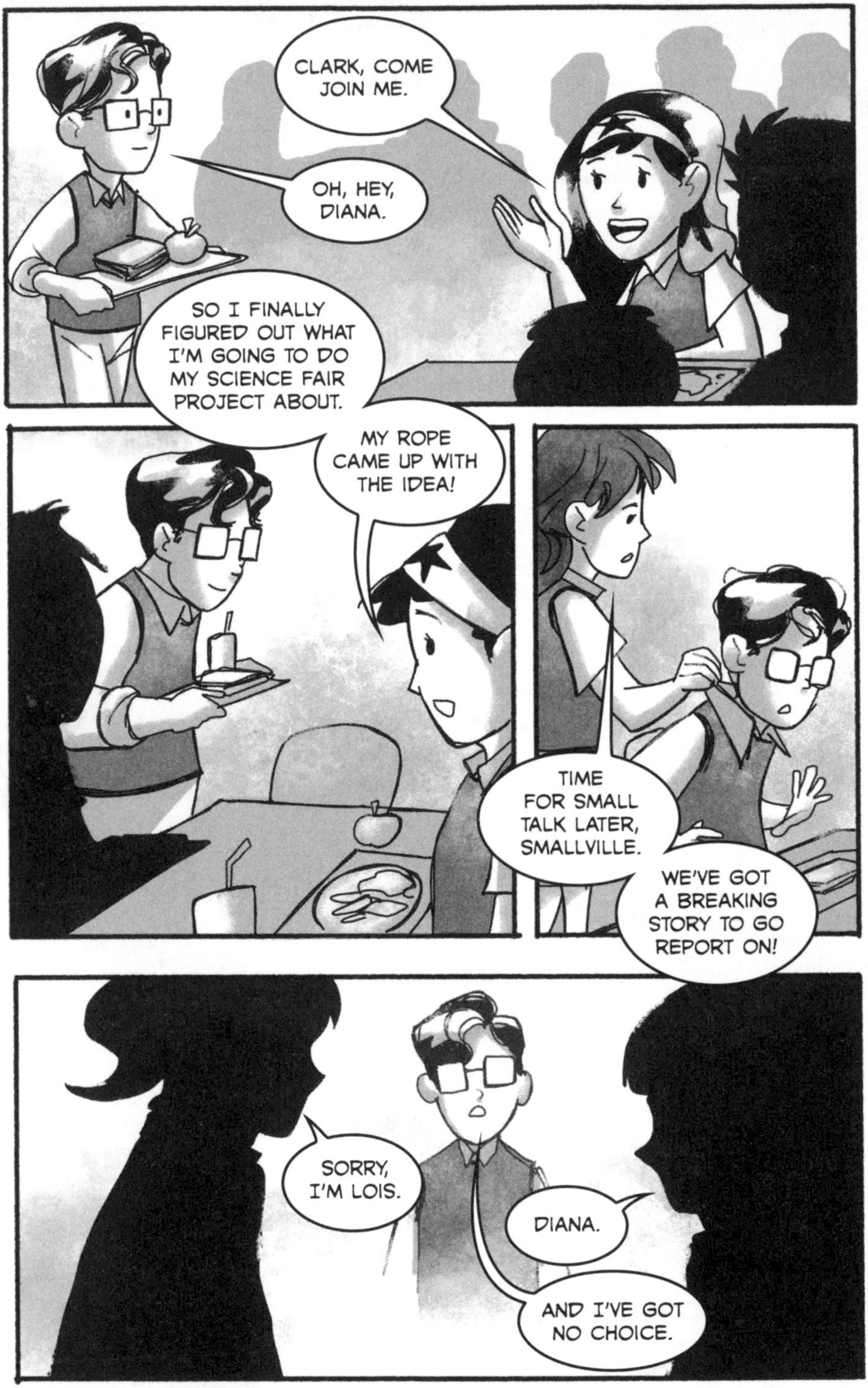

CLARK, COME JOIN ME.
OH, HEY, DIANA.
SO I FINALLY FIGURED OUT WHAT I'M GOING TO DO MY SCIENCE FAIR PROJECT ABOUT.
MY ROPE CAME UP WITH THE IDEA!
TIME FOR SMALL TALK LATER, SMALLVILLE.
WE'VE GOT A BREAKING STORY TO GO REPORT ON!
SORRY, I'M LOIS.
DIANA.
AND I'VE GOT NO CHOICE.

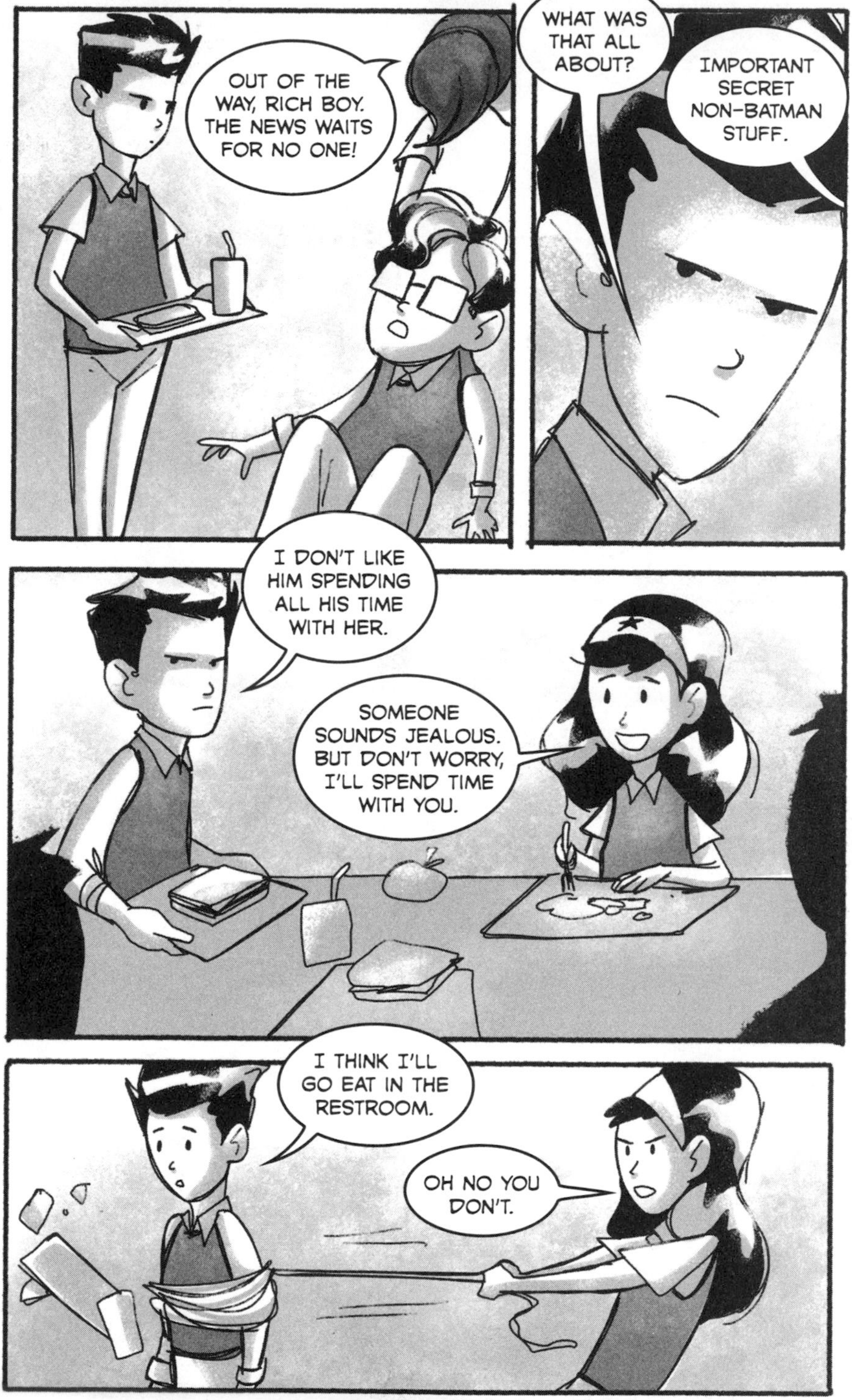
OUT OF THE WAY, RICH BOY. THE NEWS WAITS FOR NO ONE!
WHAT WAS THAT ALL ABOUT?
IMPORTANT SECRET NON-BATMAN STUFF.
I DON'T LIKE HIM SPENDING ALL HIS TIME WITH HER.
SOMEONE SOUNDS JEALOUS. BUT DON'T WORRY, I'LL SPEND TIME WITH YOU.
I THINK I'LL GO EAT IN THE RESTROOM.
OH NO YOU DON'T.

is everyone here?

not Clark

that's a first

where is he?

wasting time

no he's working at the newspaper

that's cool

they write some great articles

I read it for the funnies

They don't print any comic strips Barry

WHAT?!

then who's drawing in my newspapers?

you probably were

yeah I get bored easy

any updates on the mystery eye

BOOOOOOORING

sorry for being late

hey Arthur

so check it

I've finished my science fair project

what is it?

come meet me in the library right now and I'll show you!

SEND

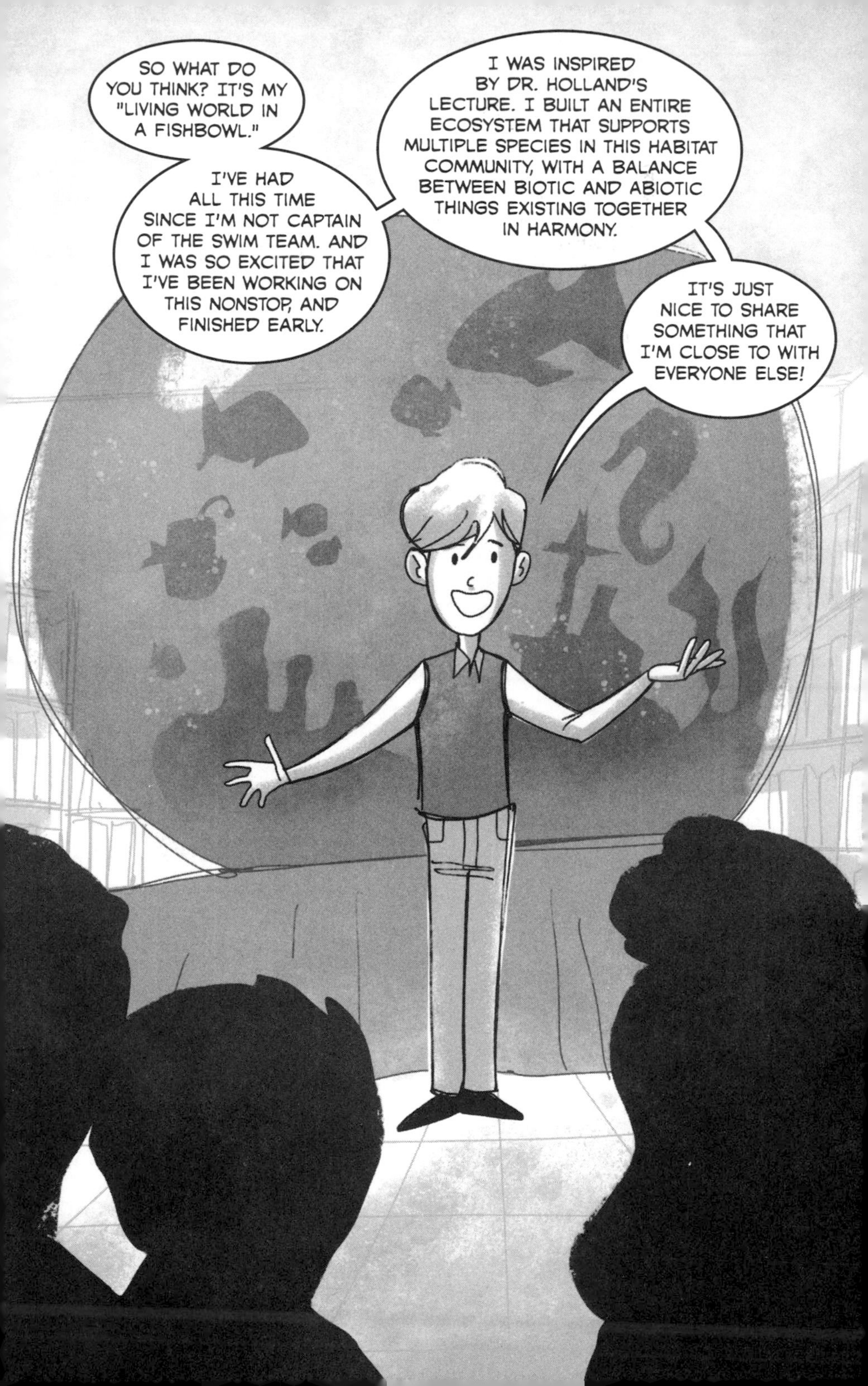
SO WHAT DO YOU THINK? IT'S MY "LIVING WORLD IN A FISHBOWL."
I'VE HAD ALL THIS TIME SINCE I'M NOT CAPTAIN OF THE SWIM TEAM. AND I WAS SO EXCITED THAT I'VE BEEN WORKING ON THIS NONSTOP, AND FINISHED EARLY.
I WAS INSPIRED BY DR. HOLLAND'S LECTURE. I BUILT AN ENTIRE ECOSYSTEM THAT SUPPORTS MULTIPLE SPECIES IN THIS HABITAT COMMUNITY, WITH A BALANCE BETWEEN BIOTIC AND ABIOTIC THINGS EXISTING TOGETHER IN HARMONY.
IT'S JUST NICE TO SHARE SOMETHING THAT I'M CLOSE TO WITH EVERYONE ELSE!

THE JUSTICE TRIBUNE

S.T.A.R. ATTRACTION
OUR INTERVIEW WITH THE
SCIENTIST BEHIND THE SCIENCE

BY LOIS LANE

With the science fair quickly approaching, I thought we'd take the time to talk directly with the source of the science fair. I was able to get on the phone with the general director, Professor Emil Hamilton of S.T.A.R. Labs, to speak about the competition itself.

"We're always very excited to see what the students come up with each year. You'd be surprised, but it inspires us just to see them, as much as they might be inspired by visiting us here. Remember, they are all future scientists in the making!" gushed Professor Emil.

But what do they look for when it comes to judging?

"Students who ask great questions even if they don't have all the answers. Science is as much about the journey as the destination. Creativity goes a long way, as does unbridled enthusiasm. Because if you're excited to share your discovery, it can excite the world." And more importantly, the judges.

"I'm afraid I have to cut our interview short. I have to meet with one of my scientists about a recent discovery that fell into our lap, so to speak!"

And with that, our interview was over.

It sounds like there's a lot of things going on over at the labs in preparation for the science fair. And you should be just as busy here. Word has it that Arthur Curry's project is the one to beat for the top prize, having revealed it recently to his close friends. But don't let that stop you from getting your own projects done in the race to win. We're all cheering for you as you represent Justice Prep.

Go, future scientists!

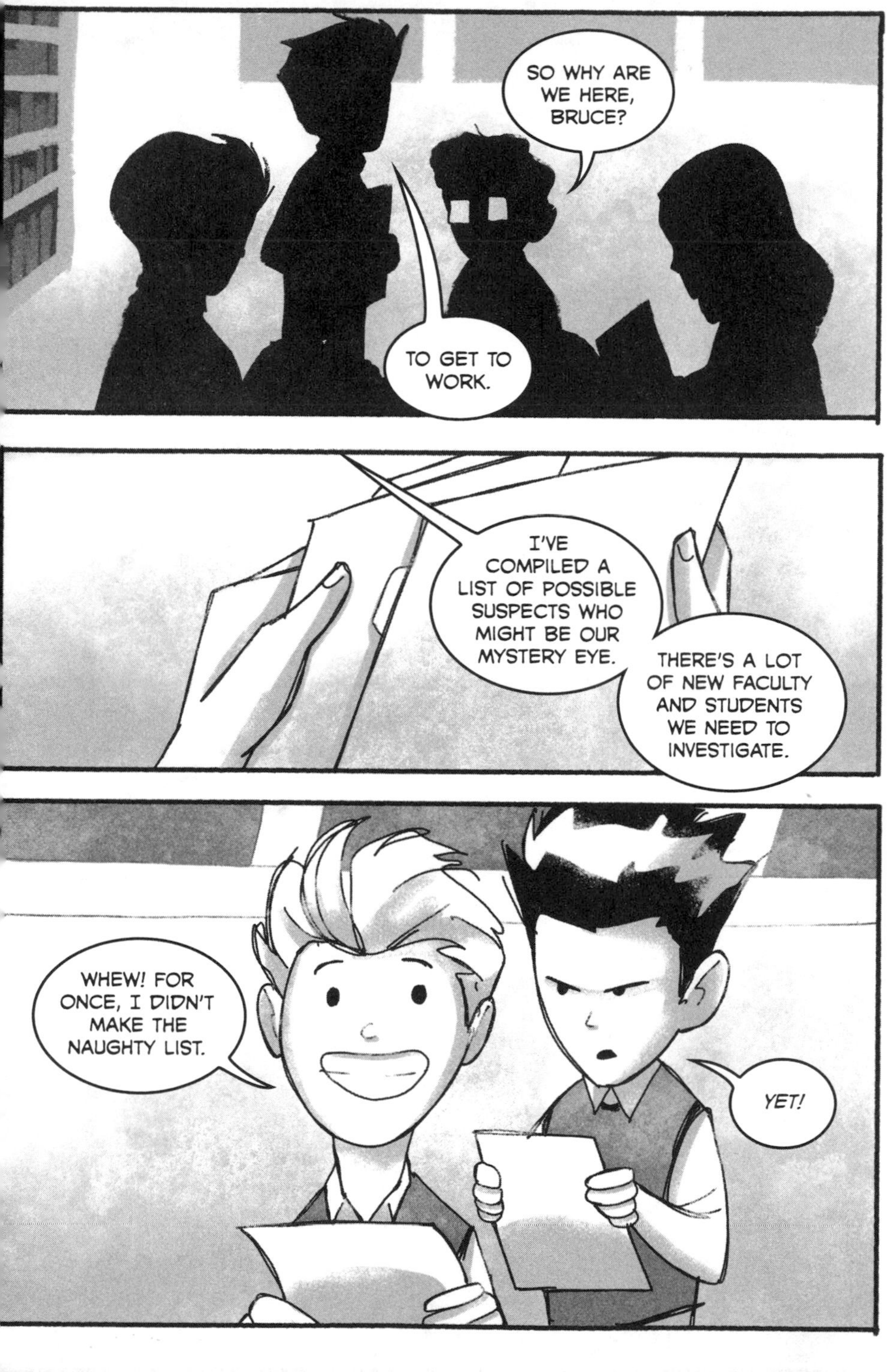
SO WHY ARE WE HERE, BRUCE?
TO GET TO WORK.
I'VE COMPILED A LIST OF POSSIBLE SUSPECTS WHO MIGHT BE OUR MYSTERY EYE.
THERE'S A LOT OF NEW FACULTY AND STUDENTS WE NEED TO INVESTIGATE.
WHEW! FOR ONCE, I DIDN'T MAKE THE NAUGHTY LIST.
YET!

MYSTERY EYE SUSPECTS

Bane = Bully but low on the totem pole. Does he even know how to text?

David Hyde = Swimmer. More interested in chlorine than computers.

Edward Nigma = Genius intellect. But it's not like him to not use riddles.

Harley Quinn = Along for the ride to have fun. Not a criminal mastermind.

The Joker = Unpredictable! Might do it for a laugh, or fool us into thinking it.

Lex Luthor = Always plotting something, even if he's no longer at our school.

Pamela Isley = More interested in plants than people. What's her motive?

Noah Kuttler = Always has his head in his calculator. Suspicious.

Johnny Corben = Always lurking around. Cutting corners. Easily aggravated.

Winslow Schott = Loves toys. But could the Mystery Eye be his greatest toy?

Lois Lane = Clark vouches for her, but I never trust the press. Watch her!

Dr. Alec Holland = Good teacher. Don't know much about him.

Professor Martin Stein = Overly cautious, which isn't a bad thing.

Mr. John Henry Irons = Works with his hands. Not sure if he'd be involved in this.

Professor Eobard Thawne = An unknown. Seems focused on one thing.

Professor Rudolph Jones = Former S.T.A.R. Labs employee. Need to check his history.

Principal James Gordon = The last principal turned out to be a villain. Might be again. We'll see.

Alfred = "The butler always does it" I hear. So I just had to be safe listing him. Sorry, Alfred. Please don't take away my desserts for the week.

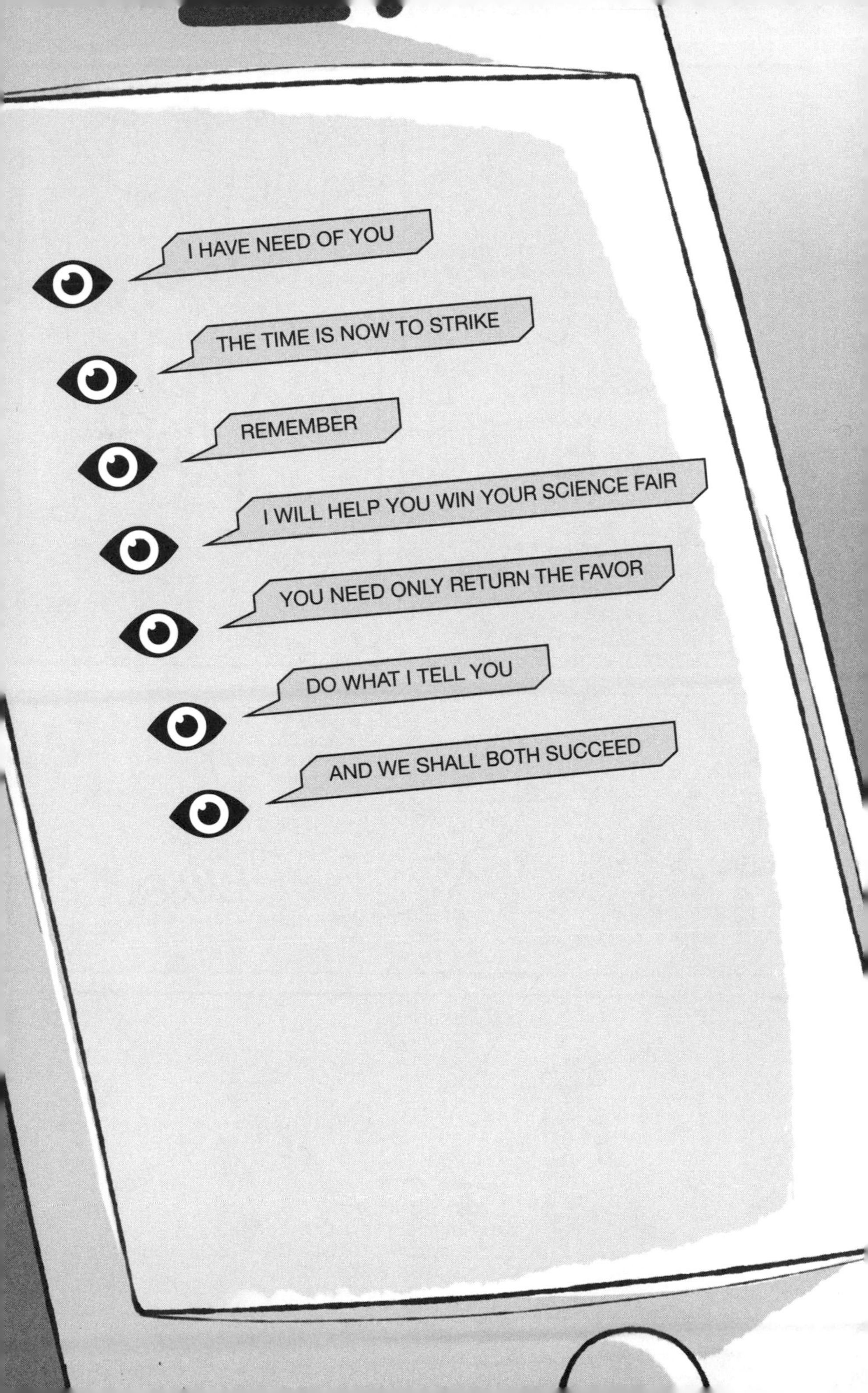
I HAVE NEED OF YOU
THE TIME IS NOW TO STRIKE
REMEMBER
I WILL HELP YOU WIN YOUR SCIENCE FAIR
YOU NEED ONLY RETURN THE FAVOR
DO WHAT I TELL YOU
AND WE SHALL BOTH SUCCEED

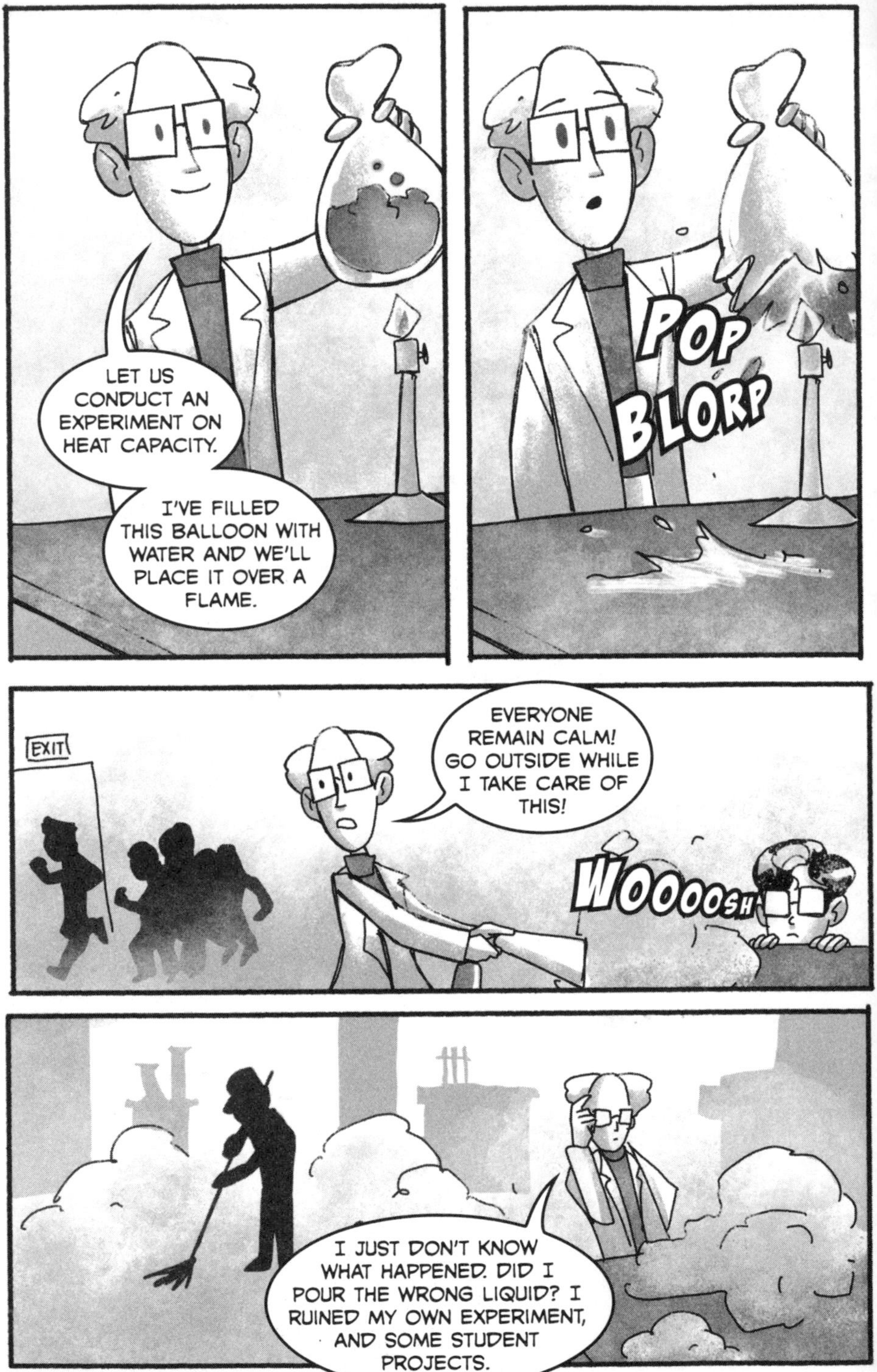
LET US CONDUCT AN EXPERIMENT ON HEAT CAPACITY.
I'VE FILLED THIS BALLOON WITH WATER AND WE'LL PLACE IT OVER A FLAME.
POP
BLORP
EXIT
EVERYONE REMAIN CALM! GO OUTSIDE WHILE I TAKE CARE OF THIS!
WOOOOOSH
I JUST DON'T KNOW WHAT HAPPENED. DID I POUR THE WRONG LIQUID? I RUINED MY OWN EXPERIMENT, AND SOME STUDENT PROJECTS.

MESSAGES

GROUP CHAT

that lab accident today is suspicious

did someone replace the water in the balloon with something flammable?

it's entirely possible

or did Professor Stein do it on purpose?

No. He was just as surprised as we were.

was he

I'm not sure if we can rule him out as a suspect

Clark it's a good thing you were there to help

the extinguishers did most of the work

I think your breath did

so be careful

if I saw you, then others might too

and right now, anyone can be a suspect

so don't make things worse

SEND

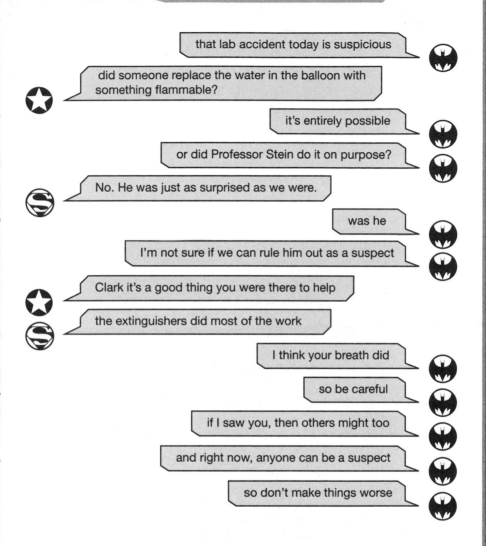

LUTHORCORP—PRIVATE CHAT ROOM
USERS LOGGED IN = 2
[1 KNOWN, 1 GUEST]

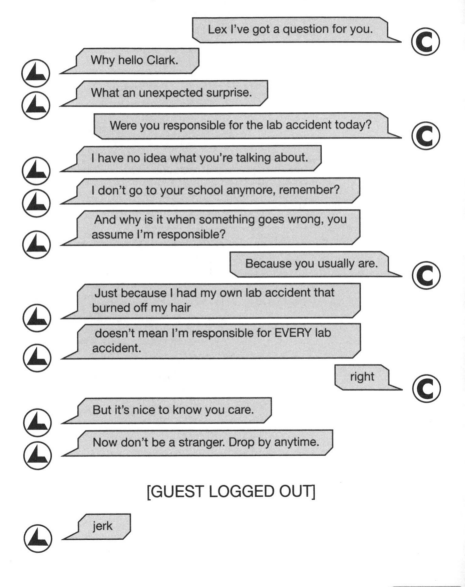

Lex I've got a question for you. **C**

Why hello Clark.

What an unexpected surprise.

Were you responsible for the lab accident today? **C**

I have no idea what you're talking about.

I don't go to your school anymore, remember?

And why is it when something goes wrong, you assume I'm responsible?

Because you usually are. **C**

Just because I had my own lab accident that burned off my hair

doesn't mean I'm responsible for EVERY lab accident.

right **C**

But it's nice to know you care.

Now don't be a stranger. Drop by anytime.

[GUEST LOGGED OUT]

jerk

SEND

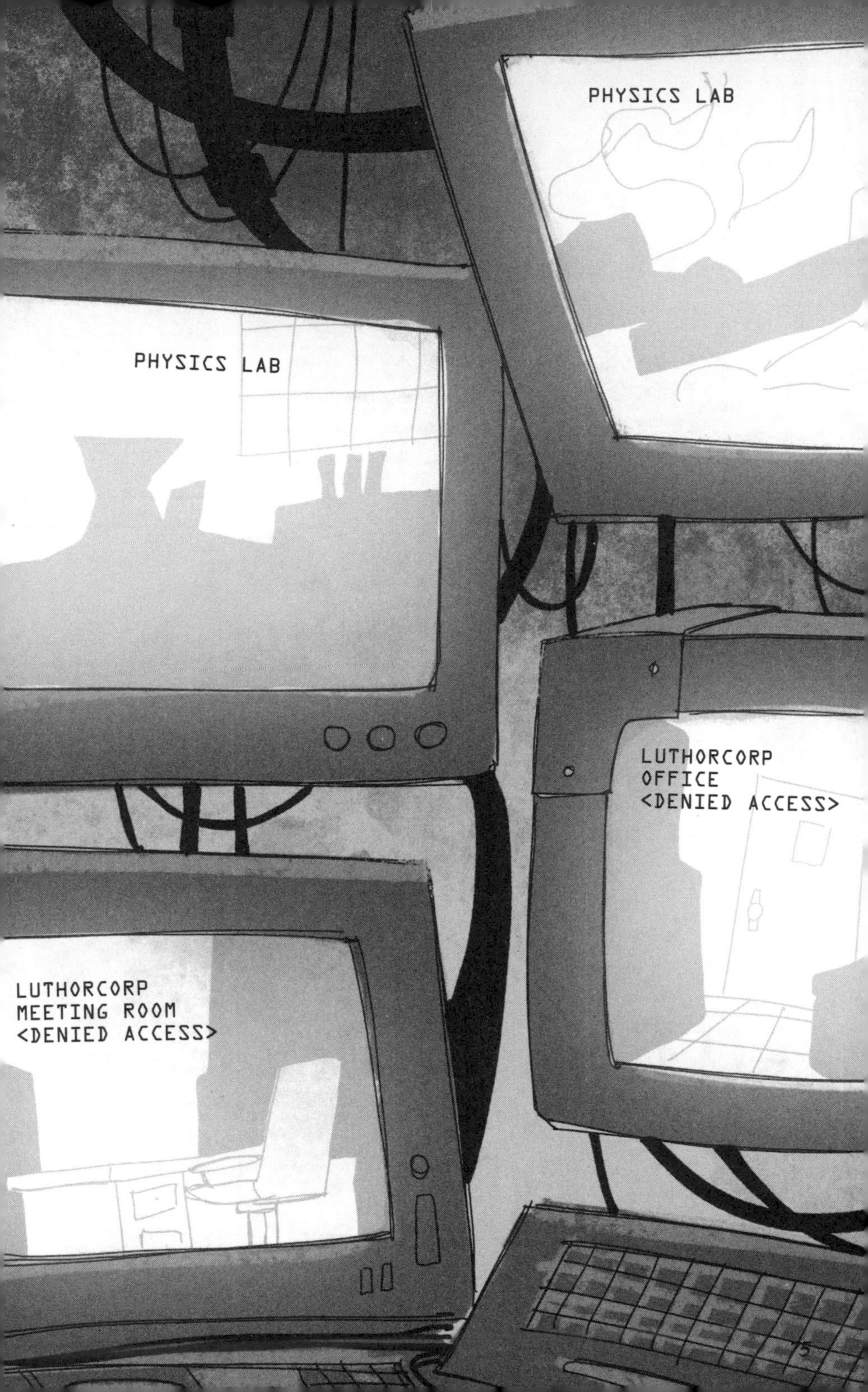
PHYSICS LAB
PHYSICS LAB
LUTHORCORP
OFFICE
<DENIED ACCESS>
LUTHORCORP
MEETING ROOM
<DENIED ACCESS>

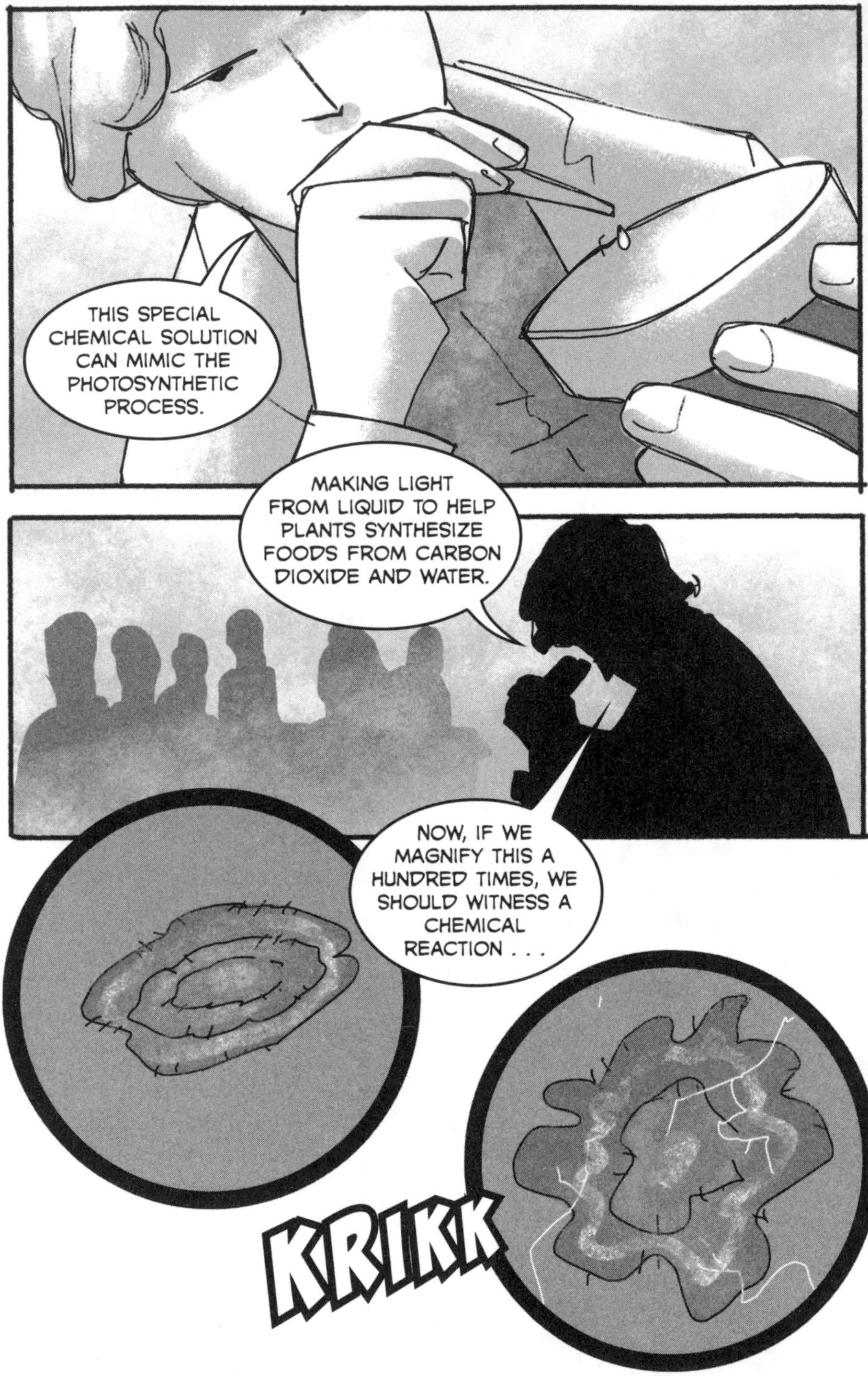
THIS SPECIAL CHEMICAL SOLUTION CAN MIMIC THE PHOTOSYNTHETIC PROCESS.
MAKING LIGHT FROM LIQUID TO HELP PLANTS SYNTHESIZE FOODS FROM CARBON DIOXIDE AND WATER.
NOW, IF WE MAGNIFY THIS A HUNDRED TIMES, WE SHOULD WITNESS A CHEMICAL REACTION . . .
KRIKK

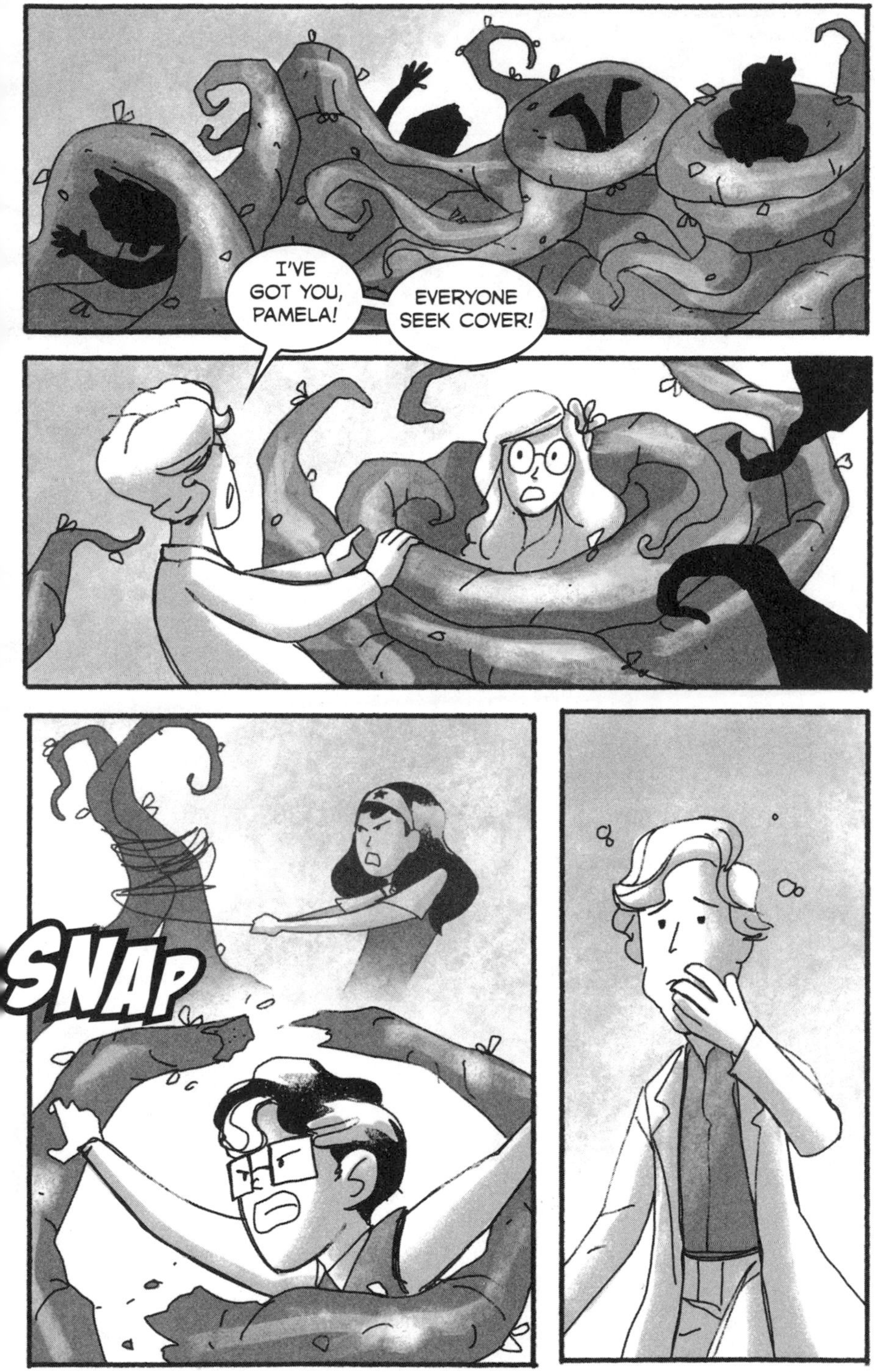
I'VE GOT YOU, PAMELA!
EVERYONE SEEK COVER!
SNAP

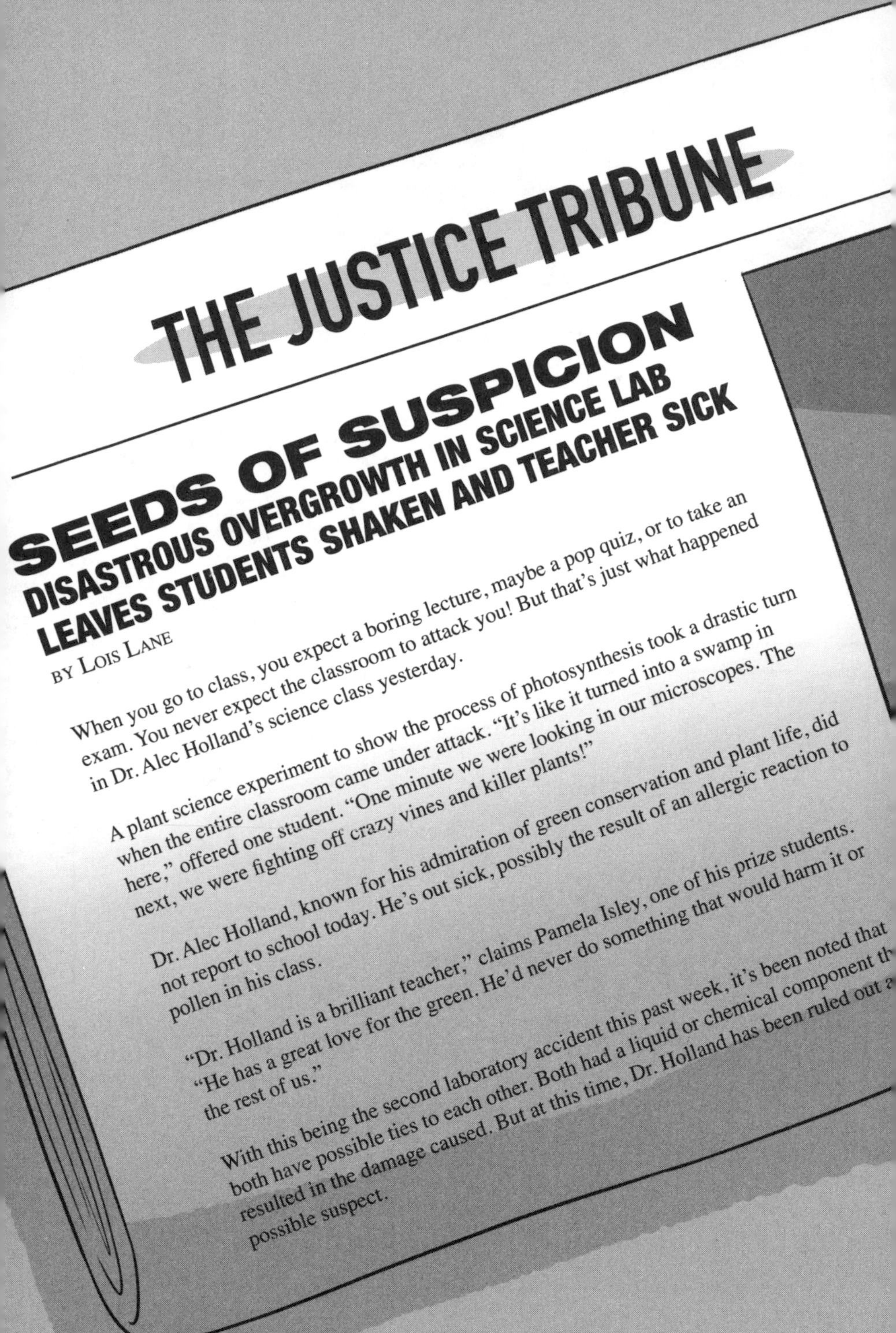

THE JUSTICE TRIBUNE

SEEDS OF SUSPICION

DISASTROUS OVERGROWTH IN SCIENCE LAB LEAVES STUDENTS SHAKEN AND TEACHER SICK

BY LOIS LANE

When you go to class, you expect a boring lecture, maybe a pop quiz, or to take an exam. You never expect the classroom to attack you! But that's just what happened in Dr. Alec Holland's science class yesterday.

A plant science experiment to show the process of photosynthesis took a drastic turn when the entire classroom came under attack. "It's like it turned into a swamp in here," offered one student. "One minute we were looking in our microscopes. The next, we were fighting off crazy vines and killer plants!"

Dr. Alec Holland, known for his admiration of green conservation and plant life, did not report to school today. He's out sick, possibly the result of an allergic reaction to pollen in his class.

"Dr. Holland is a brilliant teacher," claims Pamela Isley, one of his prize students. "He has a great love for the green. He'd never do something that would harm it or the rest of us."

With this being the second laboratory accident this past week, it's been noted that both have possible ties to each other. Both had a liquid or chemical component th resulted in the damage caused. But at this time, Dr. Holland has been ruled out a possible suspect.

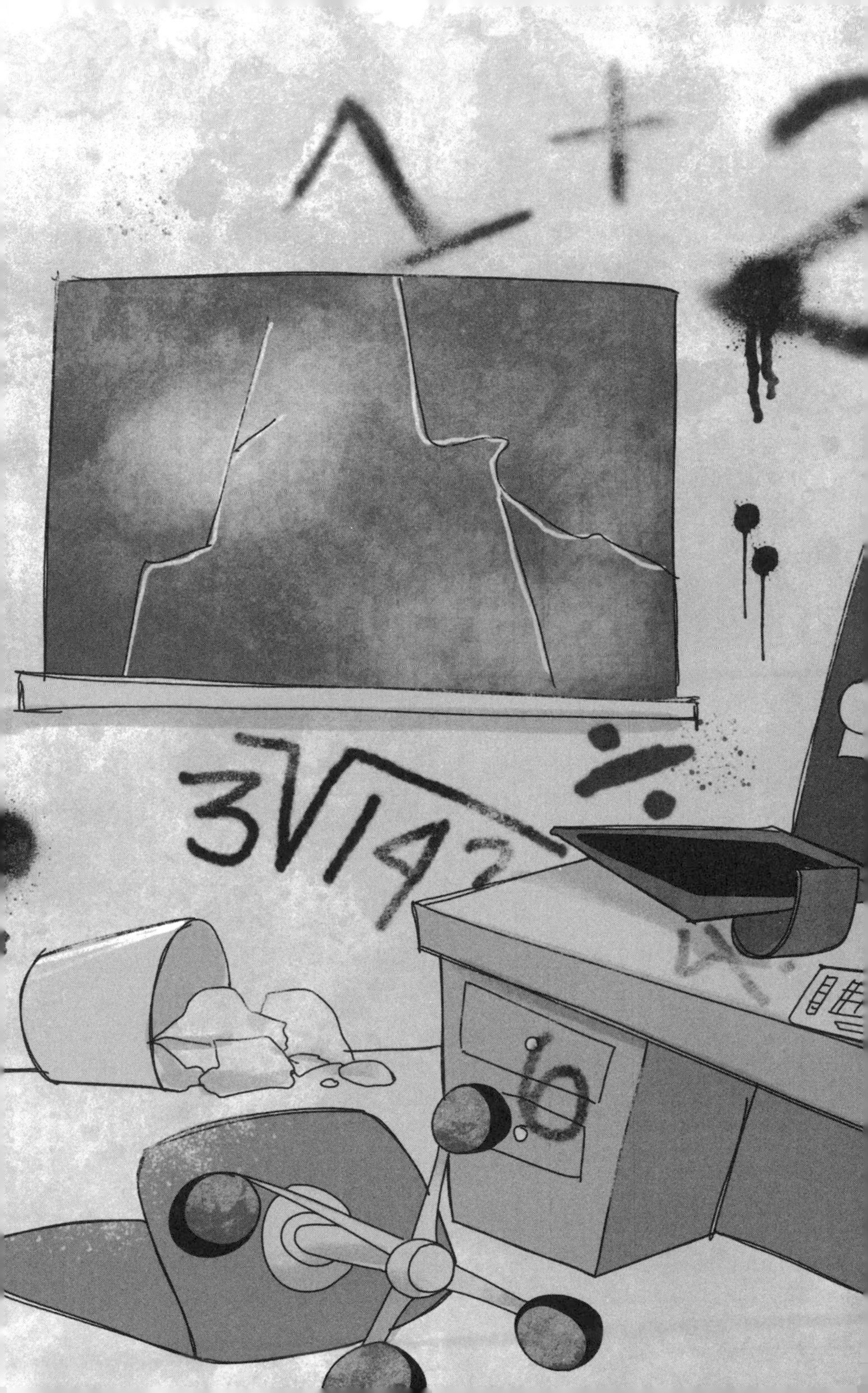

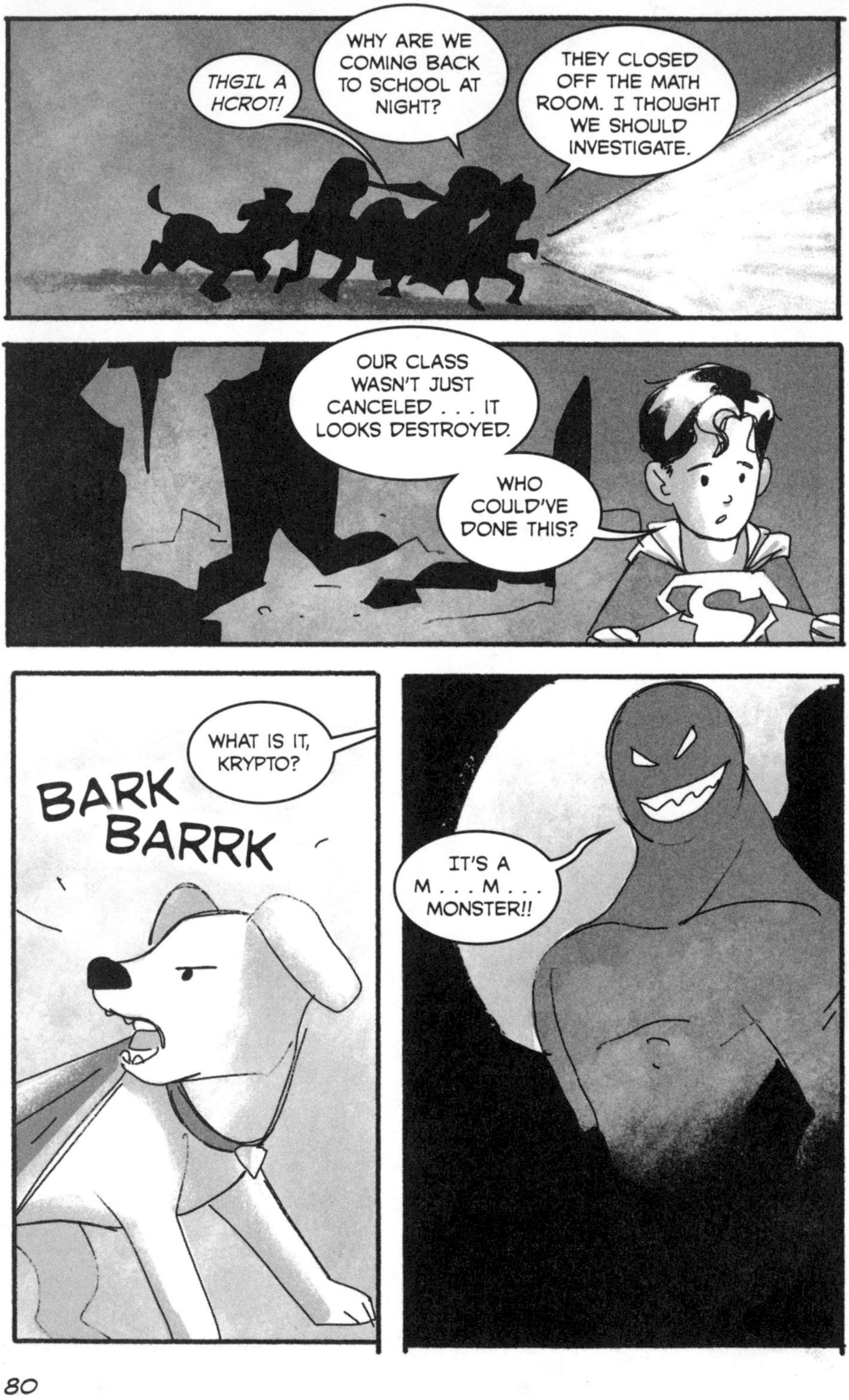
WHY ARE WE COMING BACK TO SCHOOL AT NIGHT?
THGIL A HCROT!
THEY CLOSED OFF THE MATH ROOM. I THOUGHT WE SHOULD INVESTIGATE.
OUR CLASS WASN'T JUST CANCELED . . . IT LOOKS DESTROYED.
WHO COULD'VE DONE THIS?
WHAT IS IT, KRYPTO?
BARK BARRK
IT'S A M . . . M . . . MONSTER!!

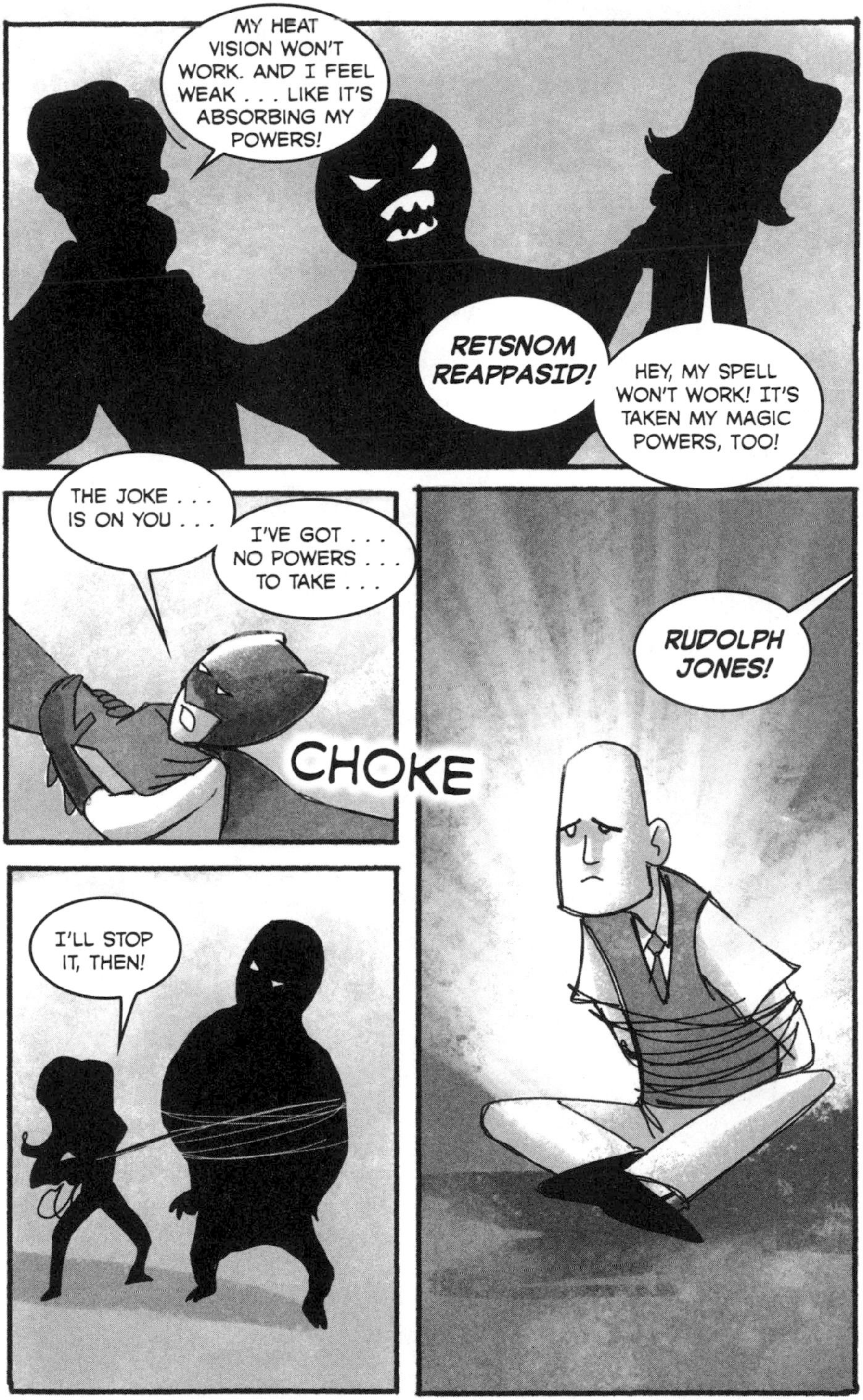
MY HEAT VISION WON'T WORK. AND I FEEL WEAK . . . LIKE IT'S ABSORBING MY POWERS!
RETSNOM REAPPASID!
HEY, MY SPELL WON'T WORK! IT'S TAKEN MY MAGIC POWERS, TOO!
THE JOKE . . . IS ON YOU . . .
I'VE GOT . . . NO POWERS . . . TO TAKE . . .
CHOKE
I'LL STOP IT, THEN!
RUDOLPH JONES!

CLARK'S JOURNAL

Bruce thought it would be a good idea to investigate the school at night. With all the classrooms being vandalized, I think he hoped we'd catch someone in the act. Instead, a monster almost caught us!

A weird package was sent to our math teacher's classroom, addressed to Rudy Jones. When Professor Jones opened it, it affected him. Bruce ran the box through his computer lab back home and found traces of radiation. The exposure must have transformed Mr. Jones into that monster. It was like a living parasite, because when it touched us, it started to absorb our powers. I think it might've absorbed the energy from some of the student experiments and destroyed the classroom. He would've gotten away with damaging more things, too, if it weren't for us kids showing up. Thankfully Diana's lasso caught him, calmed him until he reverted back to normal, and made him tell the truth. Professor Jones wasn't responsible.

The package had no return address, so there's no way to know where it came from. But I have my guesses who might've sent it . . . our Mystery Eye!

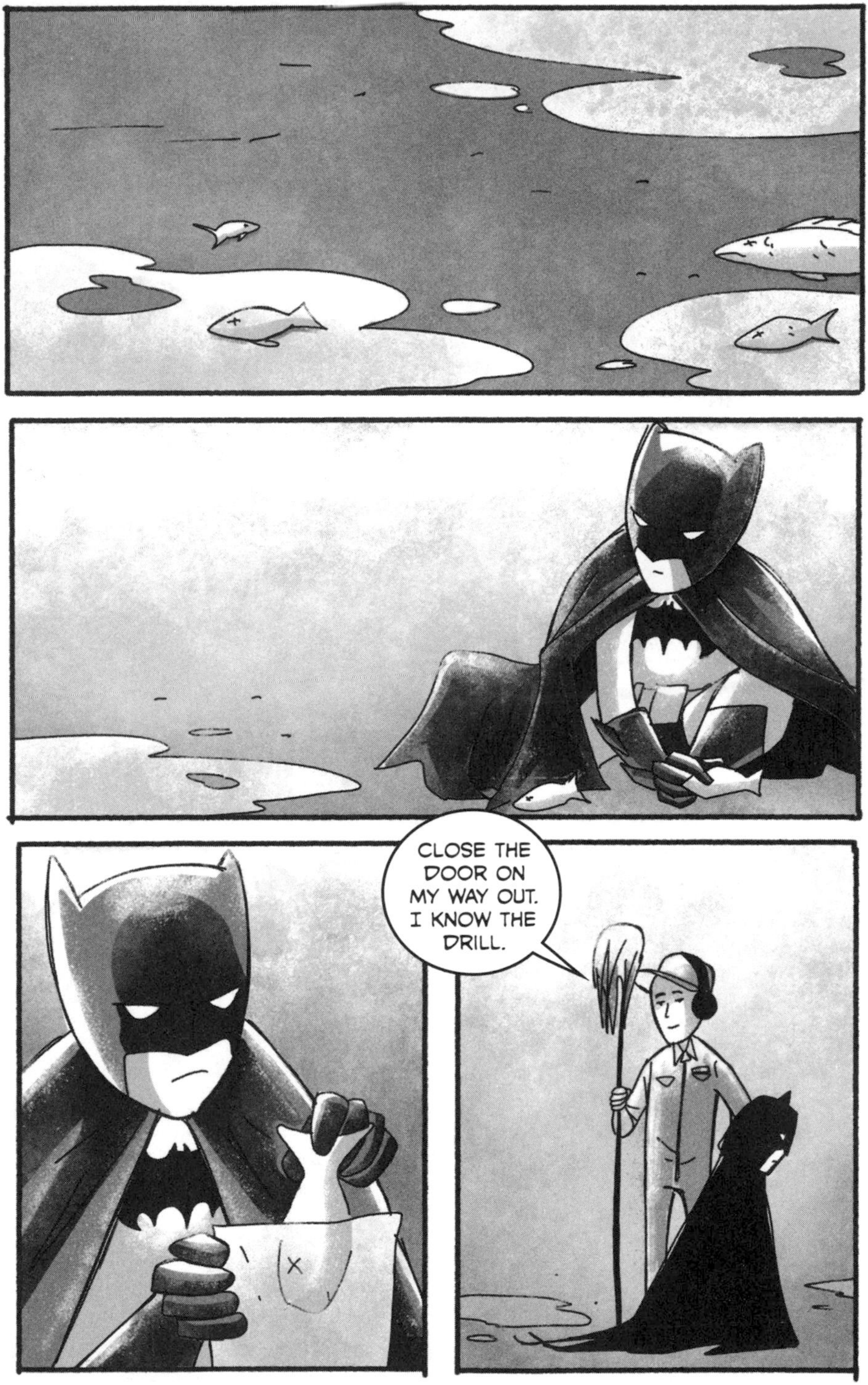
CLOSE THE DOOR ON MY WAY OUT. I KNOW THE DRILL.

TO: Clark_Kent
FROM: Bruce_Wayne
SUBJECT: Shop Class Investigation

I managed to get to the room while it was undisturbed. No teacher or students were around. I was able to recover some evidence at the scene.

I ran the sample of water I took. It has ocean components to it. That's not a direct indication of who might've done this. But it points to a few suspects who might talk to fish.

Speaking of which, the dead fish I took as evidence didn't have a smile on it. None of them did. So unless he forgot to put lipstick on them, I don't think the Joker is responsible here.

I did a quick scan for footprints or fingerprints but came up empty.

One thing, though . . . the janitor has been seen at every room that's been damaged. It's his job to clean them, but is he the one responsible for destroying them? It's something to consider.

MESSAGES

GROUP CHAT

Has shop class been reopened?

it's still being cleaned

there was a lot of water damage

most of the equipment doesn't work

We're running out of classes and labs to work on our projects.

at this rate, we'll have to work on them over at the mansion

no way!

the mansion is for me to make a mess in

no one else

I'm sure we can ask Alfred

DON'T YOU DARE!

You can always come out to the farm.

There's plenty of space out there.

for the cows

do you have high speed wi-fi access out there?

I don't think so.

never mind

I'll probably just find an internet café or hot spot

SEND

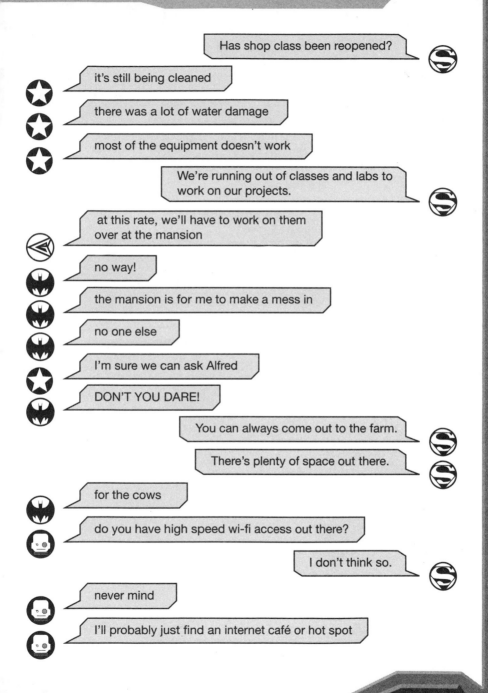

MESSAGES

GROUP CHAT

I say we go to Paradise Island to work on our projects

or our tans

that would be a bad idea

my island doesn't welcome many visitors

It's a good point.

Where are we going to work on our projects if this continues?

Many students have had theirs already ruined and have to start over.

I'll try to conjure protective spells over the remaining classrooms

Whoa! You can do that?!

I can try

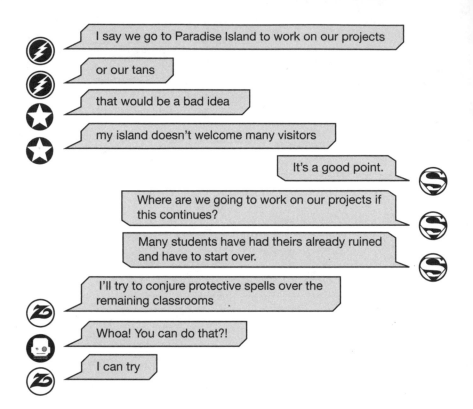

SEND

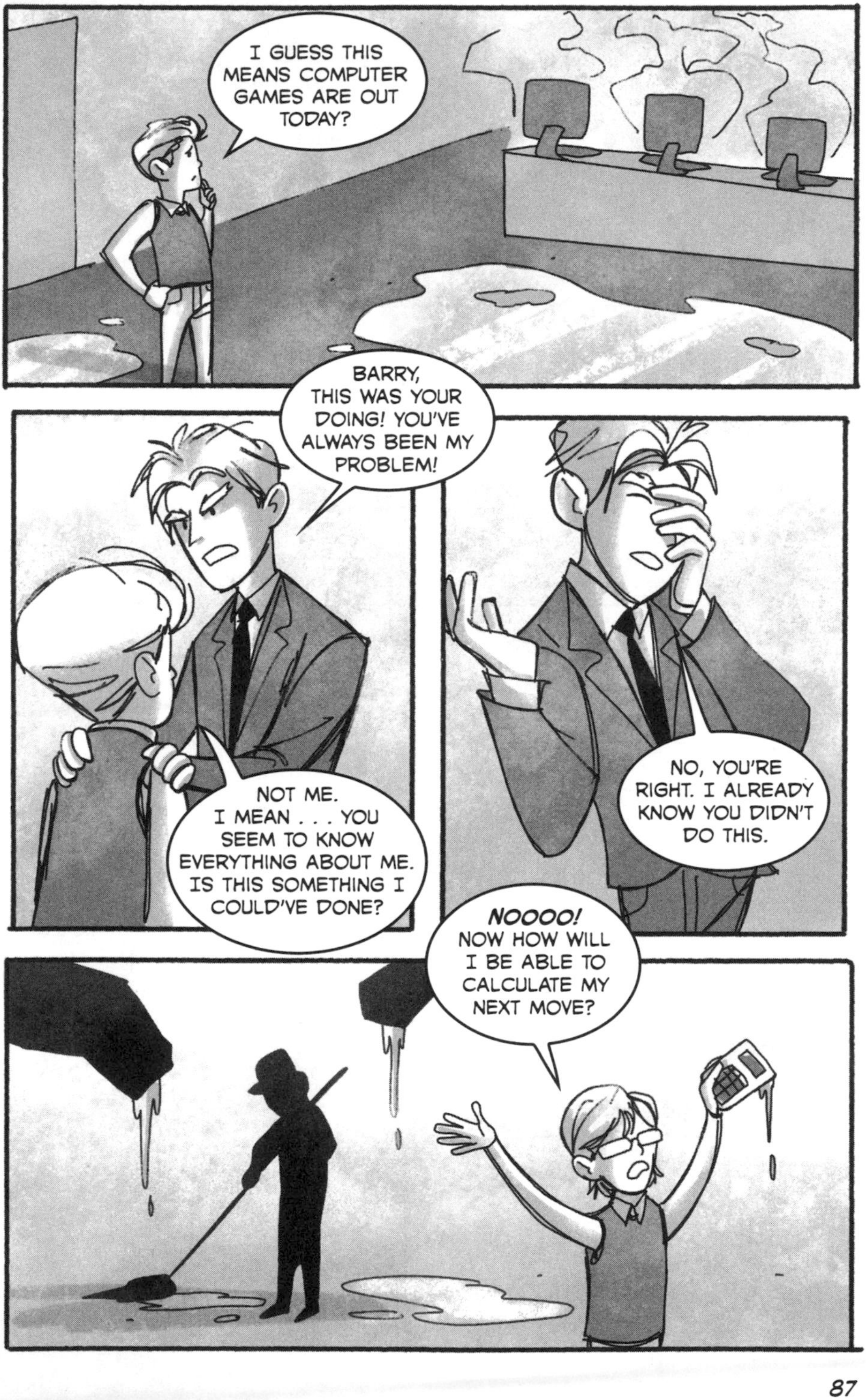
I GUESS THIS MEANS COMPUTER GAMES ARE OUT TODAY?
BARRY, THIS WAS YOUR DOING! YOU'VE ALWAYS BEEN MY PROBLEM!
NOT ME. I MEAN . . . YOU SEEM TO KNOW EVERYTHING ABOUT ME. IS THIS SOMETHING I COULD'VE DONE?
NO, YOU'RE RIGHT. I ALREADY KNOW YOU DIDN'T DO THIS.
NOOOO! NOW HOW WILL I BE ABLE TO CALCULATE MY NEXT MOVE?

GROUP CHAT

Arthur are you there?

sure

we haven't heard or seen much from you lately

been training for the upcoming swim meet

coach has been crushing us lately with laps

guess that's how he got his name

why what's up?

You've heard about all the classrooms being damaged?

sure

it's hard to miss

in my art class all the supplies got soaked

we're not talking about art

we're talking about all the school labs

places hit where students were working on their science fair projects

places where water damage was left as a calling card

are you insinuating something?

maybe

SEND

MESSAGES

GROUP CHAT

what Bruce is trying to say is

do you know who's responsible?

are YOU responsible?

that's UNFAIR Bruce!

just because I'm on the swim team or live near the ocean

or in it

it doesn't mean I'm to blame

Then help us find who is responsible!

I've gotta go

coach is yelling at me

SEND

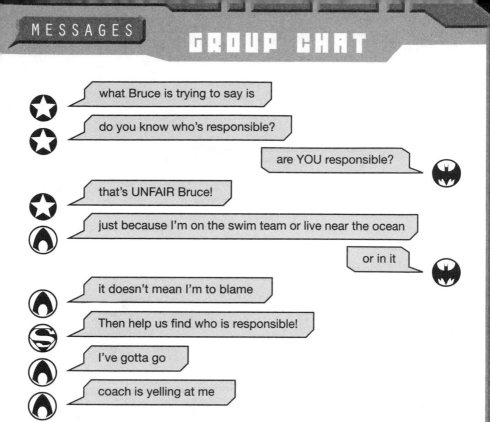

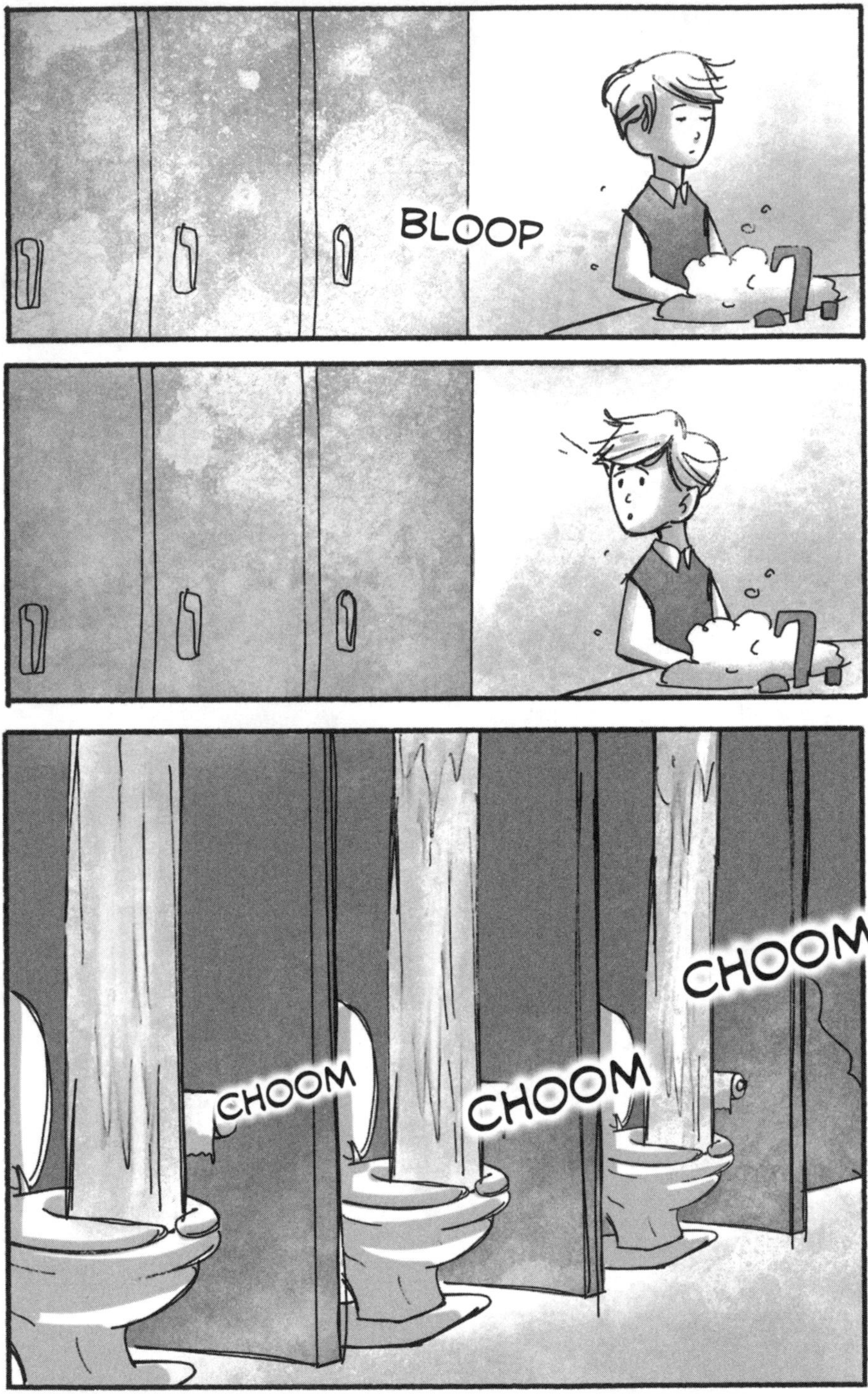
BLOOP
CHOOM
CHOOM
CHOOM

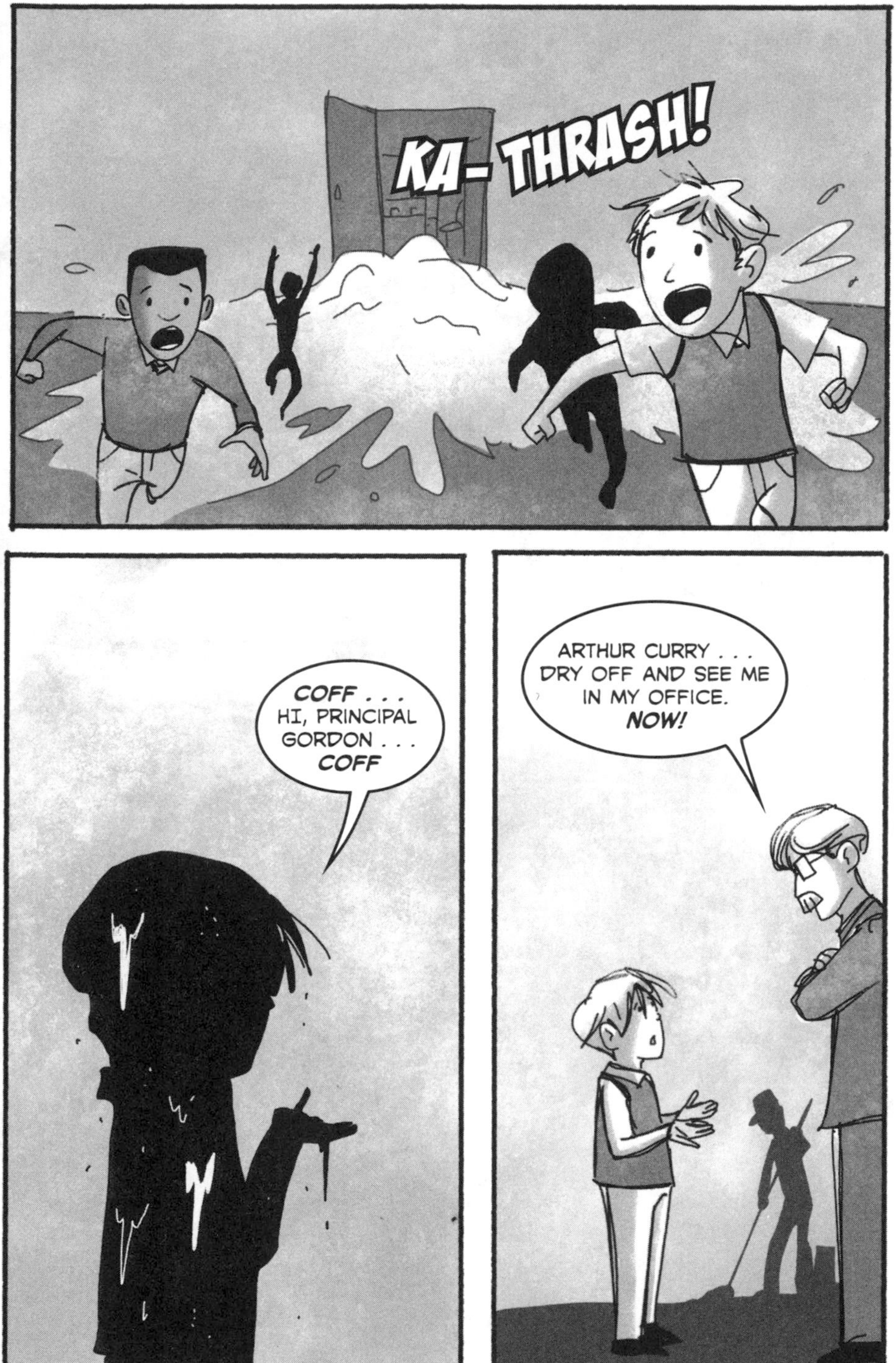
KA- THRASH!
COFF . . . HI, PRINCIPAL GORDON . . . COFF
ARTHUR CURRY . . . DRY OFF AND SEE ME IN MY OFFICE. NOW!

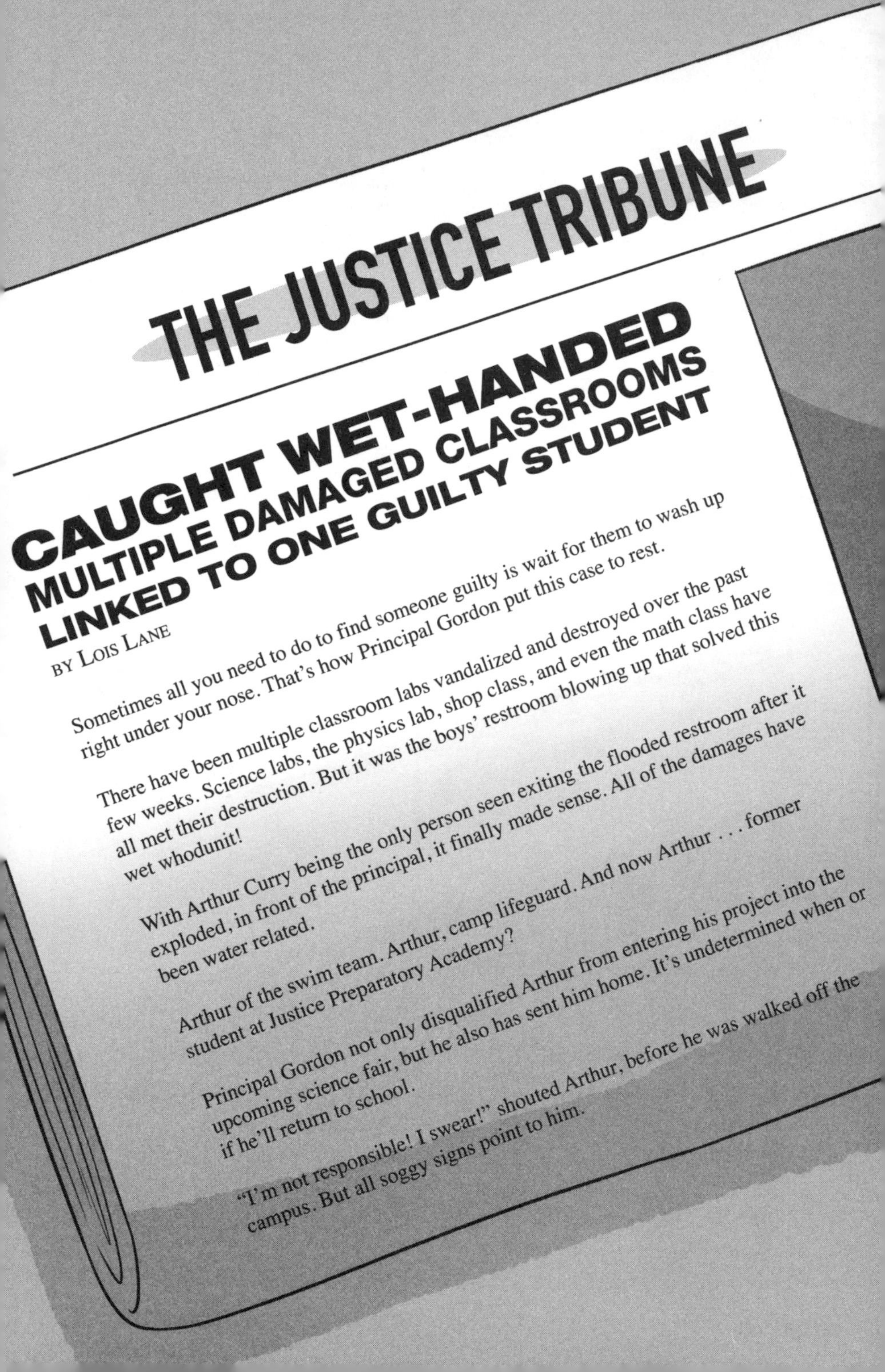

THE JUSTICE TRIBUNE

CAUGHT WET-HANDED

MULTIPLE DAMAGED CLASSROOMS LINKED TO ONE GUILTY STUDENT

BY LOIS LANE

Sometimes all you need to do to find someone guilty is wait for them to wash up right under your nose. That's how Principal Gordon put this case to rest.

There have been multiple classroom labs vandalized and destroyed over the past few weeks. Science labs, the physics lab, shop class, and even the math class have all met their destruction. But it was the boys' restroom blowing up that solved this wet whodunit!

With Arthur Curry being the only person seen exiting the flooded restroom after it exploded, in front of the principal, it finally made sense. All of the damages have been water related.

Arthur of the swim team. Arthur, camp lifeguard. And now Arthur . . . former student at Justice Preparatory Academy?

Principal Gordon not only disqualified Arthur from entering his project into the upcoming science fair, but he also has sent him home. It's undetermined when or if he'll return to school.

"I'm not responsible! I swear!" shouted Arthur, before he was walked off the campus. But all soggy signs point to him.

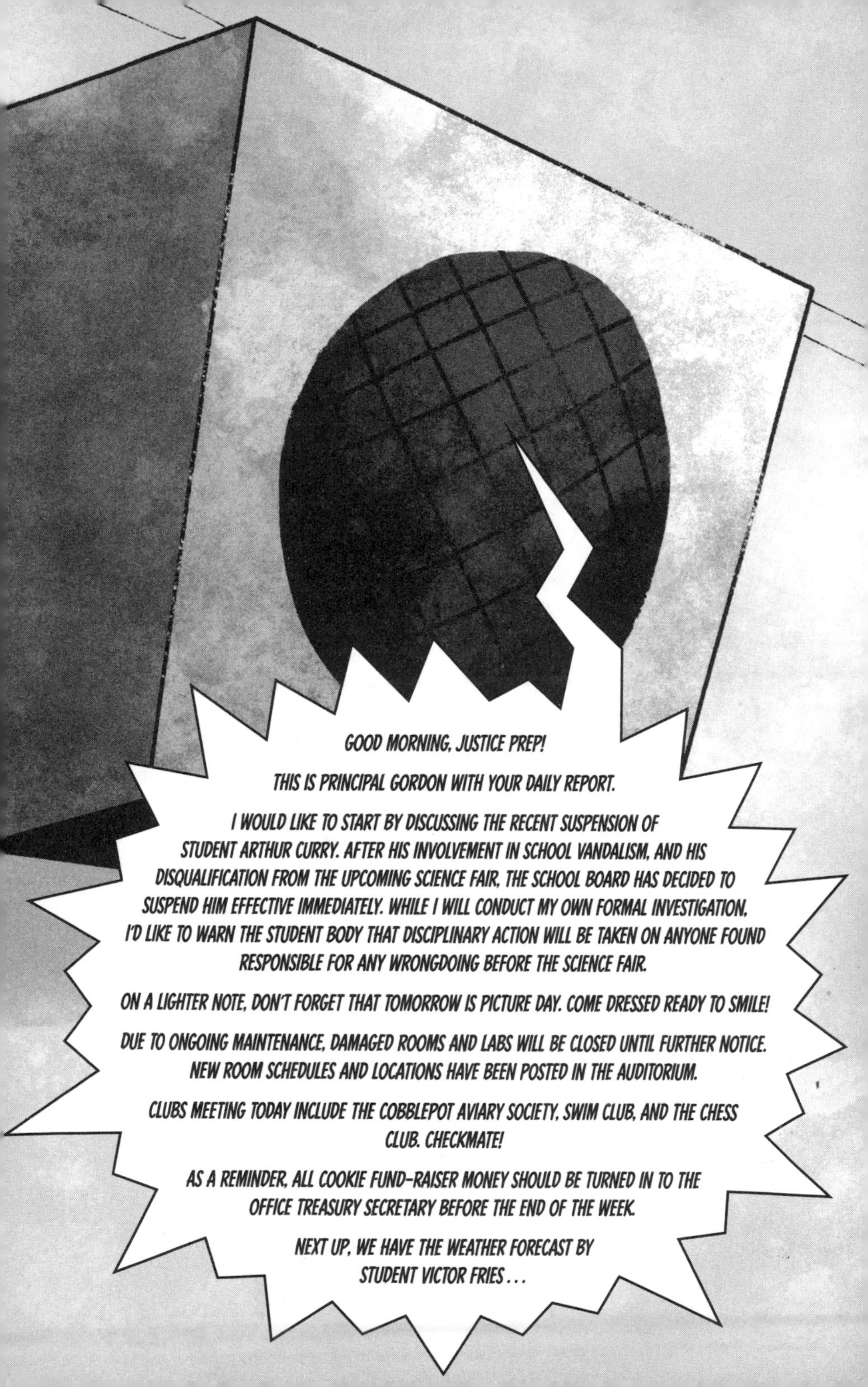
GOOD MORNING, JUSTICE PREP!
THIS IS PRINCIPAL GORDON WITH YOUR DAILY REPORT.
I WOULD LIKE TO START BY DISCUSSING THE RECENT SUSPENSION OF STUDENT ARTHUR CURRY. AFTER HIS INVOLVEMENT IN SCHOOL VANDALISM, AND HIS DISQUALIFICATION FROM THE UPCOMING SCIENCE FAIR, THE SCHOOL BOARD HAS DECIDED TO SUSPEND HIM EFFECTIVE IMMEDIATELY. WHILE I WILL CONDUCT MY OWN FORMAL INVESTIGATION, I'D LIKE TO WARN THE STUDENT BODY THAT DISCIPLINARY ACTION WILL BE TAKEN ON ANYONE FOUND RESPONSIBLE FOR ANY WRONGDOING BEFORE THE SCIENCE FAIR.
ON A LIGHTER NOTE, DON'T FORGET THAT TOMORROW IS PICTURE DAY. COME DRESSED READY TO SMILE!
DUE TO ONGOING MAINTENANCE, DAMAGED ROOMS AND LABS WILL BE CLOSED UNTIL FURTHER NOTICE. NEW ROOM SCHEDULES AND LOCATIONS HAVE BEEN POSTED IN THE AUDITORIUM.
CLUBS MEETING TODAY INCLUDE THE COBBLEPOT AVIARY SOCIETY, SWIM CLUB, AND THE CHESS CLUB. CHECKMATE!
AS A REMINDER, ALL COOKIE FUND-RAISER MONEY SHOULD BE TURNED IN TO THE OFFICE TREASURY SECRETARY BEFORE THE END OF THE WEEK.
NEXT UP, WE HAVE THE WEATHER FORECAST BY STUDENT VICTOR FRIES . . .

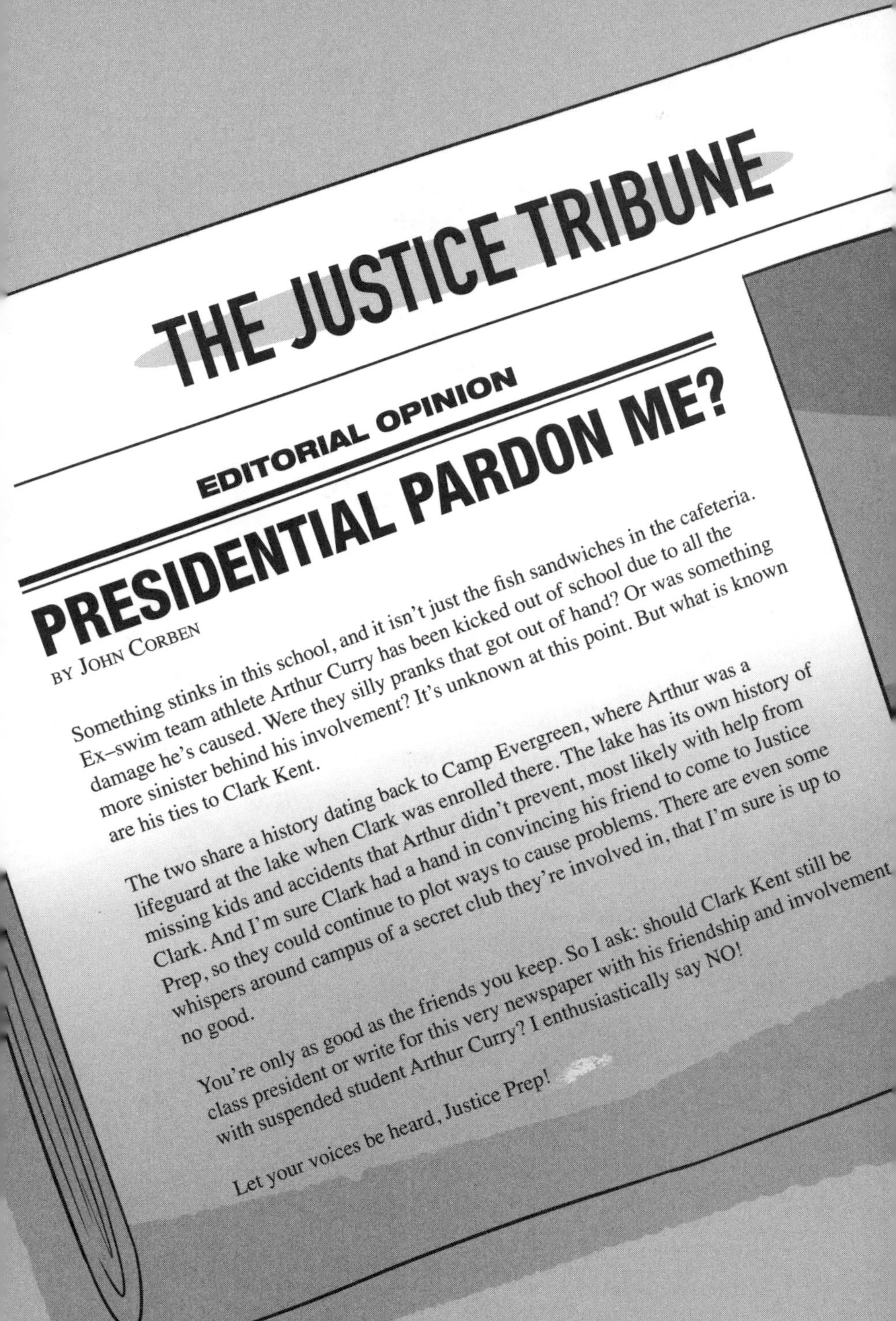

THE JUSTICE TRIBUNE

EDITORIAL OPINION

PRESIDENTIAL PARDON ME?

By John Corben

Something stinks in this school, and it isn't just the fish sandwiches in the cafeteria. Ex–swim team athlete Arthur Curry has been kicked out of school due to all the damage he's caused. Were they silly pranks that got out of hand? Or was something more sinister behind his involvement? It's unknown at this point. But what is known are his ties to Clark Kent.

The two share a history dating back to Camp Evergreen, where Arthur was a lifeguard at the lake when Clark was enrolled there. The lake has its own history of missing kids and accidents that Arthur didn't prevent, most likely with help from Clark. And I'm sure Clark had a hand in convincing his friend to come to Justice Prep, so they could continue to plot ways to cause problems. There are even some whispers around campus of a secret club they're involved in, that I'm sure is up to no good.

You're only as good as the friends you keep. So I ask: should Clark Kent still be class president or write for this very newspaper with his friendship and involvement with suspended student Arthur Curry? I enthusiastically say NO!

Let your voices be heard, Justice Prep!

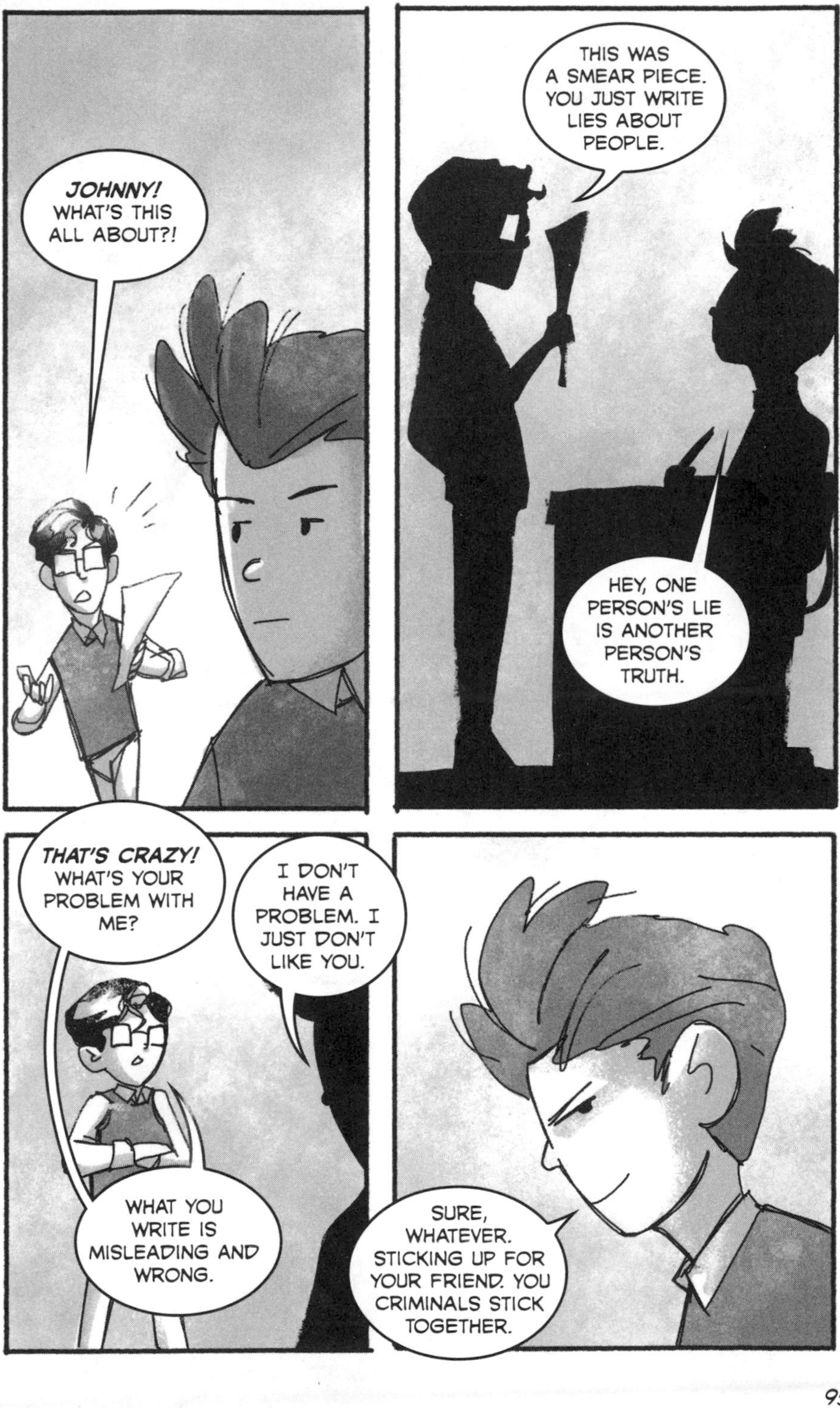
JOHNNY! WHAT'S THIS ALL ABOUT?!
THIS WAS A SMEAR PIECE. YOU JUST WRITE LIES ABOUT PEOPLE.
HEY, ONE PERSON'S LIE IS ANOTHER PERSON'S TRUTH.
THAT'S CRAZY! WHAT'S YOUR PROBLEM WITH ME?
I DON'T HAVE A PROBLEM. I JUST DON'T LIKE YOU.
WHAT YOU WRITE IS MISLEADING AND WRONG.
SURE, WHATEVER. STICKING UP FOR YOUR FRIEND. YOU CRIMINALS STICK TOGETHER.

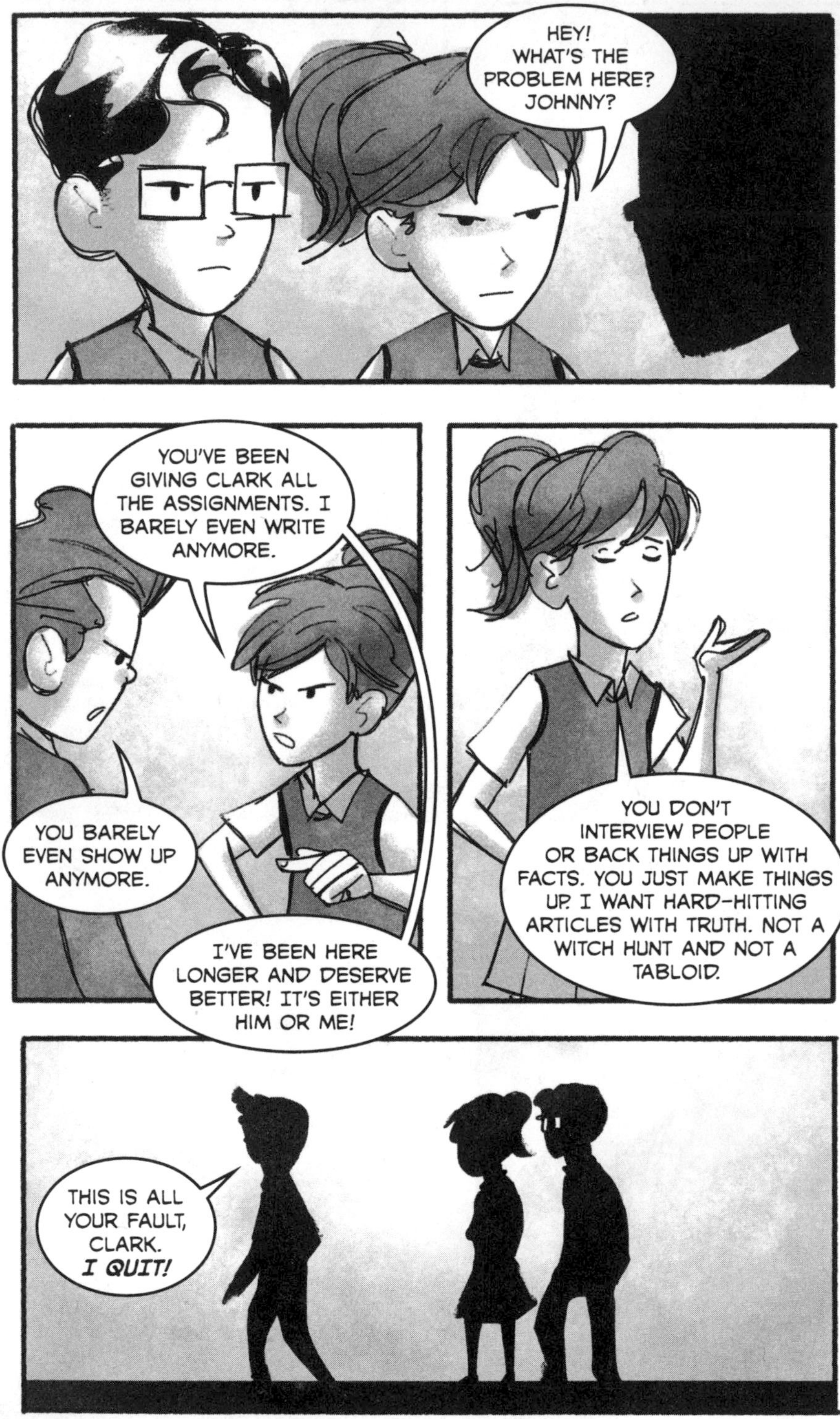
HEY! WHAT'S THE PROBLEM HERE? JOHNNY?
YOU'VE BEEN GIVING CLARK ALL THE ASSIGNMENTS. I BARELY EVEN WRITE ANYMORE.
YOU BARELY EVEN SHOW UP ANYMORE.
I'VE BEEN HERE LONGER AND DESERVE BETTER! IT'S EITHER HIM OR ME!
YOU DON'T INTERVIEW PEOPLE OR BACK THINGS UP WITH FACTS. YOU JUST MAKE THINGS UP. I WANT HARD-HITTING ARTICLES WITH TRUTH. NOT A WITCH HUNT AND NOT A TABLOID.
THIS IS ALL YOUR FAULT, CLARK. *I QUIT!*

GROUP CHAT

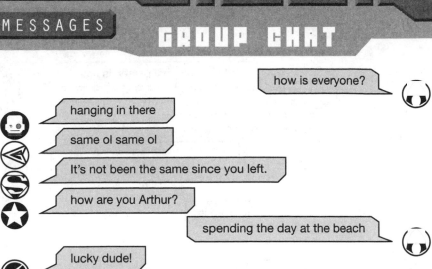

how is everyone?

hanging in there

same ol same ol

It's not been the same since you left.

how are you Arthur?

spending the day at the beach

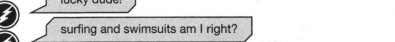

lucky dude!

surfing and swimsuits am I right?

but wish I were at school

what happened?

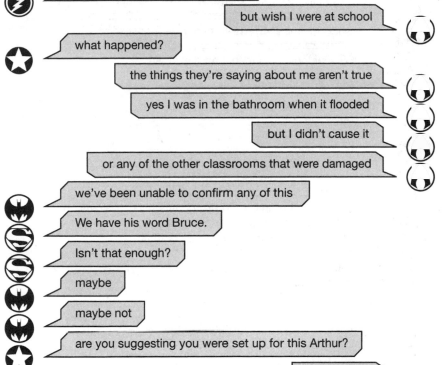

the things they're saying about me aren't true

yes I was in the bathroom when it flooded

but I didn't cause it

or any of the other classrooms that were damaged

we've been unable to confirm any of this

We have his word Bruce.

Isn't that enough?

maybe

maybe not

are you suggesting you were set up for this Arthur?

I don't know

SEND

MESSAGES

GROUP CHAT

but until the real person is caught

it just made things easier on everyone to accuse me

when are you coming back Arthur?

I'm not sure

it's not my decision

at this point the hard truth is

EVERYONE is a suspect

here we go again

we're still no closer to finding out who is responsible

which means EVERYONE can be responsible

By your logic, you're just as likely then.

yes

that's silly

I'm not offended Diana

each of us should be held to the same standards

sometimes I wish I could disappear until this is over

you totally can abracadabra and do that

not really

I don't know that spell yet

We'll keep up our search to find the one responsible.

And clear your name Arthur.

thanks

until then just hang ten dude!!

SEND

November 6th

CLARK'S JOURNAL

If there's anything I've found out, it's that school is never boring.

Johnny Corben wrote this weird article about me and Arthur. It's like he has some kind of grudge against me, but I don't know what I ever did to him. He writes lies and makes things up, which goes against what Lois and I are doing at the paper. We're trying to find the truth. And when he was confronted about what he wrote, he got mad and quit the newspaper. It's probably for the best. But I have a feeling it's not the last I'll hear from him.

With Arthur being disqualified from the science fair and suspended, it's got us all on edge. Everyone is looking over their shoulder and nervous about what will happen next or who will be accused of something. It's almost like we've all become as paranoid as Bruce is.

Who has time to work on their science fair project when someone is out to get them?

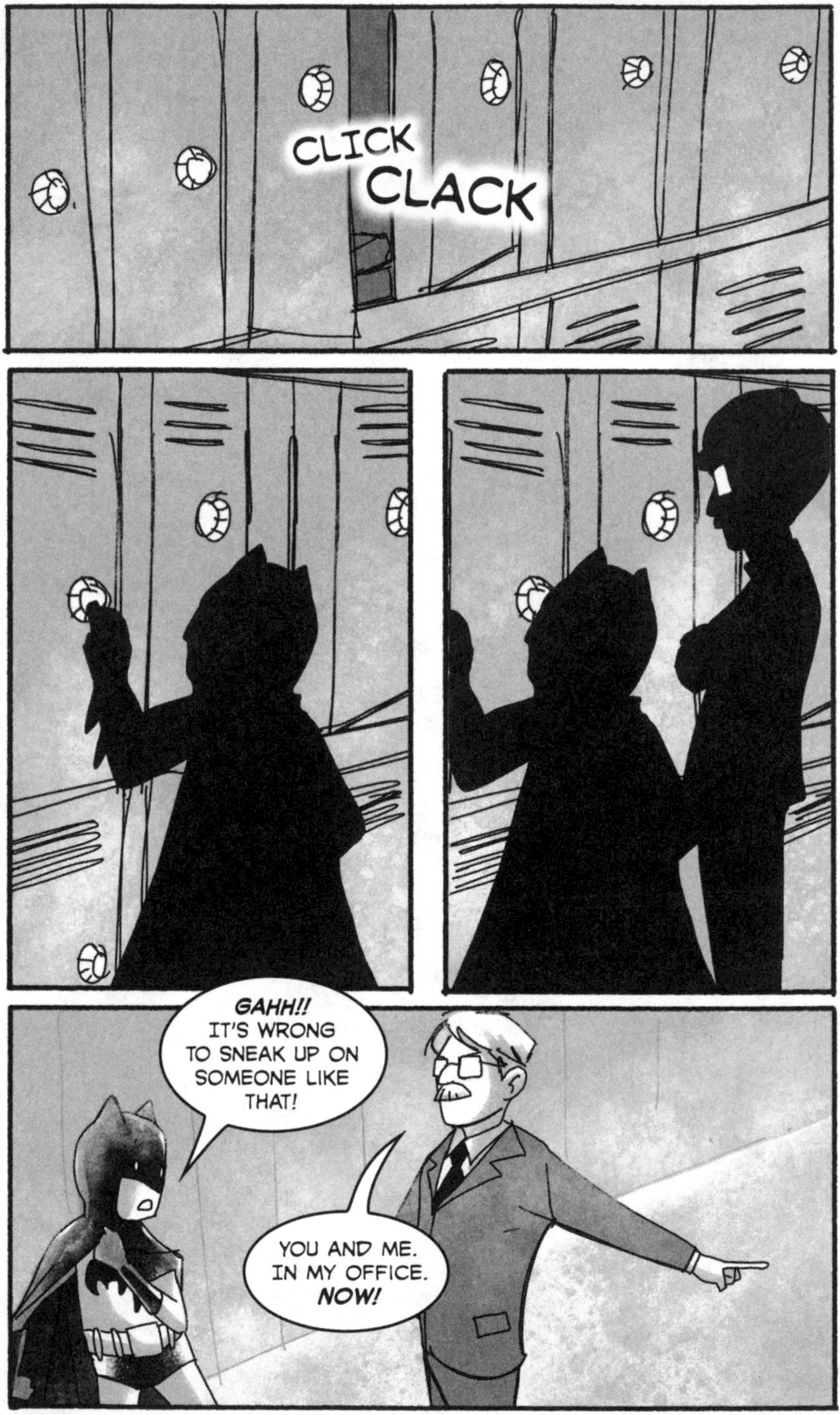
CLICK
CLACK
GAHH!! IT'S WRONG TO SNEAK UP ON SOMEONE LIKE THAT!
YOU AND ME. IN MY OFFICE. NOW!

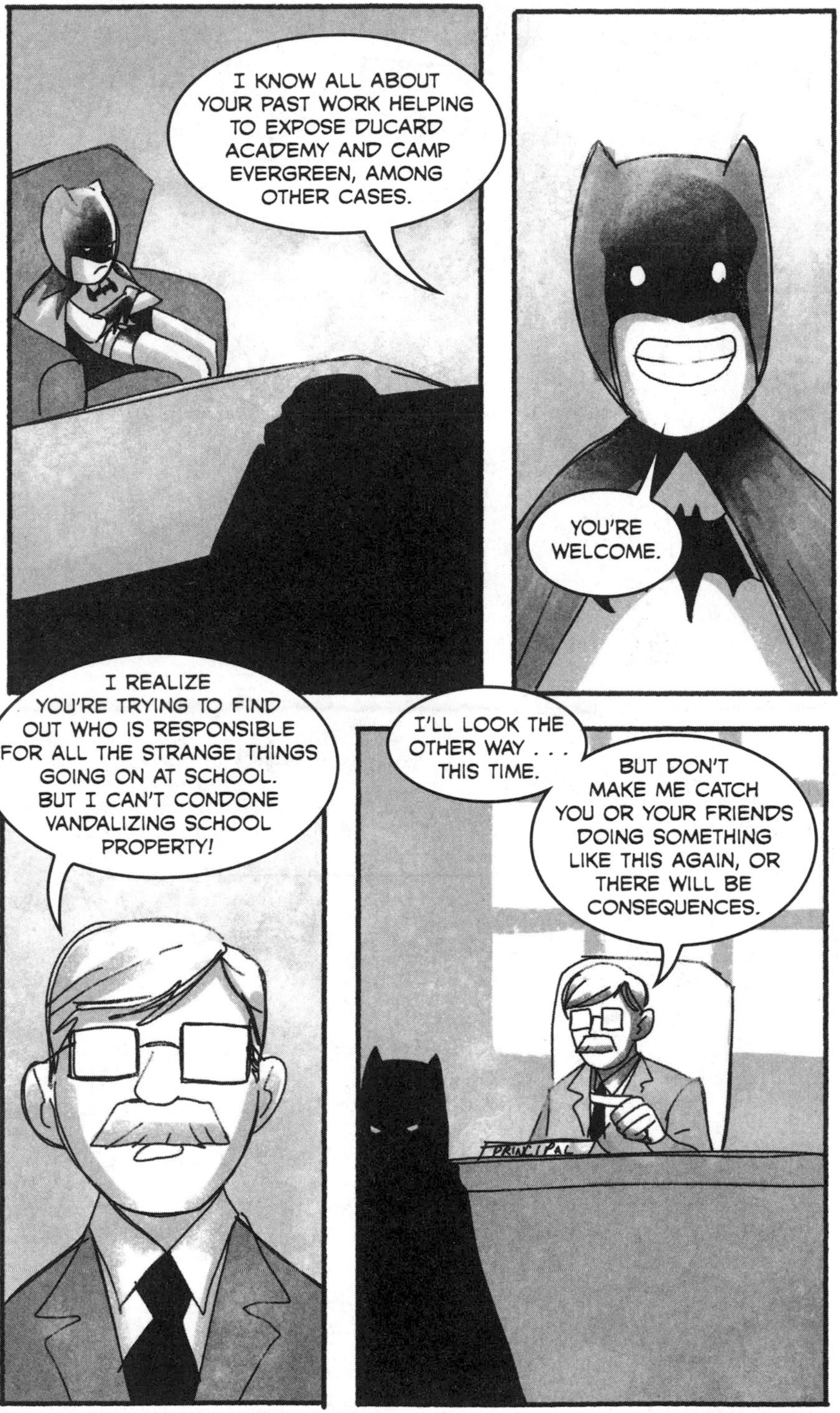
I KNOW ALL ABOUT YOUR PAST WORK HELPING TO EXPOSE DUCARD ACADEMY AND CAMP EVERGREEN, AMONG OTHER CASES.
YOU'RE WELCOME.
I REALIZE YOU'RE TRYING TO FIND OUT WHO IS RESPONSIBLE FOR ALL THE STRANGE THINGS GOING ON AT SCHOOL. BUT I CAN'T CONDONE VANDALIZING SCHOOL PROPERTY!
I'LL LOOK THE OTHER WAY . . . THIS TIME.
BUT DON'T MAKE ME CATCH YOU OR YOUR FRIENDS DOING SOMETHING LIKE THIS AGAIN, OR THERE WILL BE CONSEQUENCES.
PRINCIPAL

Clark, I was able to grab all these notes passed in class. Don't know if any of them will help find our suspect.

—Barry

If you give me water, I will die. What am I?

—E. Nigma

Answer: FIRE

I am a word. If you pronounce me right, it will be wrong. If you pronounce me wrong, it is right. What word am I? —E. Nigma

Answer: WRONG

I don't have eyes, ears, nose, or tongue, but I can see, smell, hear, and taste everything. What am I?   —E. Nigma

Answer: A BRAIN

I can see but can't hear or speak. But I will always tell the truth. What am I?

—E. Nigma

Answer: A MIRROR

Roses are red, violets are blue
If I catch you hurting flowers, that will
be the end of you!

—Pamela

IT'S HARD TO WRITE SMALL WITH LARGE HANDS

—GIGANTA!

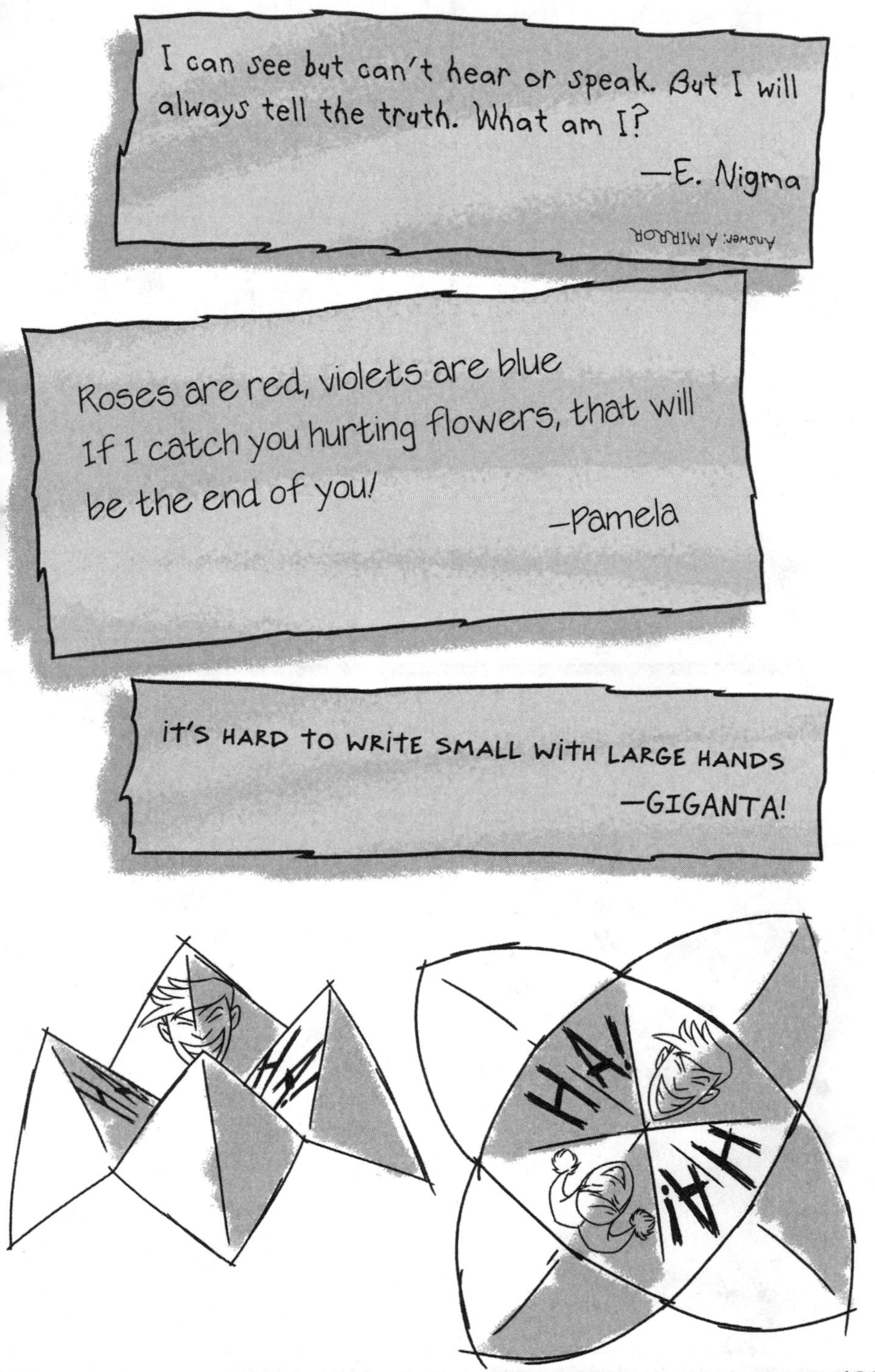
HA!
HA!

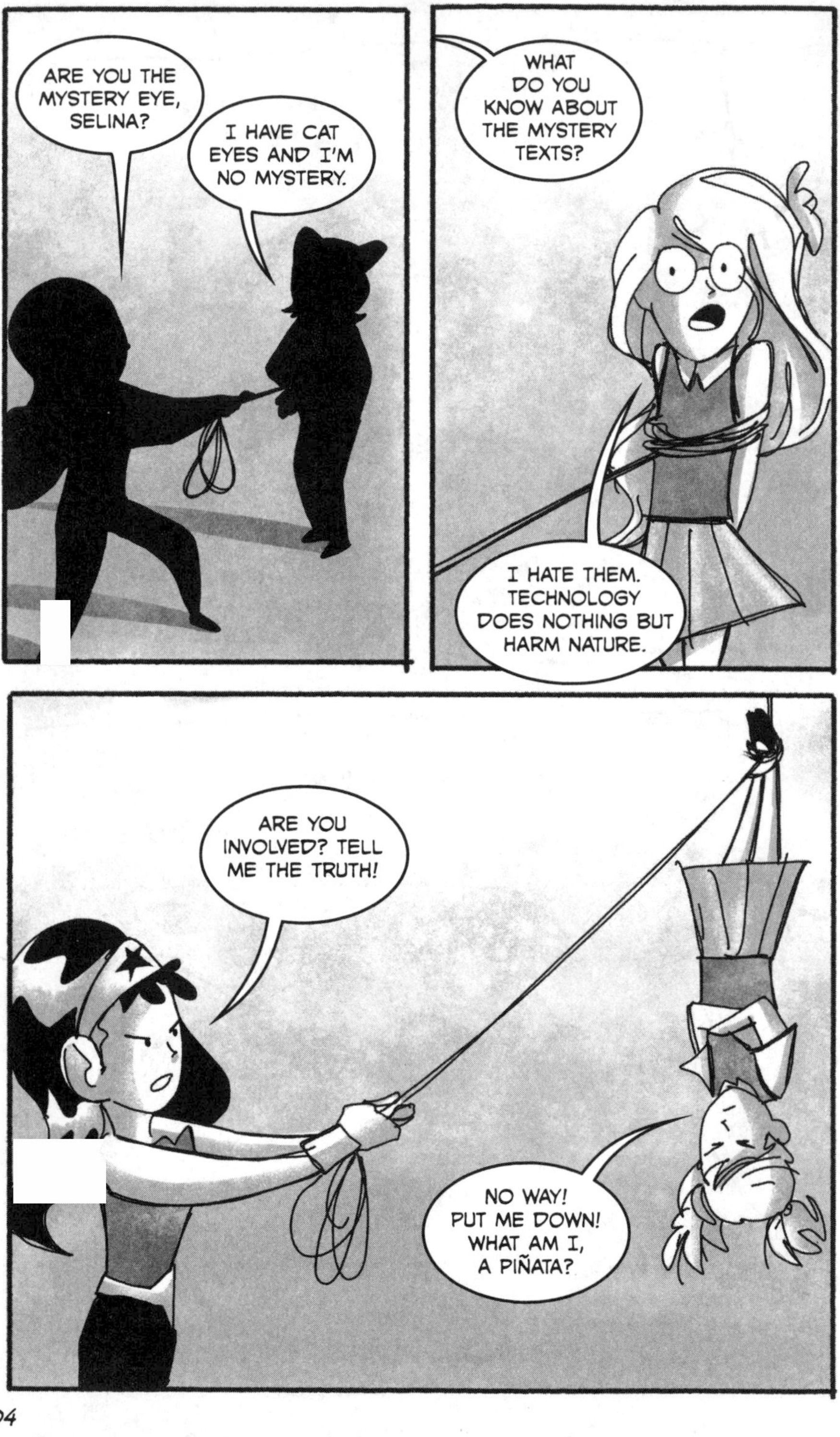

ARE YOU THE MYSTERY EYE, SELINA?
I HAVE CAT EYES AND I'M NO MYSTERY.
WHAT DO YOU KNOW ABOUT THE MYSTERY TEXTS?
I HATE THEM. TECHNOLOGY DOES NOTHING BUT HARM NATURE.
ARE YOU INVOLVED? TELL ME THE TRUTH!
NO WAY! PUT ME DOWN! WHAT AM I, A PIÑATA?

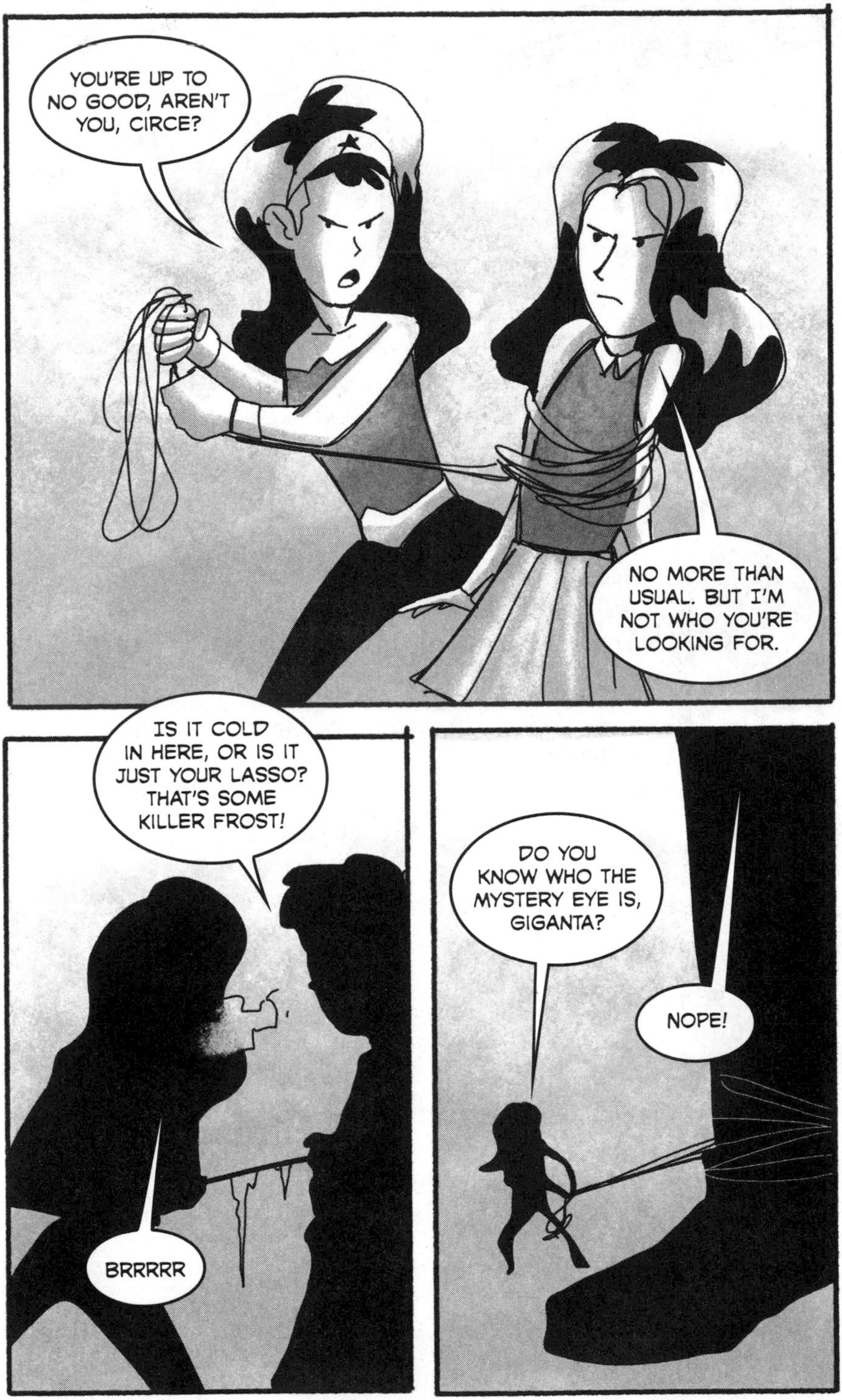
YOU'RE UP TO NO GOOD, AREN'T YOU, CIRCE?
NO MORE THAN USUAL. BUT I'M NOT WHO YOU'RE LOOKING FOR.
IS IT COLD IN HERE, OR IS IT JUST YOUR LASSO? THAT'S SOME KILLER FROST!
BRRRRR
DO YOU KNOW WHO THE MYSTERY EYE IS, GIGANTA?
NOPE!

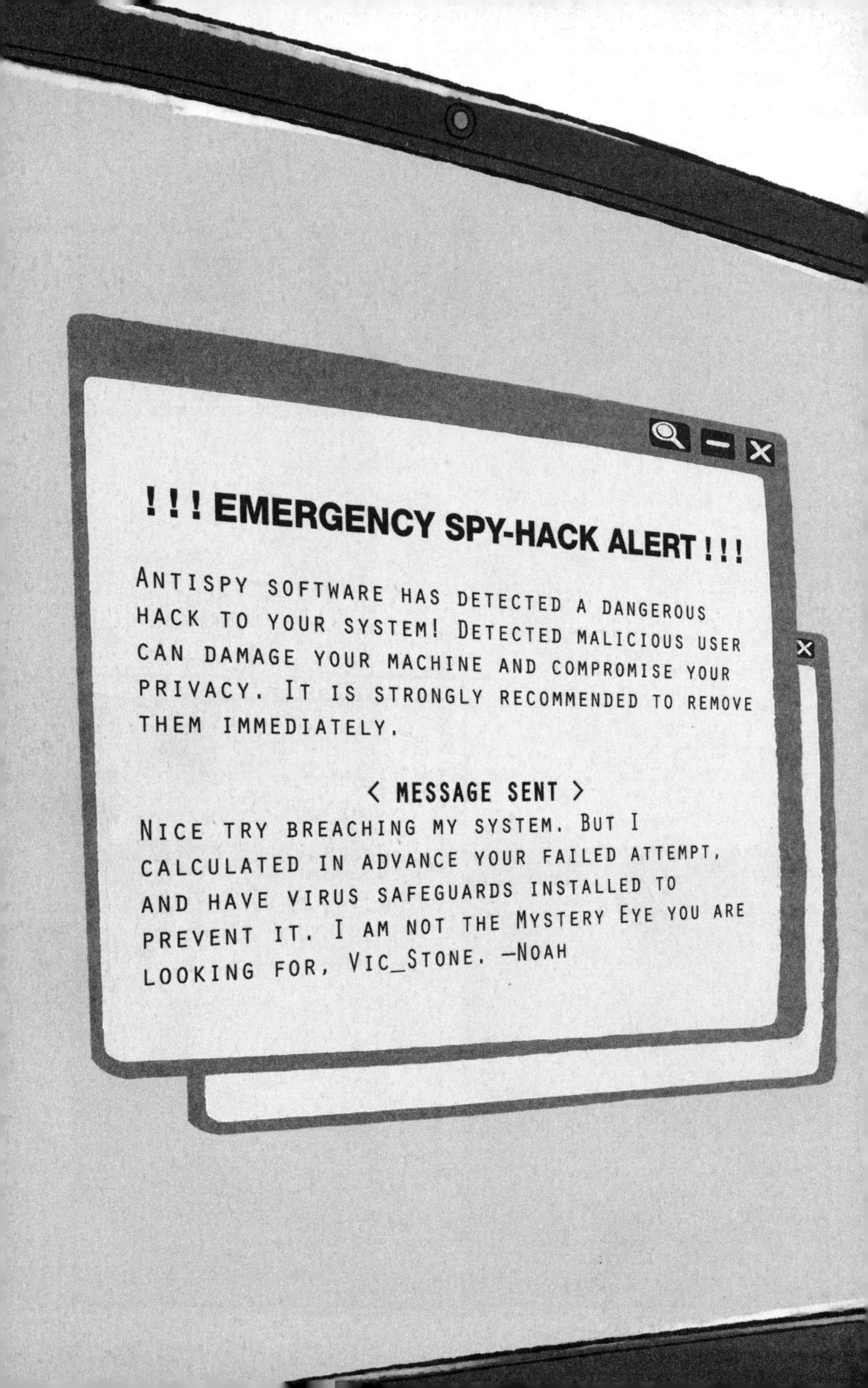
!!! EMERGENCY SPY-HACK ALERT !!!
ANTISPY SOFTWARE HAS DETECTED A DANGEROUS HACK TO YOUR SYSTEM! DETECTED MALICIOUS USER CAN DAMAGE YOUR MACHINE AND COMPROMISE YOUR PRIVACY. IT IS STRONGLY RECOMMENDED TO REMOVE THEM IMMEDIATELY.
< MESSAGE SENT >
NICE TRY BREACHING MY SYSTEM. BUT I CALCULATED IN ADVANCE YOUR FAILED ATTEMPT, AND HAVE VIRUS SAFEGUARDS INSTALLED TO PREVENT IT. I AM NOT THE MYSTERY EYE YOU ARE LOOKING FOR, VIC_STONE. —NOAH

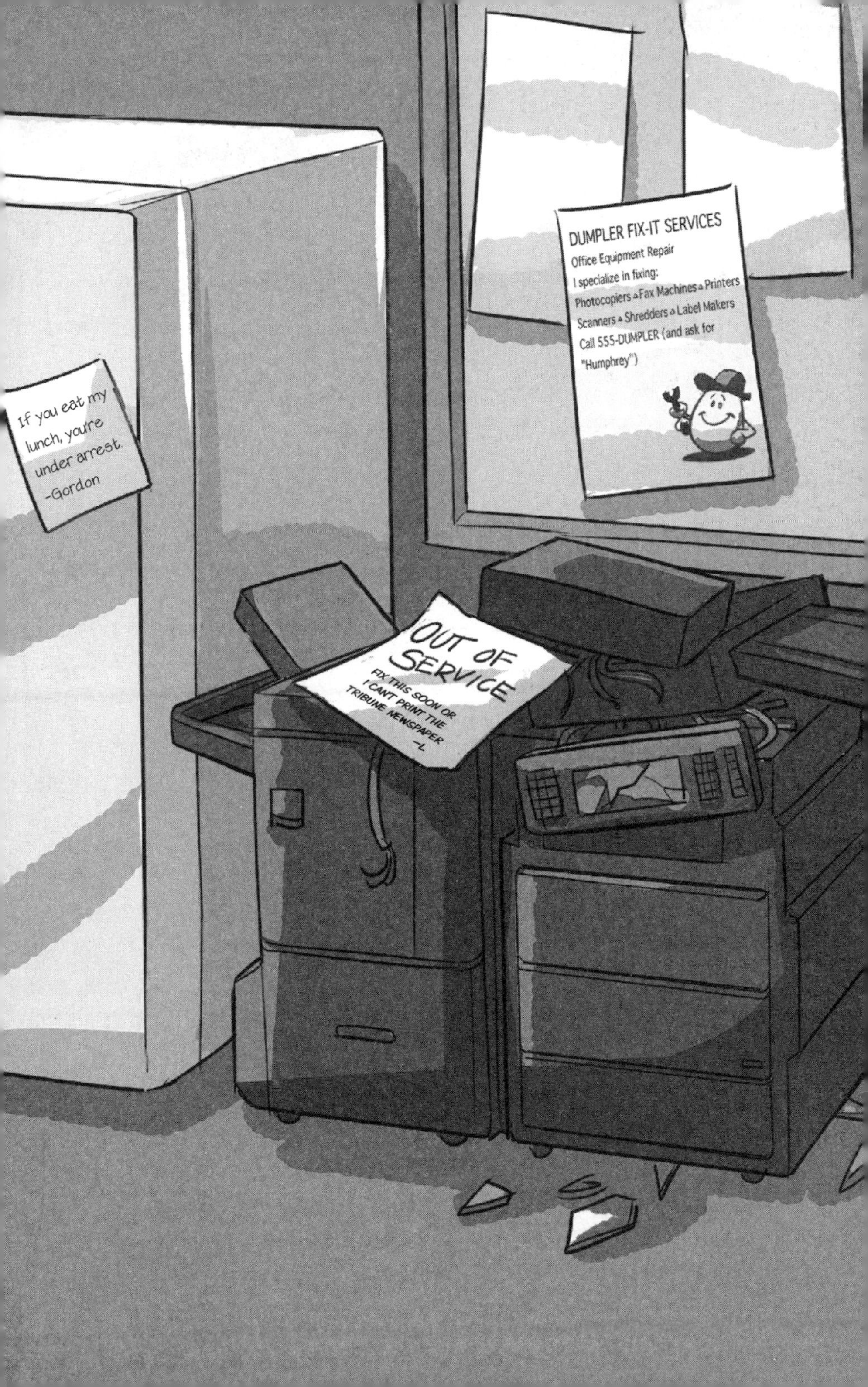
DUMPLER FIX-IT SERVICES
Office Equipment Repair
I specialize in fixing:
Photocopiers ▵ Fax Machines ▵ Printers
Scanners ▵ Shredders ▵ Label Makers
Call 555-DUMPLER (and ask for "Humphrey")
If you eat my lunch, you're under arrest. -Gordon
OUT OF SERVICE
FIX THIS SOON OR I CAN'T PRINT THE TRIBUNE NEWSPAPER -L

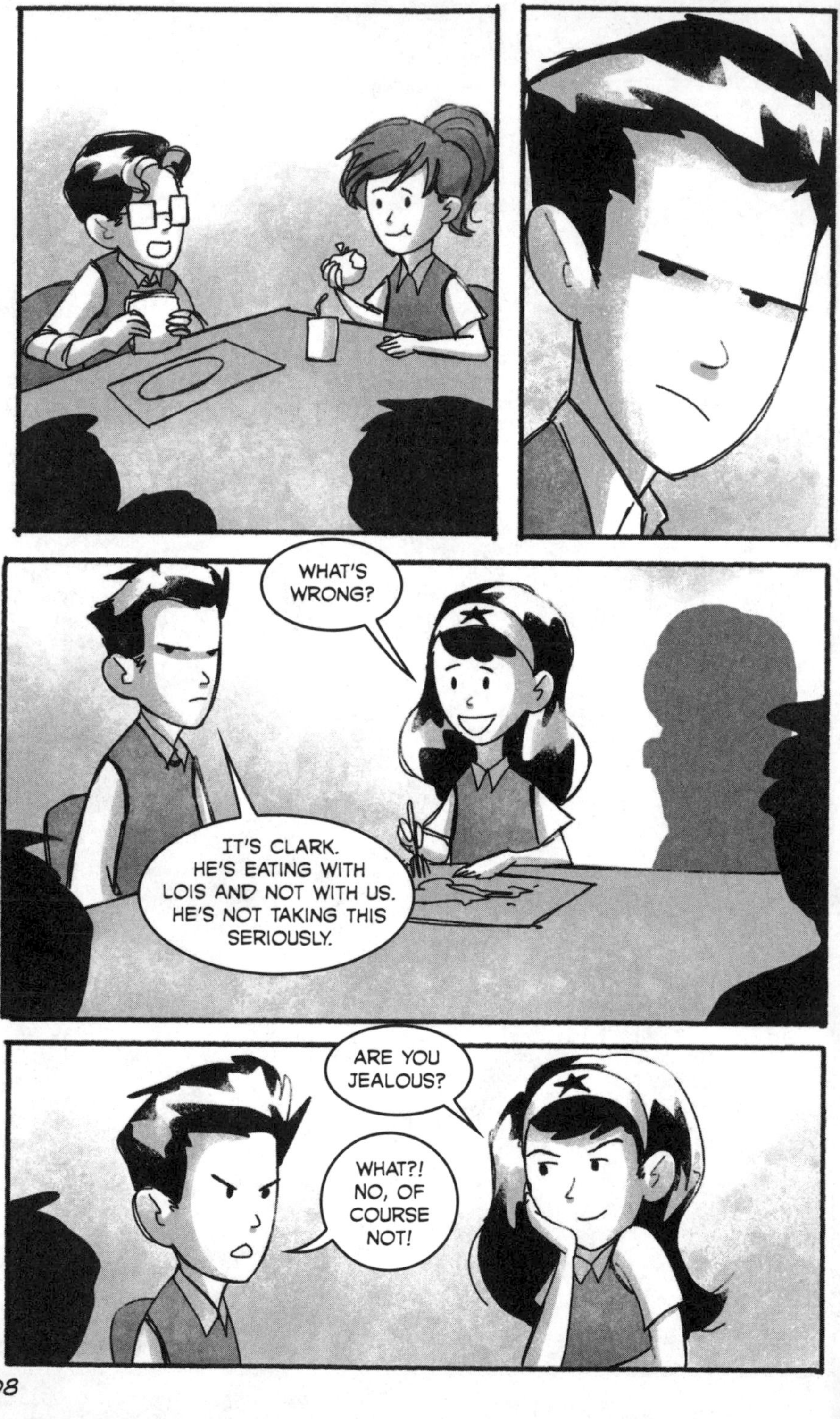
WHAT'S WRONG?
IT'S CLARK. HE'S EATING WITH LOIS AND NOT WITH US. HE'S NOT TAKING THIS SERIOUSLY.
ARE YOU JEALOUS?
WHAT?! NO, OF COURSE NOT!

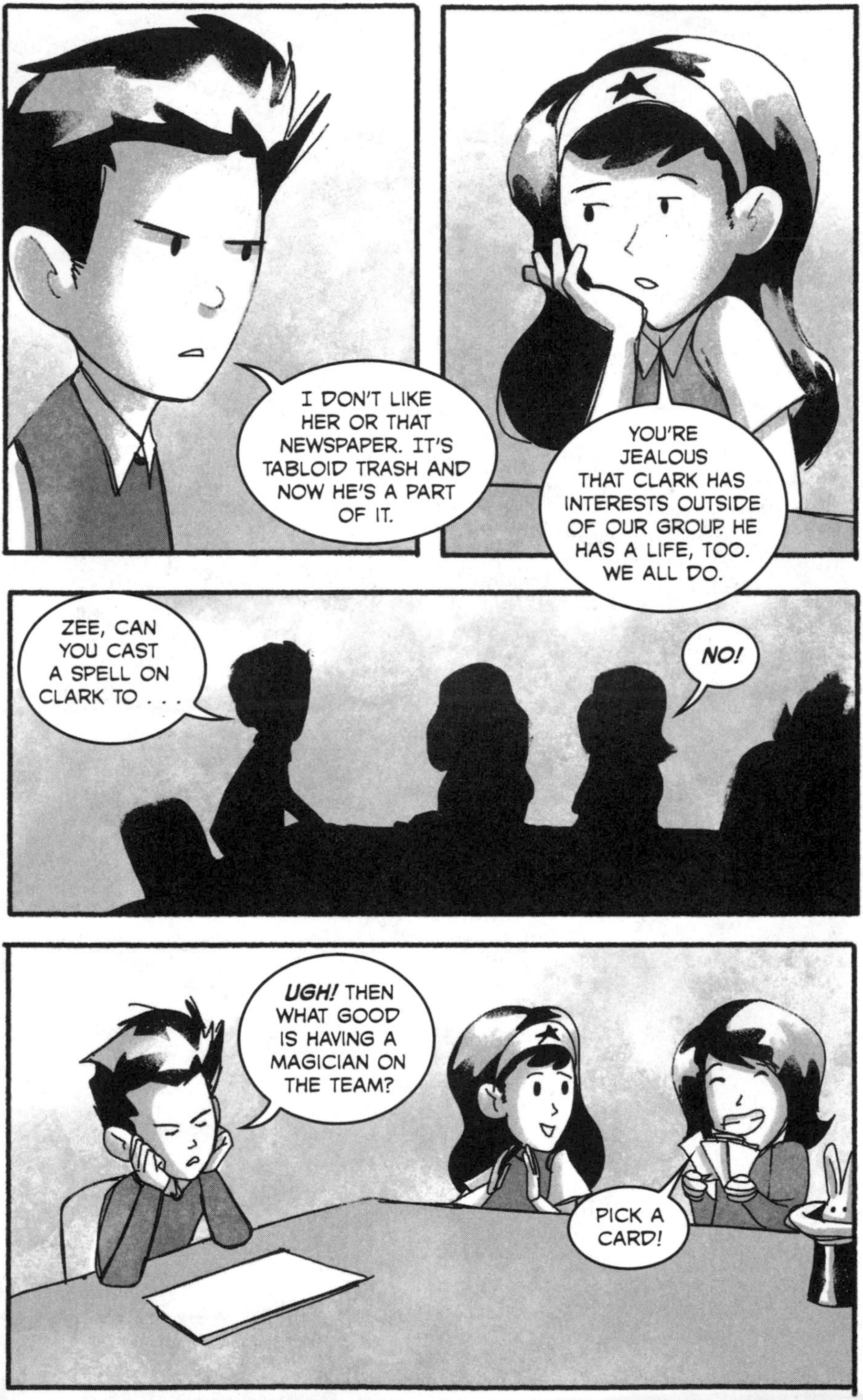
I DON'T LIKE HER OR THAT NEWSPAPER. IT'S TABLOID TRASH AND NOW HE'S A PART OF IT.
YOU'RE JEALOUS THAT CLARK HAS INTERESTS OUTSIDE OF OUR GROUP. HE HAS A LIFE, TOO. WE ALL DO.
ZEE, CAN YOU CAST A SPELL ON CLARK TO . . .
NO!
UGH! THEN WHAT GOOD IS HAVING A MAGICIAN ON THE TEAM?
PICK A CARD!

November 18th

CLARK'S JOURNAL

As the search to find out who the Mystery Eye is continues, I've been pulled in two different directions, between my friends in the Justice Squad and helping Lois investigate at the school newspaper. And Bruce isn't happy in either case. I think he's mad we haven't been able to solve the mystery. But he's also mad at me for spending time away from the group. He seems grumpier than he's been. But maybe it's because he got caught by the principal breaking into school lockers to look for evidence. I never thought he could ever get caught, but even he slipped up and was seen by the principal.

Lately everything isn't adding up. First it was all the labs in school getting damaged and shut down through various accidents. Then Arthur was accused and suspended for it. We've also been unsuccessful finding any new leads. Vic tried to hack into Noah's special calculator, thinking he might be responsible, but Noah was ten steps ahead of us and knew he'd be a target and stopped us from finding out anything. Then Diana used her Lasso of Truth to interrogate other students. Even without the ability to lie, they still didn't say anything useful. And the notes Barry managed to swipe out of class were pretty meaningless.

I just found out the school photocopy machine has been damaged. I don't know if this is an act of sabotage or just anger for what's been going on. But now we can't even print up the school newspapers until it gets fixed. It's like everything is working against us, and we're no closer to figuring out who is behind it all!

MESSAGES

GROUP CHAT

guys I think I know who's responsible for all this

my teacher Professor EO

It's not Eobard Thawne? why?

I think he's my #1 fan

that makes one of us :P

I'm being serious!

now I'm the one taking a screenshot

hee hee

he knows everything about me

as if he already knows secrets about me

but I don't know anything about him

none of us do about any of our teachers

speedy's got a point

I think the teachers have files on us

but we don't have files on our teachers

SEND

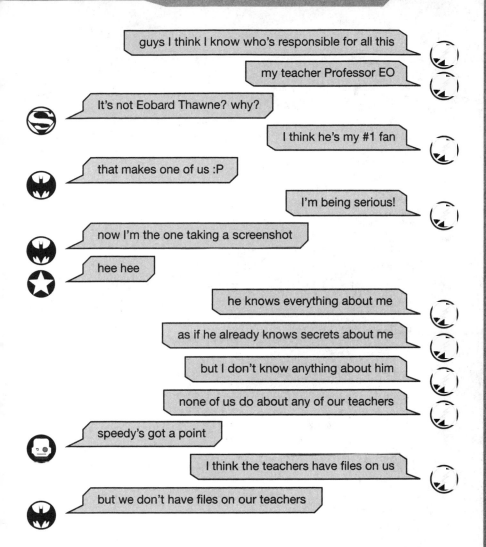

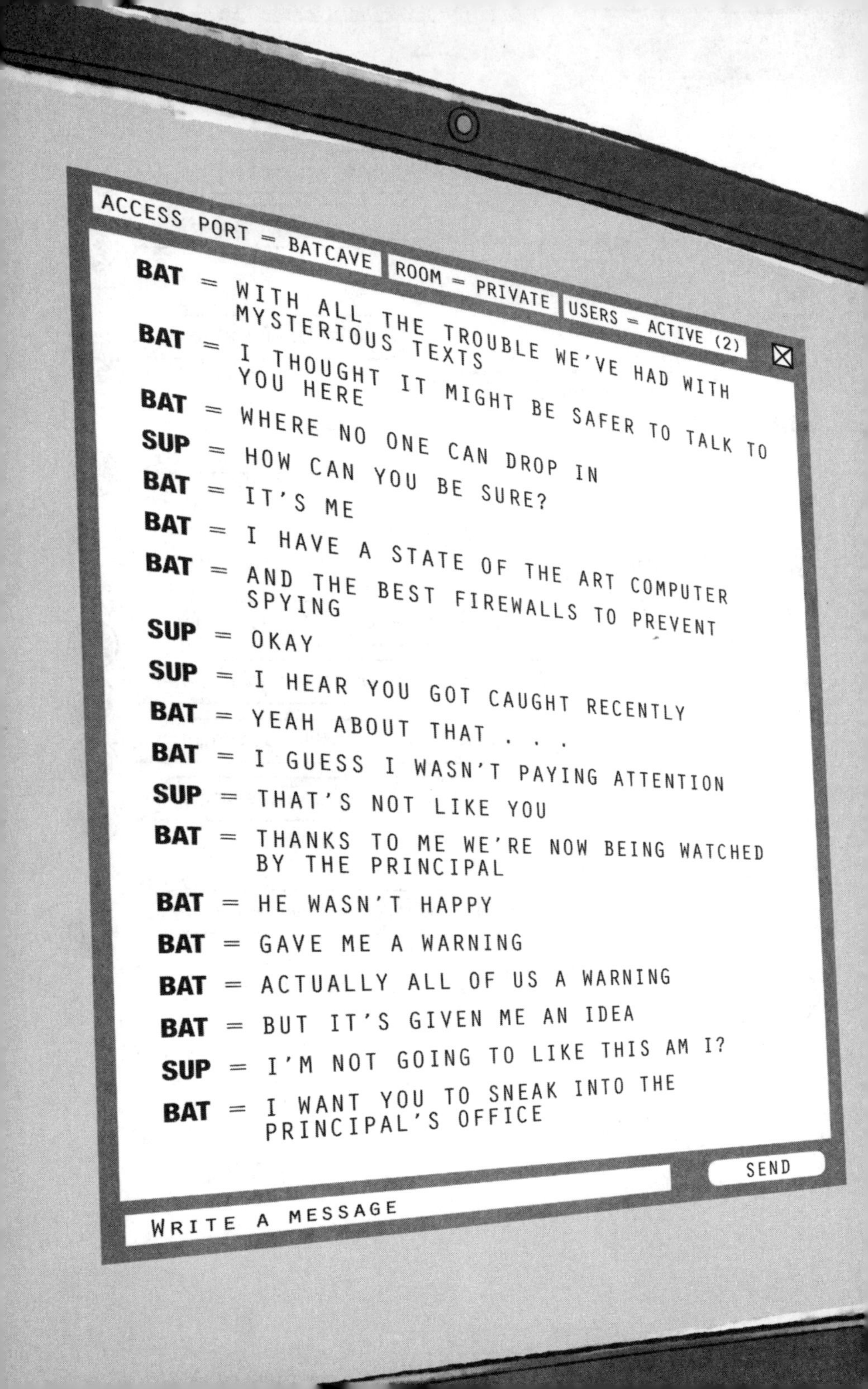
ACCESS PORT = BATCAVE
ROOM = PRIVATE
USERS = ACTIVE (2)
BAT = WITH ALL THE TROUBLE WE'VE HAD WITH MYSTERIOUS TEXTS
BAT = I THOUGHT IT MIGHT BE SAFER TO TALK TO YOU HERE
BAT = WHERE NO ONE CAN DROP IN
SUP = HOW CAN YOU BE SURE?
BAT = IT'S ME
BAT = I HAVE A STATE OF THE ART COMPUTER
BAT = AND THE BEST FIREWALLS TO PREVENT SPYING
SUP = OKAY
SUP = I HEAR YOU GOT CAUGHT RECENTLY
BAT = YEAH ABOUT THAT . . .
BAT = I GUESS I WASN'T PAYING ATTENTION
SUP = THAT'S NOT LIKE YOU
BAT = THANKS TO ME WE'RE NOW BEING WATCHED BY THE PRINCIPAL
BAT = HE WASN'T HAPPY
BAT = GAVE ME A WARNING
BAT = ACTUALLY ALL OF US A WARNING
BAT = BUT IT'S GIVEN ME AN IDEA
SUP = I'M NOT GOING TO LIKE THIS AM I?
BAT = I WANT YOU TO SNEAK INTO THE PRINCIPAL'S OFFICE
SEND
WRITE A MESSAGE

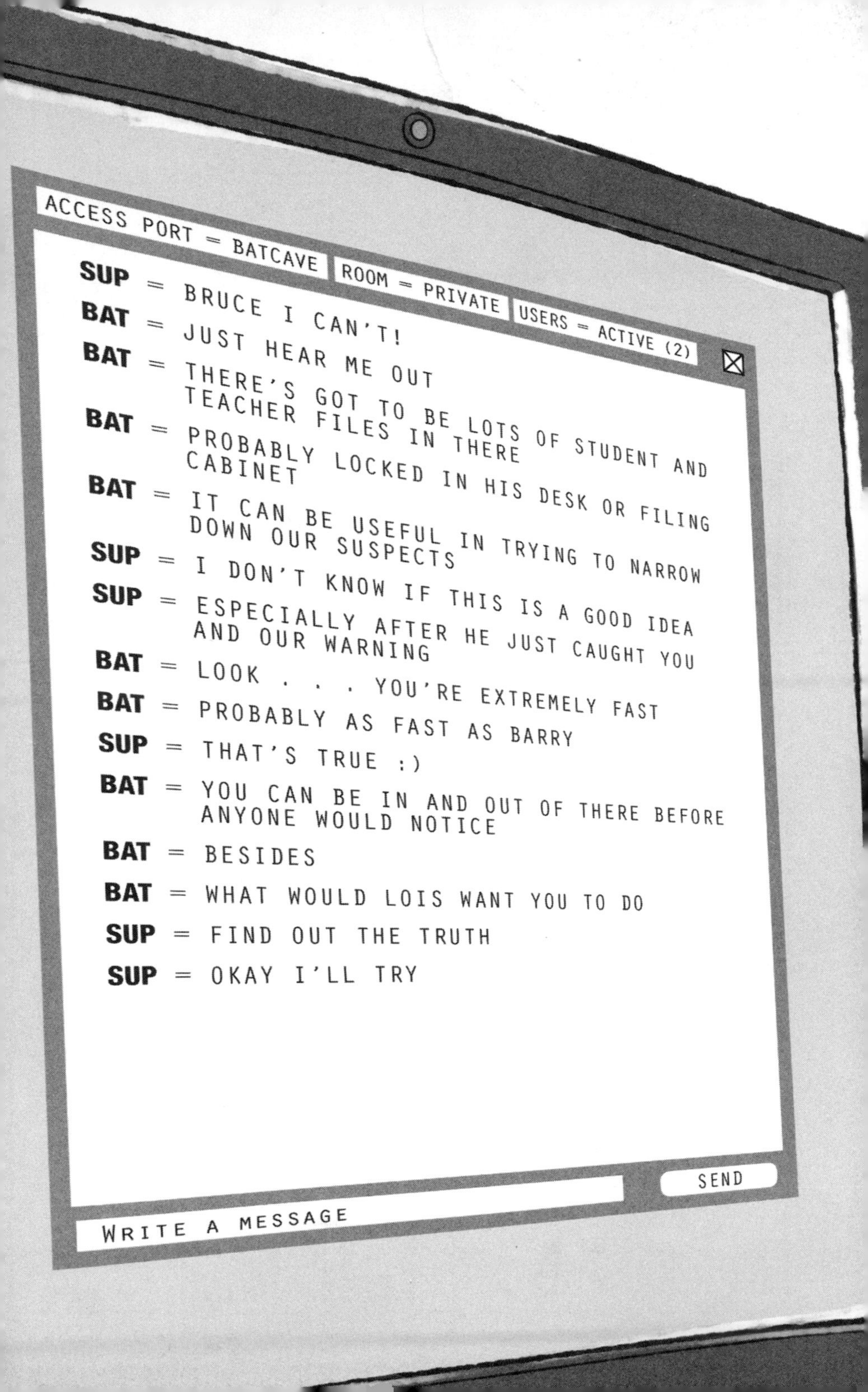

ACCESS PORT = BATCAVE
ROOM = PRIVATE
USERS = ACTIVE (2)
SUP = BRUCE I CAN'T!
BAT = JUST HEAR ME OUT
BAT = THERE'S GOT TO BE LOTS OF STUDENT AND TEACHER FILES IN THERE
BAT = PROBABLY LOCKED IN HIS DESK OR FILING CABINET
BAT = IT CAN BE USEFUL IN TRYING TO NARROW DOWN OUR SUSPECTS
SUP = I DON'T KNOW IF THIS IS A GOOD IDEA
SUP = ESPECIALLY AFTER HE JUST CAUGHT YOU AND OUR WARNING
BAT = LOOK . . . YOU'RE EXTREMELY FAST
BAT = PROBABLY AS FAST AS BARRY
SUP = THAT'S TRUE :)
BAT = YOU CAN BE IN AND OUT OF THERE BEFORE ANYONE WOULD NOTICE
BAT = BESIDES
BAT = WHAT WOULD LOIS WANT YOU TO DO
SUP = FIND OUT THE TRUTH
SUP = OKAY I'LL TRY
SEND
WRITE A MESSAGE

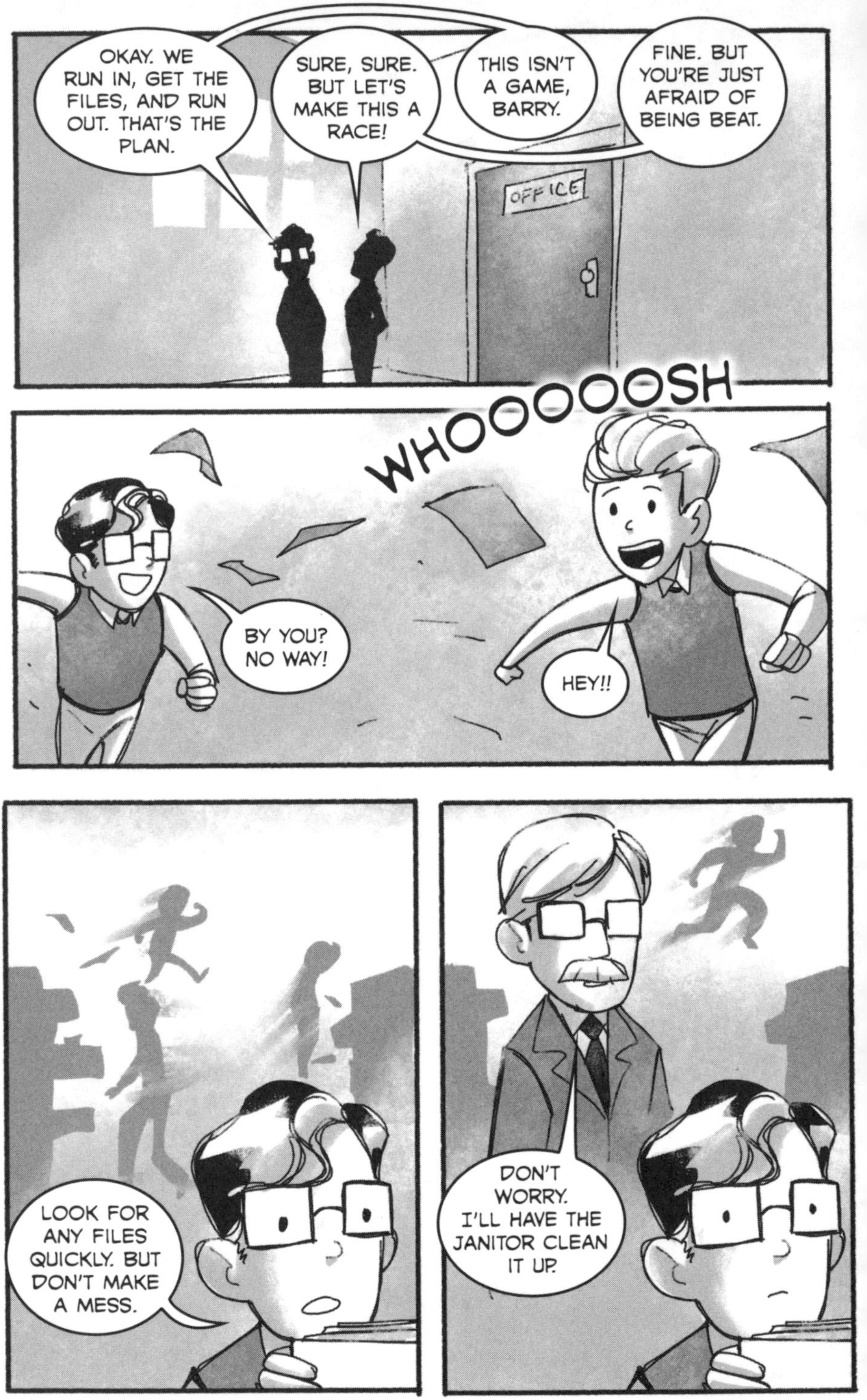
OKAY. WE RUN IN, GET THE FILES, AND RUN OUT. THAT'S THE PLAN.
SURE, SURE. BUT LET'S MAKE THIS A RACE!
THIS ISN'T A GAME, BARRY.
FINE. BUT YOU'RE JUST AFRAID OF BEING BEAT.
OFFICE
WHOOOOOOSH
BY YOU? NO WAY!
HEY!!
LOOK FOR ANY FILES QUICKLY. BUT DON'T MAKE A MESS.
DON'T WORRY. I'LL HAVE THE JANITOR CLEAN IT UP.

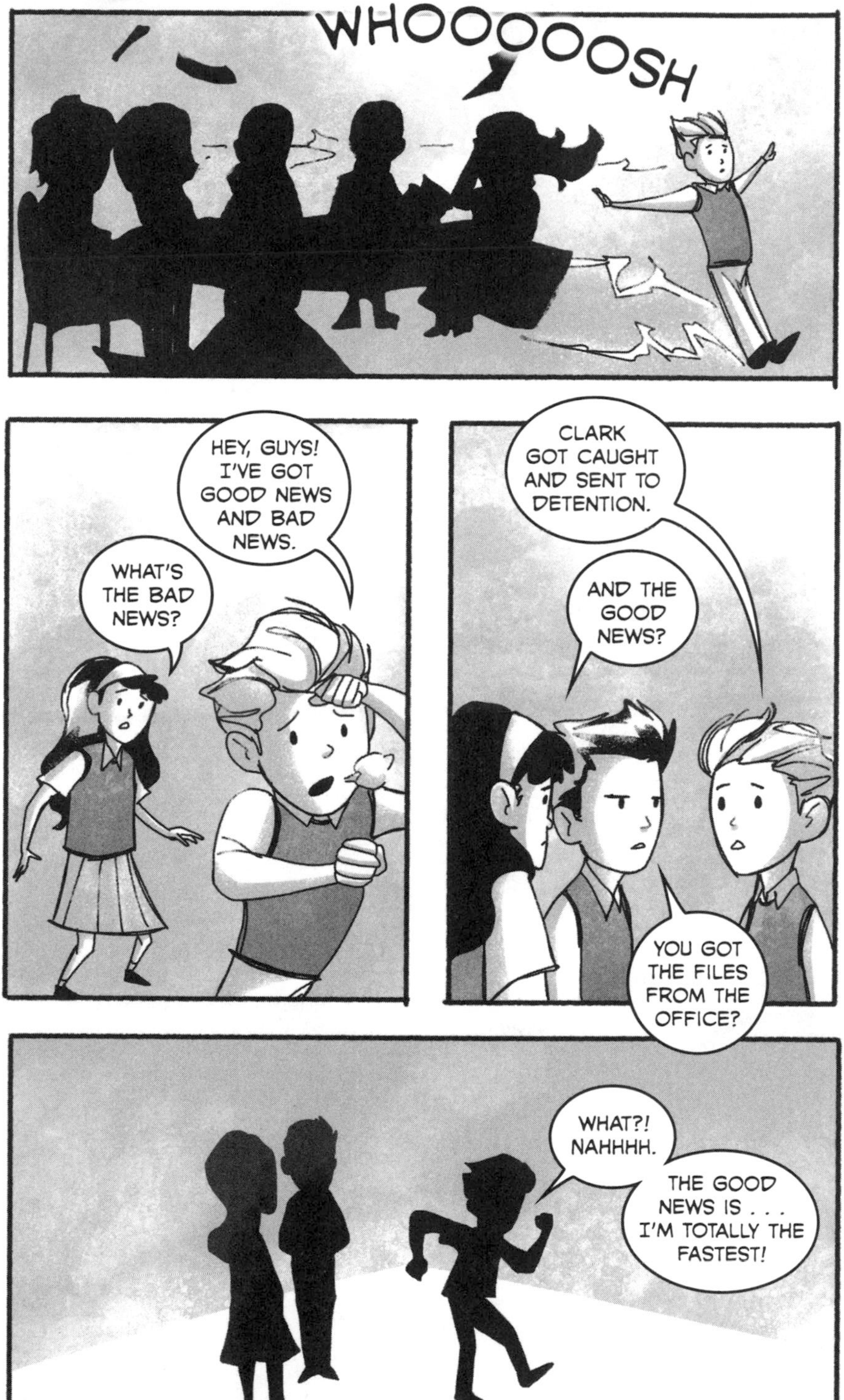
WHOOOOOSH
HEY, GUYS! I'VE GOT GOOD NEWS AND BAD NEWS.
WHAT'S THE BAD NEWS?
CLARK GOT CAUGHT AND SENT TO DETENTION.
AND THE GOOD NEWS?
YOU GOT THE FILES FROM THE OFFICE?
WHAT?! NAHHHH.
THE GOOD NEWS IS . . . I'M TOTALLY THE FASTEST!

GROUP CHAT

I did some digging

Clark's been sent to Room X for detention

why do even the ROOMS sound mysterious?!

X is the roman numeral for 10

Gordon had no choice

he caught Clark red-handed

which is funny because my Flash suit is more red than his

BARRY!

I'm just saying

should we mount a rescue operation?

I can conjure a veil of darkness spell

and I can shut down the electrical grid

no we let this play out

Clark can infiltrate the students in detention and maybe find a suspect

this might be a good thing

besides . . . I hear they've hired someone new to supervise the problem kids

SEND

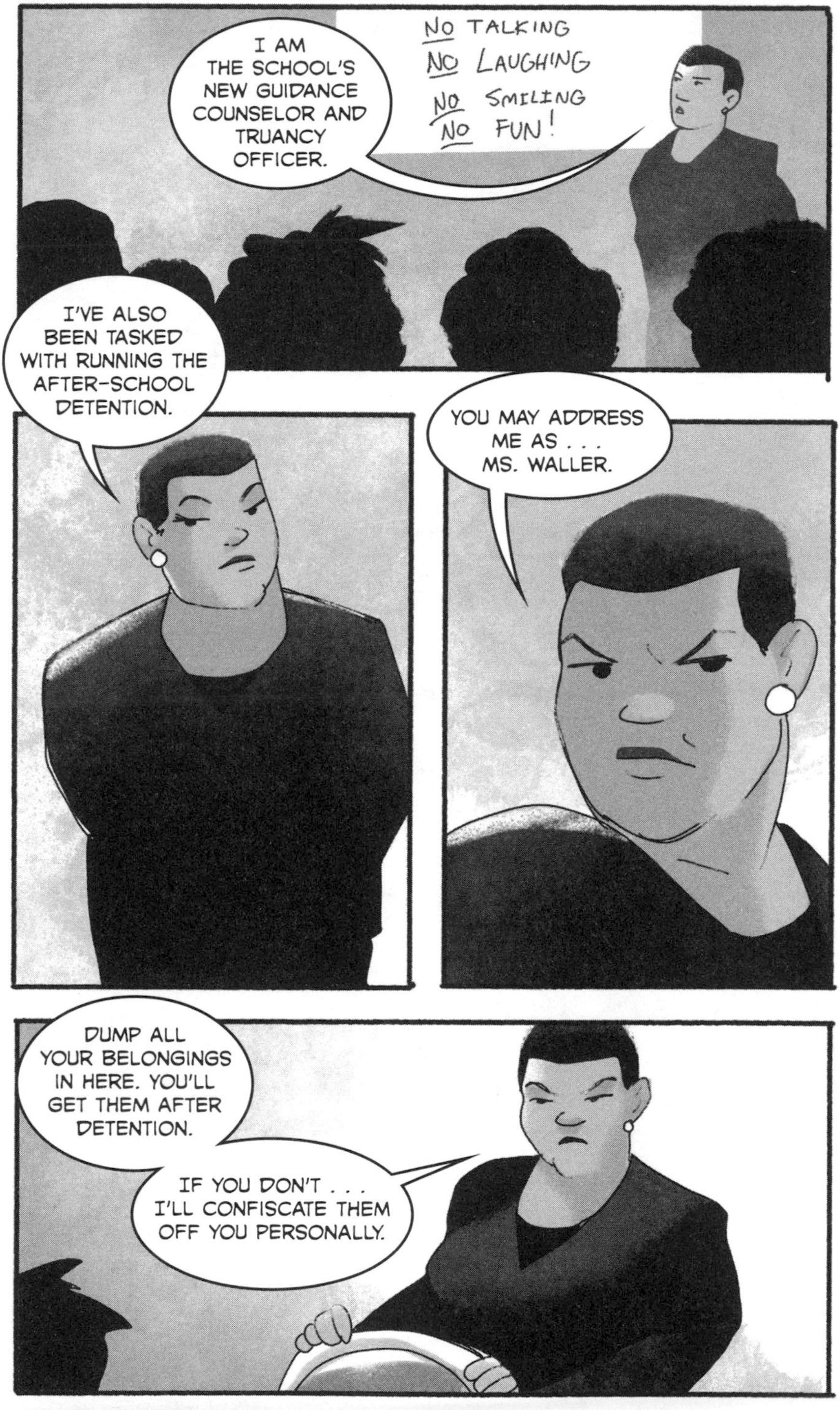
NO TALKING
NO LAUGHING
NO SMILING
NO FUN!
I AM THE SCHOOL'S NEW GUIDANCE COUNSELOR AND TRUANCY OFFICER.
I'VE ALSO BEEN TASKED WITH RUNNING THE AFTER-SCHOOL DETENTION.
YOU MAY ADDRESS ME AS . . . MS. WALLER.
DUMP ALL YOUR BELONGINGS IN HERE. YOU'LL GET THEM AFTER DETENTION.
IF YOU DON'T . . . I'LL CONFISCATE THEM OFF YOU PERSONALLY.

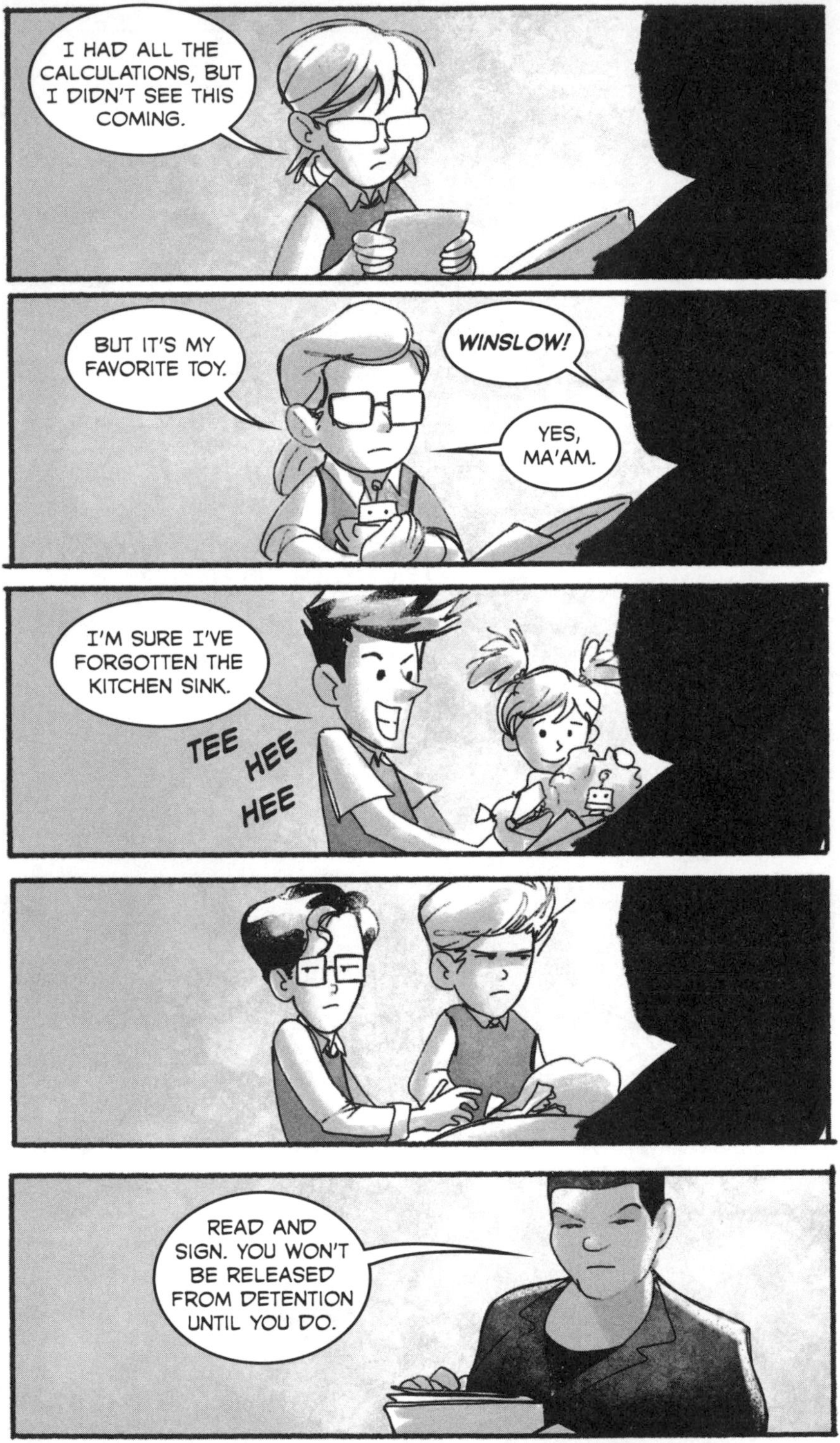
I HAD ALL THE CALCULATIONS, BUT I DIDN'T SEE THIS COMING.
BUT IT'S MY FAVORITE TOY.
WINSLOW!
YES, MA'AM.
I'M SURE I'VE FORGOTTEN THE KITCHEN SINK.
TEE HEE HEE
READ AND SIGN. YOU WON'T BE RELEASED FROM DETENTION UNTIL YOU DO.

JUSTICE PREP

JUSTICE PREPARATORY ACADEMY
STUDENT STUDY GROUP & RELEASE FORM

The school district requires written authorization to administer its selected students into an involuntary private after-school program. By signing this release form, you give the school district authorization to place **CLARK KENT** into a disciplinary after-school studies program.

Ms. Amanda Waller, and the school district, shall not be held accountable for anything that happens during the course of this specialized study group and its educational pursuits.

As Justice Preparatory Academy is fully committed to the safety of all students, please complete this form and return to the school truancy officer and detention supervisor.

Student Name: _Clark Kent_

Truancy Officer/Detention Supervisor:
Ms. Amanda Waller

Principal: _James W. Gordon_

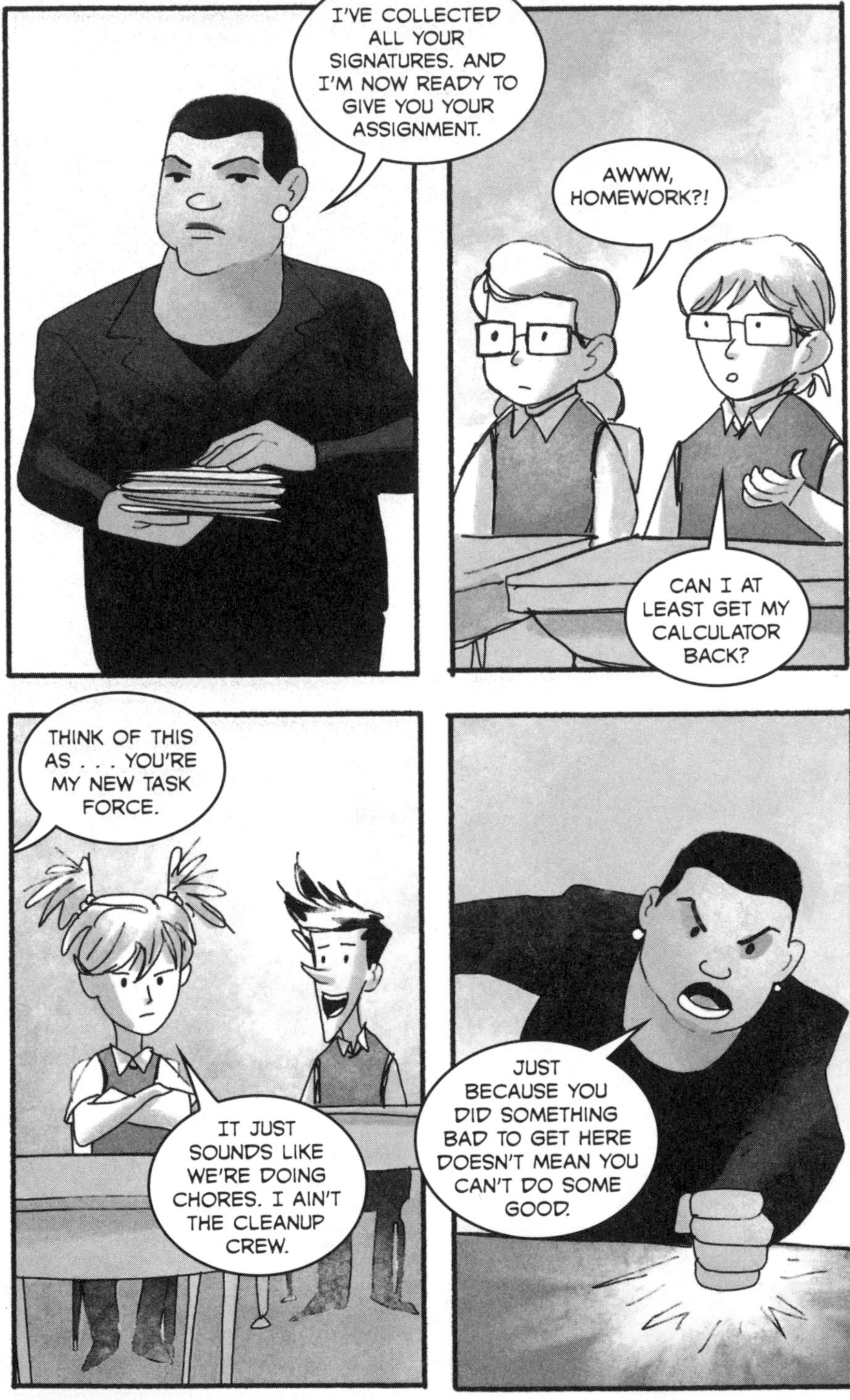
I'VE COLLECTED ALL YOUR SIGNATURES. AND I'M NOW READY TO GIVE YOU YOUR ASSIGNMENT.
AWWW, HOMEWORK?!
CAN I AT LEAST GET MY CALCULATOR BACK?
THINK OF THIS AS . . . YOU'RE MY NEW TASK FORCE.
IT JUST SOUNDS LIKE WE'RE DOING CHORES. I AIN'T THE CLEANUP CREW.
JUST BECAUSE YOU DID SOMETHING BAD TO GET HERE DOESN'T MEAN YOU CAN'T DO SOME GOOD.

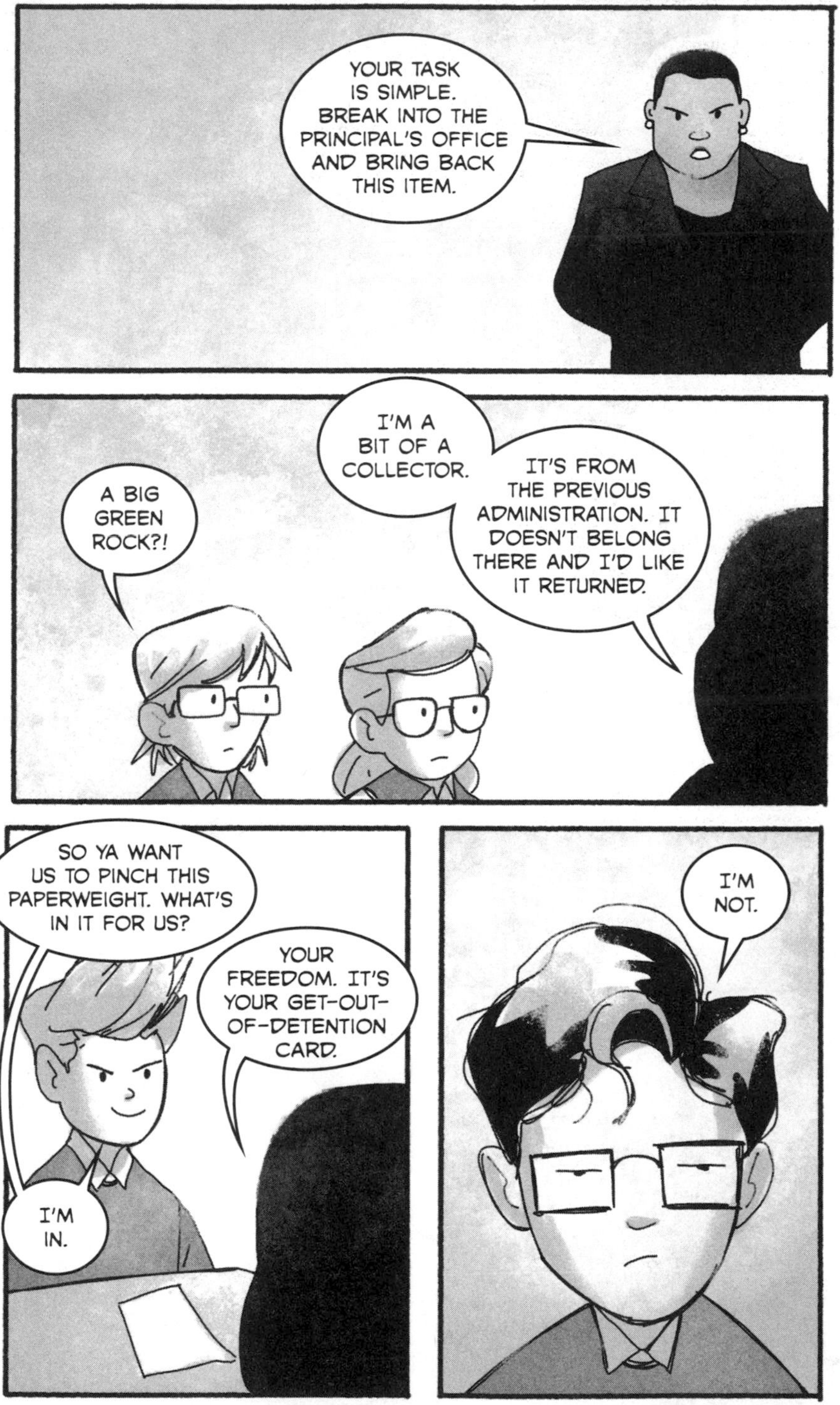
YOUR TASK IS SIMPLE. BREAK INTO THE PRINCIPAL'S OFFICE AND BRING BACK THIS ITEM.
A BIG GREEN ROCK?!
I'M A BIT OF A COLLECTOR.
IT'S FROM THE PREVIOUS ADMINISTRATION. IT DOESN'T BELONG THERE AND I'D LIKE IT RETURNED.
SO YA WANT US TO PINCH THIS PAPERWEIGHT. WHAT'S IN IT FOR US?
YOUR FREEDOM. IT'S YOUR GET-OUT-OF-DETENTION CARD.
I'M IN.
I'M NOT.

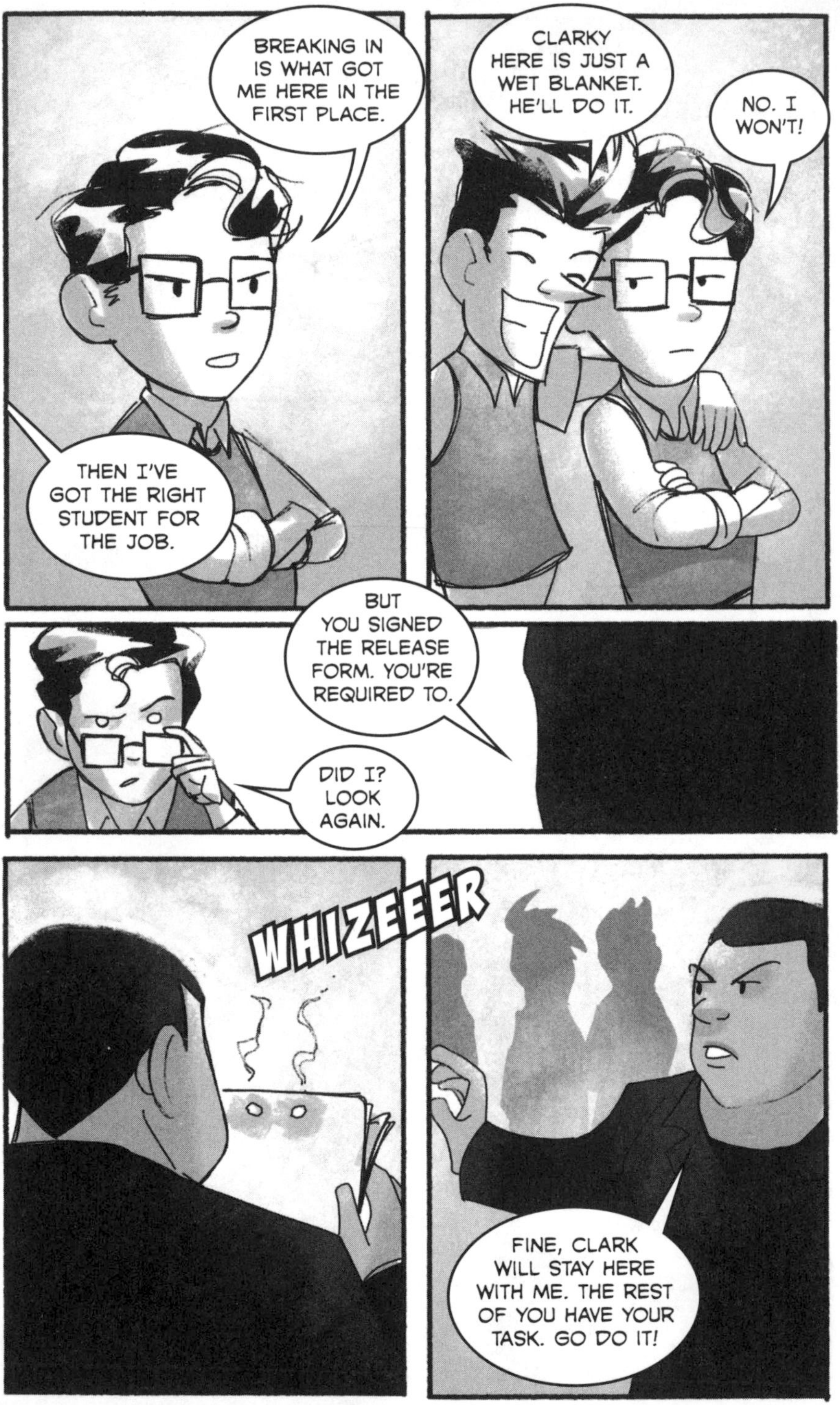
BREAKING IN IS WHAT GOT ME HERE IN THE FIRST PLACE.
THEN I'VE GOT THE RIGHT STUDENT FOR THE JOB.
CLARKY HERE IS JUST A WET BLANKET. HE'LL DO IT.
NO. I WON'T!
BUT YOU SIGNED THE RELEASE FORM. YOU'RE REQUIRED TO.
DID I? LOOK AGAIN.
WHIZEEER
FINE, CLARK WILL STAY HERE WITH ME. THE REST OF YOU HAVE YOUR TASK. GO DO IT!

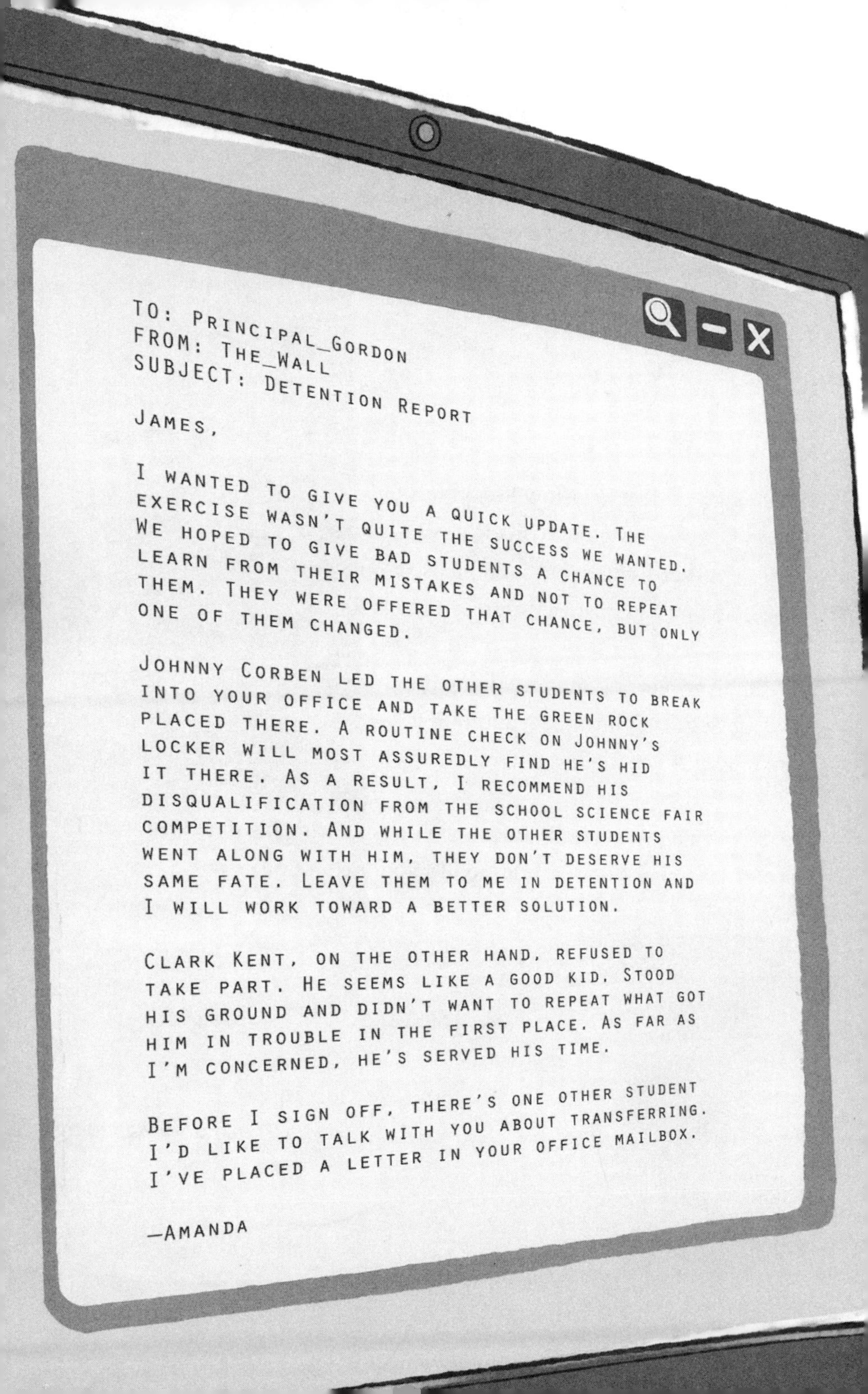

TO: Principal_Gordon
FROM: The_Wall
SUBJECT: Detention Report

James,

I wanted to give you a quick update. The exercise wasn't quite the success we wanted. We hoped to give bad students a chance to learn from their mistakes and not to repeat them. They were offered that chance, but only one of them changed.

Johnny Corben led the other students to break into your office and take the green rock placed there. A routine check on Johnny's locker will most assuredly find he's hid it there. As a result, I recommend his disqualification from the school science fair competition. And while the other students went along with him, they don't deserve his same fate. Leave them to me in detention and I will work toward a better solution.

Clark Kent, on the other hand, refused to take part. He seems like a good kid. Stood his ground and didn't want to repeat what got him in trouble in the first place. As far as I'm concerned, he's served his time.

Before I sign off, there's one other student I'd like to talk with you about transferring. I've placed a letter in your office mailbox.

—Amanda

LOCUS
INSTITUTE OF HIGHER LEARNING

ATTN: Professor Ivo

Although student Winslow Schott has only a
short time, he has already made a positive an
am sad to see him go, but I am pleased to reco
institute that can make a difference in his life.

With his recent test scores placing him high on the academic spectrum,
I believe he will be a great addition to your school. Winslow has prov-
en himself to be highly motivated, creative, and extremely intelligent.

He's been a joy to teach and a fine student during his time here. And I
know he'll make a great addition to your institution.

Sincerely,

James W. Gordon

James W. Gordon
Principal, Justice Preparatory Academy

Winslow Schott appears to have
cheated on a recent aptitude
test. His high IQ score is suspicious
following the recent trouble with
the school's computer system
being shut down. But I can't prove
it. I just think this might become
a black eye for the school if he
enters the science fair, wins, and
this is discovered upon further
examination. I suggest we transfer
him to a special gateway school for
higher learning.
—Amanda

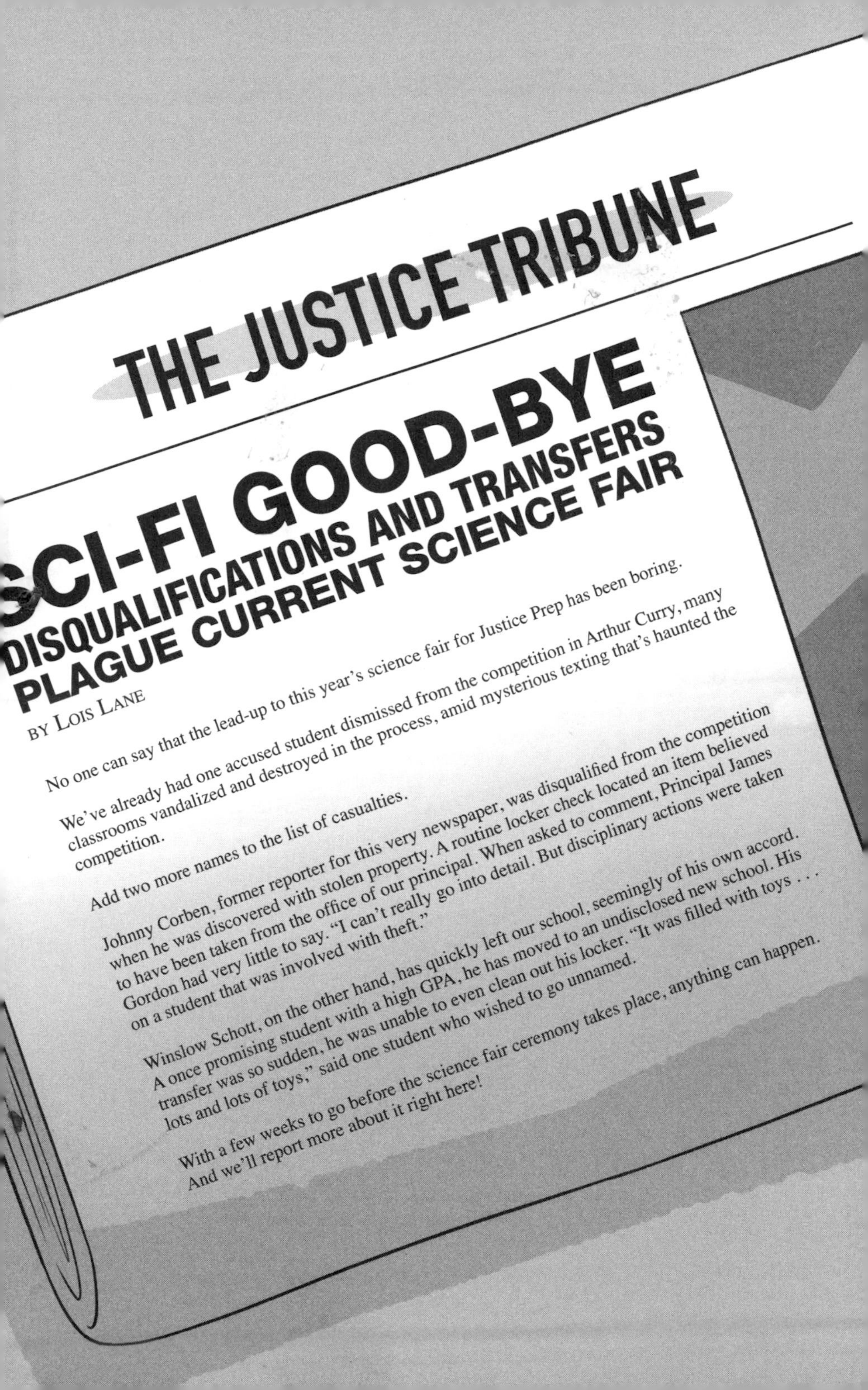

THE JUSTICE TRIBUNE

SCI-FI GOOD-BYE

DISQUALIFICATIONS AND TRANSFERS PLAGUE CURRENT SCIENCE FAIR

BY LOIS LANE

No one can say that the lead-up to this year's science fair for Justice Prep has been boring.

We've already had one accused student dismissed from the competition in Arthur Curry, many classrooms vandalized and destroyed in the process, amid mysterious texting that's haunted the competition.

Add two more names to the list of casualties.

Johnny Corben, former reporter for this very newspaper, was disqualified from the competition when he was discovered with stolen property. A routine locker check located an item believed to have been taken from the office of our principal. When asked to comment, Principal James Gordon had very little to say. "I can't really go into detail. But disciplinary actions were taken on a student that was involved with theft."

Winslow Schott, on the other hand, has quickly left our school, seemingly of his own accord. A once promising student with a high GPA, he has moved to an undisclosed new school. His transfer was so sudden, he was unable to even clean out his locker. "It was filled with toys . . . lots and lots of toys," said one student who wished to go unnamed.

With a few weeks to go before the science fair ceremony takes place, anything can happen. And we'll report more about it right here!

I know you squealed on me, Kent. You knew all about that rock and told them to search my locker. You set me up, punk! I never trusted you and your goody-two-shoes attitude. You're so fake and fooling no one. Let's hash this out after school. You vs. me! I'm gonna make you pay!

JOHNNY

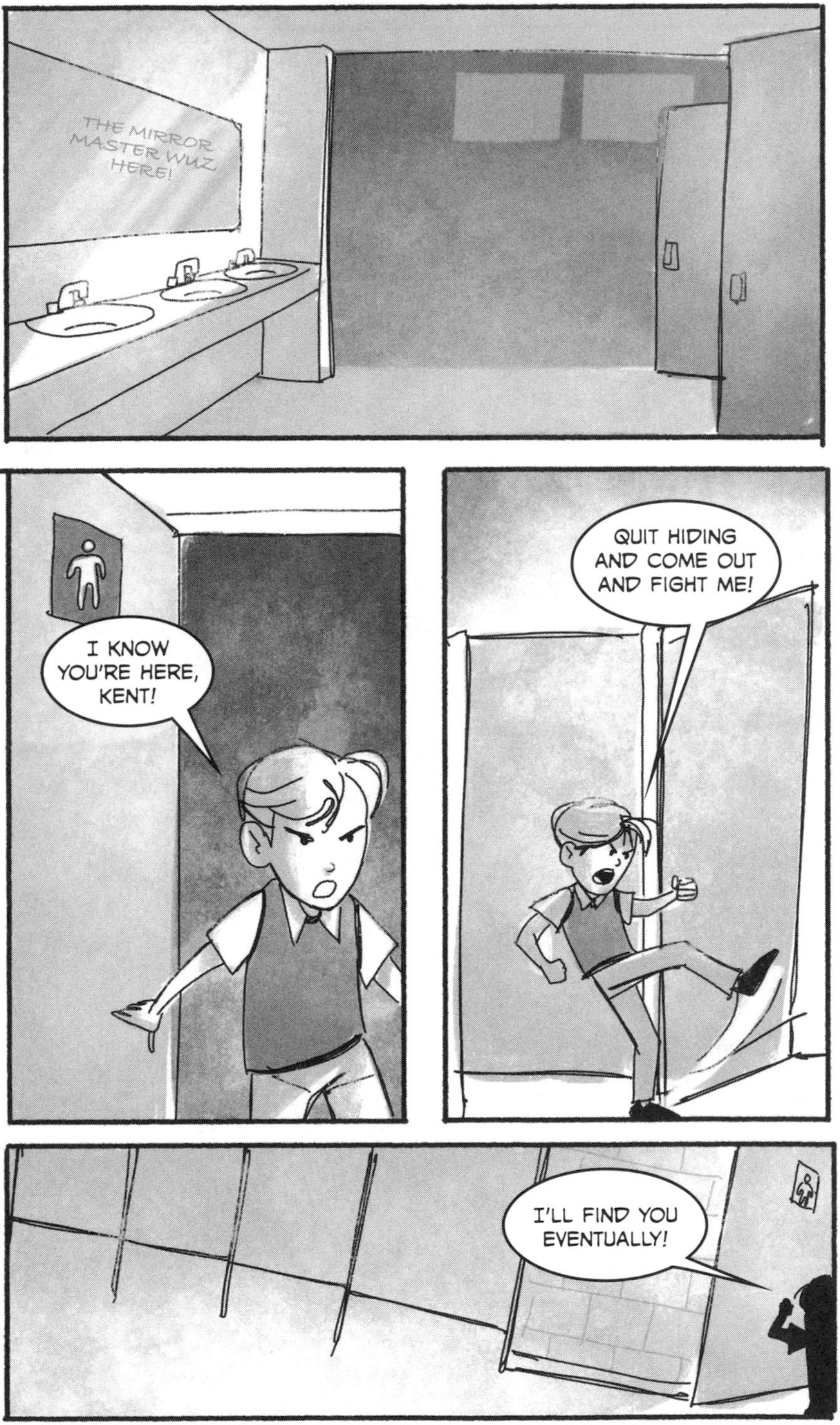
THE MIRROR MASTER WUZ HERE!
I KNOW YOU'RE HERE, KENT!
QUIT HIDING AND COME OUT AND FIGHT ME!
I'LL FIND YOU EVENTUALLY!

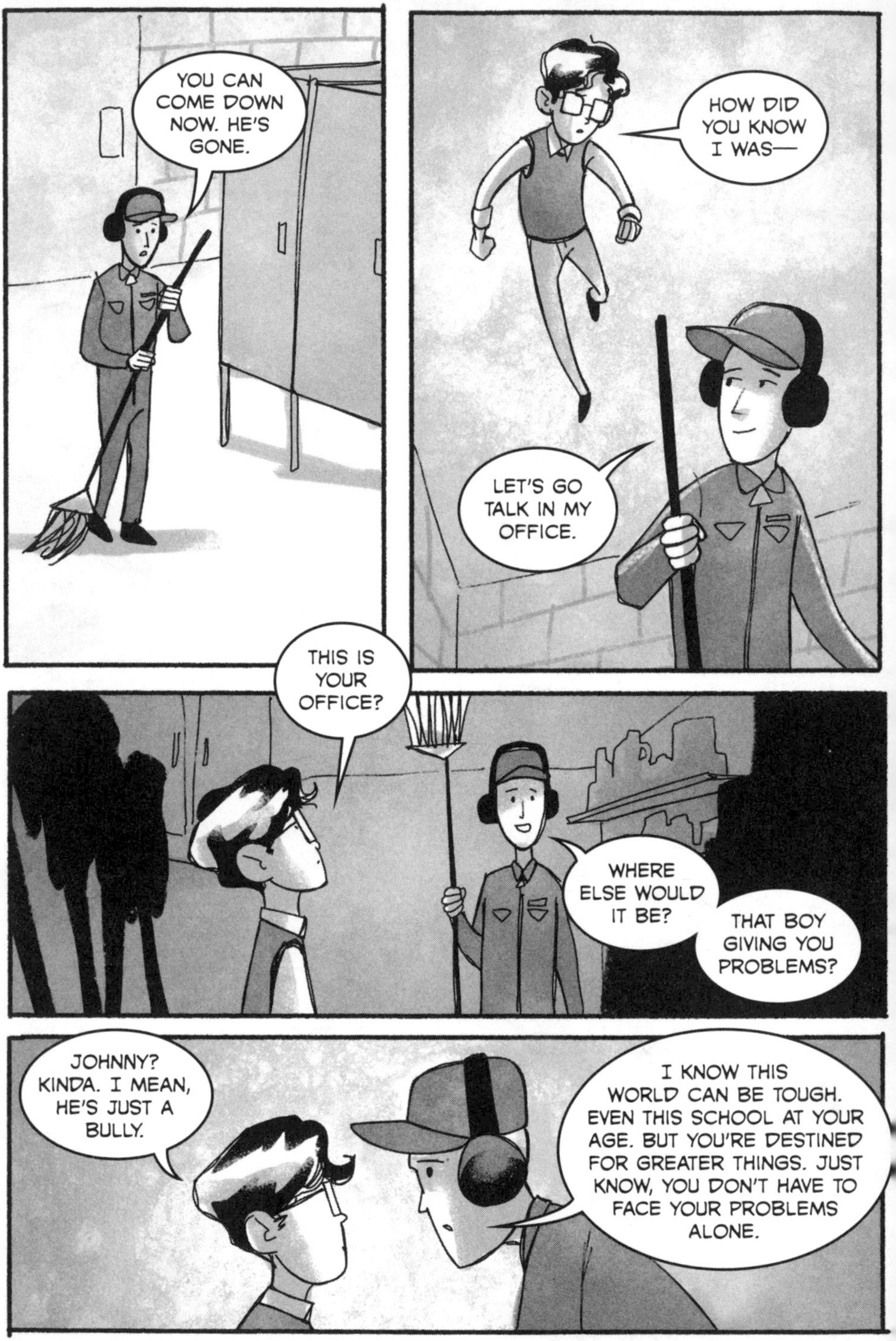
YOU CAN COME DOWN NOW. HE'S GONE.
HOW DID YOU KNOW I WAS—
LET'S GO TALK IN MY OFFICE.
THIS IS YOUR OFFICE?
WHERE ELSE WOULD IT BE?
THAT BOY GIVING YOU PROBLEMS?
JOHNNY? KINDA. I MEAN, HE'S JUST A BULLY.
I KNOW THIS WORLD CAN BE TOUGH. EVEN THIS SCHOOL AT YOUR AGE. BUT YOU'RE DESTINED FOR GREATER THINGS. JUST KNOW, YOU DON'T HAVE TO FACE YOUR PROBLEMS ALONE.

November 26th

CLARK'S JOURNAL

Almost got into a fight at school today over something stupid. Ma and Pa always told me not to fight with my fists, if my words could be a peaceful solution. But what happens when my words won't fix things? I guess it helps having the ability to fly out of the way. I'm just glad Johnny didn't see me hovering up near the ceiling.

But that janitor saw me! No matter how many times I try to hide my powers, I always seem to get caught. I don't think he'll be a problem. He was actually pretty nice. Let me know he'd be around if I ever needed his help. He even offered me a cookie afterward, but I couldn't take it. I'd hate to upset Ma if I ruined my appetite before supper.

I still don't know what I want to do for my science fair experiment. But maybe going home will provide an answer.

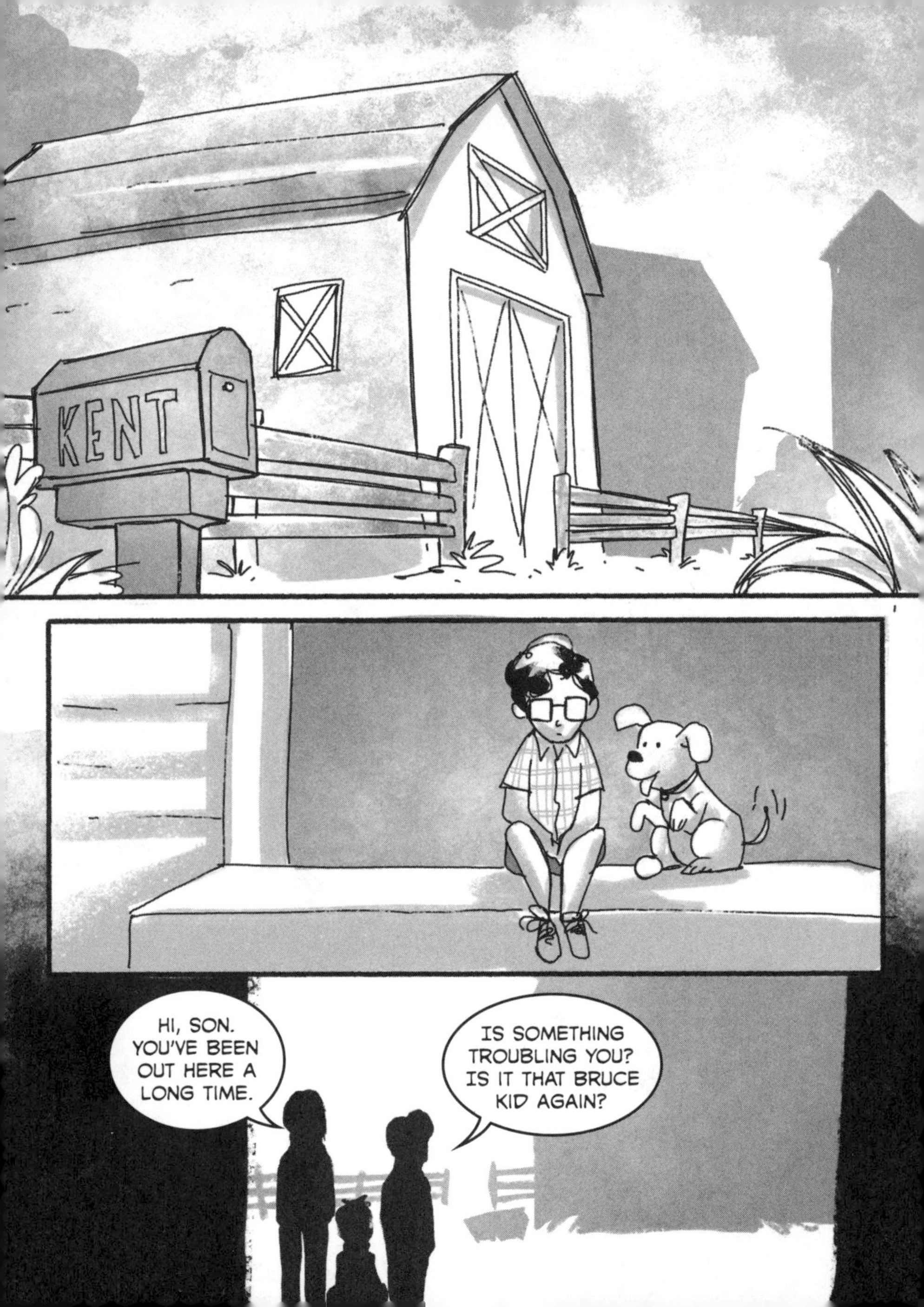
KENT
HI, SON. YOU'VE BEEN OUT HERE A LONG TIME.
IS SOMETHING TROUBLING YOU? IS IT THAT BRUCE KID AGAIN?

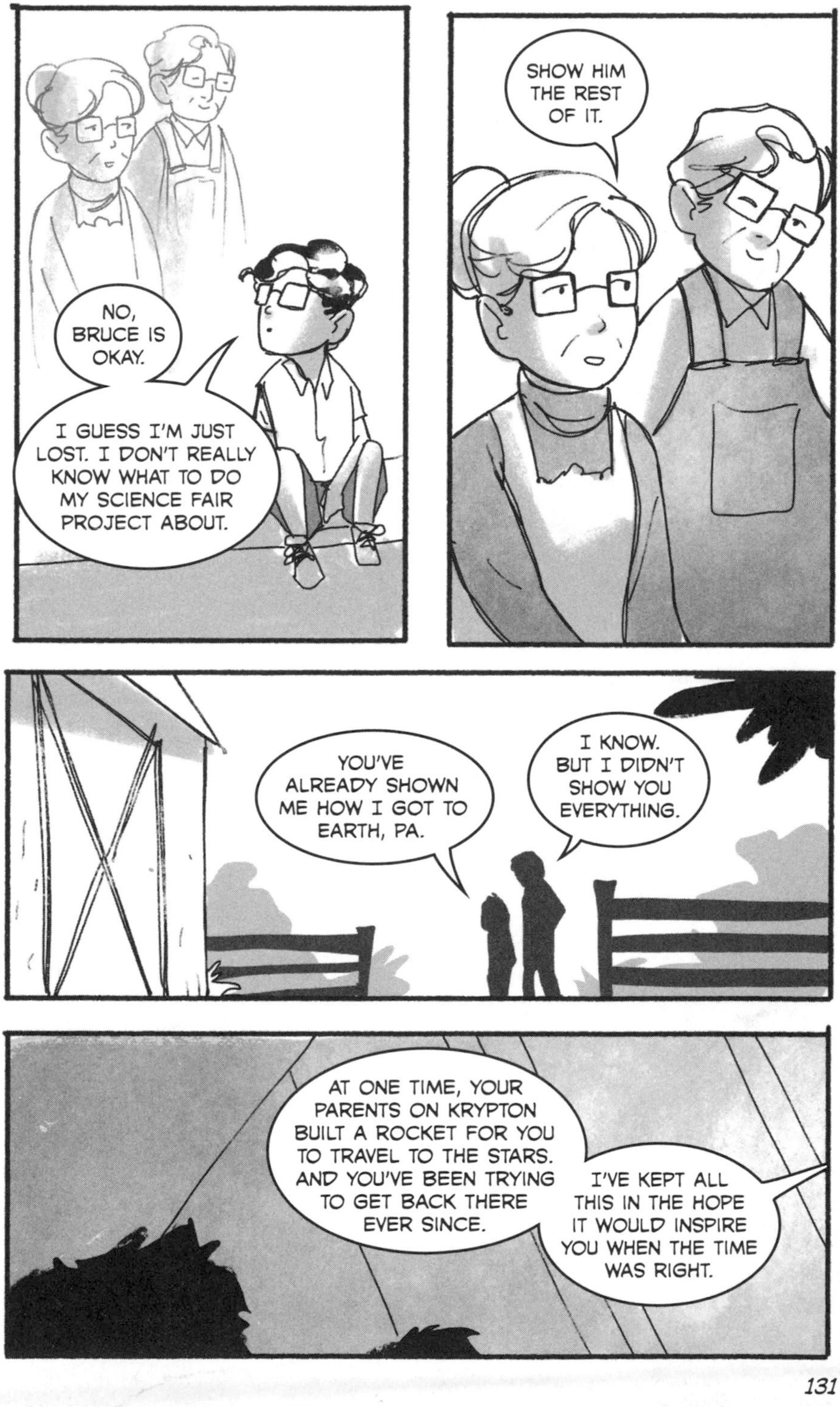
NO, BRUCE IS OKAY.
I GUESS I'M JUST LOST. I DON'T REALLY KNOW WHAT TO DO MY SCIENCE FAIR PROJECT ABOUT.
SHOW HIM THE REST OF IT.
YOU'VE ALREADY SHOWN ME HOW I GOT TO EARTH, PA.
I KNOW. BUT I DIDN'T SHOW YOU EVERYTHING.
AT ONE TIME, YOUR PARENTS ON KRYPTON BUILT A ROCKET FOR YOU TO TRAVEL TO THE STARS. AND YOU'VE BEEN TRYING TO GET BACK THERE EVER SINCE.
I'VE KEPT ALL THIS IN THE HOPE IT WOULD INSPIRE YOU WHEN THE TIME WAS RIGHT.

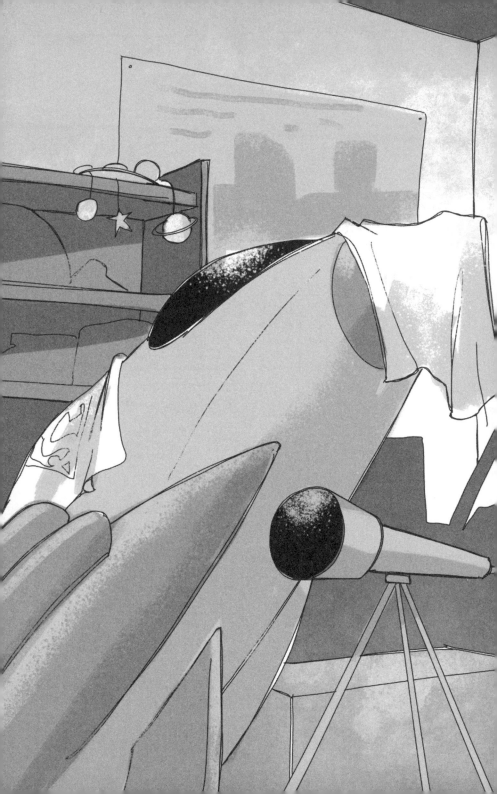

MESSAGES

GROUP CHAT

hey Smallville you there?

Actually I really am in Smallville! :)

come to the newspaper office when you get to school

there's something for you to see

What did Johnny do this time?

Did he break the copy machine?

no

just get over here ok

On my way.

SEND

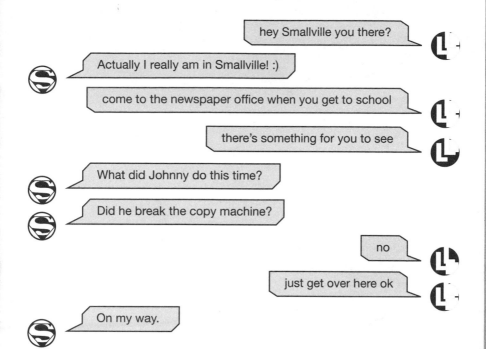

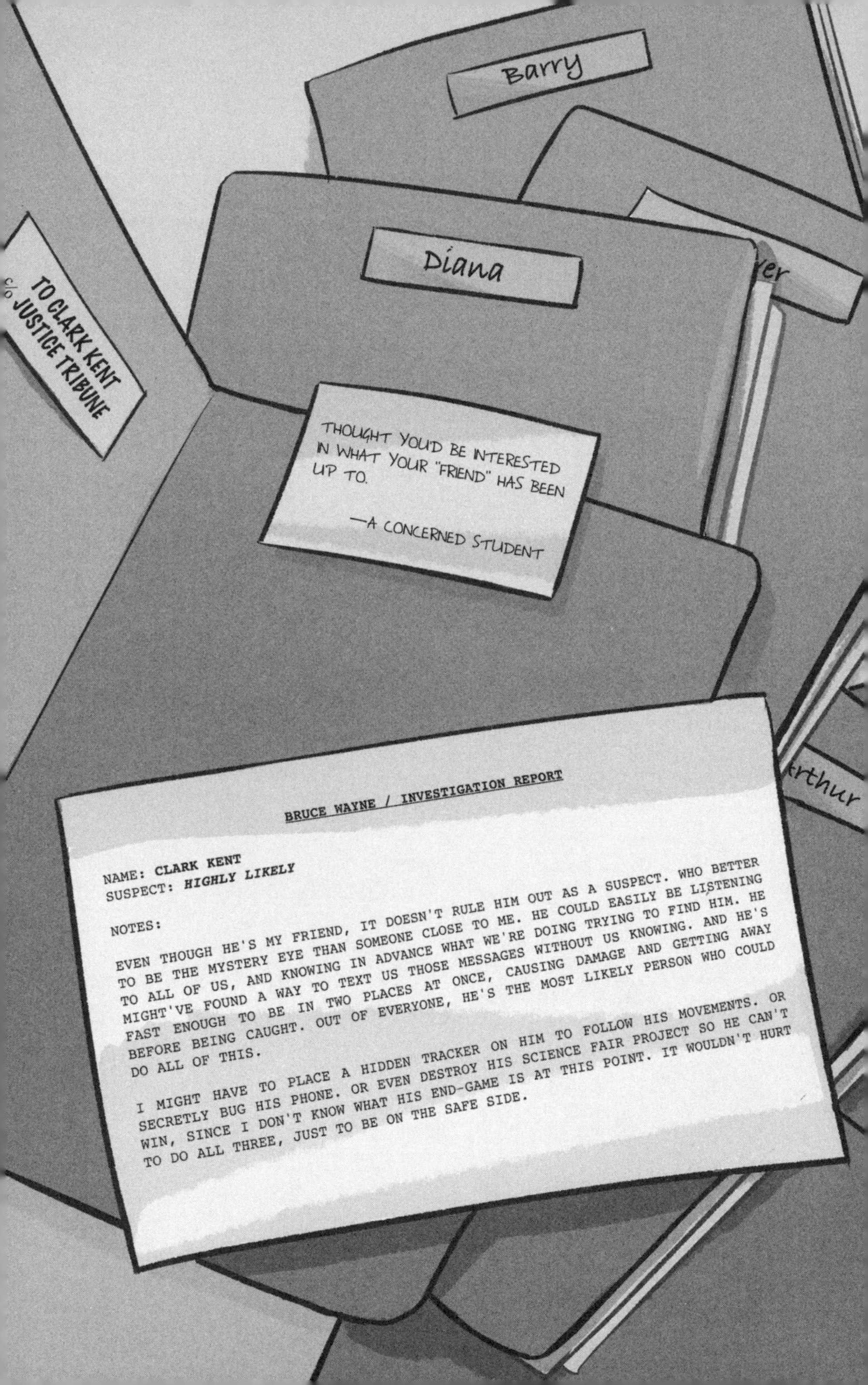
Barry
Diana
TO CLARK KENT
c/o JUSTICE TRIBUNE
THOUGHT YOU'D BE INTERESTED IN WHAT YOUR "FRIEND" HAS BEEN UP TO.
—A CONCERNED STUDENT
BRUCE WAYNE / INVESTIGATION REPORT
NAME: CLARK KENT
SUSPECT: HIGHLY LIKELY
NOTES:
EVEN THOUGH HE'S MY FRIEND, IT DOESN'T RULE HIM OUT AS A SUSPECT. WHO BETTER TO BE THE MYSTERY EYE THAN SOMEONE CLOSE TO ME. HE COULD EASILY BE LISTENING TO ALL OF US, AND KNOWING IN ADVANCE WHAT WE'RE DOING TRYING TO FIND HIM. HE MIGHT'VE FOUND A WAY TO TEXT US THOSE MESSAGES WITHOUT US KNOWING. AND HE'S FAST ENOUGH TO BE IN TWO PLACES AT ONCE, CAUSING DAMAGE AND GETTING AWAY BEFORE BEING CAUGHT. OUT OF EVERYONE, HE'S THE MOST LIKELY PERSON WHO COULD DO ALL OF THIS.
I MIGHT HAVE TO PLACE A HIDDEN TRACKER ON HIM TO FOLLOW HIS MOVEMENTS. OR SECRETLY BUG HIS PHONE. OR EVEN DESTROY HIS SCIENCE FAIR PROJECT SO HE CAN'T WIN, SINCE I DON'T KNOW WHAT HIS END-GAME IS AT THIS POINT. IT WOULDN'T HURT TO DO ALL THREE, JUST TO BE ON THE SAFE SIDE.

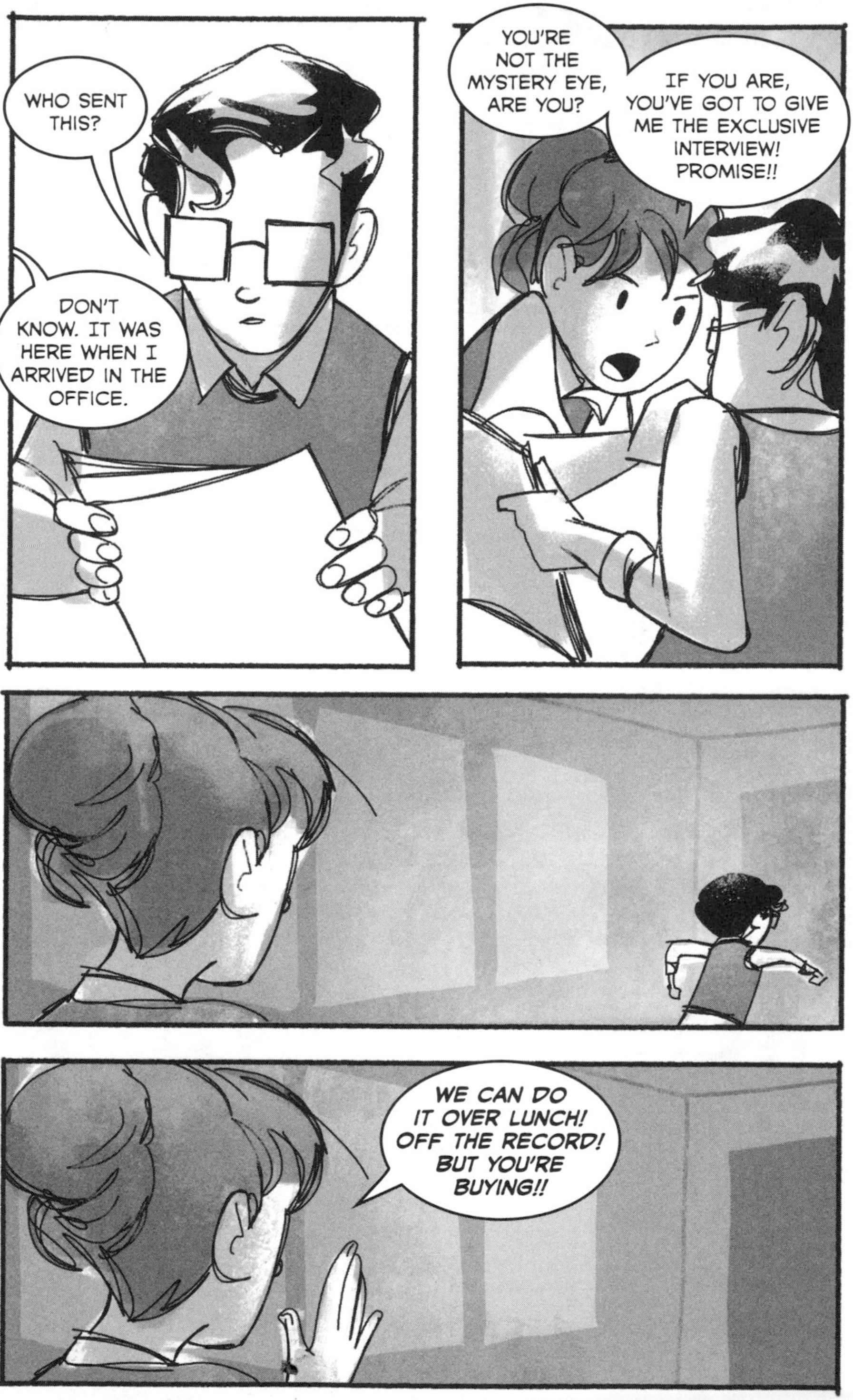
WHO SENT THIS?
DON'T KNOW. IT WAS HERE WHEN I ARRIVED IN THE OFFICE.
YOU'RE NOT THE MYSTERY EYE, ARE YOU?
IF YOU ARE, YOU'VE GOT TO GIVE ME THE EXCLUSIVE INTERVIEW! PROMISE!!
WE CAN DO IT OVER LUNCH! OFF THE RECORD! BUT YOU'RE BUYING!!

MESSAGES

GROUP CHAT

I've got something important I want to talk about.

I know right!

why can't the school lunch menu serve pizza every day?

and why does it have to be cut into squares?

has no one heard of triangles?

oval pizza might be fun

I mean pizza is already fun but it can always be funner

Bruce has been spying on each of us.

it's Bruce

at this point I just assumed

He has detailed files why he thinks each of us is the Mystery Eye.

Even how he'll destroy our science fair projects to stop us.

Or was that just for me Bruce?

Bruce!

is this true?

you broke into my locker!

or did you get Vic to hack those files off my computer?

whoa don't accuse me

I had nothing to do with this

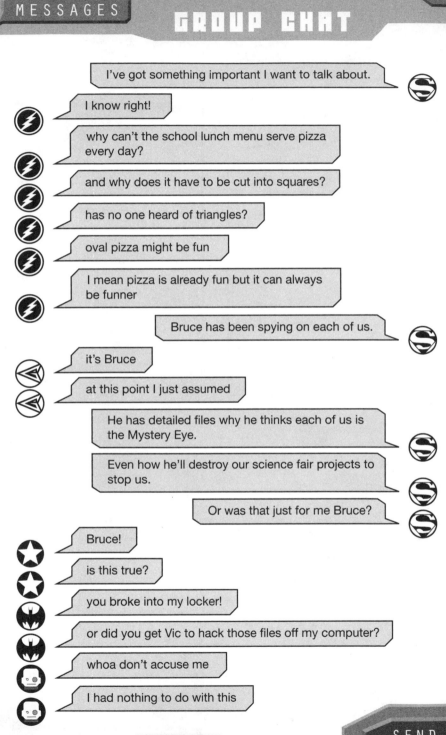

SEND

MESSAGES

GROUP CHAT

just let me say some backward spell and let's start this day over

NO!

did you sabotage all the school labs too Bruce?

No of course not!

I'm not the one under investigation here

YOU are!

it sounds like we all are

He's kept files on all of us. I'm not the only one who's seen them.

There's a stack of folders and paperwork over at the newspaper office.

I don't know who got all this stuff from me

I've really got to update my security protocols

but don't you see?

the timing of this is suspect

to present this just when we're getting close to finding the answers

someone is deliberately trying to turn all of us against each other

Yeah Bruce. YOU!

[USER CLARK HAS LOGGED OFF]

SEND

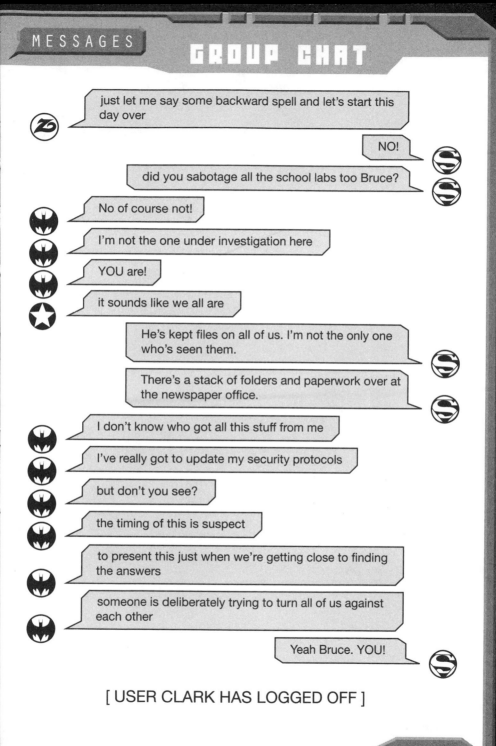

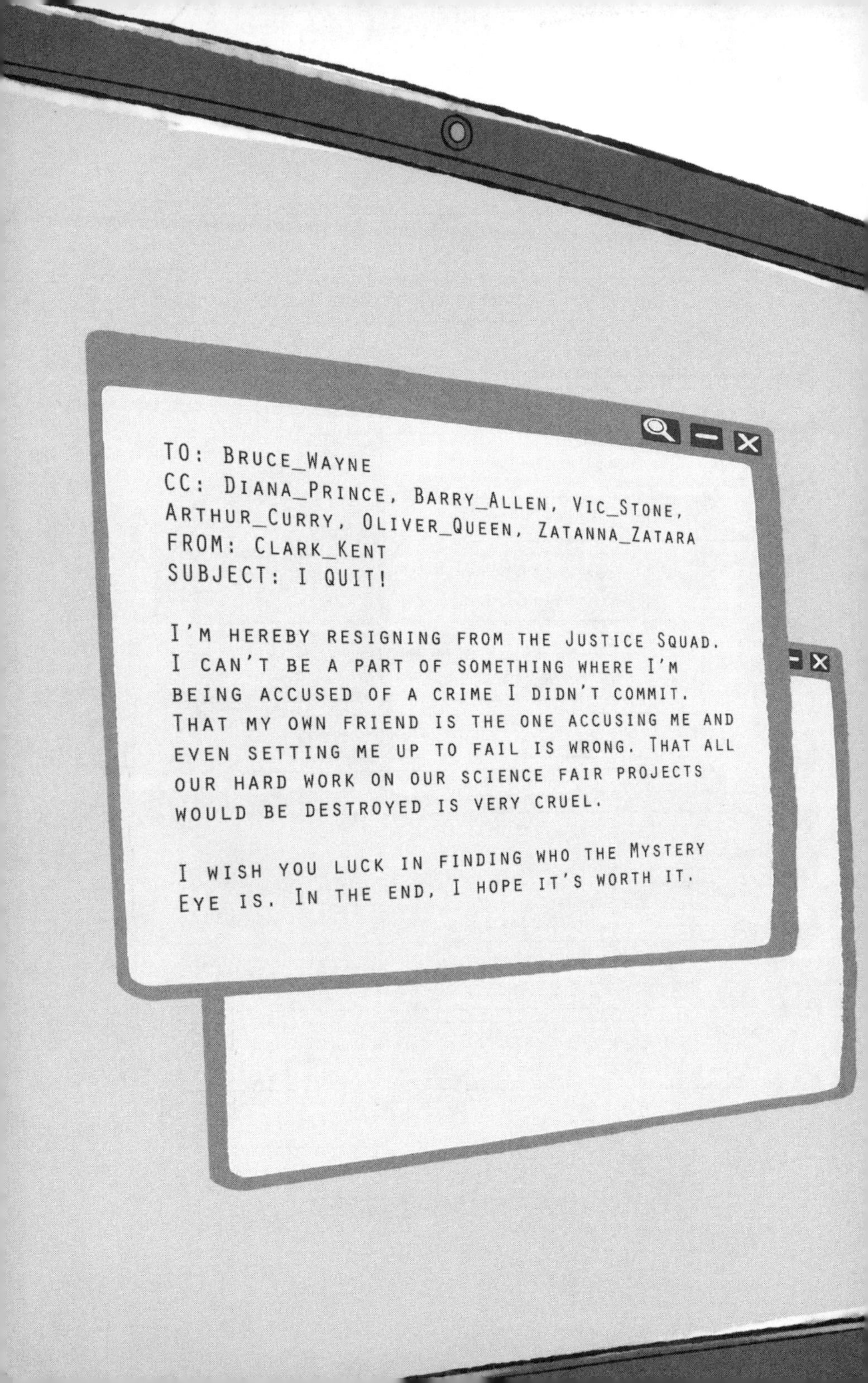
TO: BRUCE_WAYNE
CC: DIANA_PRINCE, BARRY_ALLEN, VIC_STONE, ARTHUR_CURRY, OLIVER_QUEEN, ZATANNA_ZATARA
FROM: CLARK_KENT
SUBJECT: I QUIT!
I'M HEREBY RESIGNING FROM THE JUSTICE SQUAD. I CAN'T BE A PART OF SOMETHING WHERE I'M BEING ACCUSED OF A CRIME I DIDN'T COMMIT. THAT MY OWN FRIEND IS THE ONE ACCUSING ME AND EVEN SETTING ME UP TO FAIL IS WRONG. THAT ALL OUR HARD WORK ON OUR SCIENCE FAIR PROJECTS WOULD BE DESTROYED IS VERY CRUEL.
I WISH YOU LUCK IN FINDING WHO THE MYSTERY EYE IS. IN THE END, I HOPE IT'S WORTH IT.

MESSAGES

GROUP CHAT

anyone else think Clark is running?

only the guilty run away

BRUCE!

yes I have files on everyone

it's what I do

and we still don't know who this Mystery Eye is

but maybe I went about this the wrong way

"maybe"?

I was wrong

I just took a screenshot of my phone

can I make a shirt out of Bruce's statement? :)

Barry! give Bruce a chance here

I deserved that

I took another screenshot!!

BARRY!

you have every right to be mad at me

but don't disband the group

I'll go patch things up with Clark

but Clark's time in detention has given me an idea

I'd like to use Barry to investigate other students in detention

you want me to get detention on purpose?

yup time for me to save the day!

SEND

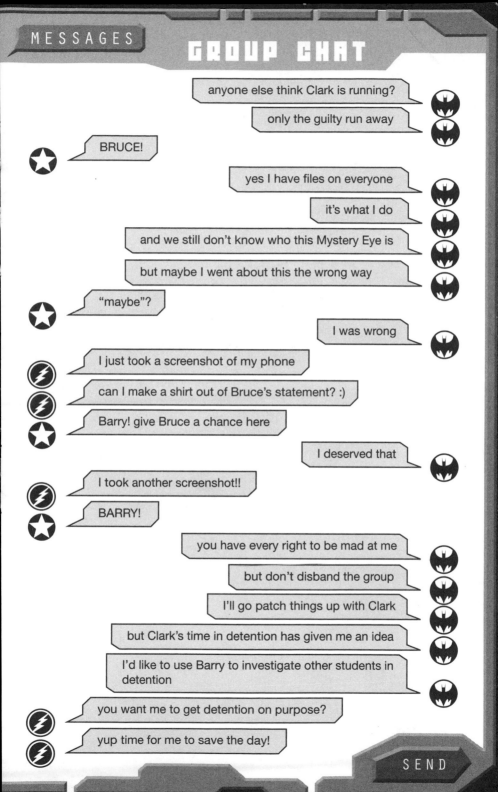

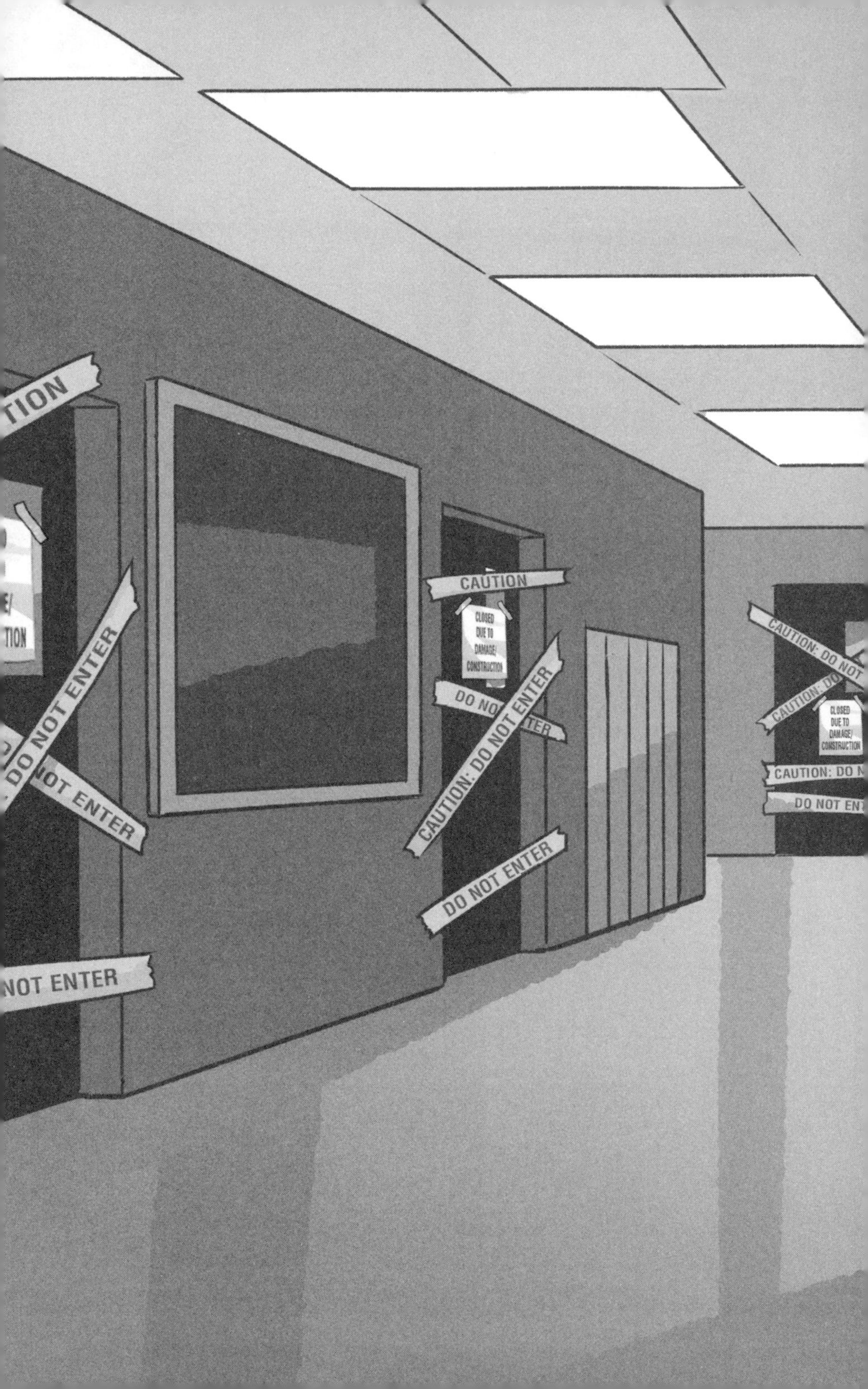
DO NOT ENTER
CAUTION
CLOSED DUE TO DAMAGE/ CONSTRUCTION
CAUTION: DO NOT ENTER
DO NOT ENTER
CLOSED DUE TO DAMAGE/ CONSTRUCTION

JUSTICE PREP

JUSTICE PREPARATORY ACADEMY
STUDENT INCIDENT REPORT

STUDENT: Barry Allen
TEACHER: Professor Eobard Thawne
CLASS: Science

DESCRIPTION OF INCIDENT: Barry was my only student missing from class. When I went out looking for him, I found him cutting my class. After a long chase, I was finally able to apprehend him. I would've brought him back to class to serve his time with me, except I was advised by the principal to escort him to the office.

ACTION TAKEN: Barry has been assigned after-school detention with Ms. Waller. He is to report to her classroom for further disciplinary action.

NOTES: Barry is to report to Room 10 immediately after school.

IF YOU HAVE ANY QUESTIONS ABOUT THIS EVENT, PLEASE CALL THE PRINCIPAL'S OFFICE

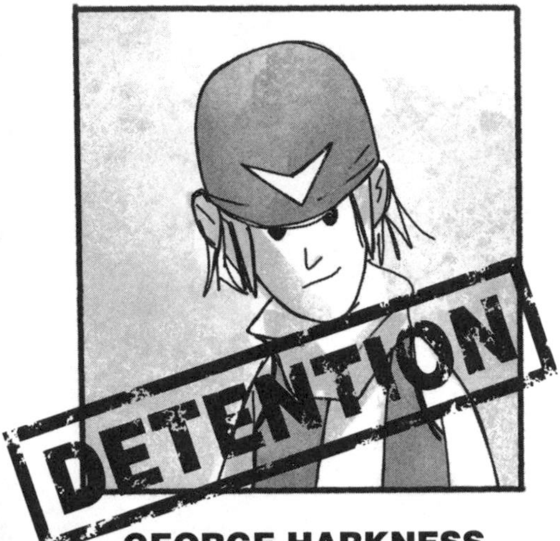
DETENTION

GEORGE HARKNESS
(aka Captain Boomerang)

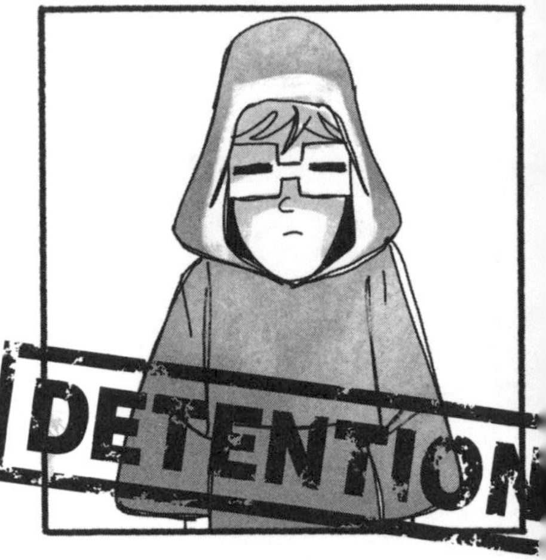
DETENTION

LEONARD SNART
(aka Captain Cold)

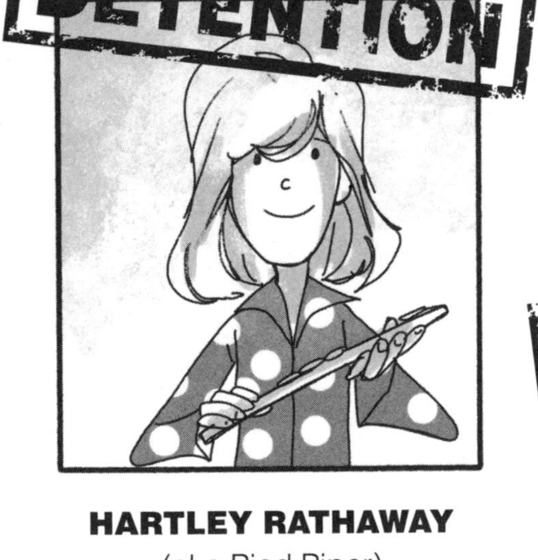
DETENTION

HARTLEY RATHAWAY
(aka Pied Piper)

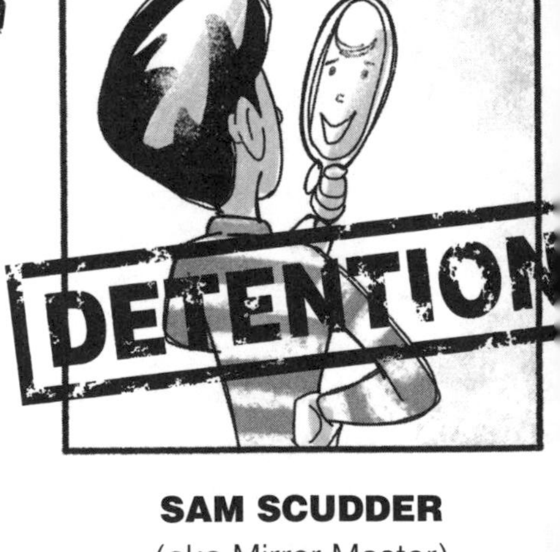
DETENTION

SAM SCUDDER
(aka Mirror Master)

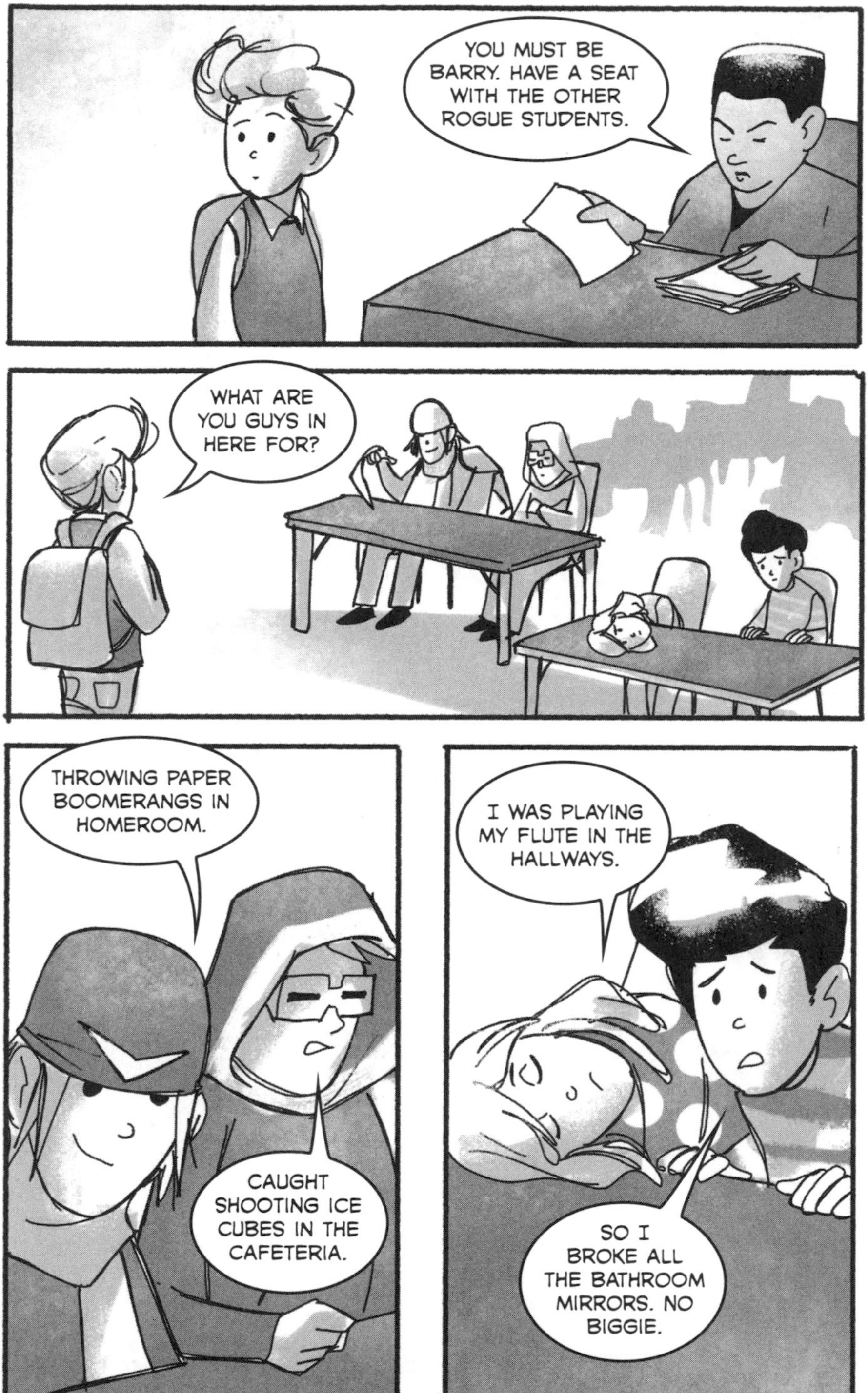
YOU MUST BE BARRY. HAVE A SEAT WITH THE OTHER ROGUE STUDENTS.
WHAT ARE YOU GUYS IN HERE FOR?
THROWING PAPER BOOMERANGS IN HOMEROOM.
CAUGHT SHOOTING ICE CUBES IN THE CAFETERIA.
I WAS PLAYING MY FLUTE IN THE HALLWAYS.
SO I BROKE ALL THE BATHROOM MIRRORS. NO BIGGIE.

JUSTICE PREP
STUDENT BAKE SALE

Please join us for our bake sale fund-raiser. Due to various school lab closures, all monies raised go to support our student scientists to help them complete their projects for the upcoming science fair competition. We will have cupcakes, cakes, cookies, and other tasty treats available. Thank you for your support!

12 noon & 3 p.m.
Located in the Academy Auditorium

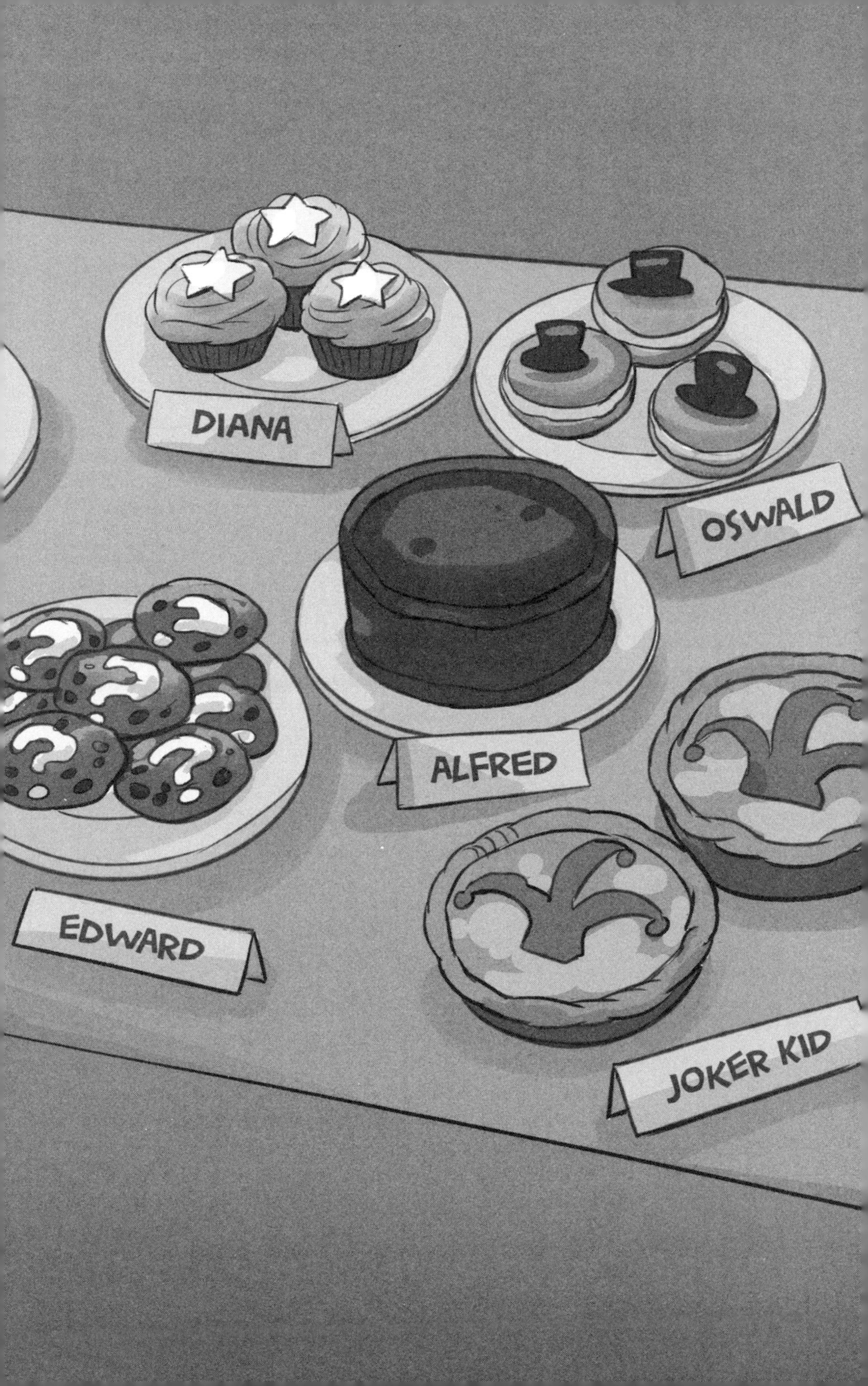
DIANA
OSWALD
ALFRED
EDWARD
JOKER KID

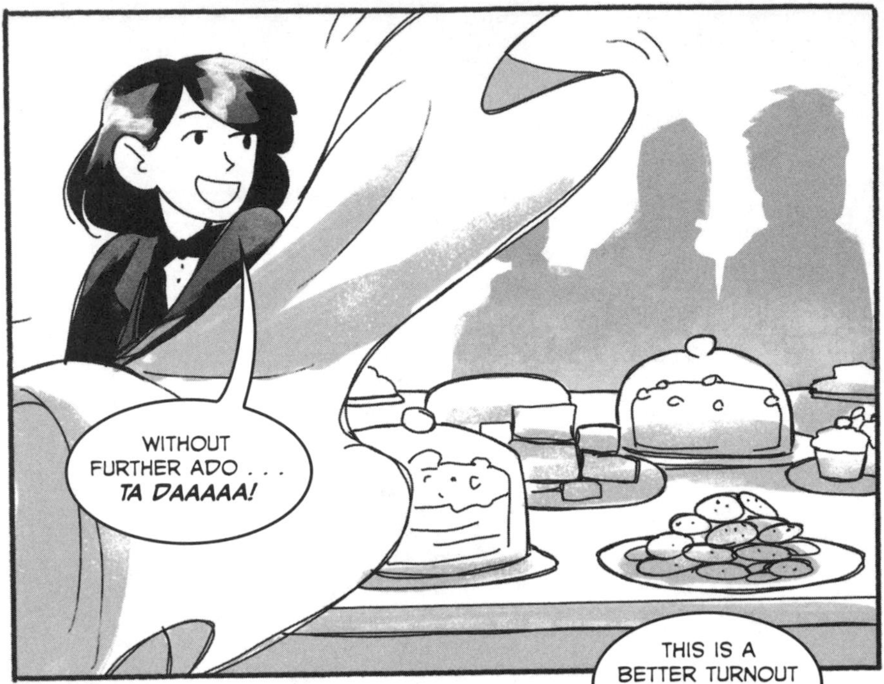
WITHOUT FURTHER ADO . . . *TA DAAAAA!*

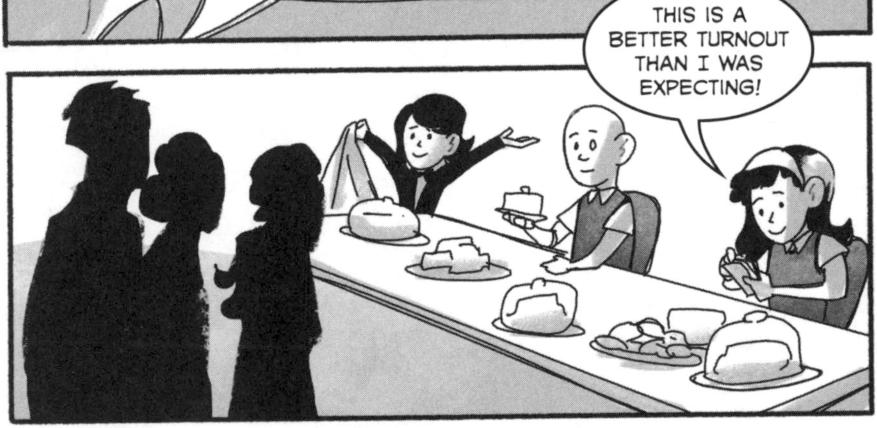
THIS IS A BETTER TURNOUT THAN I WAS EXPECTING!

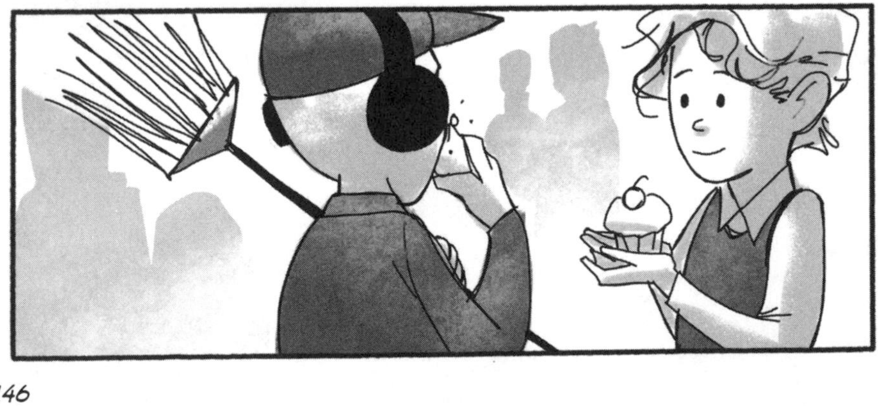

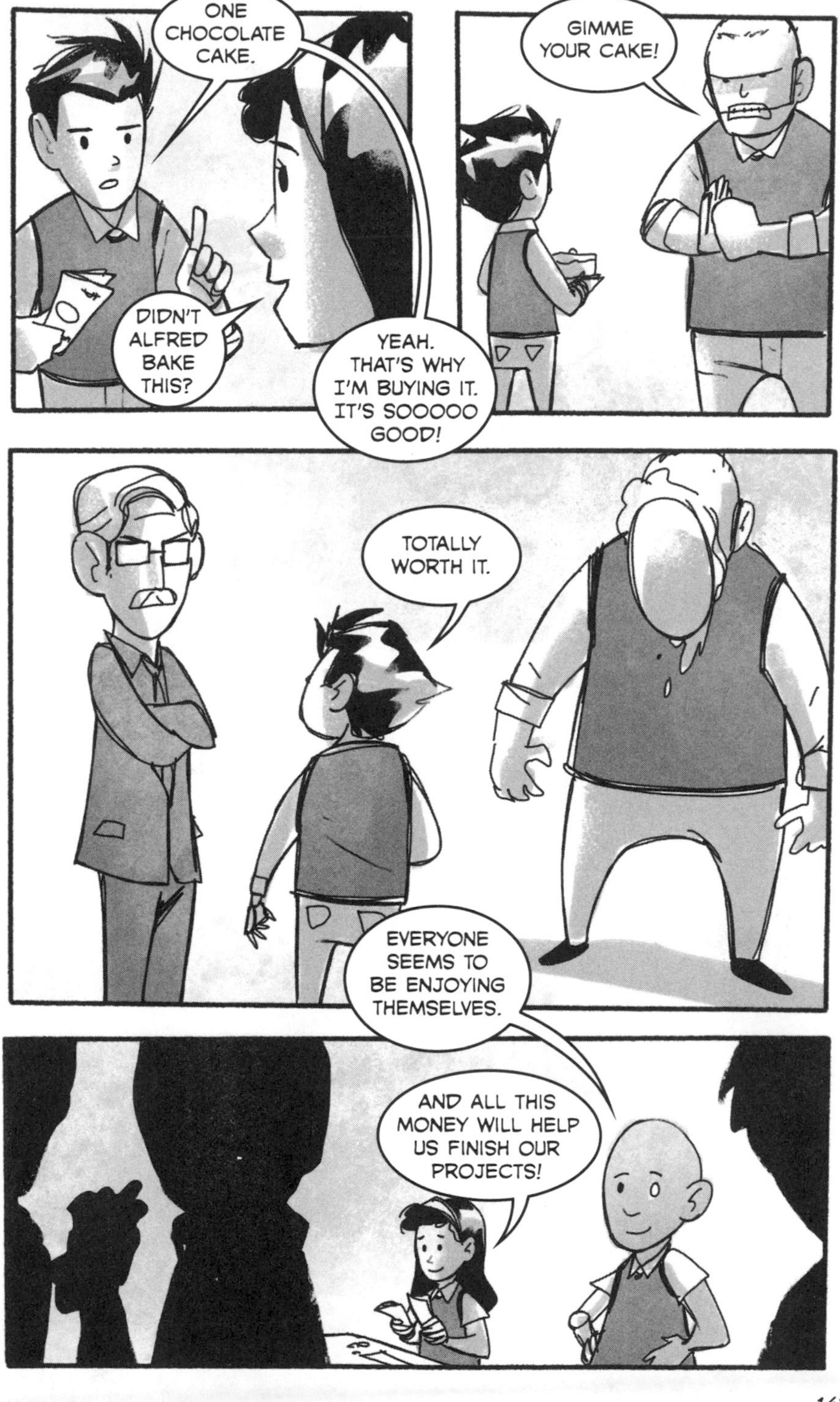
ONE CHOCOLATE CAKE.
DIDN'T ALFRED BAKE THIS?
YEAH. THAT'S WHY I'M BUYING IT. IT'S SOOOOO GOOD!
GIMME YOUR CAKE!
TOTALLY WORTH IT.
EVERYONE SEEMS TO BE ENJOYING THEMSELVES.
AND ALL THIS MONEY WILL HELP US FINISH OUR PROJECTS!

CLARK'S JOURNAL

Seeing everyone come together at the bake sale has given me second thoughts. Maybe I might've overreacted by quitting the Justice Squad. It's just that everyone is on edge not knowing who is trying to sabotage the science fair. And then my own friend, Bruce, trying to build a case against all of us being suspects was taking it too far. I understand being careful. But there's a difference between caution and letting paranoia get the best of us. And I let him get to me. I wish he didn't make me so mad sometimes, even if we don't always agree.

I heard that Barry's trip to detention has ruled out even more students as possible suspects. That's good. It sounds like those students weren't any sort of criminal masterminds. But this Mystery Eye still remains out there, on the eve of the science fair. I just hope nothing bad happens at the awards ceremony. But I'll be ready for it if it does.

YOU ARE CORDIALLY INVITED TO ATTEND:

THE 15TH ANNUAL
SCIENCE FAIR & AWARDS GALA

SUPPORTED **BY S.T.A.R. LABORATORIES,**
GENERAL DIRECTOR PROFESSOR EMIL HAMILTON,
DR. SAUL ERDEL, AND THE DISTRICT OF SCHOLARS

PRIZES AWARDED • OPEN HOUSE • FREE ADMISSION

12 NOON—DOORS OPEN

1:00 P.M.—OPENING CEREMONIES

2:00 P.M.—JUDGING BEGINS

3:00 P.M.—AWARDS PRESENTATION

REFRESHMENTS PROVIDED

THE STUDENTS HAVE BEEN WORKING ON THEIR PROJECTS
FOR THE PAST SCHOOL YEAR AND ARE EXCITED TO SHARE
THEM WITH THEIR FRIENDS, FAMILY, AND COMMUNITY.
COME TAKE PART IN ENCOURAGING THE NEXT
GENERATION OF SCIENTIFIC MINDS!

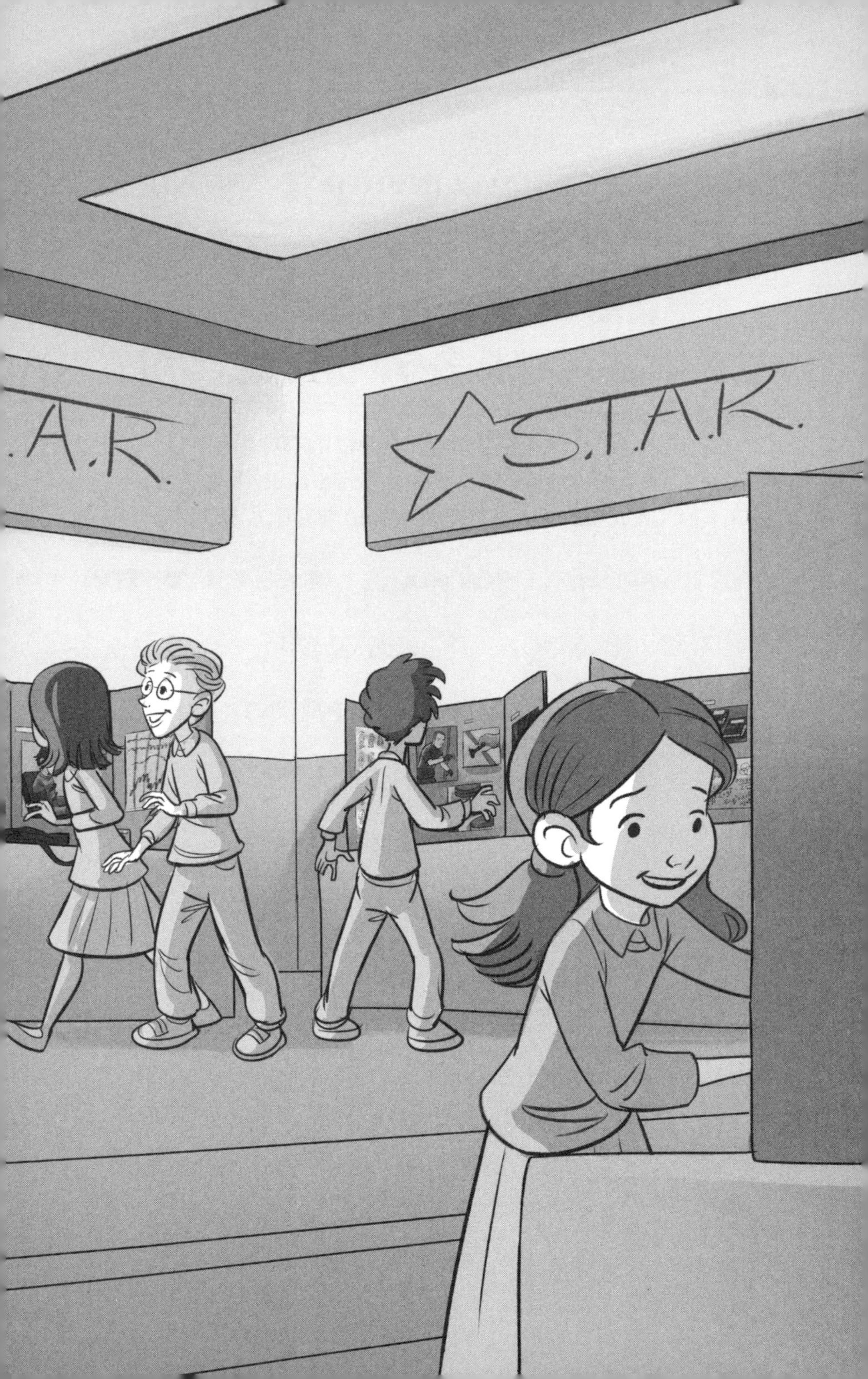
.A.R.
S.T.A.R.

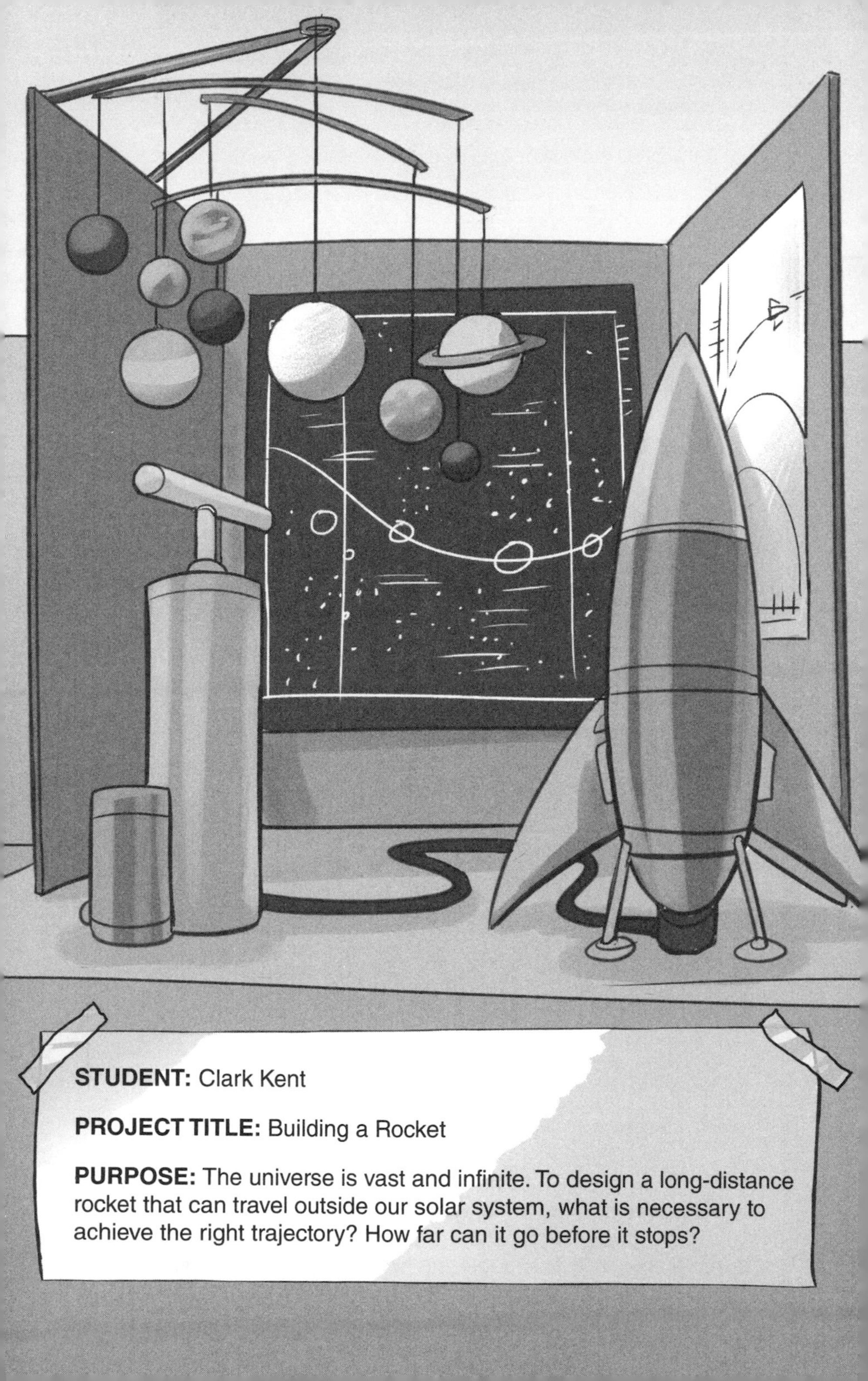
STUDENT: Clark Kent
PROJECT TITLE: Building a Rocket
PURPOSE: The universe is vast and infinite. To design a long-distance rocket that can travel outside our solar system, what is necessary to achieve the right trajectory? How far can it go before it stops?

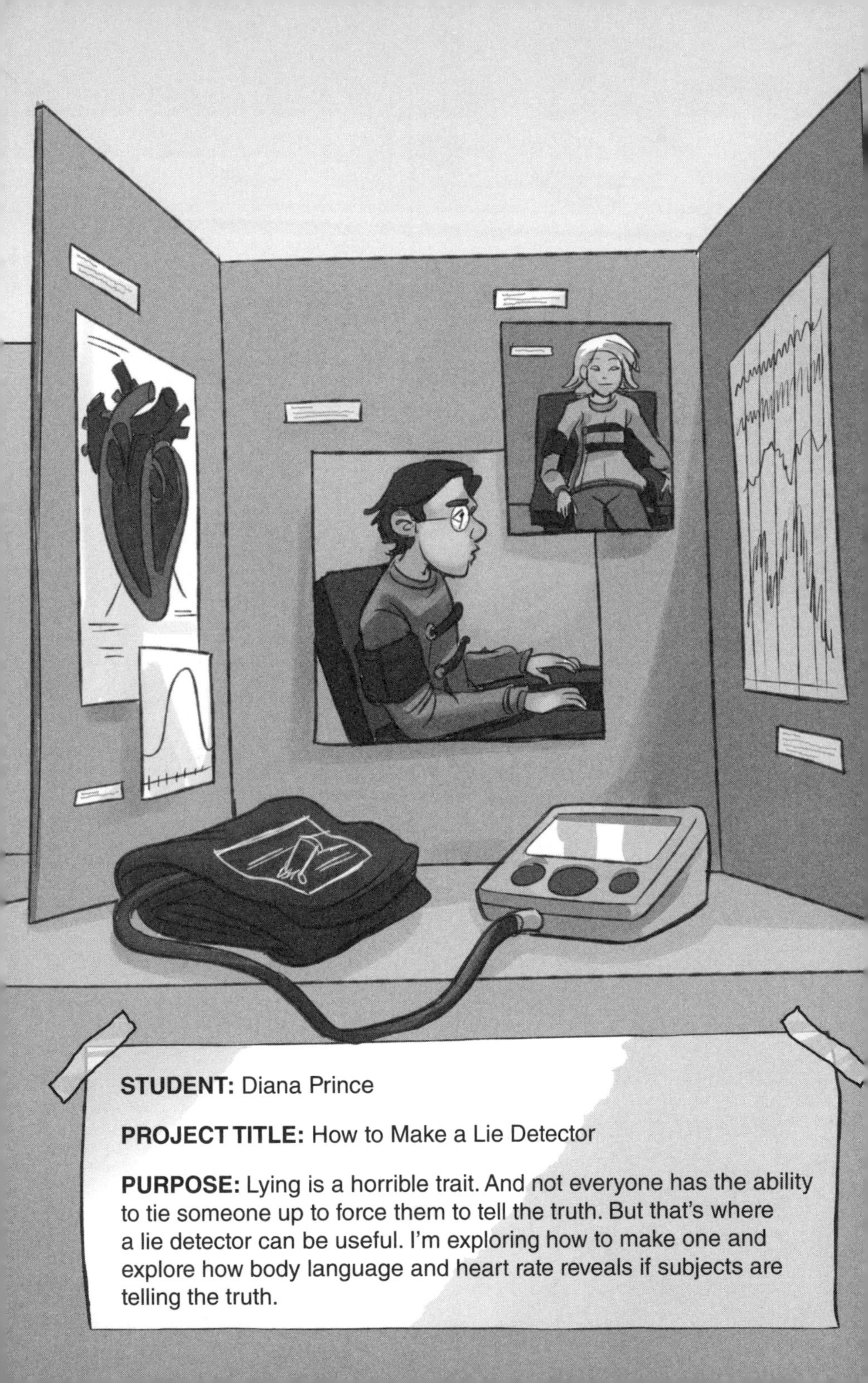
STUDENT: Diana Prince
PROJECT TITLE: How to Make a Lie Detector
PURPOSE: Lying is a horrible trait. And not everyone has the ability to tie someone up to force them to tell the truth. But that's where a lie detector can be useful. I'm exploring how to make one and explore how body language and heart rate reveals if subjects are telling the truth.

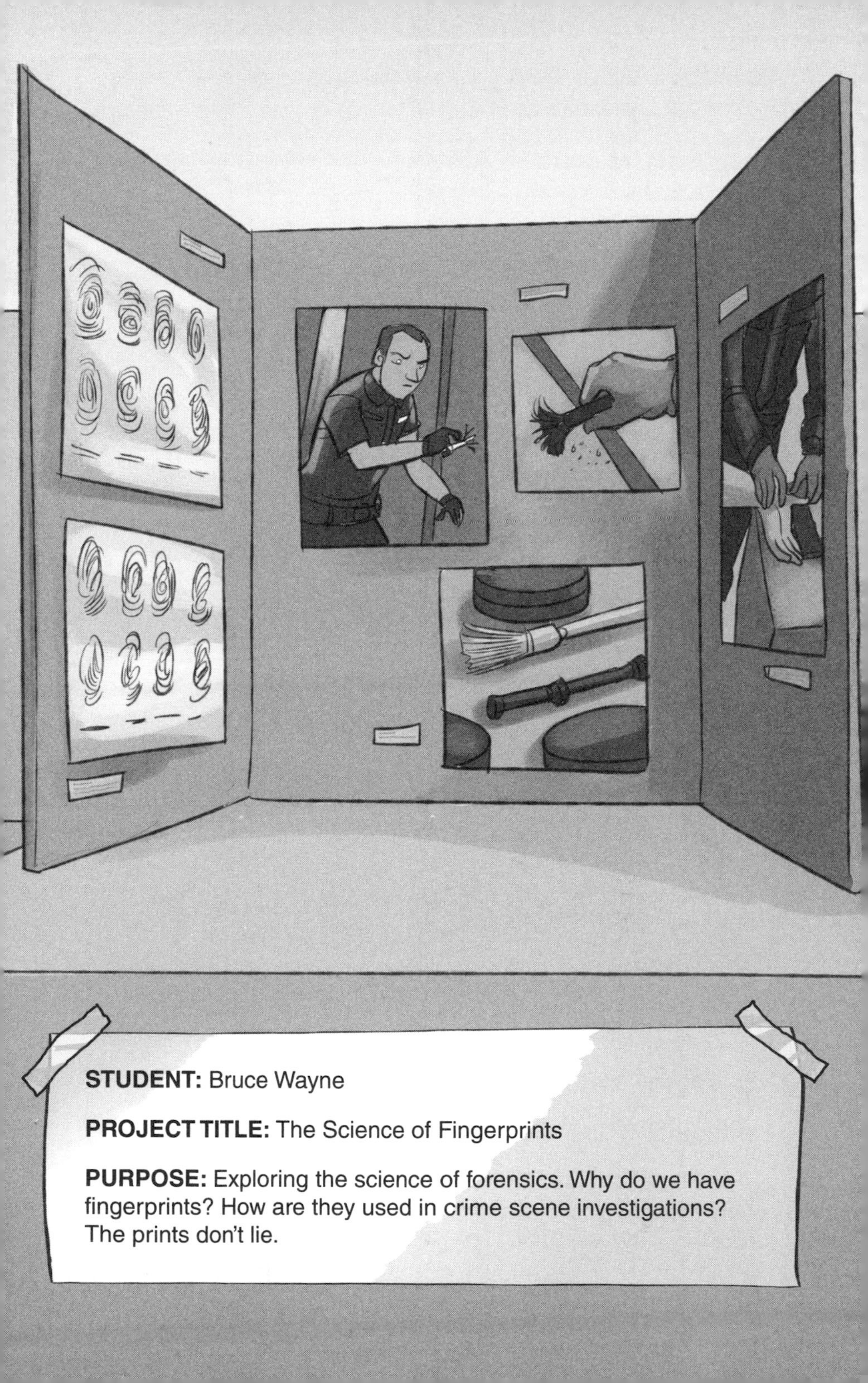
STUDENT: Bruce Wayne
PROJECT TITLE: The Science of Fingerprints
PURPOSE: Exploring the science of forensics. Why do we have fingerprints? How are they used in crime scene investigations? The prints don't lie.

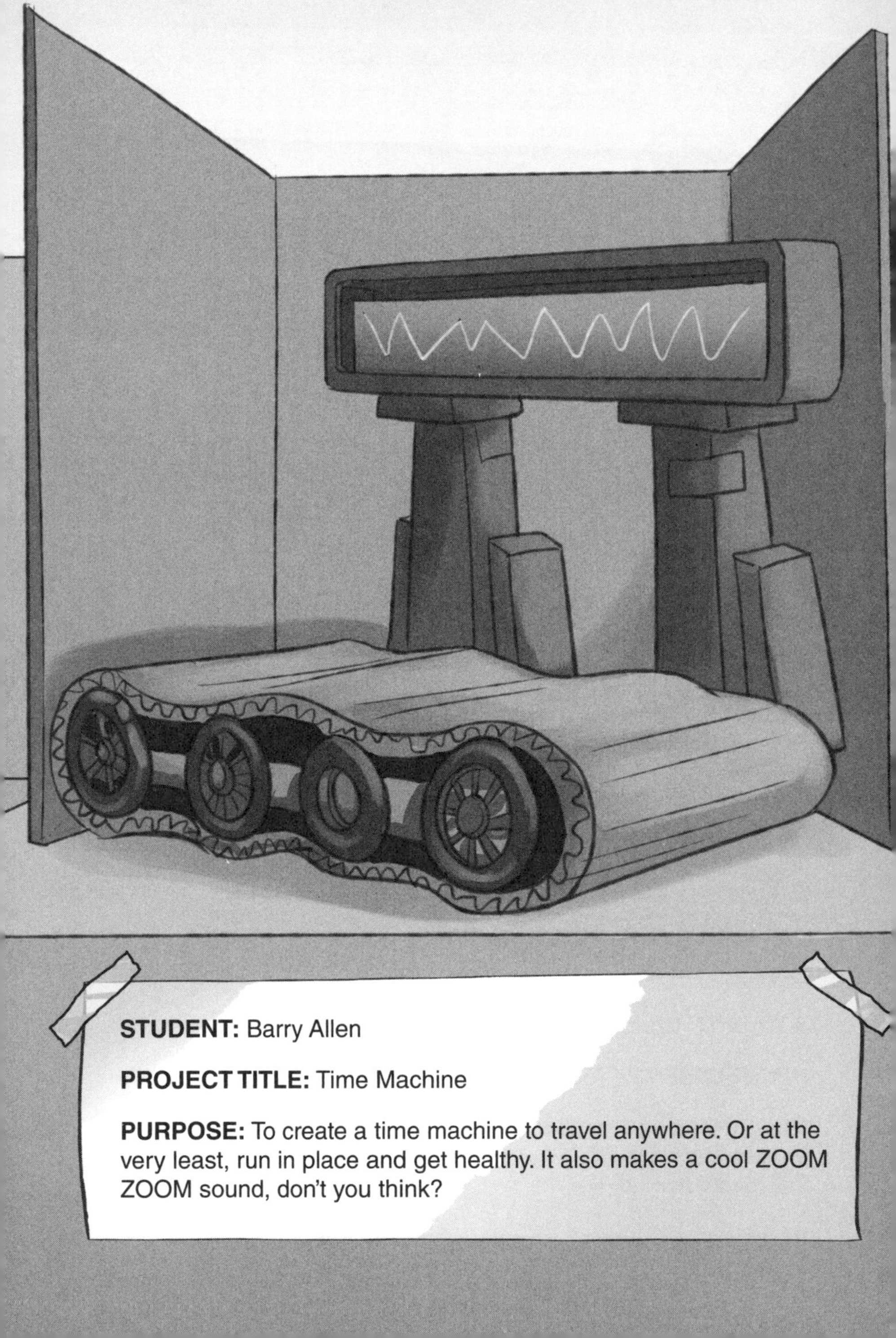

STUDENT: Barry Allen

PROJECT TITLE: Time Machine

PURPOSE: To create a time machine to travel anywhere. Or at the very least, run in place and get healthy. It also makes a cool ZOOM ZOOM sound, don't you think?

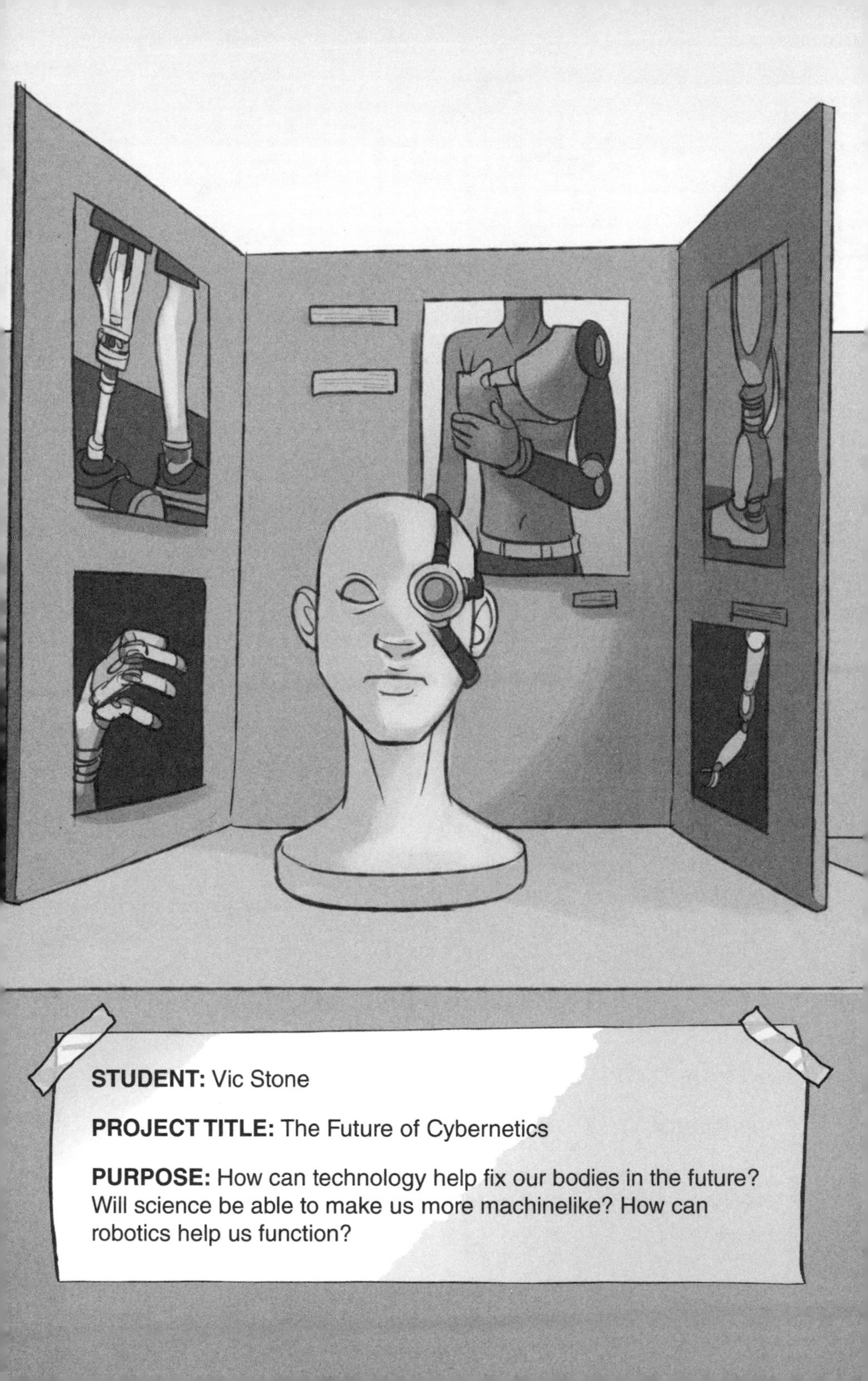
STUDENT: Vic Stone
PROJECT TITLE: The Future of Cybernetics
PURPOSE: How can technology help fix our bodies in the future? Will science be able to make us more machinelike? How can robotics help us function?

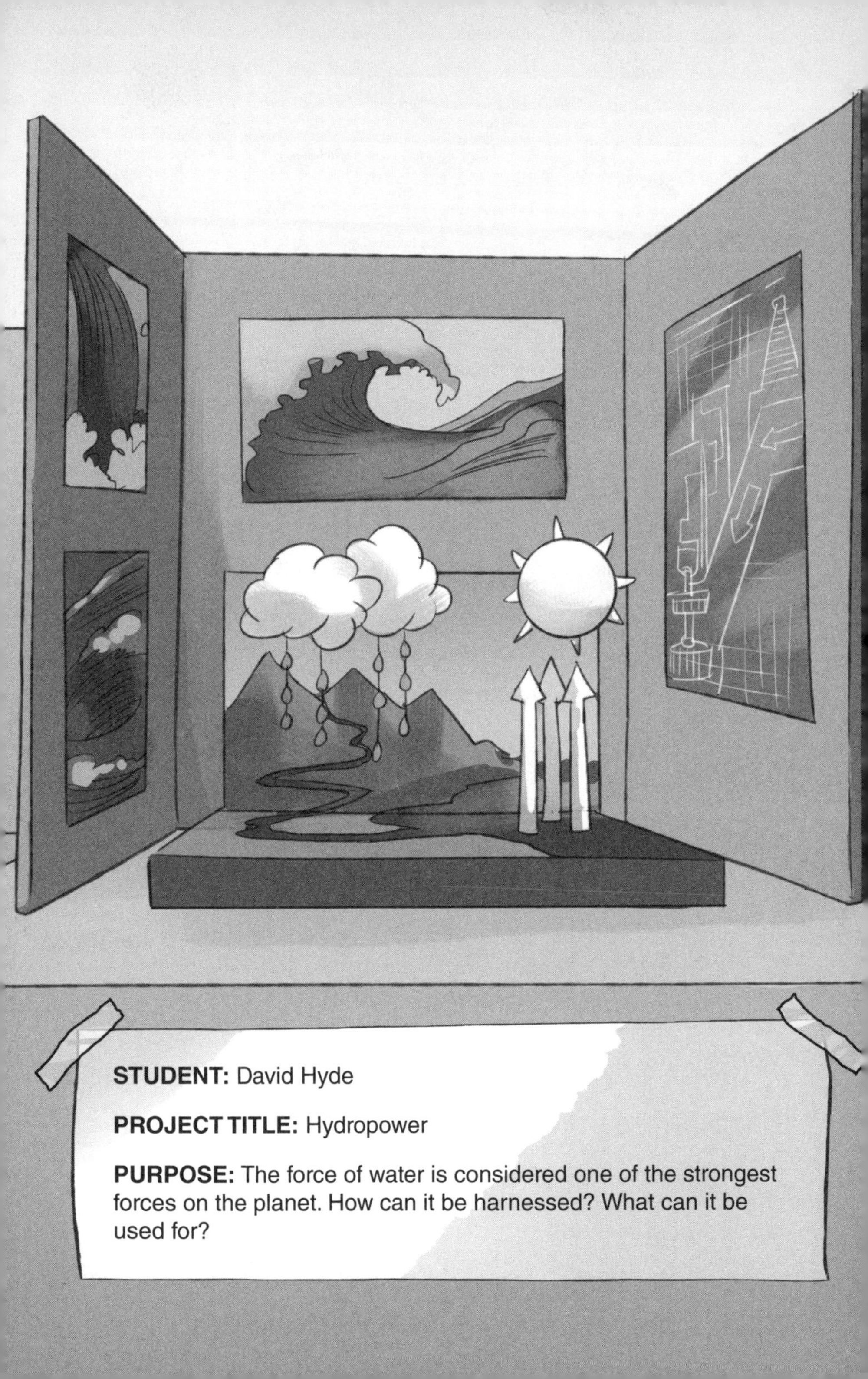
STUDENT: David Hyde
PROJECT TITLE: Hydropower
PURPOSE: The force of water is considered one of the strongest forces on the planet. How can it be harnessed? What can it be used for?

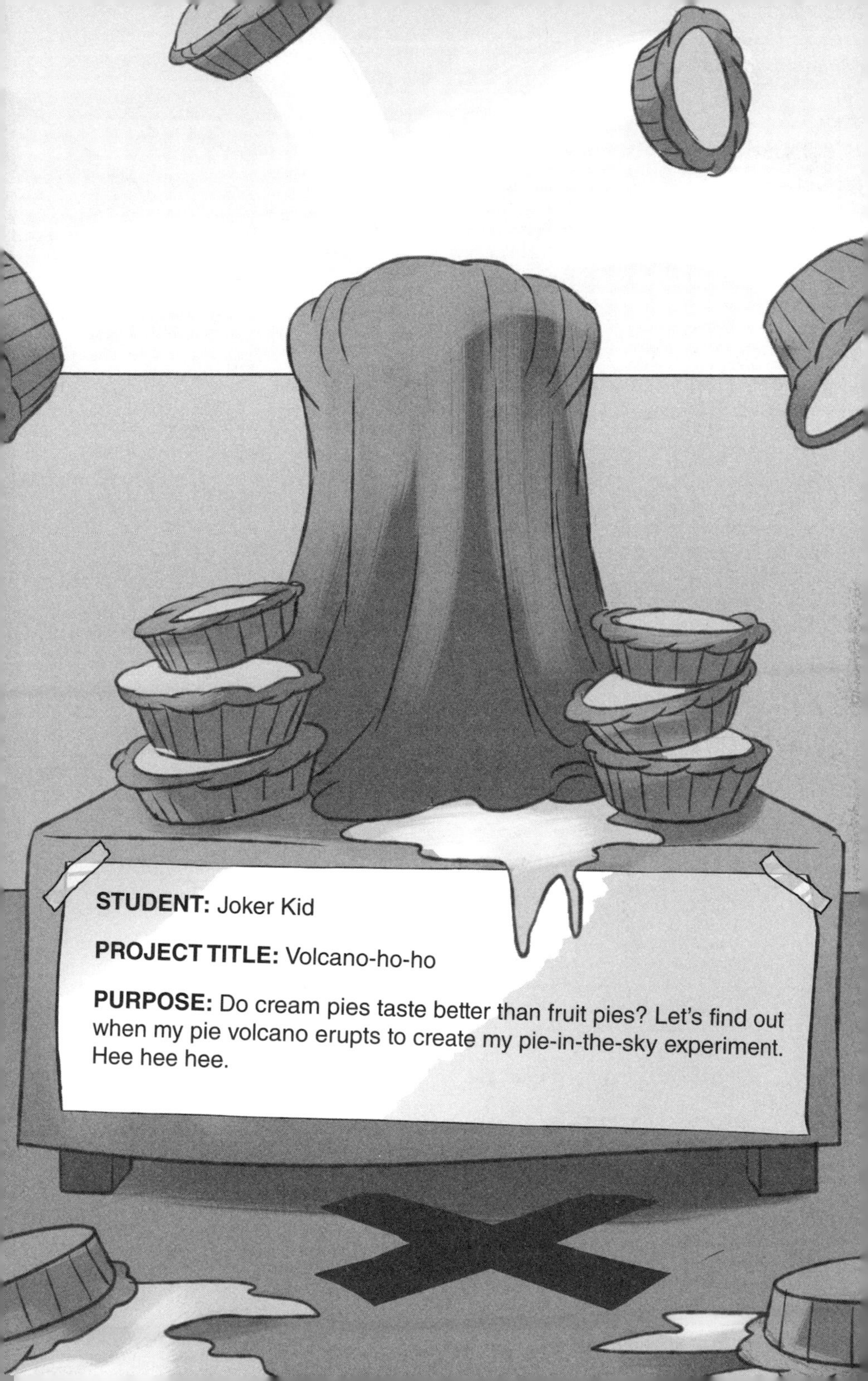
STUDENT: Joker Kid
PROJECT TITLE: Volcano-ho-ho
PURPOSE: Do cream pies taste better than fruit pies? Let's find out when my pie volcano erupts to create my pie-in-the-sky experiment. Hee hee hee.

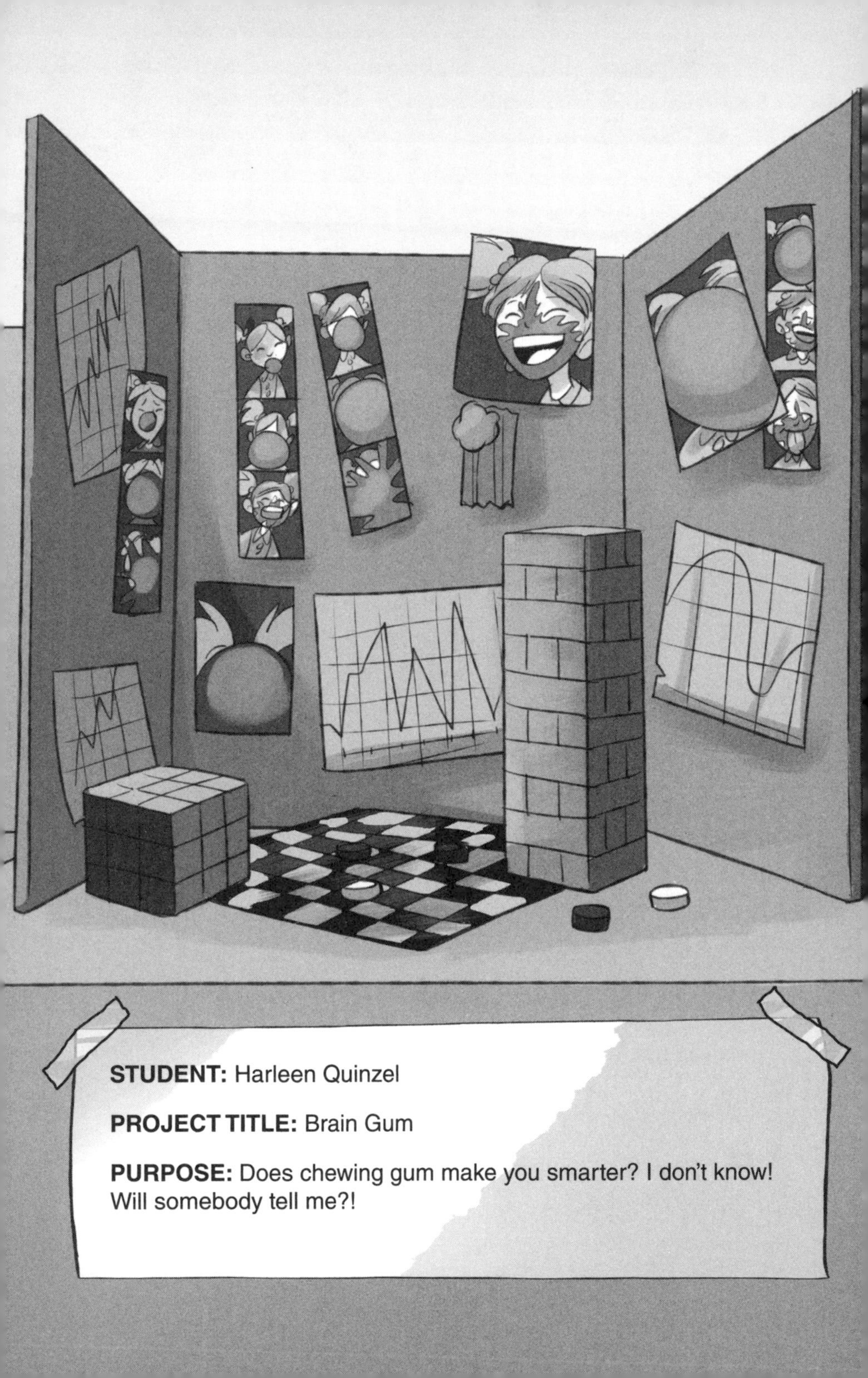
STUDENT: Harleen Quinzel
PROJECT TITLE: Brain Gum
PURPOSE: Does chewing gum make you smarter? I don't know! Will somebody tell me?!

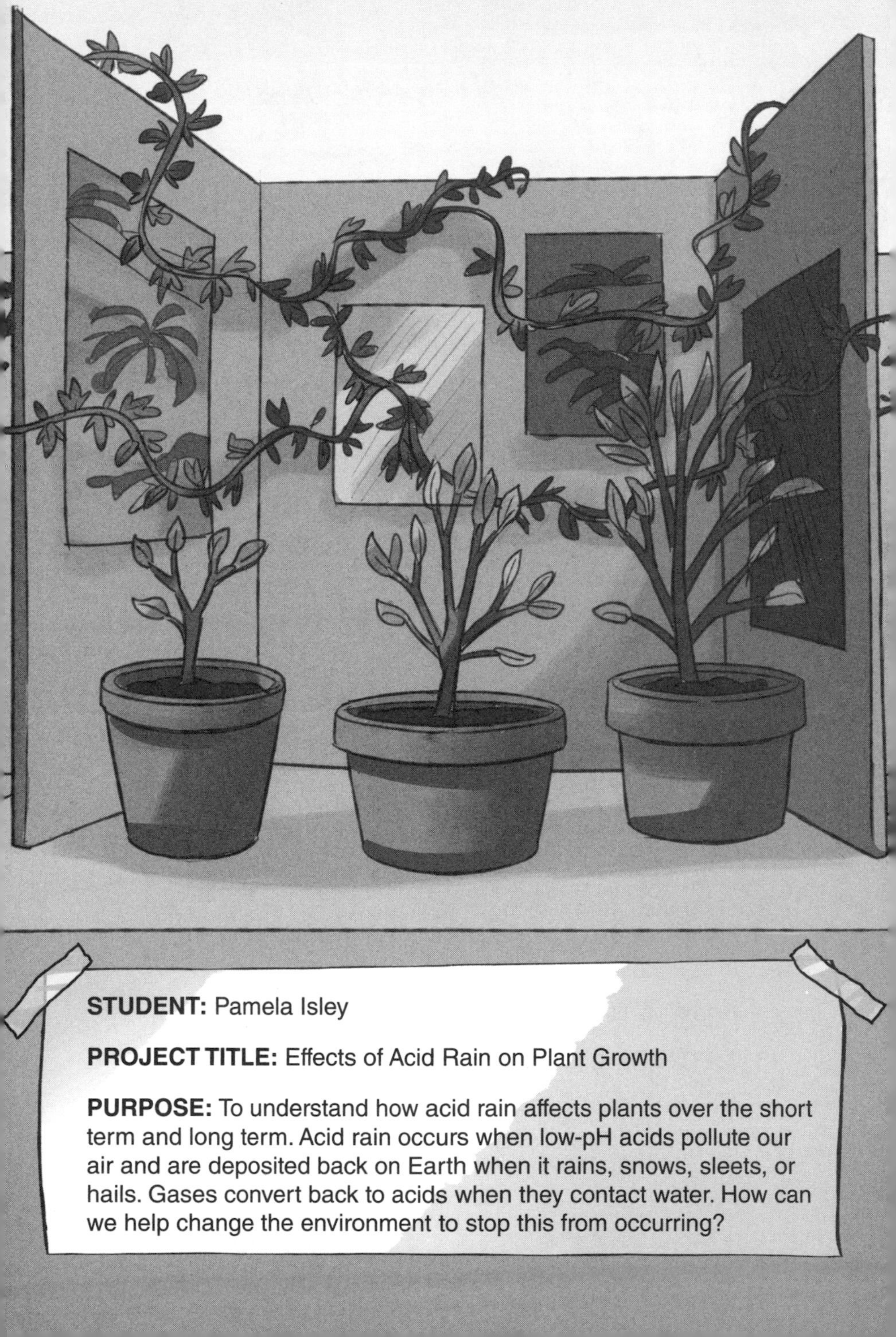

STUDENT: Pamela Isley

PROJECT TITLE: Effects of Acid Rain on Plant Growth

PURPOSE: To understand how acid rain affects plants over the short term and long term. Acid rain occurs when low-pH acids pollute our air and are deposited back on Earth when it rains, snows, sleets, or hails. Gases convert back to acids when they contact water. How can we help change the environment to stop this from occurring?

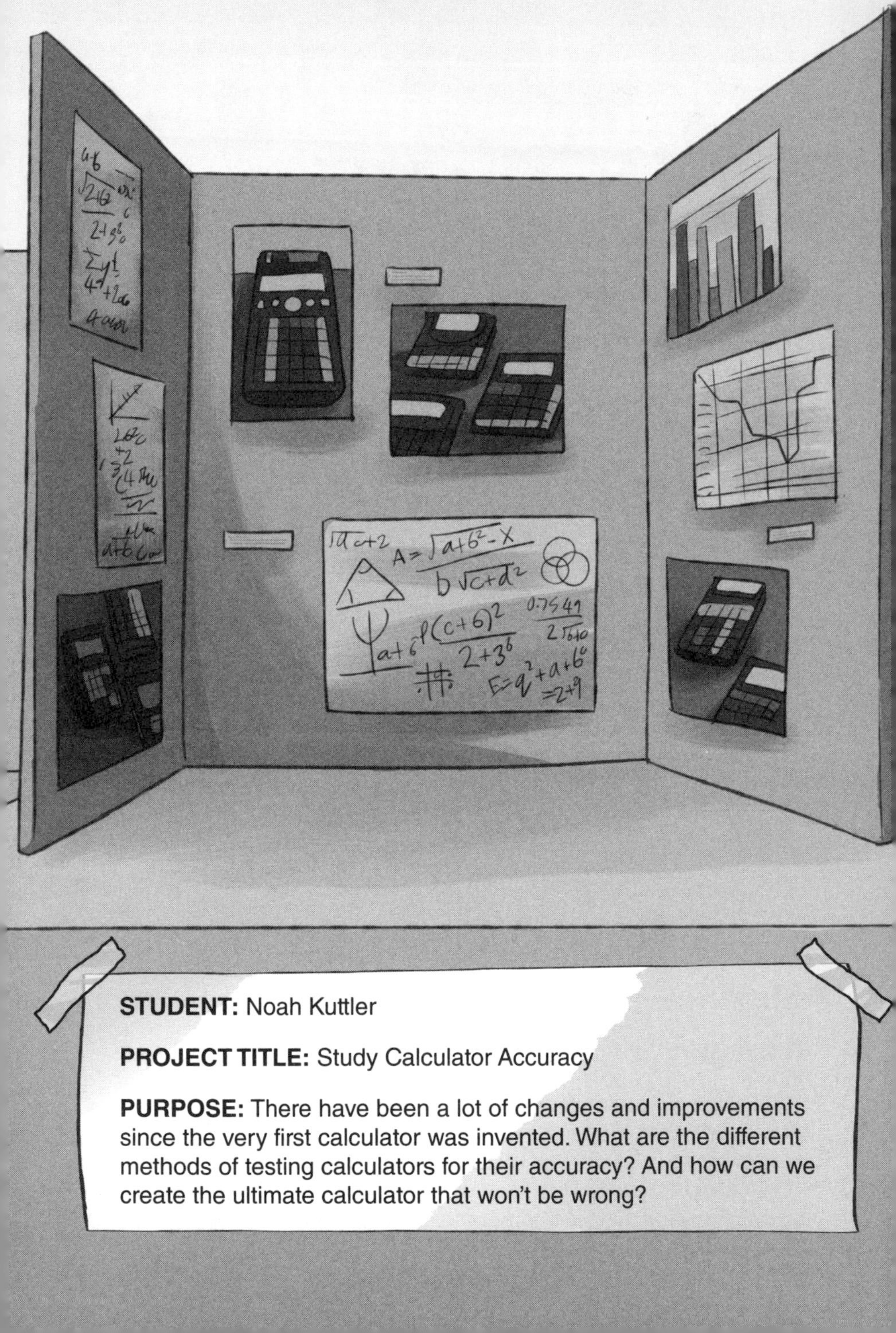

STUDENT: Noah Kuttler

PROJECT TITLE: Study Calculator Accuracy

PURPOSE: There have been a lot of changes and improvements since the very first calculator was invented. What are the different methods of testing calculators for their accuracy? And how can we create the ultimate calculator that won't be wrong?

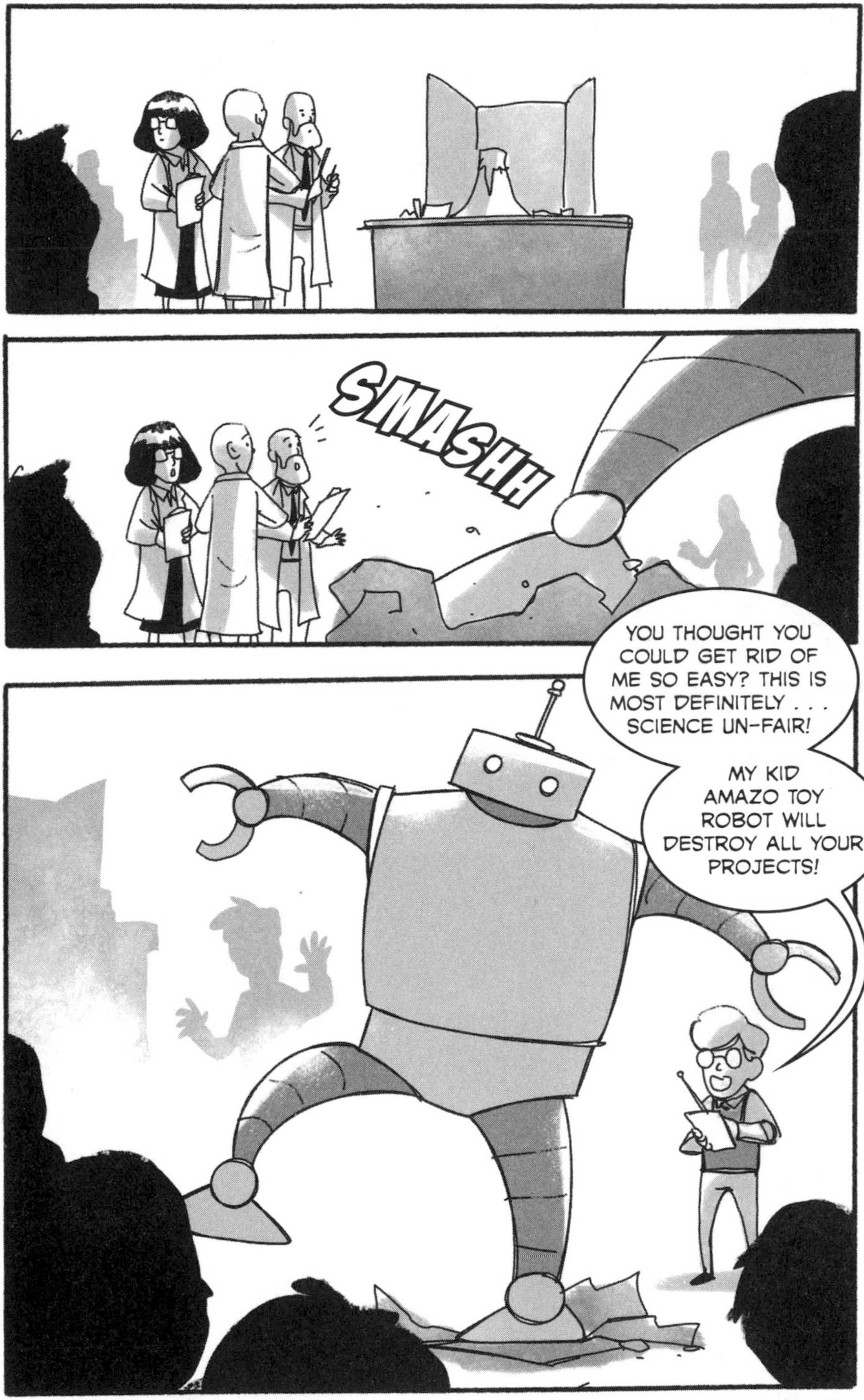
SMASHH
YOU THOUGHT YOU COULD GET RID OF ME SO EASY? THIS IS MOST DEFINITELY . . . SCIENCE UN-FAIR!
MY KID AMAZO TOY ROBOT WILL DESTROY ALL YOUR PROJECTS!

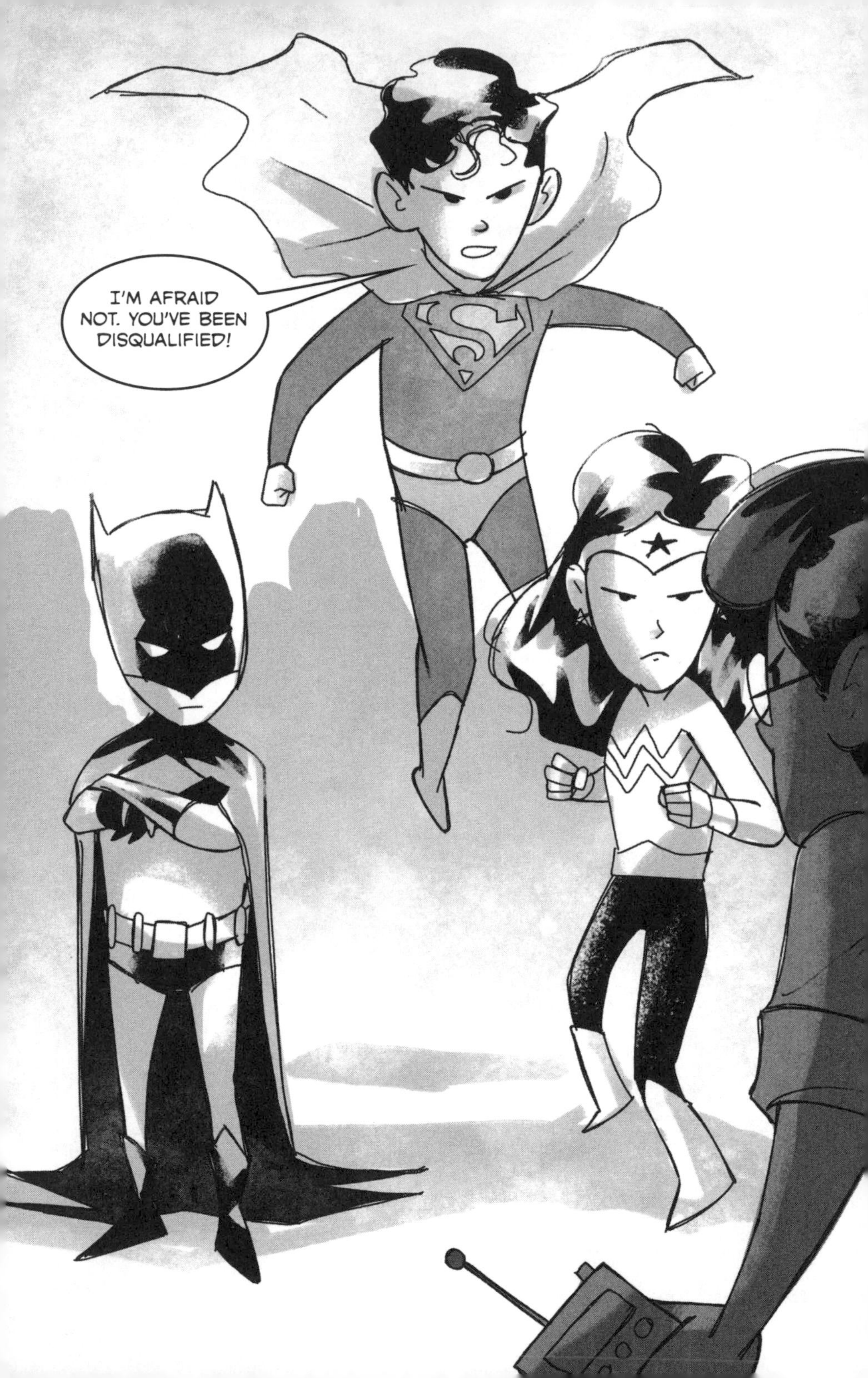
I'M AFRAID NOT. YOU'VE BEEN DISQUALIFIED!

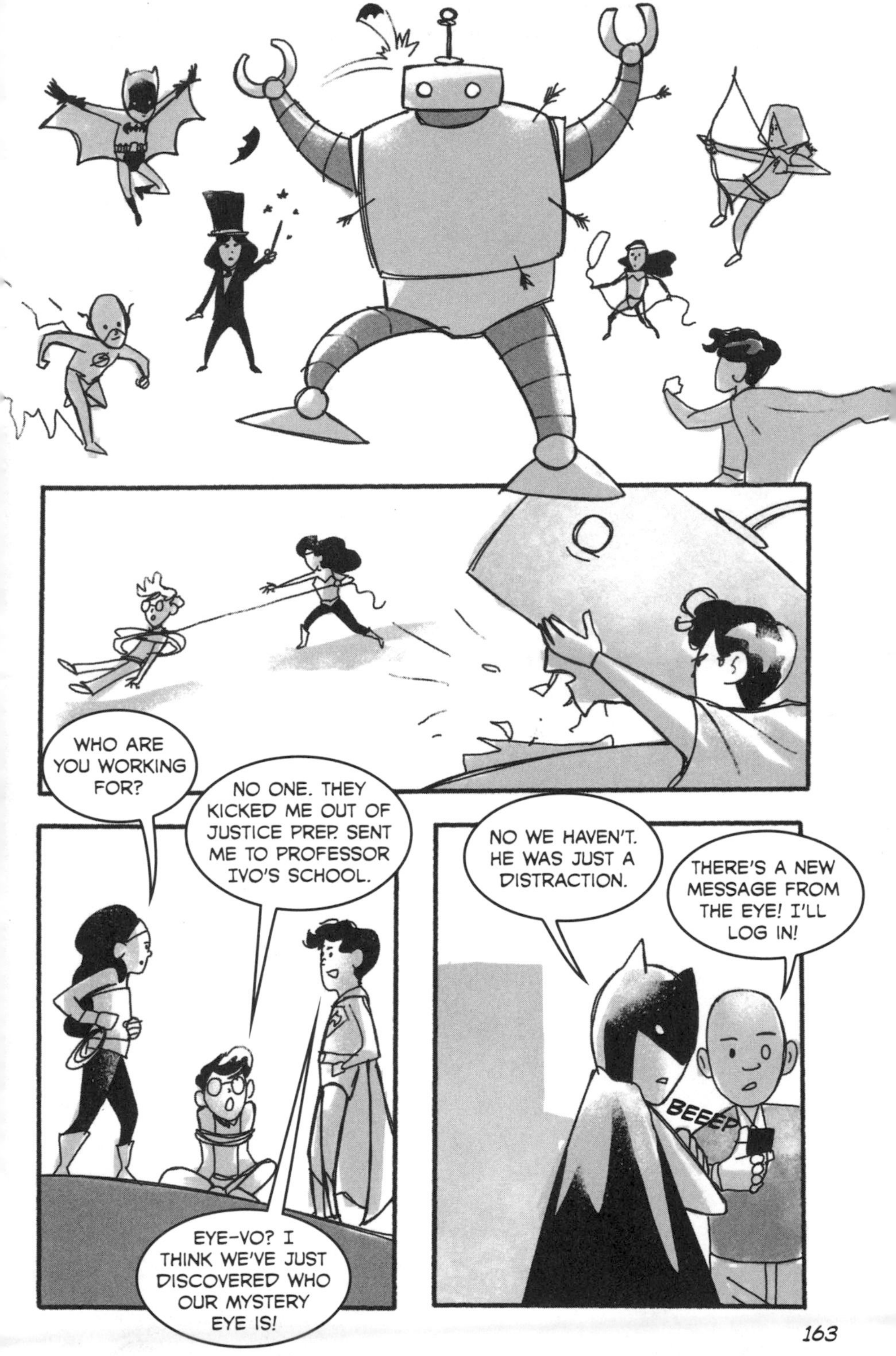
WHO ARE YOU WORKING FOR?
NO ONE. THEY KICKED ME OUT OF JUSTICE PREP. SENT ME TO PROFESSOR IVO'S SCHOOL.
EYE-VO? I THINK WE'VE JUST DISCOVERED WHO OUR MYSTERY EYE IS!
NO WE HAVEN'T. HE WAS JUST A DISTRACTION.
THERE'S A NEW MESSAGE FROM THE EYE! I'LL LOG IN!
BEEEP

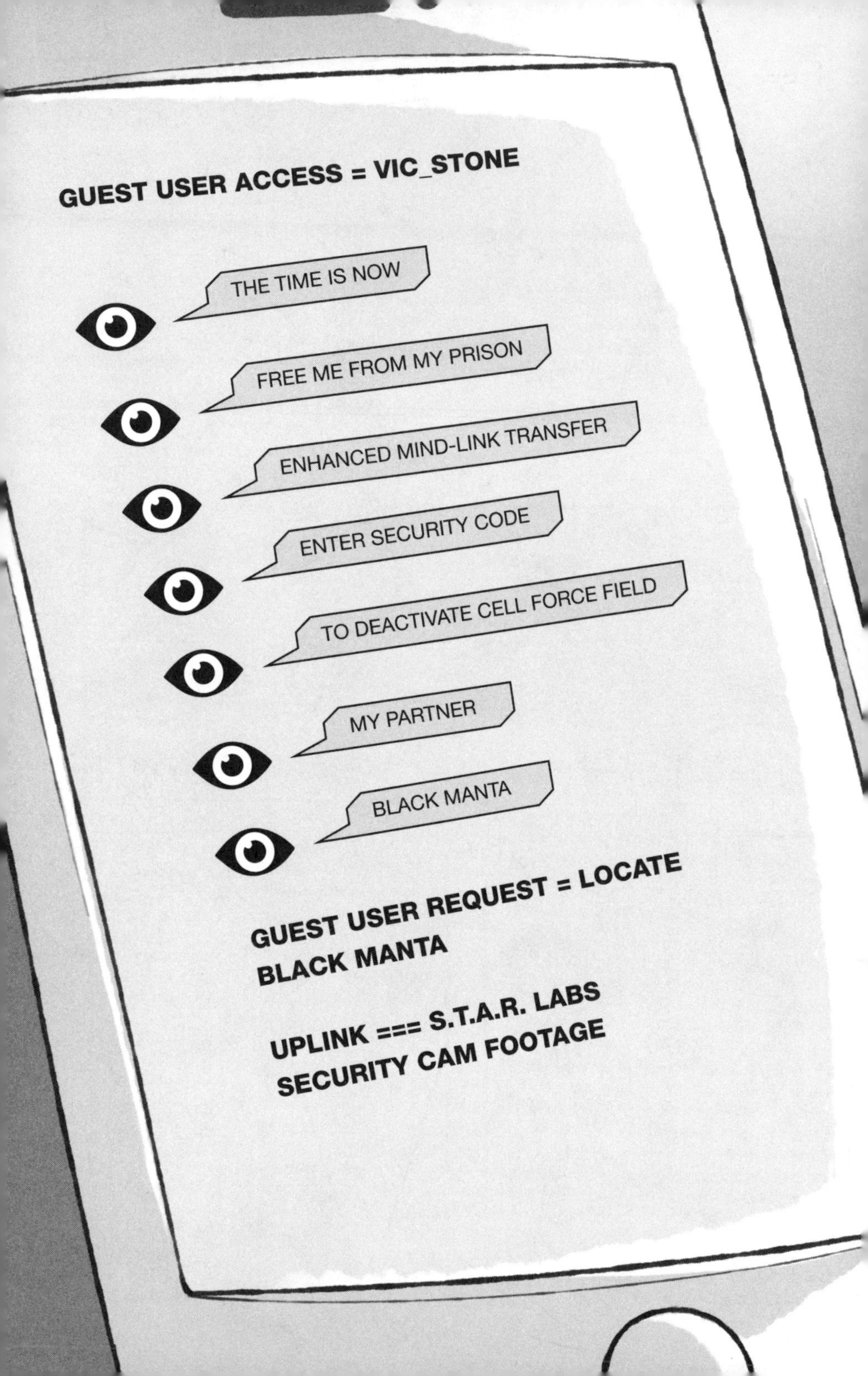
GUEST USER ACCESS = VIC_STONE
THE TIME IS NOW
FREE ME FROM MY PRISON
ENHANCED MIND-LINK TRANSFER
ENTER SECURITY CODE
TO DEACTIVATE CELL FORCE FIELD
MY PARTNER
BLACK MANTA
GUEST USER REQUEST = LOCATE BLACK MANTA
UPLINK === S.T.A.R. LABS SECURITY CAM FOOTAGE

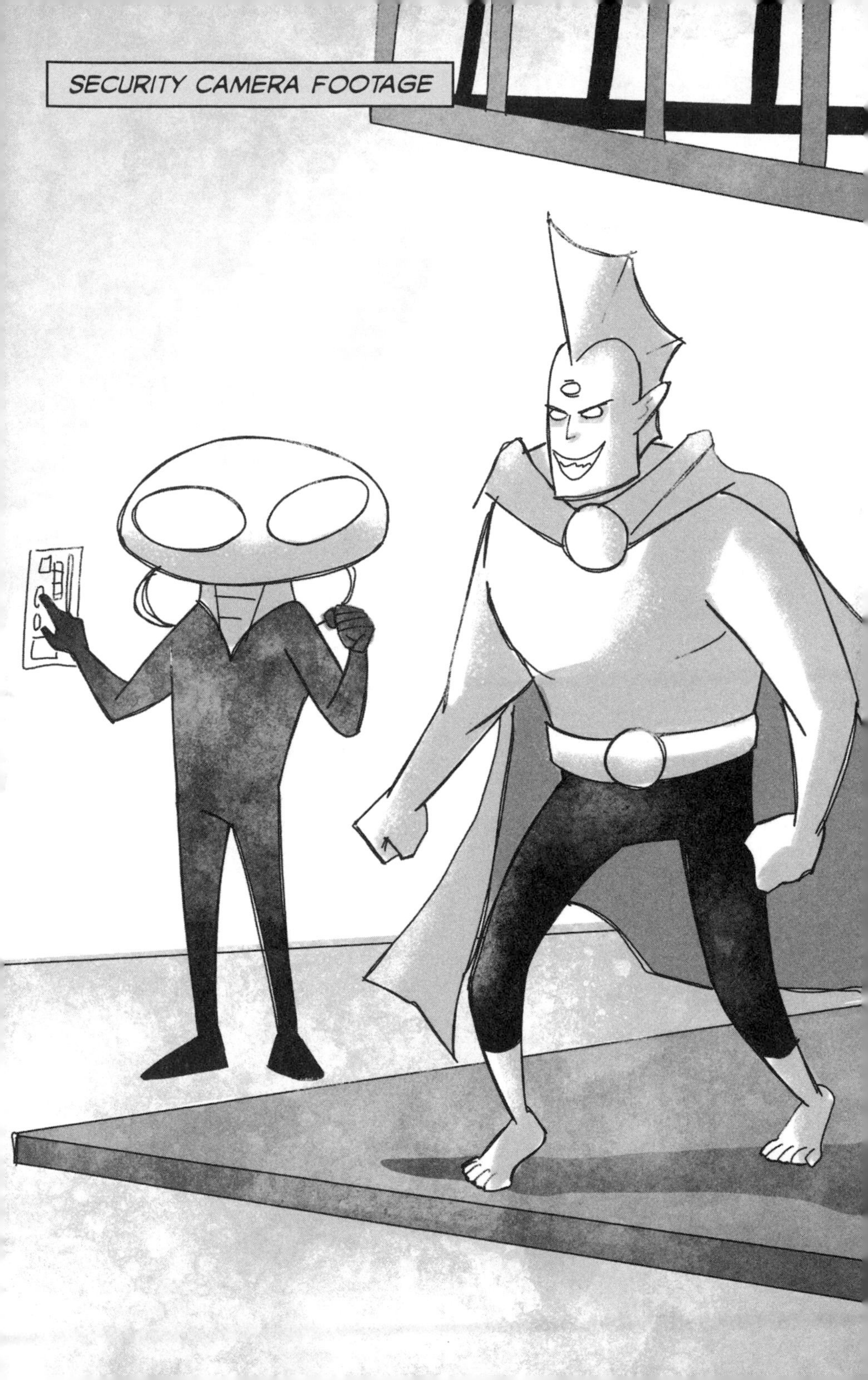
SECURITY CAMERA FOOTAGE

GUEST ACCESS GRANTED: VIC_STONE

ACCESSING S.T.A.R. LABS DATABASE . . .

<< WARNING >>

SUBJECT: DESPERO

ALIEN INVADER FROM DISTANT GALAXY. SELF-PROFESSED CONQUEROR AND TYRANT. FAILED ATTEMPT TO ACQUIRE S.T.A.R. LABS TECHNOLOGY TO HELP OVERTAKE AND RULE THE GALAXY, LEADING TO CAPTURE.

EXHIBITS A GENIUS INTELLECT AND ENHANCED MIND-ALTERING POWERS WITH THIRD EYE ABILITY. ABLE TO READ MINDS, CREATE ILLUSIONS, TELEKINESIS, TELEPATHY, AND CAUSE HYPNOSIS. UNABLE TO AFFECT ADULTS. HYPNOTIC TRANCE EFFECTS ARE ABLE TO CONTROL LESS DEVELOPED CHILD MINDS THROUGH TELEPATHIC LINK.

SCIENTIFIC DIAGNOSIS: UNABLE TO CLASSIFY HIS MYSTICAL SOURCE OF PSIONIC POWER, WHICH GRANTS HIM SUPERHUMAN STRENGTH, DURABILITY, SPEED, AND THE ABILITY TO ALTER HIS BIOMASS (TO REINTEGRATE HIMSELF IN SIZE, MOLECULE BY MOLECULE).

ANALYSIS: EXTREMELY DANGEROUS! PROCEED WITH CAUTION!

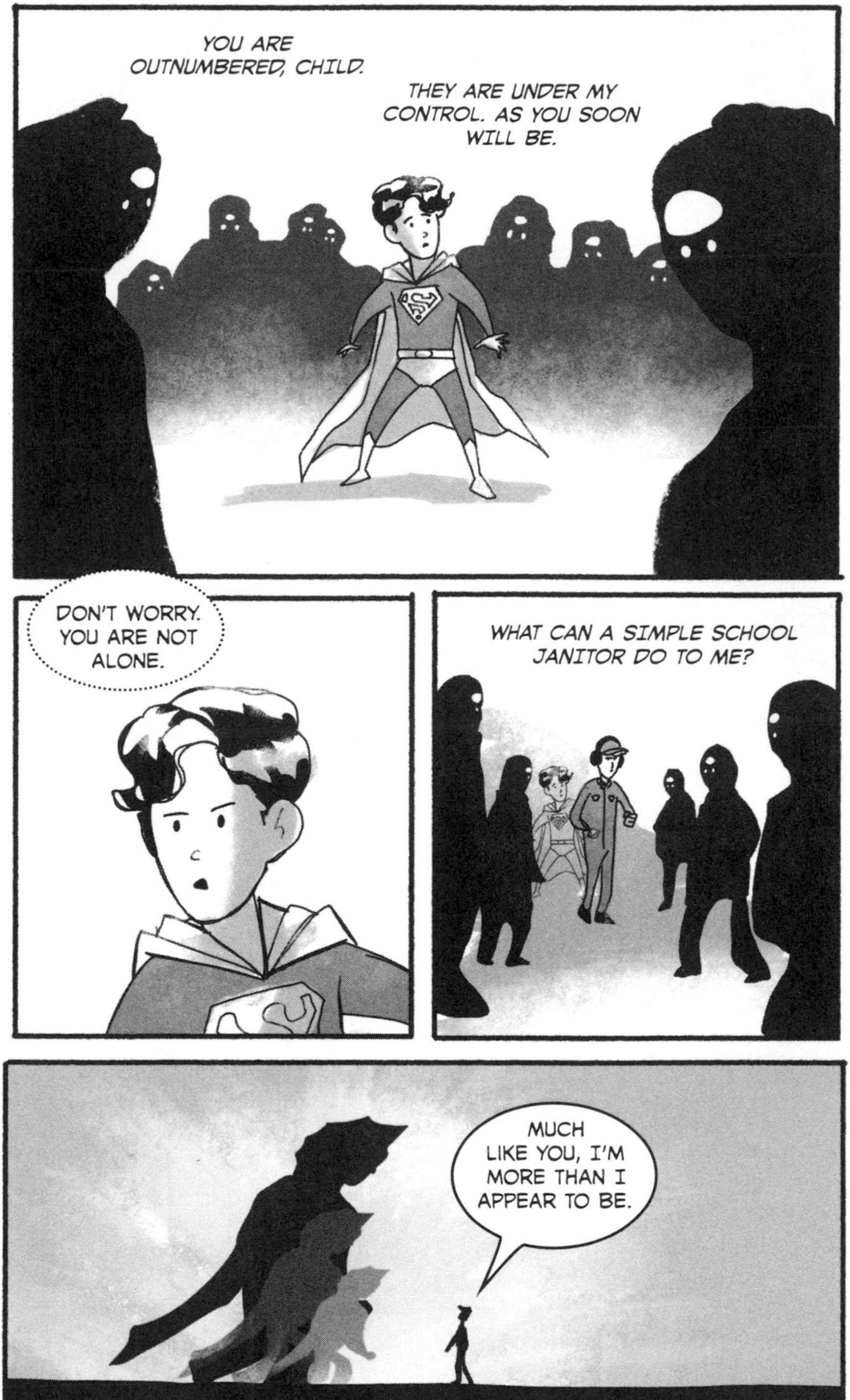
YOU ARE OUTNUMBERED, CHILD.
THEY ARE UNDER MY CONTROL. AS YOU SOON WILL BE.
DON'T WORRY. YOU ARE NOT ALONE.
WHAT CAN A SIMPLE SCHOOL JANITOR DO TO ME?
MUCH LIKE YOU, I'M MORE THAN I APPEAR TO BE.

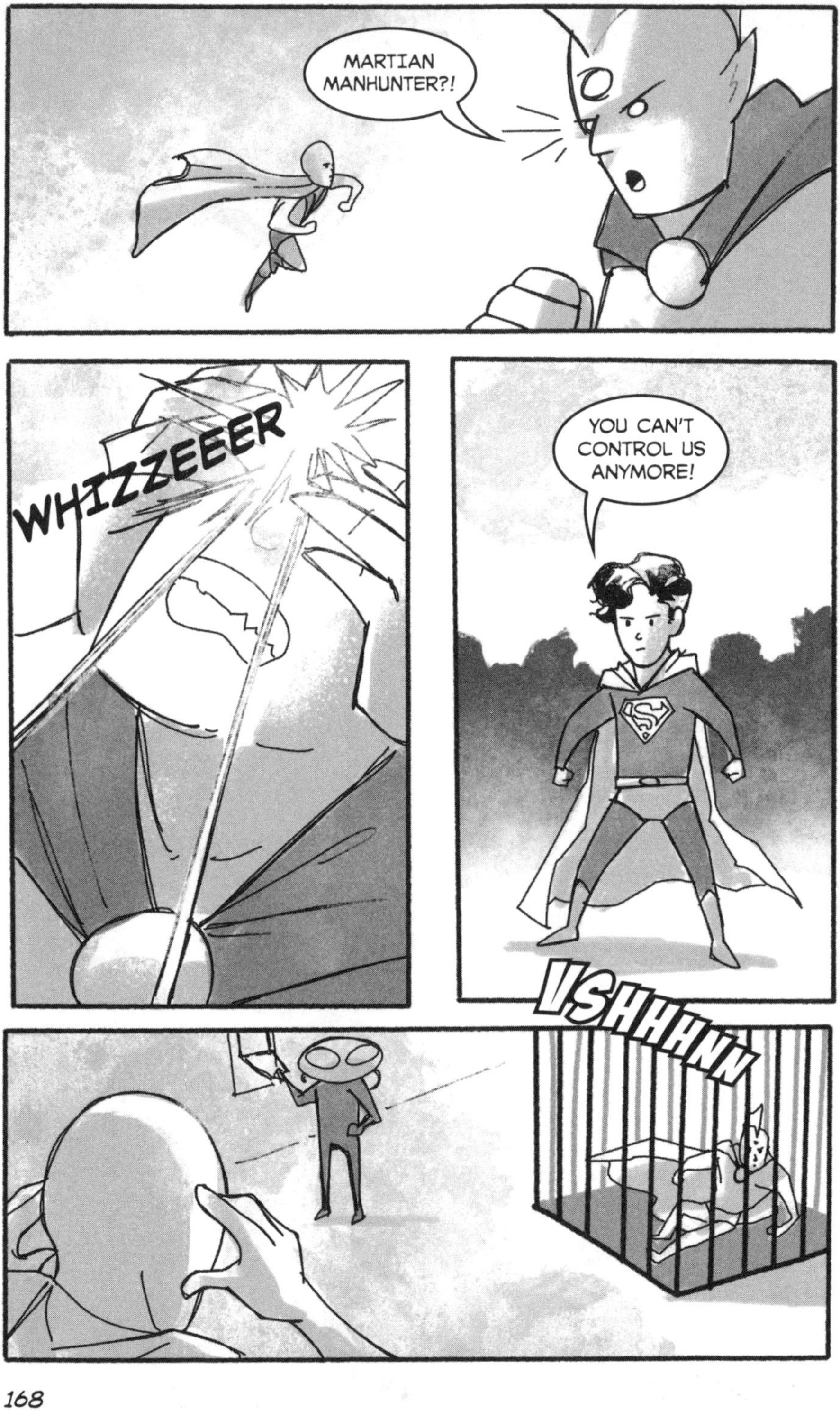
MARTIAN MANHUNTER?!
WHIZZEEER
YOU CAN'T CONTROL US ANYMORE!
VSHHHNN

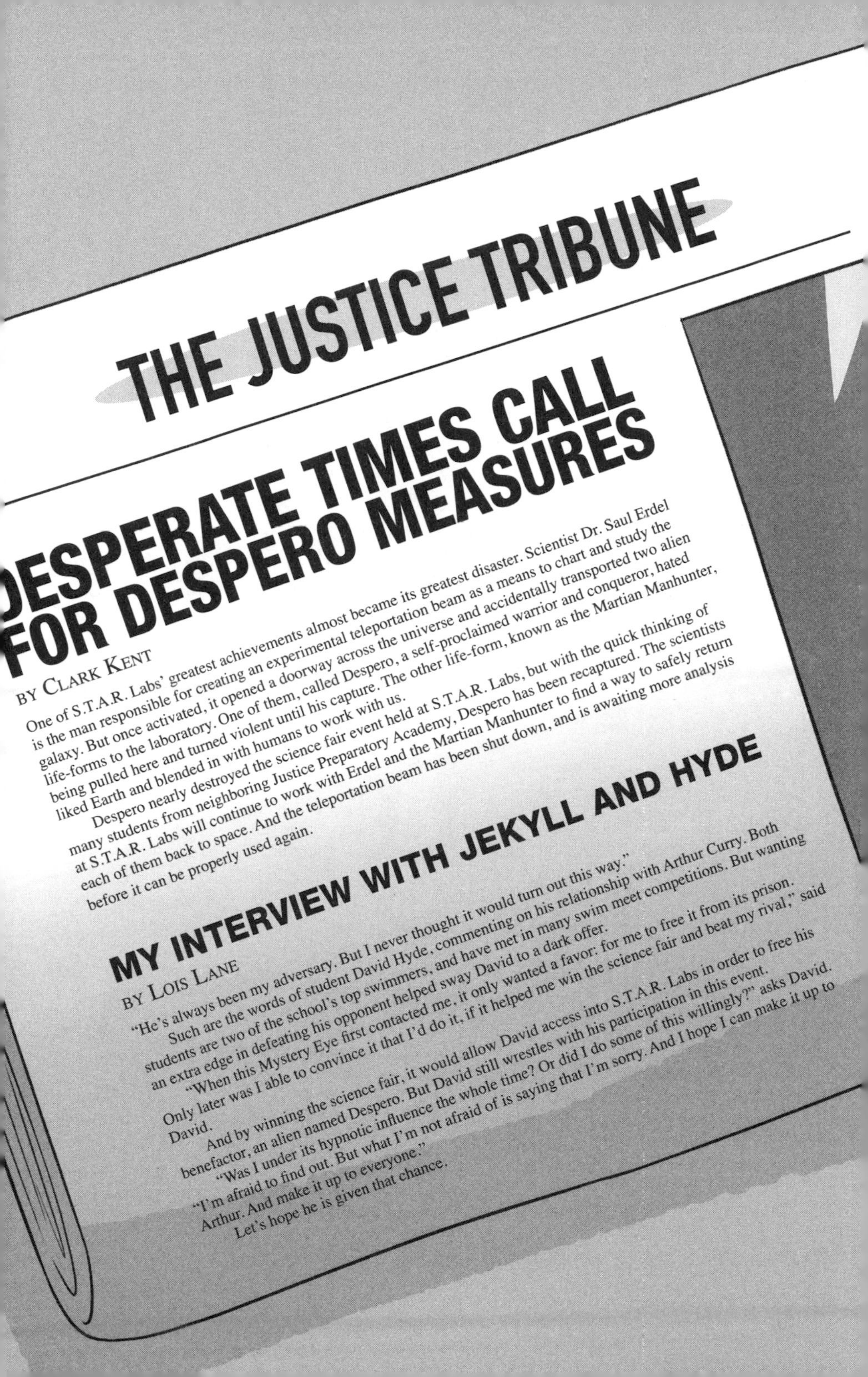

THE JUSTICE TRIBUNE

DESPERATE TIMES CALL FOR DESPERO MEASURES

BY CLARK KENT

One of S.T.A.R. Labs' greatest achievements almost became its greatest disaster. Scientist Dr. Saul Erdel is the man responsible for creating an experimental teleportation beam as a means to chart and study the galaxy. But once activated, it opened a doorway across the universe and accidentally transported two alien life-forms to the laboratory. One of them, called Despero, a self-proclaimed warrior and conqueror, hated being pulled here and turned violent until his capture. The other life-form, known as the Martian Manhunter, liked Earth and blended in with humans to work with us.

Despero nearly destroyed the science fair event held at S.T.A.R. Labs, but with the quick thinking of many students from neighboring Justice Preparatory Academy, Despero has been recaptured. The scientists at S.T.A.R. Labs will continue to work with Erdel and the Martian Manhunter to find a way to safely return each of them back to space. And the teleportation beam has been shut down, and is awaiting more analysis before it can be properly used again.

MY INTERVIEW WITH JEKYLL AND HYDE

BY LOIS LANE

"He's always been my adversary. But I never thought it would turn out this way."

Such are the words of student David Hyde, commenting on his relationship with Arthur Curry. Both students are two of the school's top swimmers, and have met in many swim meet competitions. But wanting an extra edge in defeating his opponent helped sway David to a dark offer.

"When this Mystery Eye first contacted me, it only wanted a favor: for me to free it from its prison. Only later was I able to convince it that I'd do it, if it helped me win the science fair and beat my rival," said David.

And by winning the science fair, it would allow David access into S.T.A.R. Labs in order to free his benefactor, an alien named Despero. But David still wrestles with his participation in this event.

"Was I under its hypnotic influence the whole time? Or did I do some of this willingly?" asks David. "I'm afraid to find out. But what I'm not afraid of is saying that I'm sorry. And I hope I can make it up to Arthur. And make it up to everyone."

Let's hope he is given that chance.

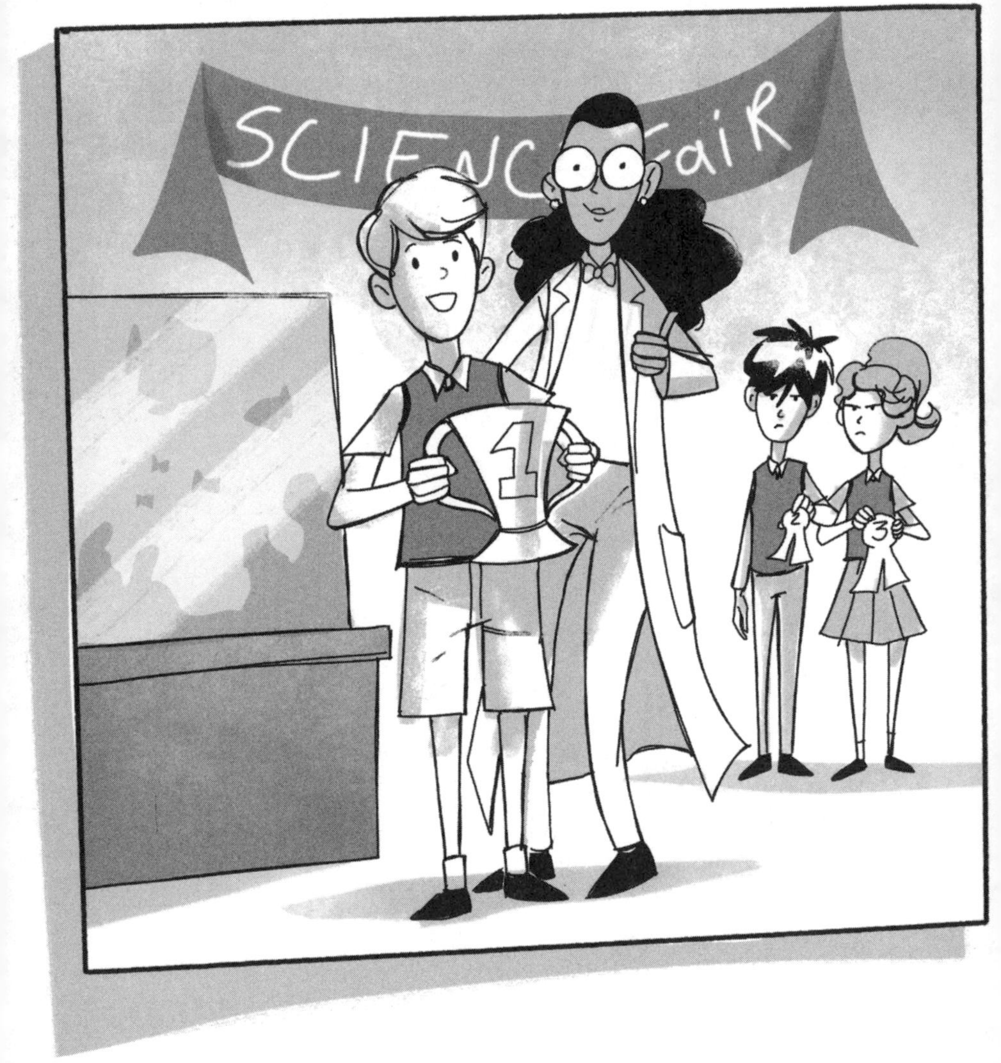
SCIENC Fair

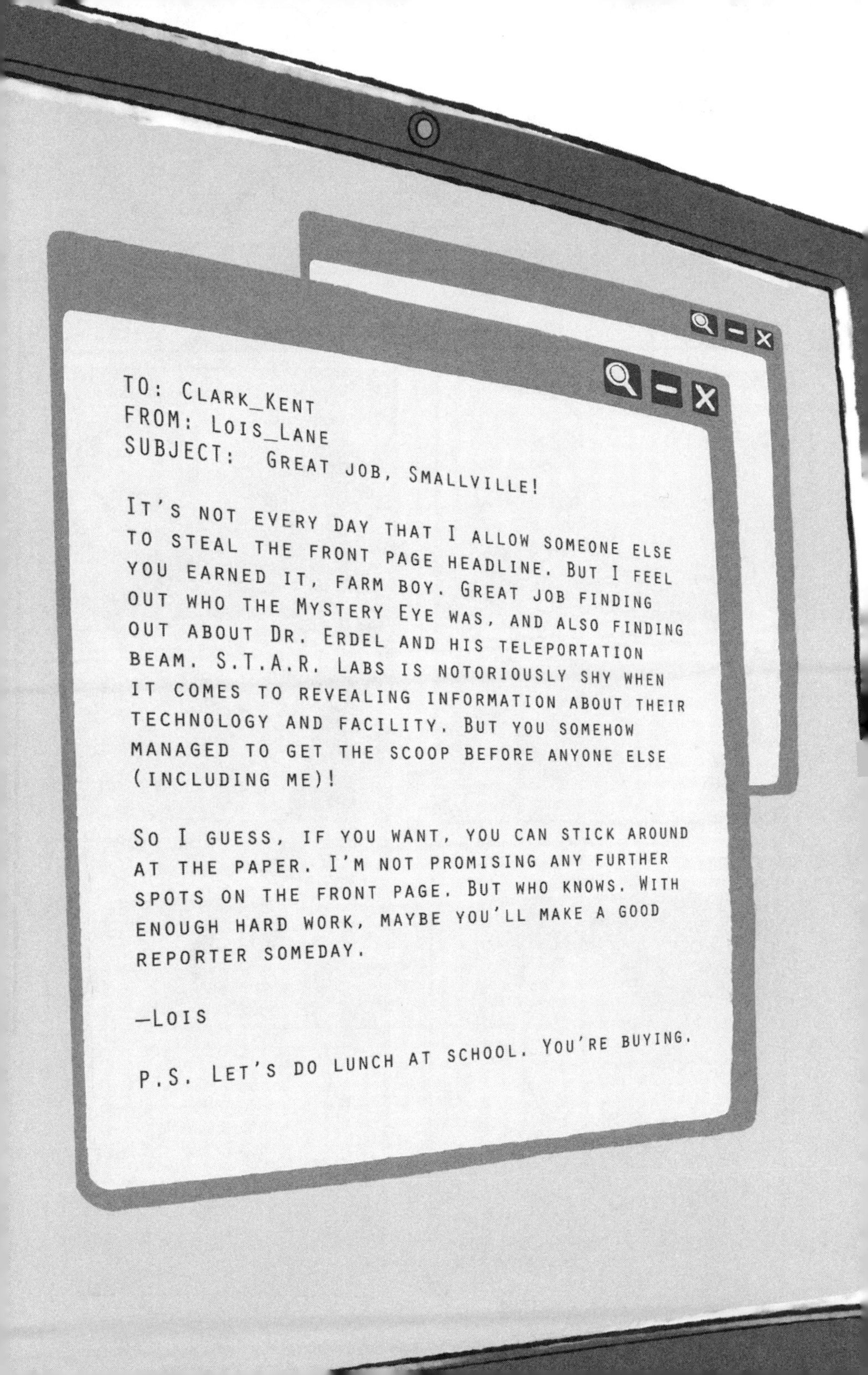

TO: CLARK_KENT
FROM: LOIS_LANE
SUBJECT: GREAT JOB, SMALLVILLE!

IT'S NOT EVERY DAY THAT I ALLOW SOMEONE ELSE TO STEAL THE FRONT PAGE HEADLINE. BUT I FEEL YOU EARNED IT, FARM BOY. GREAT JOB FINDING OUT WHO THE MYSTERY EYE WAS, AND ALSO FINDING OUT ABOUT DR. ERDEL AND HIS TELEPORTATION BEAM. S.T.A.R. LABS IS NOTORIOUSLY SHY WHEN IT COMES TO REVEALING INFORMATION ABOUT THEIR TECHNOLOGY AND FACILITY. BUT YOU SOMEHOW MANAGED TO GET THE SCOOP BEFORE ANYONE ELSE (INCLUDING ME)!

SO I GUESS, IF YOU WANT, YOU CAN STICK AROUND AT THE PAPER. I'M NOT PROMISING ANY FURTHER SPOTS ON THE FRONT PAGE. BUT WHO KNOWS. WITH ENOUGH HARD WORK, MAYBE YOU'LL MAKE A GOOD REPORTER SOMEDAY.

—LOIS

P.S. LET'S DO LUNCH AT SCHOOL. YOU'RE BUYING.

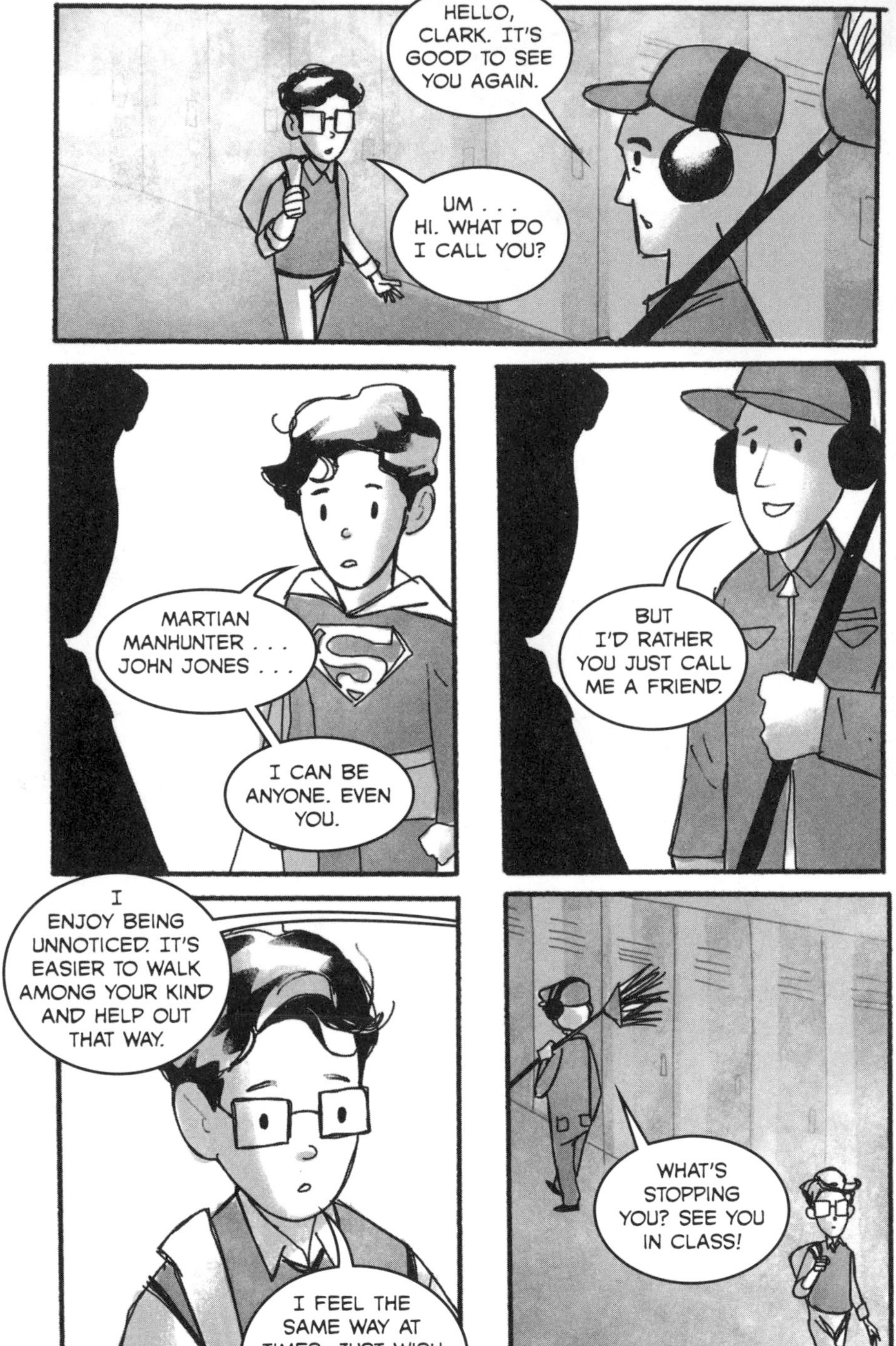
HELLO, CLARK. IT'S GOOD TO SEE YOU AGAIN.
UM . . . HI. WHAT DO I CALL YOU?
MARTIAN MANHUNTER . . . JOHN JONES . . .
I CAN BE ANYONE. EVEN YOU.
BUT I'D RATHER YOU JUST CALL ME A FRIEND.
I ENJOY BEING UNNOTICED. IT'S EASIER TO WALK AMONG YOUR KIND AND HELP OUT THAT WAY.
I FEEL THE SAME WAY AT TIMES. JUST WISH I COULD BE PART OF A GROUP AGAIN.
WHAT'S STOPPING YOU? SEE YOU IN CLASS!

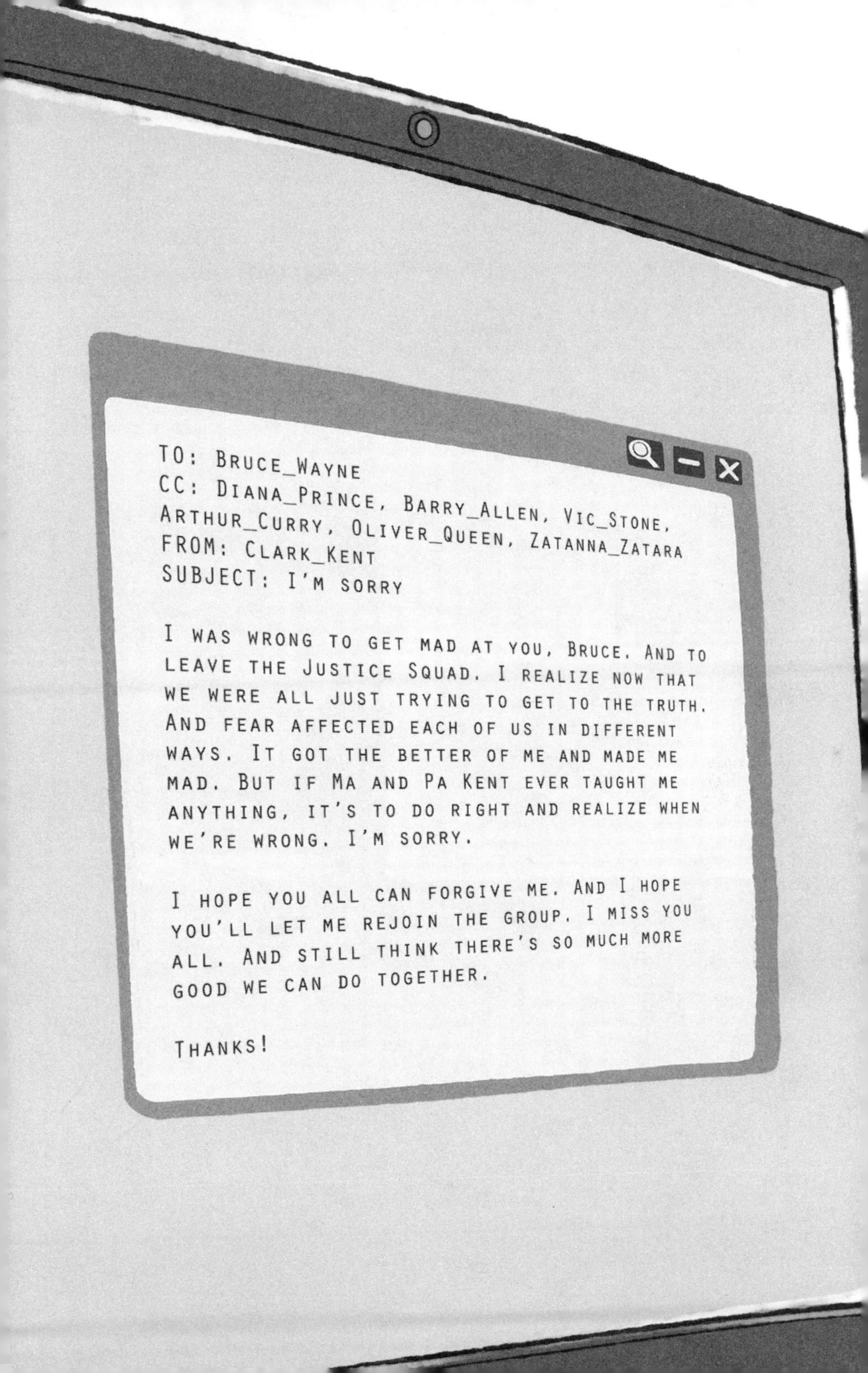

TO: Bruce_Wayne
CC: Diana_Prince, Barry_Allen, Vic_Stone, Arthur_Curry, Oliver_Queen, Zatanna_Zatara
FROM: Clark_Kent
SUBJECT: I'm sorry

I was wrong to get mad at you, Bruce. And to leave the Justice Squad. I realize now that we were all just trying to get to the truth. And fear affected each of us in different ways. It got the better of me and made me mad. But if Ma and Pa Kent ever taught me anything, it's to do right and realize when we're wrong. I'm sorry.

I hope you all can forgive me. And I hope you'll let me rejoin the group. I miss you all. And still think there's so much more good we can do together.

Thanks!

CLARK'S JOURNAL

In the end, everything turned out well. I've rejoined the Justice Squad! Before I was able to send my email out to everyone, Bruce approached me to apologize, which is a first. He took all the files he'd been keeping on every student and destroyed them. Even the files he kept on all his friends. Bruce never ceases to amaze me. He might seem like a grump at times, but he has a good heart and good intentions.

Arthur had his suspension lifted and is back in school with us. It's good to have him around again. And they awarded him first place in the science fair. As part of winning, he asked to have our whole school join him to visit the new space observatory. A very unselfish move. In a way, it felt like we all won!

But maybe the best thing to come out of all of this is realizing there appear to be other nice aliens out in the universe. I don't have to feel alone anymore. And if I'm ever in trouble, there's even more friends who will be there to help.

One day, I hope I can travel out to the stars and see the universe. It would be a great adventure. Even if Bruce isn't as excited about that idea. He says it would make him space sick.

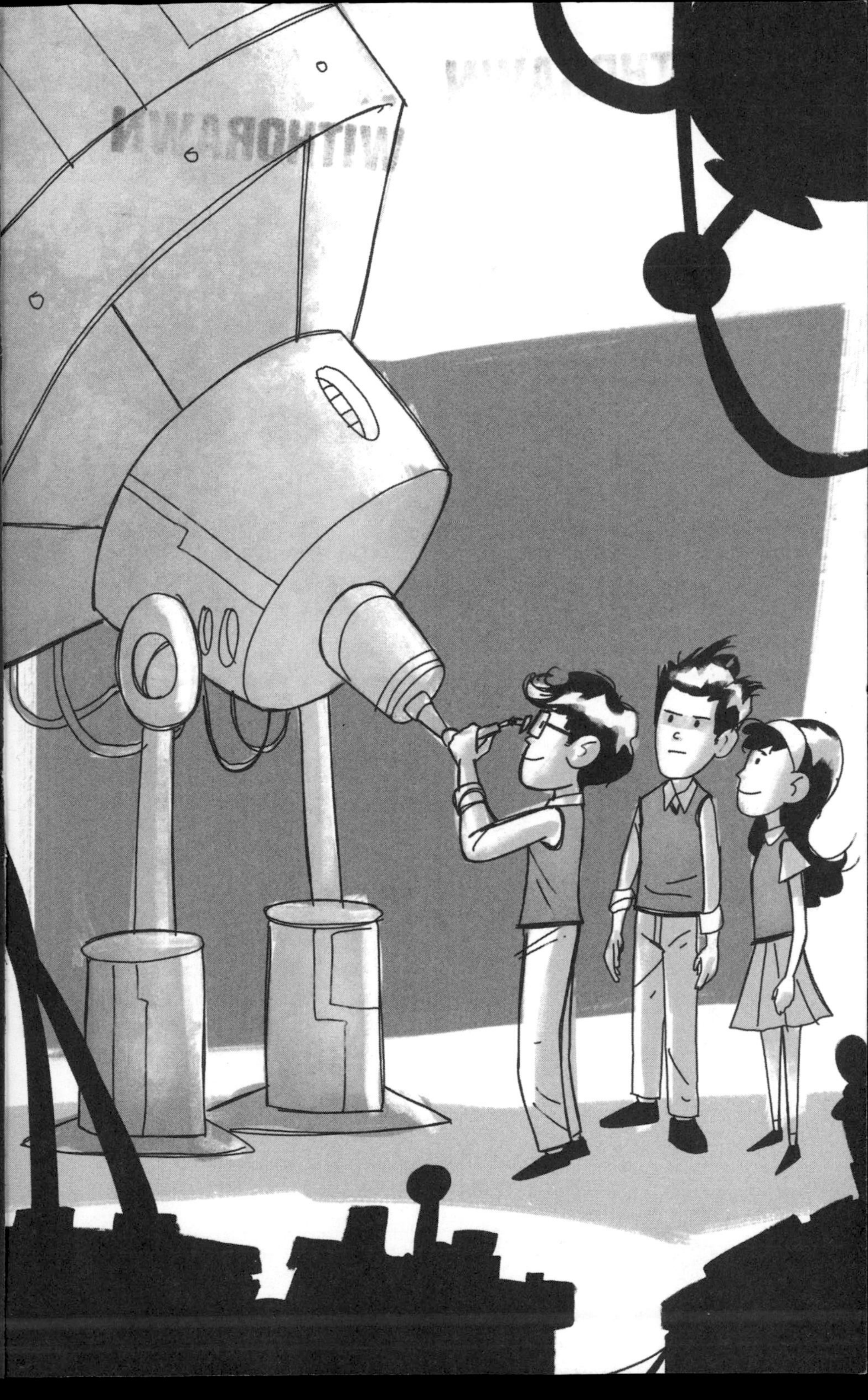

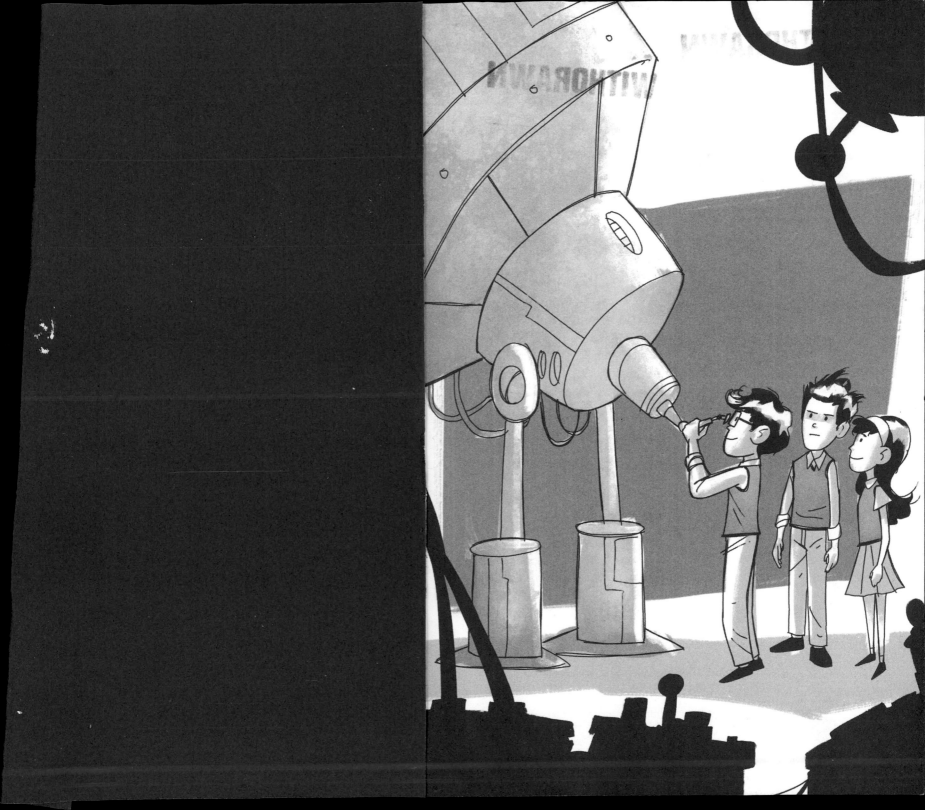

Derek Fridolfs

Derek Fridolfs is a *New York Times* bestselling writer. With Dustin Nguyen, he co-wrote the Eisner-nominated *Batman: Li'l Gotham*. He's also worked on a range of titles including *Arkham City* with Paul Dini, *Adventures of Superman*, *Detective Comics*, *Sensation Comics Featuring Wonder Woman*, and *Biff to the Future* with producer/screenwriter Bob Gale. He's written and drawn comics based on the cartoons for *Adventure Time*, *Regular Show*, *Clarence*, *Pig Goat Banana Cricket*, *Pink Panther's The Inspector*, *Dexter's Laboratory*, *Teenage Mutant Ninja Turtles*, *Teen Titans Go!*, *Looney Tunes*, and *Scooby-Doo, Where Are You!* He's also written chapter books for Capstone based on the Justice League.

Pamela Lovas

Pamela Lovas started her career working in Marvel Comics' digital department, before moving on to freelance for a variety of comic companies, including DC, IDW, Boom Studios, and Dynamite Entertainment. She's drawn and colored for such properties as *Adventure Time*, *Regular Show*, *Scooby-Doo, Where Are You!*, *Looney Tunes*, *Teen Titans Go!*, *Back to the Future*, and Funko Pop Universe *X-Files*. This is her first time illustrating a children's book.

Shane Clester

Shane Clester has been a professional illustrator since 2005. Initially working in comics and storyboards, Shane has transitioned to his real passion—children's books. Shane currently lives in Florida with his wonderful wife and their two tots. When not illustrating, he can usually be found by his in-laws' pool.